Praise for *It's a Wonderful Time*

"A satisfying, exciting ride back to post-WWII Hollywood. Jimmy Stewart's character comes alive from the page. Reading *It's A Wonderful Time* reminds me how much I miss him."

— Rich Little, Hollywood Legend

"If you've never been to Hollywood, this is your chance to see not only what it is but what it was and still should be from the comfort of your favorite chair. The sights, sounds, heart, soul and even smells of the good old days come alive on every page, paragraph and sentence. **In a word ... it's Wonderful!"**

— John Schneider, Actor in *The Dukes of Hazard, Smallville* and *Poker Run*

"Since I was child, Frank Capra's *It's A Wonderful Life* has been watched every Christmas in my home. It is still a cherished tradition. **I expect *It's A Wonderful Time* to be such a classic.** It uses time travel to reexamine the post-war Capra film with today's eyes, and is written with lots of humor and charm. *It's A Wonderful Time* comes just in time—we all need to be reminded of both the progress and decline our society is going through."

— Robert Davi, Actor in *Die Hard, License to Kill* and *The Goonies*

"I loved this idea as a script 20 years ago when I first read it. I'm thrilled to see it coming back in book form reuniting two of my favorite films of all time — *Back to the Future* and *It's a Wonderful Life*. **This is a book for film lovers to fall in love all over again as they go back in time to these classics."**

— Doug Claybourne, Film Producer of *The Fast and The Furious, The Mask of Zoro* and *War of The Roses*

"Hop into Evan West's 1938 Ford Coupe on a wild ride to Hollywood's Golden Age as Evan tries to save the classic film from cunning scoundrels. You'll walk studio backlots with Jimmy Stewart, tag along to glitzy parties, and try to keep up during breathtaking chases. **Life is even more wonderful with a pinch of time travel thrown in!**"

— Margaret McConnell, editor and publishing professional

"Combining the elements of noir, heist, time travel, and the golden era of Hollywood, the authors take the reader on a journey to post World War II when America saved the world from the clutches of the axis of evil and was about to reach her full potential. *It's a Wonderful Time* is **fun, clever and a great read!**"

—Marshall Terrill, Author of 27 books, including best-selling biographies of Steve McQueen, Elvis Presley, Billy Graham, Johnny Cash and Pete Maravich

"**Mesmerizing time-traveling Hollywood novel** effortlessly transports you to yesteryear, then makes you never want to leave." —Adam Novak, author of *Rat Park* and *Take Fountain*

"**I thoroughly enjoyed *It's a Wonderful Time*. It's a marvelous adventure** as the magic world of Hollywood movie making in its finest hour collides with an adventurous ride. Doug Stebleton and Reinhard Denke have created charming characters and an exciting plot. I highly recommend it. Hire me when you make the movie, guys!"

— Michael Mandaville, Film Producer of *Taken 1, 2 & 3*

It's a Wonderful Time

THE HOLLYWOOD TIME TRAVEL SERIES

It's a Wonderful Time

DOUG STEBLETON   REINHARD DENKE

BannerPress

Published by Banner Press
For more information, visit www.HollywoodTimeTravel.com

Edited by Andrea Vanryken
Book cover concept by Robbie Destocki, Creative Image Design Group
Book design by Christy Day, Constellation Book Design,
www.constellatiobookservices.com

ISBN (paperback): 978-1-7378525-0-6
ISBN (ebook): 978-1-7378525-1-3

I would like to dedicate this book to my mother, Ivy Stebleton, who gave me my love and appreciation of the music and films of the 1930s, '40s, and '50s and who always encouraged me in my creative pursuits while in Hollywood all these years, and to my Hollywood heroes, Frank Capra and Jimmy Stewart, for all the amazing and wonderful films they gave the world.
—Doug

I would like to dedicate this book to my parents, Fred and Marjorie Denke, who always showed me the right path. Also to my beautiful genius wife, Marilee, who always challenged me to be better, fight harder, and to always believe.
—Reinhard

PROLOGUE

Hollywood, Los Angeles

The air that morning in Los Angeles was thick and dense thanks to the coastal fog that had rolled in over the parched hills from Malibu all the way to Pasadena. By noon, it would burn off, leaving enough misty remnants behind to ensure a hazy day.

Along the Cahuenga Pass that connected Hollywood to Los Angeles, a Red Car street trolley rumbled south, loaded with morning commuters. The trolley line split both Cahuenga East and Cahuenga West, two arteries that forked off into Ventura Boulevard and led all the way up to the Conejo Valley or Burbank, depending on which Cahuenga one planned to visit that day.

At the corner of Cahuenga East and Lakeridge Road, a blue 1938 Ford Coupe, filled to the legal limit with heavy machinery in the backseat and trunk, rested just off the road. The car was hot; steam rose from the roof and hood. Two gentlemen stood near the car, surveying the surrounding landscape. They looked lost but at the same time, not so lost.

One of the men shook his head in wonder as if he were seeing something very familiar but different. Evan West was twenty-five, slightly built, not too short, not too tall, not heavy nor abnormally thin, crowned with a misbehaved mop of dark brown hair he kept tamed with Brylcreem. His face, perfectly proportioned, reeked of honesty. He was dressed in a black tuxedo and looked like he'd just left an all-night party.

The other man, Coop, also dressed in a tuxedo with a wide-brimmed fedora, joined Evan. Both looked out toward the pass. Coop was tall, dark, and gangly, with an easy smile and more confidence than most people could ever hope to have.

Evan looked at Coop, then at a clattering 1930 Chevy sedan that passed by closely. It looked like a Model A Ford but was built cheaply, seeming to be held together with sticks and airplane glue. Evan got a glimpse of the gold-on-black license plate.

Alarmed and disappointed, Evan shook his head. "When all this is over, and we get back, how do I tell everyone I know in the twenty-first century that I went to the 1940s? More importantly, how do we get out of here?"

CHAPTER 1
THE BIG HEIST

2021 AD

It was a rainy Saturday morning in December. Hardly the first. It had been coming down fairly hard for the past three days now, and as always, the city needed it. Los Angeles was one of those cities that seemed suited to the rain better than most, even though it got very little. The city came alive in the rain, even more so than normal.

And when the rain came down that hard in Hollywood, you got the feeling that anything could happen.

That Friday night, two men crossed Hollywood Boulevard from the corner of Orange and hurried briskly across the wet street. It was 4:00 a.m.; no one paid any attention to the few unfortunates who made it a point to live on Hollywood Boulevard and slowly drowned themselves in unobtainable dreams.

The pair, dressed in black and both slender, were almost invisible. Their movements seemed made with a practiced stealth, the way soldiers and law enforcement officers move—with caution and dexterity at the same time.

A ragged street woman suddenly cried out as if in pain or confusion. The men passed her without reaction—just another crazy on Hollywood Boulevard. Nothing could distract them from their mission.

The men headed with grim purpose toward the famous Grauman's Chinese Theatre, halting over the forest of famous footsteps and signatures. They exchanged a quick glance to get their bearings.

"There," the taller of the two said, pointing to the far end of the glory that was Grauman's Chinese Theatre. They hurried to a selected area and looked down, seeing a square with the names JIMMY STEWART and DONNA REED, along with their footprints and handprints (his large, hers quite small) imprinted on it. Above that, an empty square. Nothing on it, but apparently something unnamed, yet of great importance, lay underneath.

Both men carried large bags; one produced two sharp picks and handed one to his partner. With incredible strength, they hacked into the concrete, tossing chunks of ancient blocks aside.

The pick came down hard. *Clank!* A dry hit. Then another *clunk* rang out, this one wet and subdued.

The tail end of Stewart's name cracked off, the "ART" portion left dangling near the widening hole. One of the men picked that up, holding it like a souvenir. They both kneeled, working together to clear away the debris of pounded cement, wet dust, and broken stone.

At the bottom of a shallow hole, a metal container sat awaiting them. A smell arose from the box, the odor of the long-buried past, musty and pungent. It quickly dissipated in the heavy rainfall.

One of the hunters peered closer, seeing embossed on the steel sarcophagus:

IT'S A WONDERFUL LIFE – FRANK CAPRA – 1946.

The second man reached in, cracked the now-weak vault, and pulled a very old and yellowed typed script of *It's a Wonderful Life* by Frances Goodrich, Albert Hackett, and Frank Capra. The man tossed it aside; the precious script pages landed on the wet concrete, the rainfall causing the old, typed cover to bleed ink as if wounded.

The first man found another object, a framed picture with an image of a man in a striped sweater with a rope around a smiling moon. The words: **GEORGE LASSOS THE MOON** were emblazoned on it, and again, the men simply tossed the object aside, which melted in the rain along with the priceless screenplay.

Below that was a glint of steel, and both men knew it was what they had come for: a stack of 16mm film canisters. They nodded with quiet understanding. Objective reached.

A shockwave of thunder shuddered through the boulevard. The men looked to the clouds as the rain came down even harder, the storm seeming to take on biblical dimensions.

They lifted the vault, carefully stowed the canisters inside, and then threw a dark cloth over it. The two treasure hunters moved away quickly, stepping over the handprints of Clark Gable, Judy Garland, Steven Spielberg, and Fred Astaire.

The men vanished into the rain like a malevolent fog, curling and wisping into eternity.

The rain was ominous that night in its intensity and would continue another four days without pause. Soaked hillsides would collapse, and red mud would run down Highland

Boulevard for days, leaving behind a putrid odor that smelled like a cemetery.

Hollywood's past melded into its present and future and became one.

Life would upend for several people during that storm. Some would be forever altered; others would never know anything changed.

And though the world would never be the same as it was known now or as it was then, only two people would ever know the difference.

CHAPTER 2
THE PURIST AND THE PHILISTINE

Evan West in 2021 was perfectly happy with the rain; he was at the wheel of his recently restored 1938 Ford Coupe, and if there was anything that gave him that warm rush of happiness, it was driving old cars. The old, vacuum-powered windshield wipers could barely clear the accumulated rain, but Evan didn't mind.

Evan was obsessed with the past, the 1940s in particular. He drove that old car as a life statement, putting him at a level far above that of the typical hobbyist. To complete his 1940s' obsession, he splashed on Aqua Velva aftershave every morning and wore black wool slacks, a white work shirt, a pocket watch, a Hamilton wristwatch, and Florsheim Shoes that were more worn than shiny. Evan recognized himself as an old soul among the Philistines and did his best to fit in with an eternal smile and a breezy, Dean Martin-esque attitude without the booze or Marlboros.

Downshifting to second, Evan pulled his old Ford up to the gates at Raleigh Studios and slowed down enough to take in the gleaming white sound stages, the sight of which enthralled him even on a rainy day.

Hollywood had always captivated him, both in legend and in its harsh reality. He slipped in his gate card key, the arm lifted, and he was welcomed into the lot by a quick nod from the gate guard, Fred Foxman, the friendly face he saw every morning, granting him access to another day of paradise. Evan had heard the guard had been there twenty-five years and would likely remain another quarter-century. A high school dropout and former Brink's security guard, Fred just seemed happy to have a job where the likelihood of getting shot at was minimal.

To Evan, being here was a big mark of approval—he was the luckiest guy on the planet in his mind. Yes, he wasn't on the big lot at Universal or Paramount; Raleigh was an old studio, had been around a long time. Older even than Warner's Burbank Studio, Raleigh had quite a history. Built in 1915, the studio hosted the films *Whatever Happened to Baby Jane, The Best Years of Our Lives,* and *In the Heat of the Night.*

Evan's daily thoughts centered on all the Hollywood legends who made the kind of movies that had lured him from his home in Kansas City to Los Angeles. Someday, his name would be ranked up there with the likes of Steven Spielberg, James Cameron, Frank Capra, Alfred Hitchcock, and David Fincher. He was going to be a superstar writer/director—Evan had no doubt of that. He had the force of will, the talent, and the personality. He had attended the American Film Institute (AFI) film program for three years and spent most of his time in the library reading original scripts, production reports, and vintage reviews. He read every biography of every director and knew exactly what he wanted to do and who he wanted to be. The AFI had one of the best film programs in the Los Angeles area, and while not as storied as USC, it was by far the most comprehensive.

The AFI set Evan on his path, a path he could never leave even if he wanted to.

He had two years to make that dream come true. *Doable*, Evan reminded himself. After all, Capra had directed his first film at twenty-six. Orson Welles was twenty-five, Hitchcock twenty-six, Cameron twenty-eight, and DeMille thirty-three, but that was another time. He had to direct that first, great film by the time he was twenty-seven. If that didn't happen, he was unsure of what he would do. Go back to Kansas City, which was not an option. There was nothing worse than being the washed-up guy who quit on his dream. If twenty-seven came and went without his first film, however small and crummy, he'd direct one at twenty-eight or twenty-nine. He had time to be that great director; the feel of the red carpet under his feet didn't seem so far away. He'd pay his DGA dues in time, and maybe, when he was older, run for office in the Director's Guild.

Reality tended to be disappointing, and Evan, at present, was simply an editor. Not directing yet, not even writing; he was too busy editing to go to that magical, happy place where inspiration sprang from.

Editing was, Evan knew, a crucial position in the army of Hollywood, though still far from the highest peak of Mt. Everest where Evan really wanted to be. He did appreciate that he was one of the last of the legions of people to work on any given film. Movies were never made in solitude; they required a small army of technicians and construction experts, from its inception with the writer to that of the director; then on to the intricate planning that transpired with the producer, director, production designer, costumers, art directors, the cast, the battalions of camera and lighting people; and then to makeup, craft services, stunt people, and, after the film was shot, it finally got passed on to a guy like Evan.

Evan had heard the phrase "post-production rules," and he liked it. The only kicker was that Evan wasn't editing movies. He was editing movie trailers. A trailer was an entirely different animal altogether and could not exist apart from a movie.

Yes, trailers weren't the "big time." Raleigh Studios, despite a storied past, wasn't either. Raleigh was home to several commercials being filmed. Today, Ford was shooting on Stage 6, and a Lincoln commercial was in production on Stage 3. A TV comedy, *Mush Mouth and Monster Boy*, was shooting on Stage 1. *Shadamkazan!*, a show about diverse superhero teenagers in the Bronx, was underway on Stage 7.

Evan pulled his Ford into his designated parking spot for Killer Trailers, his current employer. His 1938 Ford was as out of place among the Teslas, Lexus, BMWs, M-Benzes, and Cadillac Escalades as cheap ramen at a wedding banquet. Considering his car's age, it was the equivalent of very old ramen with a very unique, acquired taste.

The elation of driving onto the lot was a short-term intoxicant for Evan. When he found himself in front of the Killer Trailers office, it hit him like a brass-knuckled punch to the nose: He was just a trailer editor, twenty-five going on twenty-seven fast, and not a member of any union, with an IMDb page that was a joke.

He glanced to his left and beheld his boss's huge Range

Rover, gleaming gray, dripping with the kind of luxury that comes from its owner throwing down six figures, and screaming out, *Behold, my employees! Look at what I can afford, thanks to you!*

Evan knew what was ahead of him today: the trailer for *Killbots*, a new Nicolas Cage movie in which Cage takes on a military division of computer viruses that have morphed from cyberspace to become a gruesome reality. Nicolas Cage was one of those guys you had to admire. An Oscar winner, a nephew of Francis Ford Coppola and even briefly Elvis Presley's son-in-law, he was known for his impressive body of work and even more impressive stack of unpaid debt that forced him to act in just about anything that came along, forgettable movies such as *Pay The Ghost*, *Vengeance: A Love Story*, and *A Score to Settle*.

Evan, as frustrated as he was, didn't let it show. A perpetual "glass is half-full" kinda guy, Evan took it all in stride. It was another day, another dollar. He got to work on a Hollywood lot across from legendary Paramount Studios, and that was enough, for now.

Evan climbed out of his Ford, lifted his umbrella, and closed the door, causing his car to clunk out its familiar, metallic *boom!* New cars didn't make that sound when their doors shut, but 1938 Detroit steel made a noise like none other on Earth. It was the sound of solid construction, the sound of *I've been around a long time, and I'm not going anywhere*, and Evan liked it.

A golf cart whirred over to him. Hank Richards was at the wheel with a perpetually bemused grin on his face. Evan didn't know his age, but he did know Hank had been around a long time. Hank had met Charlton Heston and Judy Garland, and once, Evan had spotted Martin Scorcese on the lot, and he and Hank had greeted one another like old friends. Hank was one of Evan's favorite people. He always had a kind word and a smile—especially on those days you needed it most.

Hank was a property master on staff with Paramount across the street. He would breeze by Raleigh to deliver his collection of guns, belts, tools…gizmos of every kind. The studios tended to borrow props from one another for a small fee, and Hank was more than happy to oblige. These props kept many a movie/TV police officer armed and dangerous, at least for the sake of the show.

"Mr. West, good morning to you," he purred in a low, jovial voice, a voice from the past. Hank spoke the way people used to in the movies, Evan mused, before the present age of social-media shaming and perpetual fear.

"Morning, Hank. How goes it over at the big lot today?" Evan responded.

"Same ol', same ol', every day's a blessing to be alive. If it were any better, it'd be a crime! You finishing up that crazy, computer killer movie today?"

"Yep." Evan nodded, hoping he actually could get that one done, leave work a little early, and then take a nap before the Christmas party tonight that he was not really looking forward to.

"I gave that rose to your pretty girl. Don't forget your lunch date with her." He smiled knowingly. "They don't come prettier than Gwen Sullivan! She turns every head over there at what you call the 'Big Lot.'"

Evan's thoughts went to Gwen, and his heart fell. He could feel the creeping "Can we stop dating and just be friends?" speech coming. It was inevitable with Gwen. They didn't have that much in common. She refused to sit through any movie made before 1995 and was addicted to social media. Evan found social media a repulsive blight on humanity, like the Krell labs from *Forbidden Planet*. Evan felt too much social media could easily gobble a person's soul to shreds and not even so much as belch before it reached out for its next victim. True, Gwen was a "D" girl, an executive for Rolling Stone Pictures, a company that developed, but never made, rock and roll movies. And Gwen loved her job over there despite her lack of movie history knowledge. But she was good at it according to most sources. Evan had to admit, he really liked Gwen, more than he should. He knew they had a valley of invariables between them, but she was perfect for him, or so he thought.

"I'll try not to, Hank. She is quite beautiful," Evan said, his mouth suddenly dry because it hurt to say it.

"She's better than you deserve, kiddo." Hank laughed, then wheeled away. He slowed, swiveling his head to face Evan. "Don't forget the Christmas party tonight! Have the name and address?"

Evan, whose memory was sharper than a samurai sword, nodded with a grin. "Mrs. Dorothy Paige, 1001 Orange Grove, Apartment 6. I got it!" He smiled to himself. There was something about Hank he couldn't put his finger on, but every time he spoke with him, the world felt, looked, tasted, and smelled better. Maybe it was his imagination, but he knew within seconds whatever fairy dust Hank left behind was going to vanish like a magician's rabbit at the Magic Castle.

He stepped into Killer Trailers and always appreciated that old smell of varnish, layers upon layers of latex paint, and moldy carpet.

It was the smell he equated with the past, a past he felt was probably in all regards better than the present. Evan headed to his room, clicked on the lights, which half-flickered, and took a seat in front of his iMac's enormous twin screens.

It was time to work his magic.

The iMac chimed with a piano "G" chord, and on the screens came.

Connor Alcott suddenly appeared before Evan as if having formed out of a malevolent, oily mist.

Connor Alcott, owner of Killer Trailers and that ostentatious Range Rover outside, stood at six-foot-one and carried himself with effort. He tried not to affect a slump, which came more naturally to him than did any proper form of posture, but it was impossible for the man to stretch that large, grim face into a smile. Connor was one of those guys who grew up always looking over his shoulder, absolutely certain he was about to be "found out" as an imposter. No matter where he went or what he did, the only way he could generate respect was to pretend he had more money than he had and accomplished more than anyone else. Connor's brothers were Wall Street bankers, but Connor had wanted to go to Hollywood and outdo both Steven Spielberg and James Cameron. When that goal fell through, he settled for starting his own movie trailer company, financed by his trust fund. Better to rule in Hell than serve in Heaven, words Connor never read before despite his expensive education, yet lived by.

Years before, one of Connor's friends—not so much a friend but an acquaintance—said that Connor was the kind of guy whose last words on his death bed would be "Thank God. No more fear."

"Okay, party people!" was how he greeted Evan, who naturally hated the expression and the false sentiment behind it. "Let's kick this puppy in full gear. This has gotta deliver tonight. It'll help with foreign pre-sales." Connor loved using "inside baseball" Hollywood lingo like "foreign pre-sales," "completion funds," and "financial exposure." He felt by using those terms, people would never find out Connor was too lazy and distracted to figure out their true definition and that he wasn't really a major player, just a rich kid who wanted to be James Cameron, never really tried, and wound up owning a trailer company on the Raleigh lot.

Connor took a seat by Evan, whose skin crawled the second he got close. He could smell the slight tinge of marijuana, tobacco, and tea. Connor drank tea, and it irritated Evan to no end. Real men drank coffee; poseurs drank tea—at least, that was how Evan saw the world, like one of Raymond Chandler or Dashiell Hammett's jaded private detectives.

"Okay, party people…bring up the latest cut for me, will ya?" Connor grumbled, and Evan quickly pulled it up on the left screen, using the right screen for his session. "You gonna play it or not?" Connor growled. Evan hit the space key.

On the screen, Nicolas Cage carried a silver hand cannon. He opened fire on a swarm of metallic bees—the "killbots"— that swirled around him. Music boomed and swelled. Cymbals crashed. The gun spat out a river a flame. Some of the bots caught fire; others avoided the inferno.

"Come get some of this!" Cage shouted. Evan suppressed a grin. Even though he had not been writing lately, he'd learned exactly what dialogue *not* to write while working at Killer Trailers. More action came and went. Swarms destroyed a car, a trailer park, and an office building. The pool party turned into a bloody battlefield.

"Stop there!" Evan did as Connor commanded. "Roll it back fifteen frames." Evan rolled it back half a second. "Cut it there—the shot of the bots…right there." Connor pointed to the screen and snorted. Something else Evan disliked about Connor was the constant snorting and sniffling. The man was always using a Neti pot, pouring hot water into his troubled sinuses—a byproduct of Connor's secret yet habitual cocaine use—and then sneezing afterward.

"Where's the kid being eaten by bots?" Connor asked as if offended. "The kid…the little kid? Remember?"

Evan nodded. "Oh, yeah. That seemed pretty egregious, don't you think?" he remarked, hoping that would sufficiently explain why he had omitted it.

Connor didn't buy it and fixed him with a strange, penetrating grin. "Egregious…? What the hell does that mean? Evan, Evan, Evan, listen to me. The little kid being devoured is pretty damned strong stuff. Foreign markets love kids being eaten. You, of all people, should know that."

Evan nodded, found the shot in his virtual trim bin, and cut it in within seconds. He ran the trailer again, and this time, the gruesome image of a toddler being enveloped in shiny steel bees flashed on the screen, followed by Nicolas Cage screaming. Then the shot went to a grisly pile of small bones as the swarm buzzed away. Nicolas Cage stepped in frame, regarded the bones, then raised his head to the sky and shook his fist. "Damn you! Damn you to Hell!" he shouted.

"You sure you want that?" Evan asked, disturbed by the image. When he had watched the *Killbots* trailer, it reminded him of *Hostel* or any other Eli Roth movie: the same meaningless experience of desolation and nihilism. "You might turn some people off with this. I mean, we live in a pretty insane world as it is."

Connor did *that thing*. The long silent treatment. His jaw jutted out early-man style, his chin stubble seeming to bristle. His blue eyes were without anything behind them, nearly dead but alive enough to know he'd just been questioned by an underling who was already intimidated by him.

"Evan, I want to make a statement here, and you need to respect that. I want to show the world that violence is ubiquitous, everywhere…inevitable. Damned snowflakes out there don't get it, and it's up to we, the Hollywood media, to enlighten them. We can't shy away from it," Connor intoned, keeping his voice low. Evan knew him well enough to know that when Connor used that tone, he had already practiced the speech in the mirror earlier that day. Connor looked around the room, then pointed to the fluorescent lights that were flickering. "You need to change those. I'm not gonna do it for ya."

Evan looked and nodded. "In the storage closet, right?" Evan tried to sound helpful and at the same time defuse the situation because he could see Connor building up to some kind of nasty, cutting remark that was designed to ruin Evan's day—and it usually worked.

Connor responded with that same lifeless, blue-eyed stare. Suddenly, he seemed riveted by his iPhone and walked out of the room, dismissing Evan by ignoring him and concentrating on his world of texts and emails.

Every text and email animated Connor, apparently making him feel alive, as if someone thinking of him enough to reach out was a miracle in itself.

Evan didn't mind Connor leaving silently, another one of those "Connor tricks" he used to intimidate others and keep people guessing. It didn't intimidate Evan, just made him dislike his boss even more than he already did. Considering the other thing Connor tended to do when he left an employee's room: saying the surfer 2001-era phrase, "Lates!" Connor's silent exit was preferable.

All Evan had to do today was finish this monstrosity of a trailer and change a couple of lightbulbs. He got to work, diving into tightening every shot, re-editing the music, and seamlessly overlaying dialogue. "Damn you! Damn you to Hell!" He used that audio to bridge the cut from Cage screaming to the pile of toddler bones. Before he knew it, three hours had passed. It was 12:30—nearly time for that lunch date he was dreading.

Evan felt a cup of coffee, pitch-black, the way they drank in the 1940s, was exactly what he needed at the moment. There was none of that in the Killer Trailer kitchen, only lattes, vanilla, nutmeg, and worst of all, peppermint white chocolate mocha. All of it was *yech* to Evan, who was a fan of donut-shop coffee, the blacker the better. The old guys called it "Navy coffee," and if it was good enough for the USN, it was good enough for Evan West.

As soon as he stood, Connor poked his head in the door, thumb jerked over his shoulder.

"Need you to record VO now," he said, distracted, eyes on his iPhone. "Couldn't get Grammar, but we got Dick to fill in. It's an hour session. Let's circle back after you record him, lay that track in, and mix it down, got it?"

"You want me to finish the trailer or record VO?" Evan asked indignantly.

Connor's face tightened. "Both! Get it done. J-Jo isn't here today, bro." Connor pointed to the nearby VO recording booth.

Evan bit his tongue, resentful that his workload had just doubled, putting him back two hours.

Evan hated when Connor called Jake Johannsen, the ever-faithful jack of all trades at Killer Trailers, "J-Jo," but he especially hated the phrase "circle back."

He stepped out of his room and noticed Richard Sinclair, whose voice was ubiquitous on most movie trailers. Not as famous as Kelsey Grammar, but Richard didn't care. He was happy to get work anytime, anywhere. He was an unassuming man, rail-thin, with combed-back black hair who never showed up in anything but business casual attire. Richard had grown on Evan over the years.

The man's voice was legendary, an instrument honed by years of cigarettes, coffee, and bourbon. He looked like a tax auditor with a hound-dog scowl.

"Evan, what's new on the front today?" Richard asked with that warm, friendly voice that every man, deep down inside, wished they had.

"Admiring your voice, buddy," Evan answered, sounding as positive and chipper as a young man could. Richard had that world-weary look on his face all industry veterans had after seeing so many images projected at 30 fps.

"I know you're doing great work on these trailers. I admire your craft, but I gotta level with ya—the extreme violence in this stuff gets to me sometimes. I need a breather. How about I have a smoke before we go back in to record?" He looked as worn out as his words as he withdrew a pack from his pocket and shook out a Pall Mall.

Evan declined with a shake of his head. Richard flicked out his fancy, gold-plated lighter and headed toward the door.

Evan followed. "I promise one day I'll write a movie that you'll actually enjoy being part of," Evan said to Richard.

"You say that a lot, Evan…. Could I see some of your pages? You've been building this up for a while. I'm expecting Aaron Sorkin." Richard pinned him with a dark look.

Evan shoved his hands in his pockets, fingering his pocket watch chain. He shook his head with embarrassment.

"I'm working on it, but I promise I will," Evan stammered.

Richard chuckled, sliding a cigarette in his mouth at a jaunty angle. "I'm gonna hold you to it. Remember, Evan, writers write. They don't talk about it, they just write. Until then, you're just another wage slave, and Mount Olympus is as far away as it ever was. You already set up?"

They stepped outside. The rain had diminished. Richard stared out at the dismal sky and lit up. Evan noticed a lanky man not too far away, looking completely out of place in a tuxedo. The rain didn't seem to faze him. He saw Richard, lifted a hand, and smiled. It was Matthew McConaughey, dressed like James Bond but still as recognizable as ever. He headed their way.

"All right, all right, Richard, you got another one of those for me?" He motioned to Richard's pack. Richard shook one out. Matthew took it, lit up with the help of Richard's classic lighter, and inhaled.

"What are you working on?" Richard asked.

Matthew blew out smoke and smiled. "Lincoln, my friend, right over there, Stage 3. We gotta keep those Lincolns on the road, my friend. It's an American institution." The way Matthew said it…it was clear he meant every word. He pointed at Evan's 1938 Ford. "Now this is what I've come to see. Yours?"

"Naw, that's my friend Evan's," Richard said with a glance in his direction. Matthew's eyes met Evan's, and he reached for a handshake. Evan obliged. "That a '40?"

"1938 all the way," Evan responded.

"Flathead V-8?"

"The one and only!"

"Same engine with a few modifications produced from 1932 to 1952, Old Henry's design apex." Matthew gestured toward the old, metal-framed vehicle with his cigarette hand. "You want to crank her up so I can hear her sing?"

Evan happily headed to his Ford, slid in behind the wheel, stomped his foot down on the starter, and cranked the engine. Matthew, right behind him, held up his hands in triumph. "Nothing sounds like that, Sarge! Punch it!"

Evan did as requested; the V-8 sang its opera.

"My granddaddy had a '40 truck back in Bexar County that sang this fine tune. A thing of beauty, ain't that right? Thank you, brother, for taking me back to the good times." Matthew stubbed out his cigarette and clapped Evan on the back. "See you next time, pardner."

He headed back toward Stage 3, and the rain seemed to fall around him as if he were passing through a protective cloud.

Richard and Evan headed back in, and admittedly, Evan felt a bit dizzy from Matthew McConaughey's almost supernaturally awesome aura. Back inside, Evan rounded the corner to the kitchenette. Coffee was calling to him, even if it came in the form of a latte vanilla.

A soft, female voice also called out to him.

"Hey, Evan, how're you doing?"

Evan quickly looked over his shoulder to behold Gwen, the rose from old Hank delicately clutched in her tiny hand. Evan made a move to kiss her on the cheek, and she backed away.

Uh-oh. Bad sign.

That was exactly what he had feared. He could feel the railroad tracks vibrating. The soon-to-arrive "Let's be friends" express was coming his way, the whistle shrieking.

"We were supposed to have lunch, but I'd like to talk with you in your room, if we could?" She was clipped, businesslike. *Yep, the "Let's be friends" talk.* He knew it.

Gwen was always striking in person. She was of medium height, with a Louise Brooks haircut, every dark brown strand of hair always in place. She wore a heavy sweater to ward off the chill and a pair of dark jeans that cost way more than they appeared to. Evan never saw Gwen wear extravagant footwear, always flats, usually penny loafers or boat shoes. Never sneakers either unless she went to the gym, which was every morning at 5 a.m.

Her expression could go from lively and excited to intense and serious in a second. Evan could understand why the

Paramount brass liked her so much; she was one of those who could look totally absorbed by someone and have absolutely no idea what they were talking about. Gwen had the gift of making insecure people feel important.

Evan promised himself he would take it like a man. How would Bogart have reacted? He'd light a Chesterfield and remain unfazed, and that was the plan Evan hatched in his head. He was going to be like Bogart. Totally cool, detached, barely moved. Yes, he'd act like a real man.

"Can I get you anything? Water, tea, coffee?" he offered, like a real man.

Gwen shook her head, and Evan figured it would be best to get this over with as quickly as possible. Evan led her back to his room, walking quickly like a condemned prisoner headed to the death chamber. While he knew they had no future, it always stunk to be rejected, even by someone you had already decided to reject.

He closed the door and sat down. Gwen stayed on her feet.

"Evan, I'm sure you know what's coming," she began.

Evan feigned ignorance, grinning broadly just to shove the knife in deeper. Maybe she'd feel guilty after doing this.

"I've been thinking. We're just not going to make it in the long run, so we might as well cut our losses. We're not getting any younger."

Evan's smile vanished because the hurt was real. He might have already realized they had no future, but it still stung that she realized it too and threw in the towel first. He could tell she was feeling no guilt and just wanted to get this over with. That was what hurt most of all.

"But, uh, maybe we should just be friends, you know? I think we could. I do like talking with you." Gwen looked at the floor.

Evan nodded, his face flushed. A lock of dark brown hair fell in his face, and he involuntarily sniffled like Connor.

"Yeah, well, I'm sorry it came to this," Evan said in a low, broken voice.

"Yeah, me too, but someone else will come along for you, Evan. Someone who you're right for."

Evan thought for a second, then asked the question he didn't really want to know the answer to:

"You met someone else?"

Then the guillotine fell….

"It's none of your business, but yes, I have."

"Where?" Evan should have known better than to ask, but he did anyway.

"On Twitter. He followed me and liked my Tweets."

Evan threw his arms up in despair—he was gutted. Twitter. She might as well have told him she met him while visiting a prison.

"You asked!" Gwen shouted, crossing her arms and throwing him a burning glare. "Which you shouldn't have done if you didn't want the truth!"

"You could have lied and left me in peace, but you did that to deliberately make me feel like crap!" Evan exploded, surprised by how angry he'd become. Evidently, he couldn't control his emotions Bogart-style.

"This is why we don't work, Evan. You don't act like a man. You are a little boy with your old car, your antique clothes, that silly haircut... I mean, you don't even listen to normal music. You don't Tweet, you don't Instagram, you're not getting your name out there. You're not even on IMDbPro. Look, I don't want to be hurtful. Let's just say goodbye and part as friends."

Evan had heard enough. He liked Gwen, found her attractive, smart, and witty, but now that someone else had captured her heart, he was absolutely, totally, 100 percent in love with her.

She held out her hand to shake. Evan took it, offering the limpest, most insincere handshake he could muster.

"I'll see myself out. It's better that way." Then Gwen did something Evan hadn't expected; she handed the flower Hank gave her back to him.

In a quick motion, Gwen turned on her heel, smartly opened the door, and just like that, she was gone, leaving behind her a wide wake of bruised feelings. It was the sting that came with rejection, a sting no one ever got used to.

Thoughts tumbled in Evan's mind. Maybe Gwen was right; he could have underestimated their mismatch. If he had tried to not be so "Evan West" all the time, perhaps he could have made that relationship work. But no, someone else had come along. There was always someone else. Someone smarter, stronger, faster, better looking… Someone who had "it," that thing Evan couldn't understand and certainly didn't have.

Someone who enjoyed the steaming Krell labs of Twitter and Instagram and everything else Evan detested.

Evan crumpled the flower in his hand, hoping to look like Quint in *Jaws* crushing a steel beer can, but he came off like Hooper trying to copy him with the paper cup.

The petals showered his keyboard. He brushed them away, accidentally hit the space key, and brought the computer to life.

"Damn you. Damn you to Hell!" Nicolas Cage shouted from the laptop's speakers.

It was the first thing Evan heard and the best way to end the prior conversation. He felt awful about crushing the flower, so he gathered the petals and stuffed them in his pocket.

It was only 12:38. Evan's day was halfway over and about to get worse than he could have ever imagined.

CHAPTER 3
DAY OF INFAMY

3:01 P.M.

The rain was coming down even harder than it had when Evan arrived that morning. Evan finalized his edit, finished recording Richard, went back to editing the trailer, and laid back his separate audio tracks, ready to send to the mixer across the street at Paramount.

The Big Lot. Where he wished he could be.

Evan felt a shadow looming behind him. Then he heard a sniff. Connor was back to make his already deplorable day worse. He carried several old-time 16mm film canisters. Connor lifted his eyebrows, daring Evan to ask about them.

Evan took the bait. "What are those?"

Connor smiled, leaning forward. Evan could smell the Chanel Homme, garlic, and mendacity that wafted from him. Connor looked over his shoulder with exaggerated caution—like he was being hunted. The man always liked people to think he had something up his sleeve. The reality was, he rarely did.

But this time was different. This time, he actually had something to hide, and it was unholy.

"Can you keep a secret, like, you know, dude, the biggest secret imaginable?" Connor asked, using the word "dude," which Evan despised.

"I am Mr. Secret. We've worked together two years. You've told me all kinds of stuff…."

Connor waved a hand, shushing him. "Forget it. Whatever I told you, forget it."

"I don't even know what you're talking about." Evan smiled, doing his best to be as jovial as possible with his crocodile-like boss.

Connor held up the film canister as if it were an Oscar, then lifted the top of the can to display a reel of 16mm movie film.

"You know what this is?" Connor asked.

Even crossed his arms. "16mm movie film," he answered, almost annoyed at being asked such a basic question.

"But what is it a movie of, bro?" Connor was happy, not feigning this time but really, actually happy.

The embossed lettering read: **IT'S A WONDERFUL LIFE.**

"Ooookaayyy," Evan purred, not sure where this was going. "It's one of my favorites."

"And that's where you're wrong, Evan…. This isn't the movie you know and love. It's the version of *It's A Wonderful Life* I would have directed!" Connor drew out the word "I" nice and long because he was the most important part of the sentence. "This is from a time capsule and *not* the version Capra wanted anyone to see."

Connor's eyes were lit up with glee. He was on cloud ten heading to eleven.

"There was another version?" Evan asked. His heart sped up, and sweat poured from his forehead. The hank of brown hair fell in his face again.

Things were not going well today. Gwen just left, and now his favorite movie in the world had apparently been directed in the style of Connor Alcott, a style no man on Earth would want to see.

"I mean, this has scenes that were never used in the original movie, bro! Like, uh, there's a scene of old George Bailey whopping Mary across the face, open-handed! Ka-pow! Big slap!" Connor was almost dancing with joy.

"What!?" Evan almost shouted. There was no way he would be able to be Bogart-cool with this news. "George Bailey slaps Mary? No!"

"Yes, bro, *yes!*" Connor laughed like a maniac. "And remember Uncle Billy, the drunk? George Bailey gives him a mighty beatdown after he loses the money! Right there in the old Savings and Loan! Knocks him out big time, then kicks the old buzzard in the butt!"

Evan's mind was turning somersaults. *Wait, wait, wait… if this is a dream, I have to wake up.* Frank Capra and Jimmy Stewart shot those scenes in 1946.

No way.

"And when George Bailey comes home after losing all that money, he tells Mary that they should sell the brats to an orphanage! That's just dope!" Connor was too happy, breathing too heavily.

Evan secretly wished at this point Connor would drop dead of a heart attack.

"You saw these? Tell me the truth!" Evan asked pointedly. Connor was known to lie.

"No, I didn't. I had some people view it for me, bro," Connor revealed.

"What people?" Evan squeaked.

"Can't tell you. It's that secret, and I don't trust you, but let me say they're top people."

"Who?"

"Top people!" Connor grunted, like the fat, officious government guy with the pipe in *Raiders of the Lost Ark*.

Evan's mind raced; Capra would never shoot something that awful, repulsive, or violent. Sure, *Meet John Doe* had an attempted suicide, but it was never carried through. Mr. Potter was a mean old creep, but he never had anyone killed. Capra wasn't capable of it, and Stewart wouldn't allow it. But then again, Stewart had done *The Naked Spur* and *Winchester '73* in which he went dark—like, really dark. Did those two guys wind up so deep in the throes of PTSD from World War II that they sunk into film-noir bleakness and shot those scenes in a battle-fatigue-induced fugue state?

"No one told Capra what to shoot. He'd never film scenes like that!" Evan almost shouted, and Connor loved to see how he'd riled Evan.

"I dunno, but they're there." Connor feigned a nonchalant shrug. "You know, top people—"

Evan interrupted, "Top people. Yeah, I get it. People that I would never know about."

Connor, clearly loving making Evan squirm like a worm on a hook, leaned in closer with barely hidden glee and fired his kill shot: "Look, dude, I'm releasing this for VOD and was on the phone with Amazon this morning. They're gonna buy it for the 75th anniversary of the movie's release! That's right!

It's the 75th anniversary of *It's A Wonderful Life*'s release in 1946—the frickin' Diamond Anniversary! Diamond, dude! I'm gonna have a pile of 'em after all this is over! Love those four words: *Pay per view streaming!*"

Evan didn't know how to respond except to say, "It's a classic. You can't do this! It's wrong! There must be copyright issues. Someone must own the distribution, like Turner Classics or someone!"

Connor, ruffled, got defensive. "Don't ask me about rights. This thing went into PD a long time ago, bro. The legal loopholes with this movie are like a block of Swiss cheese! And I got top people workin' for me on it, so… finders keepers, and it's gonna be my launchpad for the bigger and the better."

"Like what?" Evan asked, standing. "You gonna find the version of *The Wizard of Oz* where the Wicked Witch of the West wins?"

Connor laughed. "If I can find that, I'll do the same! Wouldn't that be awesome to see the Wicked Witch of the East set the Scarecrow on fire—and this time, he burns down? Now that would be something to see."

Connor exited the room, leaving behind a cheap aroma that only a circus clown would enjoy. Evan didn't bother to correct him; a house had crushed the East Witch at the beginning of act two, but what did it matter?

Evan burned with indignation. The only good thing about his conversation with Connor was that it had vacuumed the conversation with Gwen out of his head. Now he wanted to save George and Mary Bailey, Uncle Billy, and yes, even Mr. Potter in his own way.

That print must not ever be seen, Evan thought to himself. No, *Nyet, Nein, Non!*

No. Big fat *no!*

Connor returned to his office and closed the door. He was elated, even beyond the good news he got from Amazon, but from the devastating effect it had on Evan West. Evan, that talented little jerk, was a purist, and Connor got exactly the reaction he was looking for.

Yes!

Still woozy and light-headed from the cocaine he had used the night before, Connor opened the bottle of Absolut Mandrin, his favorite. He scooped some ice from his mini-freezer, snatched a very clean glass, and plunked in three ice cubes. Then he poured the nectar from the Swedish gods, knocking it back. The combined awesomeness of alcohol and sugar was sweet, sometimes sweeter than life itself.

And it sure took the edge off a cocaine hangover and headache.

The alcohol quickly took effect, bringing a strange clarity to his mind. The shock factor alone meant dollar signs—big dollar signs. The bigger the better. When it came to money, size always mattered, and no woke jackass was going to take this from him. The shock effect that his satanic version of *It's A Wonderful Life* would have was going to be like an atomic explosion. Twitter would burn up; he'd get more buzz than a lightning storm.

Life was good for Connor and was about to get better. He'd "circle back" to Evan later.

CHAPTER 4

THE QUEEN OF HEARTS

Evan finished the audio recording and laid back his last audio track at 5:50 p.m., the process taking longer than he had hoped. His ProTools rig was acting glitchy and cost him time.

So much for the nap he had planned on.

The foundation of his soul had been destroyed over the course of five hours, and something told him, today was one of those "fulcrum moments" in life. Nothing would ever be the same, and while he could live without Gwen, he couldn't live knowing *It's A Wonderful Life* had been desecrated by a trust-fund-moron like Connor Alcott.

Evan finished, then pulled up the trades online; it was a bad habit, but it kept him distracted from the horror he'd just heard.

He went to Variety and saw a review of a movie he'd edited the trailer for: *"Rage is not a great movie. The violence is hopelessly gratuitous, and the message is downright irresponsible. But one must give credit to the trailer utilized in marketing. The editing by Evan West of Killer Trailers is slick, and it has virtually insured at least some nominal box office magic."*

Evan was taken aback; they never mentioned movie trailers in movie reviews. The review felt somewhat like the line in *Ed Wood* when Ed reads the Variety review of his cheap play.

"Hey, it's not that bad. You can't concentrate on the negative. He's got some nice things to say, see? 'The soldier costumes are very realistic!' That's positive! We're doing good work, people!"

He slipped on his 1940s-era, Bogart-like trench coat and reached for the umbrella. The rain was still coming down, and it was going to be a tricky drive home. A 1938 Ford didn't exactly hug the road like a Tesla.

Once in his Ford, the comforting smell of cold steel, wool seats, and gasoline made him feel like life wasn't all that bad… but he still had a big choice before him: Either allow Connor to get that horrific monstrosity to Amazon, or forget about it and try to live the best life possible knowing one of his favorite movies of all time had its reputation sullied. Evan remembered something his mother told him years ago: "A reputation is a funny thing, Ev…takes years to build it up, and one day to destroy it."

Evan was not a total purist. Most 1938 Ford Coupes did not have an AM radio installed; those were only standard for the sedans and, of course, the big Lincoln Zephyrs. Driving in LA traffic was always bad, never an enlightening or enjoyable process, but attempting to do so in total silence was unbearable, a slow Chinese water torture of red brake lights and sun-baked mediocrity. To avoid that feeling of life ticking away in his car, Evan had an AM radio put in. He'd never have a digital radio in his car, much less FM or a way to hook an iPod into the sound system, but he'd settled for an antique 1947 Philco AM radio that was once in one of the first post-war Fords.

His favorite station: KNX 1070, LA's oldest. News and

weather all day, and he couldn't live without it.

He exited the Raleigh gates, heading east on Melrose. Rain beat down. Those old, vacuum-powered wipers didn't do much, but they kept the windshield clear enough. The news headlines were unmemorable: COVID vaccination spots, a big pileup on the Grapevine caused by the rain and snow, LA's mayor wanted to host a diversity celebration via Zoom at the Dorothy Chandler Pavilion…

Then the trapdoor opened—a school shooting had happened that very day. Evan winced at the announcement. Another one of those horrific events that never seemed to end, part of the chain of madness that defined the twenty-first century as far as Evan was concerned. Pandemics, riots, mass murder, civil unrest, young women twerking on police cars… the list of woes went on and on.

"A young man of eighteen years in Parrington, California, about twenty-six miles north of Los Angeles, brought a handgun to school and proceeded to open fire on his fellow students in the cafeteria.

"Theodore Martin Huckabee, eighteen, killed himself after a devastating attack that took nine lives—two teachers and seven students—and wounded twenty-three more. A manifesto online made it clear Huckabee was inspired by the early release of the trailer *Rage* on Netflix, a movie depicting a homicidal alien from another world sent to the world to exterminate humanity …"

Evan pounded the big steering wheel with frustration. "This cannot be happening! You dumb kid. It's just a movie!" Evan hissed under his breath, but there was no point—the dumb kid had already assumed RAGE was more than a movie and killed nine people and wounded twenty-three more. The breathless newscaster continued his dreadful recap of horror:

"Police interviews with witnesses on the scene and those who knew Huckabee described him as a normal, middle-class student with no criminal record but who was fascinated by violent horror films and true-crime television shows…"

Evan knew the power of cinema, its unbelievable influence on weak minds. He had read how Vladimir Putin imitated *The Godfather* in his weekly staff meetings, even using Don Corleone lines to terrify his underlings. And then there was that lonely loser John Hinckley Jr. and his attempted assassination of President Ronald Reagan after watching *Taxi Driver* too many times. According to all the headlines, Hinckley had imagined himself as Travis Bickle, a man no one should feel comfortable being. Evan had even heard whispers that those two confused walking nightmares, Eric Klebold and Dylan Harris, had possibly been influenced by *The Matrix* when they had committed atrocities at Columbine High School in 1999.

Movies had immortality, Evan knew that. They lived on forever, burned into popular imagination, and to some, they even provided a template for life. Evan shook his head and thought, *It's a wonder no one has yet been tempted to follow Arthur Fleck's path in Joker… perhaps go on an extreme diet, chain-smoke, kill businessmen on the subway, and then take out Jimmy Kimmel live on TV.*

And now *this* had happened.

Evan switched off the radio. He looked down at his buzzing iPhone. It was Connor Alcott, more than likely calling to gloat about "his" trailer or with the usual instructions.

No, no, no, no. Not Connor.

Not tonight. Not now, at least. Oscar Wilde said the only thing worse than being talked about was not being talked about, but not in this case. This was ghoulish. Evan felt he'd actually put the gun in Huckabee's hand, or worse, created the motivation for him to kill nine people and leave everyone else in that school permanently scarred. Evan conjured up an image of a Terminator-like goon walking through the school, twin .45s in hand, blasting at everyone he could lay eyes on.

Evan tried to shut the bleak image out of his mind, but it was there and would never leave, like when someone takes a flash photo of you, and the blue dot is left in your eyes after that blinding light. All he could envision was hateful rage in Theodore Huckabee's eyes, the gun shooting, and some poor high schoolers who had either lost everything physically they had, or worse, lost their innocence, something you could never retrieve.

Evan wanted someone to talk with, anyone, except Gwen. No way. She was probably still at work or with "the new guy," and Evan found that thought sickening. If there was ever a time he wished he could call his mother, it was now, but she had been gone for years, had died when he was sixteen. His father left when Evan was five; he never got to meet the man and was left with a paucity of father figures in his life. Evan then thought about all the mothers who would never get the chance to speak to their kids again after today.

Evan openly sobbed; he couldn't help it. The rain came down harder, and he had to pull over. It took all his strength just to manhandle his car, which drove like a tractor on a good day. On that rainy day, with Evan distracted by his broken heart, it handled like a WWII M4 Sherman tank missing a track.

He had never felt more alone or desolate in his life except for the day his mother died.

Evan drove to the large apartment building on 1001 Orange Grove. It was one of those buildings from the 1930s—six stories, red brick, with big fire escape ladders that snaked down the front of the building like an oversized Erector Set. Evan was still in a state of shock. He parked, not bothering with the umbrella since the rain had slackened. He walked slowly into the lobby, still wearing his work clothes. He admired the old-time LA noir décor. Evan loved the steel postboxes on the wall. Even nicer, the lobby featured an old-time cage elevator to take him up. Evan studied the antique lines and metal of the elevator as he approached. It was a dying breed in LA, and he was always happy to see one.

Evan didn't revel in that feeling for long; the thought of a bloodstained high school flashed in his brain like a crime photo. He glanced up to see a large mirror in the lobby, the kind that reflects too much.

He didn't see himself anymore. He saw a murderer, a degenerate killer who was in league with Satan, with Connor Alcott and his putrid visual poetry.

Evan got in the elevator, which smelled of grease, rust, and age. He hit the button numbered "6" and headed up. He watched the floors pass until the lift lurched to the sixth floor.

He made up his mind then and there. He'd hand in his resignation to Connor tomorrow. It was time to think about heading back to Kansas City, maybe working at the local cable station. He could start his own "movie appreciation" podcast that might get more than twenty listeners if he were lucky.

Evan took a deep breath, then knocked on Apartment 601.

Hank opened the door, a big grin on his face. "Mr. West, I presume! You made it!"

Evan couldn't find the words to express how much seeing Hank's face made him feel good again after the tunnel of shame and anguish he had just gone through.

"Well, sir, come on in. We're about to start the movie!" Hank exclaimed. The man was always in such a good mood. Evan would love to know where he got that kind of happiness, bottle it, sell half the case, and drink the rest.

"I didn't know about a movie…," Evan stammered.

Hank motioned for Evan to come in, but Evan was afraid to get near Hank, worried he might poison him with his vile evil, the price of selling his soul. "Did you hear the news?" Evan could barely croak out the words.

Hank nodded sadly, resigned. "Yeppers. Tragedy. Saw it on the Twitter. The worst kind because young people were involved. I'm so sorry for their families."

Talk about grinding a stake in Evan's heart. He didn't know how it could get any worse.

"Please tell me you don't go on Twitter?" Evan pleaded.

"Sure," Hank answered. "I go on the TikTok too. Love the dog tricks and the daredevil skiers."

Evan's face fell, and Hank laughed. "It's okay, Evan, you can live in the world, just don't be of the world."

Evan tried to collect his thoughts, then muttered, "I just edit the stuff. It's not my—"

Hank held up a hand to shush him.

A woman's voice called out. "We're about to watch the movie. Come on in. Soft drinks and popcorn!"

That was when Evan saw Dorothy, ninety-nine years old, but she could have passed for much younger, maybe even under seventy without Botox or filler. She stood up in the middle of the living room, wreathed in the glow of Christmas lights. She had that "thing" around her that said she'd walked the Earth for years and didn't let it compromise her spirit. Not one bit.

"My favorite film. *It's A Wonderful Life*," Hank chuckled.

"Yeah, mine too!" Evan chimed in. When he spoke, Dorothy suddenly perked up, seeing him. She slipped on a pair of glasses to see him better, and she had that look of someone who was thinking *Don't I know you?* She glided to Evan, no hint of arthritis in her step.

"Have we met before, ma'am?" Evan asked. She was about to nod, then a look crossed her face that Evan could not read.

"We have now. I'm Dorothy Paige, and you are?"

"Evan West," he said. Dorothy looked like she was light-headed, as if she just heard something that rang a long, silent bell in her head, a bell she hadn't heard in years.

"I knew an Evan West once long ago, even looked similar to you, but that would be impossible. Please come in. You are very welcome here." Dorothy Paige had that old-school charm and self-awareness about her that the world now so sorely missed. She took herself and the way she presented herself seriously enough to be respectable, but she didn't work too hard for approval.

"You seem out of sorts," Dorothy said but not in an accusatory way. It was as if she simply cared, which was a lot more than most people seemed able to muster these days, in Evan's opinion.

"I've had better days" was all Evan could come up with that sounded good.

Dorothy reached out and took Evan by the arm in that nice, courtly way the girls used to in the movies. She lit up with a smile bright enough to blind. "Come sit with me during the movie. I don't wiggle too much or bite. I'm in this one, did you know that? Five will get you ten you can't spot me."

"I'd be careful with that bet," Evan spoke up, suddenly feeling better than he had in hours. "I know every frame, every beat, every line of dialogue, and every note of music from that movie."

Hank looked to Evan. "She was on the set, Evan, so be careful. She worked as a waitress at a diner near the studio, and somehow, Jimmy Stewart got her a job to be in the movie."

Evan suddenly looked like he wasn't so smart after all.

"Okay, I'll play." She smiled gracefully. Her teeth were still white and shiny, almost translucent. "Did you know that when the film was made, due to sloppy paperwork at Liberty Films, *Wonderful* fell into public domain in 1974? Shame, too."

Evan was impressed. How could he not be? She might have been old, but she had her movie knowledge down better than he had his own.

"You got me there. I did not know that," Evan admitted.

Dorothy's mouth curled up in a half-smile. "Every frame, maybe. But every fact, I got ya there. The movie has made very little money since its release in 1946. None of the actors, directors, producers have made a dime from it. Jimmy learned his lesson, and it prompted him to make the deal he pushed for in *Winchester '73*. First actor to actually have an ownership stake in a movie, so at least something good came out of it."

Evan couldn't bring himself to tell her that his horrible

boss with the unmentionable name already had that figured out and planned on desecrating this movie, which to Evan was the equivalent of painting graffiti on the sanctuary floor of St. Peter's. Evan had to change the subject, considering that his secret knowledge of what was about to happen to the film was horrible and obscene.

"Are you still acting?" he asked. Dorothy broke into a laugh that came from a good place.

"Oh, my goodness, no, my dear young man. After *Wonderful*, I went into a little business, worked with Coca-Cola as a franchise partner. Afterward, I invested heavily in a company that manufactured typewriters and punch codes called IBM. It worked out fine." She motioned to the apartment and smiled sweetly. "I own the building and the others on this block. I should be okay for the next several years, God willing."

Hank burst out laughing and leaned over to Evan. "She owns the buildings the block over, too, all the way up to DeLongpre. And you know that little shopping area on Sunset and Sunset Plaza? That too." Hank winked at Evan, then looked to Dorothy. "Sometimes, we Hollywood people forget you can make a fortune elsewhere, we're so mired in our palm-tree-dappled-first-look deals and residual checks."

Evan's cell buzzed, not a few times but over and over. Incessantly. Evan blushed, shrugging.

"I'm so sorry," he said, and Dorothy gave him a look that said, *Do what you must.*

Evan knew it was Connor; only he would call like that and keep calling. That was what he did. The entire world was at his beck and call, whenever and however he chose. Evan backed away from everyone, held up an apologetic hand, then retreated into a small room that was lit only by an old-fashioned Tiffany lamp. He noticed Dorothy's apartment was really three apartments she had taken for herself, all filled with tasteful furniture and various portraits on the walls of people who had lived in a long-ago era.

He picked up. With Connor, there was no "Hello, how are ya?" He would just start talking as if in mid-sentence.

"You heard the news, right, bro?"

"Yeah, I heard. You okay with it?" Evan already knew the answer to that.

"Sure, fine. I mean, whatever. I didn't kill those people, dude. But I gotta get you to agree to this: No talking to newspeople. I'm already getting calls. No statements, no conjecture, no nothing. Got it, bro?" Connor loved sounding like "a boss."

"Sure, sure. No statements, no talking to the press. As if I would." Evan tried to regain some of his swagger.

"Well, I don't know what you'd do, dude. So, for your own sake, keep your mouth shut." Connor was threatening, but it didn't really get to Evan. It wasn't easy to be threatened by someone you didn't respect. "So, now that that's solved, tomorrow, we're screening *Wonderful Life*, my version, tomorrow at ten in room 3. We'll circle back tomorrow, got it? You better be there. I know it's Sunday and all, but that's just another day to me."

"What is wrong with you?" Evan asked. "One minute, you're worried about the press and statements about *Rage* and this clown show of a tragedy, and the next, you're gonna throw this awful abomination of a longtime favorite film out to the world?"

"Bro, I'm a Hollywood producer. Trouble is my middle name. Law of the jungle to be both reckless and fool-hearted and welcome trouble! Circle back tomorrow. Lates!" Connor mercifully ended the call.

Again, that awful phrase. *Circle back. What the heck does it even mean?* Evan wondered. *Everyone says it so much now. Kind of like the word "literally," as in literally used far too often.*

"Sorry about that. I'm coming," Evan apologized, rushing back toward the main room. Soon, the lights went down, and brilliance unfolded on Dorothy's enormous flatscreen with a picture so bright and pristine it looked like a 4k hi-def master. Evan took a seat by Dorothy, who offered him popcorn.

He lost himself in the swirl of Frank Capra's genius. The scene where George Bailey and Mary fell in the pool, the sweetness of George pressing his cheek against hers, saying, "Mary…Mary…" because he loved her so much, it hurt. The movie went by so fast, it was a blur. Evan stole a glance at Dorothy's Christmas tree in the corner. It was flawlessly decorated, a grand tree that seemed so at home in this house, it was like a movie set: Perfect in every way.

The final scene had finally come up. George Bailey had returned to his family after Clarence had shown him what a terrific life he led. In the scene, Dorothy, much younger but very much the same, was in the crowd, singing "Auld Lang Syne." Evan touched Dorothy's arm and pointed at her on the screen, his face about to crack from the size of his grin.

Dorothy looked to Evan, a tear in her eye, and nodded with the kind of vigor most ninety-somethings could never muster.

"Prettiest girl on the screen," Evan whispered. Dorothy reached for and gripped his hand. She exuded warmth that made Evan almost tingle. "Charmer."

From that moment on, Evan found himself captivated by

a woman seventy years older than himself. He monopolized her attention while Hank watched, bemused. Evan asked her about her time on the set of the movie, what Capra was like and how he approached each scene, her impression of James Stewart, and about her experience working with Donna Reed and Gloria Grahame.

Dorothy told him stories of fights, creative battles, the laughs, tears, and disputes. She described the grind of shooting with men who had just come back from World War II and still couldn't shake the memories of what they saw from their souls. She also vaguely remembered something else Evan never knew about—how a certain producer on the lot, his name long forgotten, had insisted Capra shoot certain scenes everyone on the cast and crew found repulsive. But they did it anyway because, in those days, orders were orders.

The magical night that capped off one of Evan's worst days came to an end. Dorothy and Hank walked Evan to the elevator, and she cocked her head toward him.

"Evan, I swear I've met you before. It's coming back to me now. I would swear on Frank Capra's grave I know you," she said to Evan, seeming almost in awe of her memories as they flooded back. "It's uncanny."

"You knew someone as miserable and broke as me?" Evan laughed, and Dorothy suddenly straightened as if to launch into a very serious explanation, then she softened.

"No, no…he was handsome and gentle. A wonderful man. He always made me laugh. Everyone loved him. Maybe you have a double out there, Mr. West. They say we all do."

There seemed to be something ethereal between them. It was as if time had stood still. Evan had never felt something this intense before, an emotional pull between two people who simply admired one another, nothing more. Dorothy's eyes filled.

"I sure hope we can spend more time together, Dorothy," Evan said.

"Anything's possible," she replied and handed Evan an old-fashioned calling card. "Goodnight."

Hank waved to him. "Something magical happened here tonight," Hank said, and Evan cocked his head questionably. Hank looked to Evan as if he were crazy. "You know good and well what happened here. You develop early onset Old Timer's, or something? We just watched *It's A Wonderful Life* with one of its last eight surviving cast members."

Evan nodded, smiled, and stepped into the elevator. He looked back to Hank and Dorothy, wishing he could stay. The warmth Hank and Dorothy exuded was like the smell of freshly baked bread or a newly opened carton of ice cream. It was the sensation of home and being loved.

Sometimes moments in life can be too good to ever end. But if they didn't, all the fun would go out, Evan thought.

I mean, who wants warm milk and cookies every night?

Evan got back to his small apartment on Whitley near the Hollywood intersection. His apartment was loaded with furniture and one sheets (movie posters) of *Goldfinger*, *Back to the Future*, and *Jaws*. He went to the kitchen, snatched a water bottle from the refrigerator, and thought about his day: Hank…the end with Gwen… And then he went dark as he considered Connor Alcott, the coiled, thrashing tentacles of Connor's presence and works seeming to grip his heart. Evan shook that thought away, reflecting back on Dorothy and Hank and *It's A Wonderful Life* and, of course, the glory that Frank Capra had gifted the world.

Once in bed, he could not sleep. A sudden conviction had filled him. He was going to save *It's A Wonderful Life*. He didn't know how, but he was going to do it.

God willing, as Dorothy liked to say, he would save a national treasure from desecration.

CHAPTER 5
INTO THE BREACH

The rain was still coming down hard Sunday morning, harder than any other time Evan could remember. And the wind… It was blowing something fierce, Evan could see birds in the sky that seemed to be floating, beating their wings against a headwind so powerful, they could not conquer it.

Despite the tempest outside, Evan was inwardly thrilled. He'd never done something this bold before, and he was satisfied with himself in a way only a man who'd told his tyrannical boss to "Take this job and shove it" could be.

Evan blasted east along Santa Monica as fast as he dared in that old Ford, all eight-bangers humming. The car was slippery on the rainy roads, especially with its narrow sixteen-inch tire size.

Evan relished recounting what he'd just done. It was so mind-blowing. Just thirty minutes earlier, in the screening room, Evan had been tasked with lacing the old Bell and Howell projector Connor found. He took that heavy beast up into a projection booth, and rather than start the movie, he'd grabbed those precious film canisters, dropped the entire stack on his toe (he could still feel it throbbing. It had been a five-alarm "Ouch!"), exited through the front doors, threw the cans on the front seat with a metallic shuffle, and get-awayed.

Evan thought for sure he had felt Connor watching him earlier with intensity. Like the lizard the man was, he seemed to have a sharp, innate sense for potential danger. So, he had kept a close eye on Evan, sensing his imminent betrayal.

And he sensed right.

Evan was just out of the lot when he saw the headlights of Connor's tank-like Range Rover behind him.

Evan swung left on Melrose Boulevard, switched to the right lane, then hooked a quick right onto Gower, wheeling past the old RKO globe and Astro Burgers. The rain was coming down so hard now, it was almost impossible to see through the windshield, the old wipers barely clearing the precipitation.

He blew past the Hollywood Memorial Cemetery, hoping that Providence was on his side. Evan was acting crazy, like all men on a mission tended to. Saving *It's A Wonderful Life* had suddenly become more important than exercising safety, at least on that day. History was depending on him, and he could feel its warm embrace pulling, guiding and showing him the way.

Either it was the hand of fate, or he was losing his mind. Evan shook that latter option off. This was about courage and commitment, about being bigger than he had ever been. He couldn't help but remember the great John Wayne quote: "Courage is when you're scared to death, but you saddle up anyway."

"God willing, I can do this!" Evan shouted over the heavy percussion of rain—and then hail—that pounded the steel roof of his Ford mercilessly.

Evan ran the light at Santa Monica Boulevard, pitched left, and lost control of his car for a horrific, heart-dropping second. He downshifted, correcting by steering right, then left. The Ford responded beautifully.

Evan grinned. *Say what you want about anti-Semitic, Hitler-loving Henry Ford, but the man knew how to make a fine automobile.*

Evan glanced into the rearview mirror. Connor was still behind him. He had run that light as well. Evan gritted his teeth. His boss was becoming really annoying. He was also driving a much faster car.

Evan fired through the Vine intersection, seeing Cahuenga up ahead calling his name. It was almost like a push. Evan had never experienced anything so "real" in his life. It was as if a warm presence was pushing him in the back of the head and leaning him toward the right, urging, "*Go...right...here!*"

Evan spun the huge steering wheel, and the Ford effortlessly pivoted right, the film canisters sliding off the big bench seat and clattering to the floor. Evan downshifted to second, and his big toe barked with pain from his earlier injury when he hit the clutch, but he didn't mind as he heard that big V-8 roar. To his left, he passed the Hollywood Recreation Center, noting that the baseball field was completely soaked. He pressed forward, glancing in the rearview. Connor was not far behind.

At this point, he wasn't sure why he was heading north on Cahuenga except a very loud voice in his head was telling him to.

"TAKE CAHUENGA NORTH," boomed the voice. **"NO QUESTIONS."**

Evan asked no questions—though he was wondering what he was supposed to do once he reached Cahuenga East's end-point at Barham Boulevard.

Turn right and head into Burbank...or go left and cross the 101 Freeway. Maybe double back?

He weighed those options, glancing at the gas gauge. A quarter of a tank left. Maybe he could make a quick right on Lakeridge, head toward the Hollywood reservoir, lose him there...

He shifted to third and felt the engine winding down, catching its breath. He splashed through an accumulated pool of water at the Sunset intersection. The engine coughed, suddenly drenched with water.

For a second, Evan worried the 1930's-era technology was going to let him down because, at the end of the day, old is old. He just couldn't compete against a British-made, creep-owned Range Rover.

His phone buzzed, but he wasn't about to pick it up. What could Connor say to him now? Cortez had burned his ships, and there was no going back now. It was conquer, or die.

His engine coughed again as if to shake off the wet. Evan watched Connor firing up behind him at amazing speed, and his eyes widened. Evan grabbed his gearshift and downshifted. *Ka-blam!* The car sputtered to life again, faster than ever, and he exploded forward like a rocket, blowing through the lights at Hollywood Boulevard and Cahuenga. The street before him snaked left, and he could make out the dim overhanging roof of the I-101 ahead.

His phone buzzed again, and this time Evan picked up.

"What do you want, Connor?" Evan shouted, a little too keyed up for his own good.

"What do you think I want, bro? You're in trouble, dude! You stop now, and we'll forget about it. Give me back the movie, and we'll let bygones be bygones. I mean, if you cooperate, you could have your job back, bro!"

"I don't want it back! I'm fired and plan on staying that way, Connor! Got that? I don't want it back!" Evan shouted so loud, his voice croaked. He mashed his thumb on the end button and tossed the phone to the floorboard, where it landed with a heavy clunk.

The lights at the Franklin intersection were green, making it a lot easier for Evan to push onward—one more reason to believe Providence was guiding him toward something unknown and wonderful.

Connor was still behind him, the phone was buzzing like crazy, and Evan remained laser-focused…but fear was creeping up on him. He thought back to the Duke's saying about saddling up anyway. He was strangely comforted by the fact that he *had* saddled up, and now he was doing the unthinkable: He had stolen his boss's stolen goods.

That was when he quickly realized why no police were coming his way. *It's A Wonderful Life* didn't belong to Connor. It belonged to everyone, and Evan was going to keep it that way.

It filled him with new resolve.

He banked to the left as Cahuenga dipped toward Odin Street, which ran to Highland and the Hollywood Bowl. He jerked his wheel to the right and floored it as he climbed the hill past the old Hollywood Cross and the John Anson Ford Theater entrance.

Behind him, Connor was gaining, and so was a Honda Civic that was directly behind Connor, tailgating him.

Evan checked the speedometer—70 mph, an accomplishment for his magnificent beast. Now he had to make it to Barham Blvd, and then, well, he didn't know where he would go. But for the moment, everything was at peace with the universe. He was flying along at a good clip past the Cahuenga Tennis Condominiums. It was now raining so hard that the windshield was a splatter-shield of icy rain. And then hail began to pummel his car, a deluge of hailstones battering down on the painted metal and glass.

At the Tennis Condominiums, he hit 80. He'd never gone that fast in this car. Like Matthew said, the V-8 was singing a high note, and it was beautiful.

That was when Evan West's 1938 Ford began to hydroplane. Not like a modern-day car hydroplane…more like an old car about to lurch totally out of control. Evan felt the car almost lift up and then spin around a full 360. The only good that came out of it was, he could spot Connor's Range Rover heaving to a stop and then skidding sideways. The Honda directly behind Connor smashed into his Range Rover, spinning it 180 degrees with a loud screech of steel and broken glass.

Connor's radiator erupted with a blast of steam.

Evan's car straightened, but he had no control over the machine. And he was headed directly for a heavy, concrete light pole that stood guard at the corner of Lakeridge and Cahuenga.

High-tension wires buzzed overhead.

Evan heard thunder boom; the sky above a black and blue bruise. He tried to steer away, but it was too late. His car had a rendezvous with that pole he could not avoid. It was like some manifest destiny, his Ford, that pole, and everything that was about to transpire.

The old car *smashed* into the pole; the right fender crumpled like tin foil. The car skated around, now at a right angle to the street. The sound was deafening—an explosion of iron, rubber, and concrete.

Evan's head *snapped* into the steering wheel, and for a few seconds, he was knocked unconscious.

The pole cracked, then danced off its foundation as if it were alive. The wires above snapped and sprayed blue and red sparks more colorful than a fourth of July fireworks show.

The pole toppled, landing inches from Evan's car with a massive *crash*! Concrete and steel rammed into the street, throwing up bits of debris.

The wires came down in six long, black snakes that spewed fire and electricity. The electrical currents reached out to each other and embraced, creating a magnesium-filled hot orb of electrical current that had taken on a life of its own; it was now a fusion reactor, flowing with highly charged electrons that meant business.

The two intertwined currents began to rotate and created a blue arch of electrodynamic power. The archway grew until it stood at least fifteen feet high, yet it wasn't done growing. Inside the arch was nothing but darkness as if the combined power of the two currents had created a vacuum that had sucked time and space into realms not yet discovered, and more importantly, maybe not ever meant to be.

In the car, Evan came to and could feel the enormous power of massive voltage combined with the wet charge of rain. The inside of his mouth had a coppery taste. His car engine stopped, and so did his watch. His hair stood on end. It crossed his mind that he was about to die. He had to get out of his car at the very least since he'd be cooked alive if he didn't bail out.

Evan escaped and rolled onto the ground, then looked up to see electrical sparks showering over him.

Above him, the electrical "gateway" grew as if created of electronically charged magnesium. He stood up and, distracted by the unexplainable sight, immediately tripped on the wet street and landed on his back. Ignoring the pain that shot up his spine, he rolled over with a grimace, then looked up. Any pain he was in was a forgotten memory as his eyes widened, and his mouth fell. The arch was beginning to collapse down on him.

Already, the tendrils of electric arcs laced over his car, the old Ford glowing red with indescribable heat. It soon began to glow white. He could feel its intensity burning into him, into everything.

The sight was horrible. Some things were not meant to be seen, and this huge, golden ring with an everlasting nothingness in the center was one such thing. He could feel how ancient it was, the eternal nature of it.

He scrambled to his feet, but it was too late. The tendrils of blue and red electricity rained down on him with white-hot, high-octane concentration, fed by the hailstones and rain.

Lightning flashed out of the sky, hit the ground next to Evan, and then fed into the swirling inferno of a nuclear chain reaction that kept growing with every millisecond.

Evan held his hands over his head like a character in an old sci-fi movie warding off a giant insect. He glanced inside his car to see the film canisters. That was when he thought, *This is it. This is what it's like to die. I can't stop what's about to happen. This is the end.*

Might as well go out like a man.

Evan looked to his right and saw Connor jogging toward him in the rain, a look of determination on his face.

Then it hit Evan—he had failed to save the movie. If God was really on his side, his old car would melt and take that evil print of *It's A Wonderful Life* with it.

Evan glanced back at the swirling power demon towering above him and pictured his hair turning white like Moses on Mount Sinai when he stared into the face of God.

Right before he blacked out, his last thought was *I've done my duty.*

CHAPTER 6
STRANGER IN A STRANGE LAND

Evan regained consciousness.

He was exactly where he was before; the electrical monster was now just two sputtering wires dancing on the pavement. Only the broken pole was made of wood, not concrete. No giant beast of fire and steel loomed over him, just two thin, rubber-coated wires snaking back and forth.

Dangerous, yes, but not the soul-swallowing, high voltage beast it was before.

He heard a car slowing, and he turned around to see a man in a tan, 1935 Chevrolet sedan pull over. He leaped out of his car and looked to Evan with worried, haunted eyes.

At first, Evan was convinced it was Connor and turned to flee.

"You okay, buddy?" The man was earnest with an intense face and lanky build, and he was not Connor. Not by a country mile. No sniffling, no "Better give me that film, bro."

The man wore a wide-brimmed gray fedora with a thick black band, an old-time blue double-breasted suit, and scuffed, brown, two-tone broughams. Evan shook his head, trying to clear his vision, but the man remained the same. He was not Connor.

What a relief!

"Yeah, sure, I lost control of my car and… Hey, I see you got one, too." Evan pointed at the man's car. The guy looked over his shoulder and shrugged. "Antiques are the best," Evan croaked, trying to cover up the fact that he was shaken to his core.

"Yeah, sure, I suppose, but it ain't that old, friend. And mine's a Chevy. Say, you need any help or anything?" The guy actually meant it, and Evan tried to figure out why a man with a tan 1935 Chevy sedan would not think it that old.

The man approached Evan, patted him on the shoulder, and held up two fingers.

"How many fingers am I holding up?" he asked, and Evan mirrored his gesture.

"Say it. How many?"

"Two."

Now satisfied, the man looked to Evan's car. "You're lucky. You coulda been killed. Why're you driving so fast in the rain?"

Evan shrugged. The man craned his neck to look over at Evan's car again, then jerked his thumb toward a small stairway across the street that led down.

"You go through that tunnel under the Red Car tracks. You come up over there on Cahuenga West. There's a filling station not far away. They got a tow truck. Want me to drive you over there? No skin off my nose. Happy to help."

Evan couldn't get over how earnest this guy was. He genuinely cared, and that wasn't behavior Evan was accustomed to. He glanced to his car. "It's okay. I got a phone." Evan looked around inside the interior, but it wasn't there. No iPhone on the passenger seat. No film canisters on the floor.

That's not right. Where are they?

"You do?" The man seemed genuinely perplexed over the idea. "You sure you're okay?"

Evan looked toward where the Hollywood freeway was supposed to be and saw a trolley rumble by. The freeway was there, but it was more of a wide road with three lanes on each side.

The Red Car tracks ran between both streets, right where the I-101 Freeway was in 2021.

Evan watched one Red Car rumble east, and the other rolled west. Sparks flew from the electrical roof pole.

Evan stared, soaking in the details as one wheeled along. A real Pacific Electric Red Car, red and gold on the sides… aluminum roof.

And there were people inside of it!

"Whoa! That's a Red Car!" Evan shouted.

"Yeppers, we got those in LA. Say, you sure you're okay? You sound kinda goofy. You hail from somewhere else?"

"No, I'm, um…" Evan was still trying to figure out where the heck he was. He noticed the rainstorm was just a drizzle now.

And then it hit him—the smell.

Wow.

Despite the rain, Evan detected the combined reek of exhaust fumes, stronger than anything he'd experienced before. He figured it was his car, which didn't look nearly as damaged as he assumed it would be. The Ford had a dented fender, sure, and the pole he had smashed into was still a fallen soldier; the electric lines around it danced, but not with the god-awful intensity he had witnessed before.

Evan looked back at the stranger, studying him. He looked like someone from an old photograph; the hat; the double-breasted suit was a dull blue, clearly woolen, with frayed lapels; and the wilted shirt collar hung loose around his neck. His blue necktie had a skinny knot with a bright red rose painted below.

He shook out a Lucky Strike cigarette and offered it to Evan. "No, thank you," Evan said.

The man took one for himself, flicked open a worn Zippo, and lit up. Evan noticed the cigarette was old-school, non-filtered, and smelled strong, a variation of cigar smoke as pungent as the exhaust smell that filled his lungs.

"Better get that tow truck. Go just under the tracks through there, then take a left down Highland. Sinclair station on the right at Franklin," the man continued, then added, "Sure I can't give you a lift?"

Evan wasn't sure, but he shook his head anyway. "No, I got it. I'm sure I can get it started," he said and hoped he actually could. He climbed in the car and punched the starter button on the floor. Nothing. Not even a *click*. The battery must have disconnected, or the engine was smashed.

Evan could hear sirens, not the modern *Woop! Woop!* he was accustomed to but the old-fashioned wail he knew from old movies.

"Lookie there. Cavalry to the rescue. Be careful out there, mister," the man said and climbed back in his Chevy. He cranked it up and turned back onto Cahuenga East, heading away. Evan figured the guy was like him, a daily re-enactor of the past in old clothes, driving an old car, and smoking old-time cigarettes, though that did not explain the Red Car...or what was about to happen next.

The fire trucks were on their way, two big American La-France trucks. Evan did a double take.

American LaFrance fire trucks? What is going on?!

The firemen leaped off their truck and hurried over to Evan. The one in charge, a big Irishman, red-faced and angry, shouted, "Hey, kid, you trying to get yourself killed?" The fireman pointed to the power lines on the ground, still hissing and sizzling. "Get your butt over on the other side of the road. Those wires are hot!"

The firemen went to work in heavy rubber gloves and dull brown raincoats. Their helmets were a dull black, nothing like the shiny-helmeted LAFD Evan remembered. These men were all very lean, far more slender than any of the firemen Evan had seen before.

Evan looked to the stairway leading down to the passageway the good Samaritan told him about. All the years he'd lived in LA, he had no idea this existed.

"Listen, kid, make yourself useful and get a tow truck over here, or I'll call one in myself, and it'll cost ya double."

Evan looked at the fire truck, pointing at it in wonder. He was still in a daze, woozy, barely able to take everything in at once. "That's a heckuva old truck you got."

The fireman leaned forward to Evan, sniffed him. "You been drinkin', kid?"

Evan shook his head. The fireman seemed satisfied regarding his sobriety and crossed his arms a little defensively.

"No, that is not old. City sprung for these with the surplus budget after the war ended. About time too." The fireman grunted with pride. "So, what's it gonna be, I call the tow truck or you get one yourself? I gotta get this heap outta here and on the double." The fireman looked at him closer. "Quite a bump you got on your head, kid."

Evan shrugged, rubbing his head where he hit the door. "It's not so bad," he explained.

The fireman didn't look convinced, but Evan just nodded, heading toward the underground passageway. "Yes, sir, I'll go get a tow truck," he said in passing.

"Hey!" the fireman shouted after him. "Slow it down, will ya? You only got one life, kid. Just 'cause you guys made it home don't make you bulletproof."

Evan hup-toed it to the passage, hurried down the stairs, and then peered into the tunnel that led to Highland. It was dark and musty down there, but actually *clean*. Water dripped from the ceiling, with no graffiti or discarded beer cans to be found anywhere. Evan noticed a smattering of cigarette butts, all from the non-filtered varieties of smokes.

Evan stepped into the tunnel, then stopped and just stood there, trying to bring some reason back into his life. He knew he was in Los Angeles, California, USA. He knew the streets. He knew the layout, but something was wrong.

Something? Evan thought incredulously. *Everything was wrong!*

The Red Car, the good Samaritan's car, the antique fire truck, the rainstorm that went from heavy to light… What the heck was going on?

A dark thought hit Evan like a shotgun blast. He was dead. That must be it.

He had been electrocuted, and now he was dead and in some kind of alternative universe. He had entered a long-past, long-dead version of Los Angeles.

But if he were dead, how come he could smell, taste, touch, and feel? The tobacco smoke from the Samaritan's Lucky Strike was as real as him smashing into that pole.

So, what was going on?

Evan moved into the underground passageway, noticing that the lights in this tunnel actually worked. Dim, old-fashioned tungsten lights burned overhead, not the dingy fluorescents that fouled most city-funded walkways.

The thought that he'd gone back in time crossed his mind, but he quickly dismissed that. *Back in time?* he mused. No… No way.

Time travel was impossible.

Then again, Evan remembered something he read somewhere….something about Einstein comparing time to a winding river, with all of us in a boat, drifting along between two high banks. "*We can't see the future beyond the next curve, or the past behind us, but it's all still there, as real as the moment around us.*"

But was it? *No.* Evan shook his head. *Impossible.*

He was dead. That had to be it.

He made his way toward the light at the end of the tunnel, looking down as he noticed for the first time some debris that had nothing to do with a cigarette butt.

Evan stared at it—an empty beer can that read Falstaff Beer along the side.

Evan's brow furrowed since Falstaff had been out of business since 2005. He picked up the can, and it wasn't the recyclable aluminum that weighed next to nothing.

This was heavy steel, the same type of can Quint crushed in *Jaws.* He thought back to when he had crushed Gwen's rose petals in a fit of misery, but that already seemed like it had happened a thousand years ago.

He admired the can's heft, wondering if it had just been left here sixteen years ago or so. Or maybe, just maybe, he'd gone back in time.

Again, impossible. *Had to be*, Evan reasoned, though he felt his heartbeat starting to ramp up, the heavy can becoming wet in his sweating hand.

Evan dropped the can, which thumped to the ground with a heavy sound. He picked up the pace, hurrying to the end of the tunnel and ascending the stairs there. His head popped out on Cahuenga West before it became Highland.

The rain had let up, but the skies overhead remained a baleful gray.

A dull-black 1934 Ford sedan rumbled by, the V-8 engine rumbling just as his sedan did. Then a dark-green 1940 Dodge, followed by a blue, 1939 Studebaker Dictator Coupe. Evan watched with the same awe he'd have shown if flying cars had just shot down the street.

Those cars didn't have the shimmer most antique cars did in the movies, which always came from collectors. Or from car shows. The cars rumbling past Evan looked beaten and worn… driven daily.

Evan even spotted WWII-era gas ration stickers—a white-on-black "A," white-on-green "B," and white-on-red "C"—on several windshields.

Gas ration stickers from WWII?

Evan put his hands over his ears and squeezed his eyes shut. His mind was on overload, and the smell of the musty tunnel and all that exhaust smoke had him reeling. He had to find a way back—a way back to what he'd left.

Then a lightbulb seemed to switch on. *Go back…to what,*

exactly? Back to Connor? Being chased? That rain? The electrical monster that looked like one of the creatures of the Id from the movie Forbidden Planet?

No, not an option.

Perhaps he really was dead. After all, this was Evan's idea of heaven. It just didn't get better than the 1940s in his mind. Evan had always hated the present and been obsessed with the past. And now, there he was…smack-dab in the year 1940-something.

Yep, I'm dead. No doubt about it.

He wondered if what he was experiencing was like that episode on *The Twilight Zone* during which the gangster thought he had been shot, then found himself thrust into the lap of luxury. Every pool game, he won, and every bank he robbed had compliant bankers. Finally, the guy realized he wasn't in heaven, he was in the other place.

Evan shuddered. Perhaps that was where he was now…*the other place.*

He made a smart left and headed down Cahuenga, which gradually became Highland Boulevard. Nothing had changed that much.

A dull-gray 1934 Ford pickup passed him. He smelled thick exhaust again, along with a deep ammonia stench that reminded him of rotten eggs. He wrinkled his nose, confused by the odor. Then he remembered—no catalytic converters during this time period.

He glanced over and noticed another gas ration sticker that looked as if it had seen better days on a windshield.

He remembered the fireman's words: "…*city sprung for these with the surplus budget after the war ended.*" He knew that World War II ended in September 1945.

He glanced at a big, black 1940 Packard 180 that passed, noting the license plate.

1946.

Gold with black numbers. He'd never seen a California plate in that color scheme before. He'd seen blue-on-white and gold-on-blue, but never black-on-gold.

He shook his head and blinked hard as if that might wake him up. *This couldn't really be happening…could it?* He remembered the bump on his head and rubbed it.

Ouch. His head throbbed. His car had been built solid… maybe a little too solid. The bruise on his head was real, so maybe, just maybe, he was hallucinating. But no, that wasn't impossible. Even the most far-out LSD trip he'd read about featured pink rainbows and talking frogs, never a hard, cold step back in time that was perfect to the last detail.

Perfect to the license plates, the light rainfall, the smelly exhausts, and the Red Car trolley.

Evan made his way south on Highland. Ahead, he could see the marquee to the Hollywood Bowl.

The marquee read: **BING CROSBY–TWO NIGHTS ONLY!**

A loudspeaker was blaring a Crosby song: "Did You Ever See A Dream Walking?"

Evan listened to the lyrics, the serendipity between them and his situation lost on him due to his head wound.

Evan listened to the tune, thinking, *I never woke up this morning. I'm in the middle of a dream…a very hardcore dream. That has to be it.*

The dream theory seemed a lot more palatable than death. Or maybe, just maybe, he had strayed onto a very realistic movie set for a period piece.

Evan felt the music flow through him like an old friend. He liked all of Bing's songs.

Evan figured he might as well enjoy the dream since, if he was in fact asleep, this was by far the best and most detailed one he'd ever had.

He passed the Bowl, watching as more cars from the '30s and '40s roared by. Parked in the lot were more vintage models from the same decades. Some people were heading up toward the Hollywood Bowl, presumably to see Bing Crosby's performance.

Traffic was as bad as it always was. *Guess there were no good ole days in LA when it came to that*, he realized.

He kept walking, passing the VFW Hollywood Legion Post 43. The WWI cannon was still parked out front. He hadn't known it had been there that long, then shook his head, reminding himself that this was all a dream.

He passed the Hollywood Methodist Church on the corner, which looked the same as he remembered. A majestic white building that shone down on the city.

Evan could see the Sinclair gas station ahead on the corner of Franklin and Highland. He could even see the tow truck he had been directed to: a 1940 Ford painted dull orange with black fenders that looked like it had seen better days, like most of the cars that passed.

Another song blared from a nearby radio someone had placed on their window in a beautifully maintained apartment building where the Hilton Garden should be…if it were about eighty years from now.

He got to the Sinclair and noticed the men working all wore gray shirts, black trousers, and visor caps with the Sinclair dinosaur logo. They were awaiting the next customer, and sure enough, a cream-colored Hudson Commodore with shiny, aluminum wheels pulled in.

Evan forged across the crosswalk at Franklin and walked over to the front window. He was soaked from walking in the rain, the bruise on his forehead now an angry, glowering black and blue.

The first Sinclair attendant looked to Evan and frowned. Evan noted the name on his shirt read "SAL." Sal was lively, had an easy grin and a muscular build, and although he was in his late twenties, he looked older…weather-beaten. His hair was slicked back with gallons of Pomade, and half a toothpick poked out of his lips as he chewed on the other half. His eyebrows reminded Evan of two enormous caterpillars that met in the middle. Sal and Evan shook hands.

"What can I do you for, mister?" Sal asked, noting Evan's condition and the bruise on his forehead.

"I need a tow truck, had a crash up on Cahuenga and Lakeridge," Evan explained.

Sal nodded. "Where you takin' it?" he asked. Evan couldn't help but note the people in his dream paid attention, listening to Evan whenever he spoke and responding with interest.

"I dunno. Who do you recommend?"

Sal seemed to mull that over. "I got the guy for ya. Not too expensive. Honest gentleman. This isn't some foreign model, is it?"

"No, sir, 1938 Ford."

Sal laughed and shrugged. "We can help you out, buddy, then take you to Big Mike's over on LaBrea and Sunset. He'll fix you up."

Sal put on a pair of work gloves and led Evan to that big Ford tow truck he had spotted nearby. Evan noticed Sal walked with a noticeable limp.

"Hey guys," Sal hollered, "I got a quick tow. Hold down the fort for me!" Sal waved to his guys, who then ambled over and gave that Hudson the business, cleaning the windshield, scrubbing the tires, and wiping the windows.

Evan looked over the car, stopping at the driver's side window. Beyond it, a beautiful young woman in her twenties in bright red lipstick sat at the wheel. At first, she didn't notice Evan was staring as she was busy powdering her face and pursing her lips, using the rearview mirror as her vanity.

Finally, she glanced at Evan. Her eyes held his, and she winked at him.

Evan was stunned. *Wow.*

That woman, one of the most beautiful he'd ever seen, had winked at him. Everything about her was "just so," her hair perfectly done in a Veronica Lake hairdo, and she wore a tight, blue dress from her neck to her torso. She rolled down her window to pay the attendant for her gas and smiled sweetly at him.

Evan climbed in the truck, realizing that the men at the station were also looking at her. Not that he blamed them any.

"Wow, Hollywood's got some pretty dames," Sal said, cranking the engine. He leaned over and flicked on the radio. The Andrews Sisters were crooning out "Bei Mir Bist Du Schon."

Evan noticed how worn the seats in this truck were. They smelled of cigarettes and gasoline. Sal ground the big Ford's gears, slipped out onto Highland, cut into traffic, and swung right on Odin, heading for Evan's incapacitated car.

The song by the Andrews Sisters mystified him. He'd never heard that number before. Not once. How could he dream something he'd never heard?

He felt the lump on his head. Perhaps this was all the result of a terrible concussion. Evan had never heard of a case of a concussed person who hallucinated anything this vivid, but maybe his was the one example of lucid, "concussed" dreaming.

He looked out the window; the rain had let up. Sal knew how to handle that truck like a champ. Not everyone could handle such a beast with such ease. Evan noticed Sal's hands. They were huge. Calloused and scarred, the man had obviously seen his share of life, maybe more than that.

You just get back, kid?" Sal asked.

Evan wasn't sure how to answer at first. Then he got it. Just got back from the war, Sal had meant. Evan struggled to answer.

"Nah, I was here editing patriotic films for the war effort," Evan answered. A half-truth.

"Hey, flat feet…bad eyes…whatever. You helped us win, right? I got no judgment against that. Just the bums who didn't lift a finger."

"Were you there?" Evan asked, curious as to Sal's answer.

"I was at Pearl, served on the USS *Nevada*, got burned on my legs, got invalided back home. A sailor who limps ain't much good on a battleship." Sal laughed.

Up ahead, fire trucks were parked near Evan's wrecked Ford. Sal studied it from a distance. "Aw, that don't look so bad. I'll get it hooked up and take care of it for ya." Sal pulled the truck in, backing up to the Ford with a another sharp grind of the gears.

He climbed out, shook the firemen's hands, hopped into Evan's Ford, and slipped it in neutral. Sal guided the hook below the Ford's radiator and snagged the front of the frame, the car's strongest spot.

Evan watched Sal as he shuffled around the side of the truck, climbed onto the bed, cranked the crane, and creaked the Ford into place. He did all this in less than five minutes, and Evan marveled at his proficiency. Sal did what he did with pride.

In that moment, Evan decided he liked it here, preferring it greatly to the world he left, whether he was actually in 1946 in reality or in a dream. The people in this time were more measured, seeming to respect themselves more than the people he knew. The grinding anxiety, wild-eyed paranoia, and confusion that pervaded Evan's era were not here. It didn't even seem to exist in this place, whatever this place really was.

However he got here, it didn't matter to Evan. He had nothing to go back for, nothing at all. Why not stay in this very vivid dream? It was far better than 2021, no question.

The next hour went by in a flash. Evan was continually surprised at how much easier the world worked in this Los Angeles 1946 world, though daily living seemed a lot more physically strenuous. No wonder everyone was so thin—they were always working, moving, and operating cumbersome vehicles with admirable deftness.

And there was always a radio somewhere playing pop music wherever he went. He liked this music so much better than that of Cardi B. or Taylor Swift.

Sal pulled into Big Mike's, backed Evan's Ford into an empty garage, got out, and cranked it down. Evan could hear another radio, this time playing Dick Haymes and Helen Forrest's song about chasing rainbows.

Sal headed over to Evan. "That'll be six bucks. I think that's fair enough," he decided

With that, Evan realized, whether he was actually dead or in a dream, this was not a free country. It was just like the place he came from: a very expensive country. Evan thought fast, went to the Ford's glove box, and checked the floorboard. The film cans were not there, and his cell phone had pulled a similar vanishing act.

Evan was still in too much of a daze to recall the wallet in his back pocket. Nervously, he searched the car for his other items. If they had also disappeared, things were going to get mighty rough in the next few minutes.

Relieved, he saw the other items he'd kept in the box were still there: a big flashlight, road flares, and a multi-purpose Swiss knife that was hefty and could fix just about anything known to man.

Evan took them to Sal, who wore a frown.

"It's a long story. I know, you've heard this before, but I'm traveling a little light now, and I will get you your six. Can I leave these with you as a deposit?"

Sal regarded the road flares and flashlight, then gravitated toward the man-sized Swiss Army knife. Sal took it, admiring its heft. Then his eyes shifted to Evan's vintage Hamilton wristwatch.

"If you don't have the dough, I'll take your watch as collateral. I'll give you a week, then this is mine." Sal held out his hand.

Evan unfastened his watch and handed it over.

"This is worth twenty bucks, kid," he reminded Evan. "I like Hamilton, good make."

Sal slipped the watch in his shirt pocket and patted it. Evan nodded, knowing this was a dream and he might as well go with the flow.

"So long, kid. See you soon, right?" Sal climbed in his Ford, backed onto LaBrea, and rumbled away.

Evan watched him go, then turned at the sound of

approaching footsteps. A very big man was heading his way. Big Mike, Evan presumed. The man was the size of a mountain, with overalls that could have doubled as a pup tent. Big Mike was endowed with a shiny, bald head and close-set eyes. Mike nodded to Evan as he slowly advanced toward Evan's Ford to look it over. After a brief inspection, he lumbered back toward Evan and scratched his head.

"Okay, kid. This should take me a week. I'm guessing it's gonna be about sixty bucks. You got insurance?" Big Mike asked.

Evan shook his head. He doubted his AAA policy would work here, wherever here was.

Big Mike shrugged. "Might want to correct that, mister. It don't cost but five bucks a month, and it sure can come in handy. But yeah, give me a week."

Evan looked to the other cars Big Mike was repairing, all showing various stages of damage. The calendar on the wall read: APRIL 1946. A Varga girl, complete with rosy cheeks and a seductive smile, graced this month.

One thing you can say about April 1946, Evan thought, *people certainly were trusting.*

But was it really April 1946? Evan doubted it but recalled the words of a psychologist he knew through Gwen who had said that when in a dream, you should "just go along with everything."

Big Mike ripped out a receipt and handed it to Evan. Evan pocketed it, they shook hands, and he was off.

Evan walked from Big Mike's shop on LaBrea and Sunset north to Hollywood Boulevard. Traffic was fairly heavy, and every car on the road looked like a collector's item to Evan, with brands most people had long since forgotten about: Nash,

Packard, Hudson, Franklin, Auburn, Studebaker, and DeSoto. The exhaust fumes were overwhelming—a combination of odors leftover from thousands of cigarettes mixed with fried food, rotten eggs, and human sweat.

Hollywood Boulevard felt alive, like an animal with a deep hunger. Some things, Evan felt, never changed.

The women on the street were dressed elegantly, enjoying the post-war prosperity only the Americans had benefitted from at the conclusion of the Big One. Some carried shopping bags; others led children who were dressed as adults. Little boys wore suits; little girls were clad in starched dresses. All the men sported suits and ties, some more frayed than others. The trousers were always cuffed at the ankle.

Not one man was hatless. No derbies, top hats, or baseball caps. Just fedoras. No sneakers either; he could hear the clicking of dozens of leather shoes on concrete. He made a quick note: Men in 1946 didn't dress like teenage boys with jeans, T-shirts, and baseball caps. They dressed like adults. That was classy. Another reason to enjoy this bizarre journey.

Evan continued to walk on Hollywood, and there it was: Grauman's Chinese Theatre. The place looked the same, minus the cheap souvenir shops flanking it on either side.

Big klieg lights swept far above his head as big men manually operated them, sweeping them so that the light crisscrossed in the clear skies.

A huge banner read THE BLUE DAHLIA. Crowds were gathering, and photographers lined up along a red carpet bordered by velvet ropes.

Evan was so astonished at the sight of Grauman's, the red carpet, and the movie that was soon to premiere that he had to stop for a second. All his life, he'd been chasing his dreams, in such a hurry to direct a motion picture before thirty. He'd never been in any fulfilling relationships. Everything had to be transactional because that was how things worked, at least in Evan's mind. That was certainly how Hollywood worked.

Now, all his plans had been blown way off course. Maybe permanently.

But does it matter? Evan wondered. *Dream, illusion, or the afterlife...whatever this is, I'm gonna make the most of it. Might as well enjoy the ride. No turning back.*

The sun was going down; massive black Cadillacs pulled up to the theater for the premier. Evan crossed Hollywood at LaBrea, hoping he'd catch a glimpse of Humphrey Bogart, one of his favorite actors of all time.

So if I see him, what should I do, ask for an autograph? Anticipation buzzed through his body. *Who am I kidding? Asking Bogart for an autograph is about as lame as dressing up in a Star Wars costume for Comic-Con.*

He was in front of the theater now, where a crowd had quickly multiplied until people were jostling each other for a glimpse. Evan slipped into the throngs and quickly noticed most people from this time either wore too much perfume or not enough. The smell of sweat, Old Spice, tobacco, and sickly sweet perfume was heavy, nauseating.

A heavyset girl of eighteen pushed in front of him, blocking his view of the Cadillac that had just pulled up. She was among those who weren't wearing near enough perfume, and it was thickly noticeable.

"Excuse me?" Evan muttered.

"Take a powder. I was here first!" she hissed at him. She

was an angry ginger, freckles splashed across her face like polka-dotted paint. A farmer's daughter-type, Evan surmised, and not someone to be trifled with. The big ginger already had enough high-octane anger in her to power a jet engine.

Evan moved to another position, finding an unobstructed view. The big ginger pushed someone beside Evan, who then barreled into Evan and propelled him forward. He stumbled past the rope onto the red carpet, arms pinwheeling as he tried to regain his balance. He landed on one knee, just in time to look up and behold a stunningly beautiful bare leg stepping out of the big Caddy. He regained his feet and found himself staring directly at Lauren Bacall at the peak of her beauty, dressed in a shimmering gown with a tasteful pearl necklace and diamond bracelet.

What a terrible way to meet Lauren Bacall, he mused with a sigh. Evan got to his feet and tried to get out of Lauren's way.

Lauren, who had seen everything, headed toward Evan and pointed to the big ginger girl.

"You need to behave yourself, sweetie. It's only a movie," she purred, wagging her finger at the big ginger. Lauren flashed a smile at Evan, who couldn't believe this was all happening in front of him.

Humphrey Bogart, dressed in a dark, double-breasted suit, with a lit Chesterfield in hand, had also stepped out of the limo. He looked to Evan.

"You okay?" Bogart asked, his lined face lit up in the bright lights, eyes creased but calm.

Evan froze, face-to-face with his matinée idol. It was like staring right at the sun or moon. There was nothing he could think to say that would have been right, so he simply nodded with a dumb grin on his face. Evan couldn't believe how small Bogart seemed in person: same face, same voice that Evan remembered from every line, every scene. His hair was perfectly combed and slicked back in his trademark style. He was compact, perfectly shaped for the camera: small body, large head, and graceful moves.

"Enjoy the picture. I hear this one's actually good." Bogart winked, then took Lauren's arm, and they swept toward the front doors. A smattering of golf applause followed them.

Evan watched them float away from him, legends so big they didn't seem real. People like Bogart and Bacall walked on water, as far as Evan was concerned. They were made magical simply by who they were, but with the dynamic supercharge of Hollywood behind them, they became immortal. It was all a kind of ethereal magic, the very thing that made Evan's heart beat fast, made him feel alive.

Evan backed into the crowd just as Alan Ladd walked by with his wife and waved to the crowd, smiled that big, phony smile required for public events, and then headed in. Veronica Lake, who was actually tiny, followed behind him without an escort.

Evan stepped back, too astonished to say anything or even think straight.

Keep moving, Evan, his mind, still struggling to find sense in all of this, urged him.

With reluctance, Evan headed away from the premiere, doubled back to LaBrea Avenue, crossed the street to the south side of Hollywood Boulevard, and then headed east.

He passed scores of people dressed in their Sunday best. Thoughts were still tumbling through Evan's head as his logic and rationale grappled with a lack of any way to explain this situation. Everything looked, sounded, and smelled real enough. Cars motored by, the streetcar on Highland lumbered by, every detail perfect and real. Evan wondered what would happen if he dashed out into the middle of Hollywood Boulevard and got hit by a Chrysler. If he were dead or in a dream, he'd be fine. Maybe the car would pass through him.

Evan stopped, thought about it, then started for the middle of the busy street.

A strong hand grabbed him by the shirt collar and yanked him back.

"What's the matter with you, mister?" A woman's voice yelled in his ear. "You want to get yourself killed?"

Evan pivoted around to see a small woman in her fifties with genuine concern on her face. She spoke with a heavy Italian accent.

"Sorry, I was daydreaming," was all Evan could come up with.

"Better you wake up, mister. Last time I saw a contest between an automobile and a man, the automobile won!" she exclaimed. "Sorry to grab you so hard, but you almost got smacked by that Buick."

Evan grew acutely embarrassed as a crowd gathered to watch. They thought he was crazy—he could see it in their eyes.

A smallish man with ink-stained hands and green-shaded eyes shook his head at Evan and waved a hand as if to ward off a bad smell.

"Youse guys seen a lotta stuff over there, and now you're kerplunked in the head. Watch yourself!" the smallish man said, then stepped back into his typesetting shop.

"I'm very sorry," Evan said, looking around at their concerned faces. "I don't know what came over me. It was like my brain rebooted, or something," Evan tried to explain, though it was clear nobody believed him. Evan shrunk away from the gathered group of curious-bordering-on-judgmental onlookers, threw one last glance over his shoulder at them, then shrugged.

Maybe I am crazy....

The wave of excitement Evan had been riding about this magical place had eroded. Fear was taking its place. He didn't like where he was. He wanted to go back.

Evan crossed Highland Boulevard, glancing over at where the Ripley's Museum in 2021 was. At the moment, a Rexall drug store sat in its place. Evan glanced inside and spotted a soda fountain with high school-age kids gathered in front of it, engaged in a lively conversation.

The sun was now gone. Streetlights flickered on, not nearly as bright as he remembered them being. Evan made mental notes. In his dream world, it smelled bad, the lights were dimmer, and people seemed to actually care about one another.

He kept walking, not knowing where he was going exactly. He passed the Hollywood Theater. Its marquee read, HOUSE OF DRACULA and DETOUR. He walked past the Holly-wood Book Store and smelled meat sauce and spaghetti from the Italian Kitchen he stopped to look at.

A loud crash startled him. Two sweaty men in torn suits crashed out of the kitchen door, both throwing haphazard punches. Every punch made contact, crunching bones and flesh. Blood dripped on the pavement in front of him. Evan stepped back in shock.

Two waiters in white shirts, black trousers, and bow ties hurried out and separated the men with headlocks. Both waiters were huge; in another age, both could have easily tried out for the Tampa Bay Buccaneers.

"Louie, call the cops, will ya?" One of the waiters called out toward the door. Louie must have been inside somewhere.

Evan sidestepped the fracas; the last thing he needed was trouble, especially after what people assumed had been a strange suicide attempt earlier. Though in reality, he had just been trying to figure out where he was…and maybe *what* he was.

Anger filled Evan's thoughts. Why had this happened to him? He had just been trying to save an iconic film, and now he was…here. He didn't fit in in this world. Or did he?

He crossed at Cahuenga, and it hit him suddenly—he was exhausted. Odd, feeling sleepy while in a dream—if that was what this was. He sighed, considering the reality of his situation. He had very little money, plenty of credit cards, a twenty, and a ten, but he knew no place in this time period would take either credit cards or currency from 2021.

Evan headed back down Hollywood, got to the Security Pacific Bank, and turned right.

Up ahead was the Hollywood Methodist Church, looking reassuringly like he remembered. As Evan recalled, churches tended to be open for the weary—and he really needed a little sleep. Not that much, just enough to hopefully wake up back near his car on Cahuenga.

Or not wake up at all. Perhaps he was simply dead.

Evan closed his eyes. *God, if you're listening, please give me a safe place to sleep for a while. Then, when I wake, please get me back home.* He realized he was suddenly sounding a lot like George Bailey: "I want to live. I want to live." Although, in George's case, he actually had something wonderful to go back to.

Evan felt he did not. What did he have, really? No girlfriend, a horrible job he'd been fired from, and stalled dreams of being a director/writer that weren't coming true anytime soon.

He made it to the Hollywood Methodist Church. The front doors were locked, so he went around to the side and located a door near the rear of the church that was unlocked.

Evan stepped inside, finding the area dark. Fatigue overwhelmed him; he couldn't remember being so tired his entire life. He stepped into the sanctuary, marveling at the size of this church. Better yet, there were cushions on the pews, the softest he'd ever seen. He sat on the nearest pew with a creak and looked at the cross. *God, please get me home…or wherever I'm supposed to be.*

And then a terrible feeling rushed over him like a tidal wave—the feeling that he was, in fact, dead. This was his afterlife: a place that was familiar but wasn't at the same time.

He had never achieved any of his goals. All he had set out to do was not going to happen. He'd stolen film cans that didn't belong to him, he'd gone crazy and died in a terrible car crash.

I really am dead.

Fear welled up inside him. Evan had never been afraid before, really afraid of anything.

But now he very much was. Whatever was going on with him, it was scary and depressing.

And so very, very lonely.

He reclined on the pew and fell asleep within seconds. Not just a light doze, more like a very, very deep sleep.

Sleep without dreams.

At least none he could remember.

CHAPTER 7

THE FELLOW TRAVELER

Evan woke, nearly face-to-face with a worried man leaning over him. Evan sat up with a start, and the first thing that hit him was pain, sharp, biting, deep pain. And a lot of confusion.

His mind raced as quickly as it could, considering the fact that it had been jump-started from a sleep deeper than any he'd ever experienced.

"Son, can I get you anything?" The man wore a dress shirt, tie, and slacks but no jacket. "I'm Reverend Campbell…" He was a little older than Evan, and Evan noticed he had a hook for a left hand.

Evan struggled for words. "I'm so sorry," he finally managed. "I'm new here and couldn't find a place to sleep. The door was unlocked, and…"

"I'm glad you found us," the reverend said. "Let me get you some water." He hurried away.

The pain from Evan's toe hit him again, and with that pain came flooding back in all his memories. He'd crashed his precious, antique car and woken up in a peculiar world filled with strangers who dressed like they were all actors in an old movie. He'd given his watch to a tow truck driver who'd fought at Pearl Harbor, left his car at Big Mike's on LaBrea Boulevard, seen Lauren Bacall and Humphrey Bogart up close, and almost stepped out into traffic before being saved by a concerned Italian woman.

And his foot… It hurt like the dickens. Evan pulled off his sock and shoe. His toe was screaming with agony and smudged black and blue, looking like something from another planet.

Suddenly, he remembered why—he'd banged his toe on the stack of the film cans he stole from Connor Alcott. Now it was swollen to twice its normal size. He felt the bump on his head; it hurt far less than before, but with every beat of his heart his toe was throbbing as if a jackhammer was thumping it.

And then it dawned on him… He was alive. The terror he fell asleep with last night was gone, replaced with a wonderful feeling. *I'm alive.*

He looked around, took in his surroundings, and then half-shouted out, "Thank you, God!" It had clearly all been a bad dream. He was going to walk out of this church and be back in the world he knew from before.

He put his shoe back on, painfully tying it. Pain…that was a good thing. Pain meant not dead. He made up his mind that he was going to enjoy whatever else came his way because life was a lot better than the alternative. If he never got to direct a movie in his life, no big deal. He decided that he would just be a good man.

The reverend returned with some water, and Evan slipped his sock and shoe back on. Going barefoot in a church hardly seemed classy. The reverend handed him the glass, which Evan drank in one thirsty gulp.

"Thank you so much for being here, reverend," Evan began. "And for allowing me to stay here."

"The church isn't mine. What is your name, sir?" Campbell asked.

"Evan West, sir." Evan reached out for a shake and got a firm one in return.

"The doors of the church are always open," Campbell explained. "For I was hungry and you gave me food, I was thirsty and you gave me drink, I was a stranger and you welcomed me."

Evan thought there was a certain familiarity to his words. Reverend Campbell smiled, though Evan could see the man had more pain behind his eyes than happiness.

"Anything else we can do for you, sir?" Campbell asked. Evan shook his head, got up, and limped to the door. Campbell noticed his uneven gait. "You have an injury? Just back home from over there?"

Considering where he was and who he was talking to, Evan felt pretty compelled to tell the truth. He grinned. "I'm a movie editor and dropped some cans of film on my big toe. This is only a daily reminder that I'm actually alive."

"Praise God!" Campbell exclaimed and laughed.

Evan hobbled out of the same door he came in. The sun was up, the sky was blue above, and the air smelled like exhaust fumes and ammonia.

A huge revelation hit him.

I'm still here…in April 1946. It wasn't a dream. I'm not dead. This is the past. Evan sighed, then nodded. He was still a glass-half-full kinda guy at heart. He couldn't change who he was.

I'll just have to make the most of it, he decided.

He breathed in the terrible air and coughed a bit, watching the line of turtle-like cars snaking down Highland Avenue toward the Hollywood intersection. The Sinclair station was still across the street, and he knew Sal was waiting for his $6.

A hunger so strong that it made him nauseous overcame him, and he felt woozy. Like an icy claw, it grabbed at his stomach and squeezed. He hadn't eaten anything since 2021.

Evan headed across the Franklin intersection and toward Hollywood. He glanced at a large clock on the Security Pacific Bank building. It was 10:30 a.m.

He'd slept at least twelve hours and was refreshed and ready to accept whatever came his way. He'd done well most of his life being alone in 2021. No reason he couldn't tackle any challenges 1946 threw at him.

He reached into his pocket, feeling four quarters and three dimes. He exhaled in relief. Coins hadn't changed in almost one hundred years. And money he could spend meant food.

Evan reached the Hollywood and Highland crosswalk, heading east on Hollywood. He passed the bank building and quickly spotted a burger stand called Frank's Hamburgers. Not very imaginative, but the location was perfect…and so was the aroma. The smell of grilled burgers, eggs, bacon, and onions hit him hard. His mouth watered; he just hoped nothing there cost more than $1.30.

Frank's was a small place; only five tables in front and a grill beyond the counter that two acne-spotted teenagers were tending. A big man with hairy arms, presumably Frank, leaned on the cash register and read the racing forum.

Evan's eyes hit the menu behind Frank. Cheeseburger with pickles: 75 cents. Coca-Cola: 25 cents. Evan's mouth watered as he approached the counter. Frank glanced at him, not looking too friendly.

"One cheeseburger and a Coca-Cola," Evan requested. Frank glanced to one of the two teenagers hovering over the steaming grill.

"Dollar even," Frank growled. Evan handed over the quarters. Now he was worth thirty cents. The smell of burgers on the grill was enough, though. It reminded him again that he was alive. If they had cost a million dollars, it would have been worth it.

Evan watched the passersby on the street, realizing they were all long dead, or if they were children here, very old in Evan's time. Evan shook his head. His time was apparently now. Not 2021.

He always felt he was born in the wrong time anyway. He didn't like anything about 2021, least of all his being there.

"You're up!'" Frank shouted, and Evan broke out of his trance. His burger was in a real basket made from wicker, and his Coca-Cola sat next to it on the counter—in a real glass with ice.

Evan took them to a table and sat, offering a silent prayer to God in thanks that he could afford this. Then he threw back a few swallows of the Coca-Cola and almost choked. The flavor was incredible—an explosion of sweetness that blew his mind. *It was that good.* There was no corn syrup in the soda, just pure sugar, probably from Cuba or another Caribbean island, maybe even Martinique.

He took a bite of the burger, and again, the meat, ketchup, pickles, onion, and bread tasted better than anything he'd ever had. Nothing compared. He had another sip of Coke, and again savored the atomic blast of flavor.

Evan chewed, closing his eyes and thinking, *The past stinks, but it tastes so good.*

His eyes jolted back open as a hand clamped down on his shoulder. Evan turned. A Black man about his age, dressed in a black suit, green tie, and ubiquitous fedora stared down at him. He was impossibly tall but dressed very dapper and perfect, not a thread out of place.

"I'm sorry to bother you, but I require a few minutes of your time. Mind if I sit?" the man asked.

Evan gave him a wary look, to which the man responded with a smile, and without waiting for an answer from Evan, took a seat across from him at his table.

Evan immediately took a liking to him. His smile was open and honest, and Evan didn't detect the glint of a user in the man's eyes, quite the contrary.

"This is concerning your accident on Lakeridge and Cahuenga East yesterday. I was there and saw everything." He leaned in conspiratorially. "I came through there too. Can't tell you how happy I am to see you?"

Evan was about to take another bite but froze before the food quite reached his lips, astonished.

"William Cooper." The man jutted his hand across the table. "Just call me Coop. Not Will, William, or Bill. Just Coop. I'm from 1899."

Evan released one side of the burger long enough to shake the offered hand, then re-grasped his sandwich and took a glorious bite, chewing and trying to take in what Coop just told him.

Coop appraised him. "So, what time are you from?" he asked.

CHAPTER 8
CHANCE ENCOUNTERS

Evan was dumbfounded. There he was, in 1946, and he hadn't even been there a full day before someone had discovered he was a being from another time. In one way, it comforted him. He had confirmation that he'd traveled back in time somehow like Marty McFly or the two American scientists in the old Irwin Allen show *The Time Tunnel.* Then he seized upon Coop's words. *1899?*

"Time out," Evan said, leaning back.

Coop furrowed his brow. "Time out? What's that mean? I have a hard enough time keeping up with how people in 1946 speak. The vocabulary is rich and inventive," Coop marveled. "Not at all the way most educated people from the nineteenth century speak."

Evan listened to Coop's delivery; he spoke like the early Edison recordings he had listened to in the past. Every word was enunciated clearly.

"Time out… It just means 'wait a second,'" Evan clarified. "I need to collect my thoughts. I mean, I'm not sure you're real. My name is Evan West, by the way."

Coop grinned broadly, and then laughed, a little too loud. Suddenly feeling like he was being watched, he snuck a glance at Frank.

Sure enough, Frank had leaned in and was listening, his eyebrows up with interest.

"How about you finish your late breakfast, and we'll talk more somewhere …a little more private," Coop suggested.

Evan wolfed down the rest of his burger, then inhaled the Coca-Cola. The combination of sugar, meat, cheese, onions, and bread in his stomach energized him and threw off the jet lag (or maybe time-lag) that had overwhelmed him before.

Coop stood and nodded to Frank. Frank just stared at them with cold, curious eyes, clearly struggling to determine who they were.

"Thank you. Burger was great!" Evan gratefully said to Frank, who gave him a silent nod of acknowledgment. They *vamanosed* out the door and turned right toward Highland.

Coop has a fast gait; Evan had a hard time keeping up with the tall man. Coop headed directly for the Red Car trolley stop at Hollywood Boulevard and Highland. There, Coop stopped at the counter and bought two all-day passes for him and Evan. The men waited at the stop in silence as Evan eyed him curiously. Then, together, they climbed on board the next trolley. Coop led Evan to a seat in the back.

Evan looked around, noting that there weren't that many people on this ride. He wondered why they were seated at the back but figured Coop was just trying to stay under the radar.

"Where're we going?" Evan asked.

"Down to the LaBrea station. There's a place I know," Coop answered, then shook his head. "Best we not talk until we arrive."

Evan nodded and directed his head out the window, marveling at the sight of 1946 Los Angeles, the air brown with pollution, the endless lines of cars zipping back and forth like huge, clumsy beasts on four wheels. The honking, New York-like in its frequency, was far more aggressive in this time than in 2021.

At the LaBrea junction, they disembarked. Coop led them to a nearby bar called The Zebra. They went in, and Evan almost stopped in his tracks, nearly overwhelmed by the smell of beer, cigarettes, and cigars mixed with cheap cleaning fluid. He held his breath and let Coop lead them back to a corner table.

Velvet portraits of African women and American Indians adorned the dark-red-painted walls. Evan studied the bar; it wasn't nearly as stocked as any of its 2021 counterparts he had visited. This era, so much simpler and less grandiose than the one he came from, was okay by him.

At least there was no Twitter or TikTok.

Coop threw a wave to the bartender, a Black man with a bald head who seemed to recognize him. Coop held up two fingers. The barkeep nodded.

"Why here?" Evan asked honestly. Coop looked to him as if he were crazy.

"They don't mind Black people here. Frank's Hamburgers, maybe not so much. Other places, it's a strict no-no. But, all in all, not as bad as 1899. The world has evolved a little but not much."

Evan then remembered—there was racial segregation in the 1940s. The era he looked back upon so fondly would have been great for a White person, but for anyone else, each day represented a minefield of danger. No wonder Coop had sat at the back of the bus—it was the expectation. Evan recalled the internment of so many Japanese in 1942 and the specter of Jim Crow in the American South, though he had been blissfully unaware that Mr. Crow had extended his odious reach into Los Angeles.

Coop met Evan's gaze. "So, shall I begin?" he asked.

Evan nodded, still woozy from the combined reek of the 1946-era bar.

"I'm from 1899. Originally from Tennessee. My folks moved us up to New York when I was a kid. A few years later, I was lucky to get a job with a man you probably never heard of."

"Try me. Maybe I have," Evan offered.

"Nikola Tesla," Coop answered. "Great man. Smartest human being on—"

Coop looked flummoxed as Evan's laughter interrupted him.

"You worked for Nikola Tesla?" Evan asked. "Why do I find that hard to believe?"

Coop's face went flat. "How do you think I got here?" His voice was tinged with irritation.

Evan stopped laughing. "Go ahead," Evan said meekly, sorry that he had been such a jerk.

"I worked for Nikola Tesla. Helped him with the move to Colorado Springs," Coop explained. "He was working on something that you just wouldn't believe." The barkeep brought them both cups of coffee—black, without any offer of milk or sugar—which Evan found refreshing. "You drink coffee, right?" Coop asked. Evan nodded and took his first sip.

Again, he was vaulted into heaven. No vanilla latte mocha. This was genuine Navy coffee, strong as heck and not taking any prisoners. He was sure this was the same recipe that won World War II for the Americans.

"It doesn't matter what Tesla had created. It's too complicated to explain, and to be honest, I'm not even sure what he'd achieved." Coop paused. "But life got a whole lot more interesting for me that night in July 1899, two months after we moved to Colorado.

"Tesla had a lot of equipment at that time and was doing some experiments with electricity, trying to get it to run between places without the use of any wires, as I understood the process anyway." Coop frowned, squinting his eyes. "I have to tell you, Tesla was doing something…groundbreaking. He told me he once generated several million volts through the enormous coil he had built with my help. Tesla even told me he had a theory that the communications might be from another world, perhaps alien in origin."

Evan leaned forward, listening intently.

"That's what led me to think irrationally," Coop continued. "I had to crank up the voltage so these communications could come through more clearly."

Coop described how he went into the lab one night when Tesla was meeting with Astor, his main investor, at the hotel in town about ten miles away. A lightning storm had been ravaging the skies. Coop turned on the generator and had it generating nine million volts of electricity, which was aided by the flashing lightning above. Coop described an enormous "gateway" that had formed in the cascade of blue electricity that showered from the generator. Behind Coop, a generator overheated and exploded, throwing him into the gateway. Evan wondered if Coop had flown through space at 80 mph, the same speed he had been driving when…it happened.

"I woke up during a thunderstorm, same place you were, Lakeridge and Cahuenga Boulevard. Except I wasn't in a car, and I was in August of 1944." Coop laughed. "That area is a gateway, and when there is a storm with lightning, I get over there as quickly as I can. So far, since 1944, only one other storm has happened before yesterday's, so my seeing you come through was miraculous. I'd very much enjoy it if you informed me how you passed through."

Evan was at a loss for words, but a lot of what Coop said made sense. Coop was clearly projected by the generator explosion into a similar gateway, created by a combination of man-made and heaven's own lightning.

"I'm from 2021," Evan began, and Coop's jaw fell open. Evan waited for Coop to recover, though his heartbeat was already speeding up, his excitement over finally being able to describe his experience to a "fellow traveler" making him grin foolishly.

"Time out!" Coop exclaimed. "From 2021? That's astonishing!" Coop went silent, thinking for a moment. "I don't know your particulars yet, but why did the portal send me forward forty-five years and you back seventy-five? This is something we must study!" Coop slammed his hand down with excitement. "Are you also a scientist?"

Now it was Evan's turn to be embarrassed. "No, I'm a movie editor. I edit trailers."

Coop burst into laughter. "I work in the movies too! Well, at least, here I do."

Evan inwardly thanked God for this man he had injected into his life. Another industry guy! "What do you do?"

"I am an assistant to a production sound engineer and also work as an on-set recordist."

Evan furrowed his brow.

"If you find that difficult to believe, you should know I helped develop an optical-to-magnetic sound transfer machine that made the recordist's job a heck of a lot easier. I've put my Tesla skills to work in 1946, and quite honestly, the technology isn't at all what I'm used to. It's extremely primitive. After working with Tesla…," he trailed off wistfully.

"In 2021, Tesla's tech would be better than ours, I'm sure. You know, in my time, Tesla is worshipped! A very wealthy man named Elon Musk has an electric car company named after him," Evan told him.

Coop beamed with pride. "I wish I could see him again. I very much do." He sighed. "When I came through, he was already gone. Dead and buried, apparently penniless. Thomas Edison was a skunk. He might as well have shot him after all he did to disgrace the man. If only both of those brilliant scientists had not been consumed with ego…if they'd worked together, who knows where the world would be now?"

"Just give it seventy-five years, and you'll see!" Evan exclaimed. Then he dove into his story, describing the day when he went through, his theft of *It's A Wonderful Life*, the high-speed car chase, and his crash into the pole. Coop listened, absorbing every word.

"Never heard of that movie," Coop remarked. "But what you say makes sense. The crash released electricity from the power lines, and the lightning enhanced it, just as it did mine. You ended up in the same geographical location, whereas I was transported 1,082.3 miles here. You went back in time.

I went forward. We'll need to make some calculations, and that will take some time, Evan West."

Evan leaned back in his chair, absorbing all this information while Coop eyed him thoughtfully.

"You have a wife? Kids?" Coop asked. Evan shook his head, and Coop was visibly relieved. "So, we're two lonely time travelers, stuck here in 1946 for reasons I can't begin to understand. Science rarely has concrete answers, but we can always guess around the edges," he mused.

Evan finished his coffee, feeling the rich, black liquid coat his throat and stomach like a comforting old friend. He closed his eyes, clinging to the familiar taste for a moment.

This is too crazy, Evan thought. *Too much to take in…*

"I got this, don't worry," Coop said, seeming almost to read his thoughts. "I must confide in you and be honest. We need each other, Evan. We can figure out how to get back home together, I'm convinced of that." Coop smiled. "You also need a job. Can't survive without money." Coop's eyebrows raised knowingly as he took a swallow of his coffee. "I'll take you to the movie I'm working on. They're always looking for skilled people, and with your futuristic skills, Mr. West, you'll be quite an asset to them. I can't promise you anything, but proximity is helpful."

Evan was astonished at Coop's generosity. "What's the movie you're working on?"

"I don't remember the title. We're up at Encino, just started shooting. I never can remember the titles or who's in them. Most of these movies are on the intellectually vapid side, Evan West. I'm sure in 2021, you have your own form of entertainment that is far more fulfilling."

Evan didn't bother to answer Coop's hopeful observation because he didn't want the guy to hear how far humanity had climbed, and at the same time, succumbed to levels of obscene absurdity. If he tried to describe reality TV, or pointless obsessions like the Kardashians, most pop music from 2021, or Prince Harry and Meghan, Coop would have lost all hope for the future. The man would've assumed the world had reverted back to the pre-Flood orgies and mindlessness Noah built an ark to escape from.

They left The Zebra and took the Red Car all the way west through Cahuenga Pass. The pole was already back in place, the power lines mended. Evan was impressed. LA city services in 1946 were efficient.

Coop pointed at the pole and looked at Evan. "Next time we have a lightning storm, we're going to be right there," he announced.

Evan was half-listening, more interested in the passing sights. As they crested the pass, he looked around, studying the few houses—mostly Victorians—and the rows of orange groves beyond them that seemed to stretch into infinity.

Evan faced his companion, eyes wide. "Just wait until 2021, Coop. It looks nothing like this," Evan almost shouted, then noticed people were staring at him. "Look at the orange groves!" Evan enthused, more to himself than anyone else.

The Red Car stopped at Lankershim, then trundled west toward the next stop at Laurel. The pole above showered sparks off the roof, the car's wheels making high-pitched braking sounds that reminded Evan of the chirp of NYC subways trains.

They approached the Laurel Canyon Boulevard exit. The Red Car stopped; Coop stood and headed for the exit. Evan followed.

Evan looked at Laurel Canyon Boulevard with awe; what would one day be a modern marvel of asphalt engineering over the hills that divided Hollywood from the San Fernando Valley was now only a dirt throughway of uneven ground and gravel. Few houses occupied the hills in 1946, and even fewer businesses lined the boulevard.

They caught the bus at Ventura, which in 1946 was a winding, two-lane road headed east and west. Then they stopped at Burbank Avenue. The only landmarks on that street that Evan could see were a Signal gas station and a dry cleaner's.

Coop pointed across the street. At Evan's questioning look, he said, "Shooting in Encino today."

Evan, still jazzed by the rustic nature of the 1946 San Fernando Valley and the fact that he was about to see a movie set from the era, forgot basic safety rules and unwisely entered Ventura without looking both ways.

A 1937 Bentley Torpedo Roadster careened around the corner far beyond the legal speed limit. Evan glanced to his right just in time to start running. The Bentley swerved violently, just kissing his arm before slamming into a mailbox on the corner of Burbank and Ventura with a loud *smash*.

Evan cringed at the sight of the Roadster's warped bumper. Steam vented from the broken radiator. He hurried over to the car and looked at the driver and his passenger.

Coop wisely shuffled away and watched from a distance, no doubt aware of the consequences of a Black man potentially causing an accident, especially one involving a Bentley that his boss drove.

Evan realized he was on his own as he watched a tall man, lean and balding, in a crisp, three-piece suit hop out of the car to inspect the damage. This man was not like the typical welcoming faces Evan had come to associate with this era; he seemed to be one of those men who'd frowned so much over the course of his life that his face had twisted into a perpetual perma-frown. To counterbalance his bald head, he had shaggy, salt-and-pepper eyebrows that looked as mean as the rest of him.

"Look what you've done to my car! Idiot!" he screamed, the veins on his neck standing out. The man was pouring sweat and breathing heavily.

Evan bristled at the insult, at being looked down upon by some jerk in a Bentley—or a Land Rover. Just another creep with money assuming everything was everyone else's fault.

"Look here, I was just crossing the street. You came around that corner at 90 miles per hour, and I did absolutely nothing to your car. Your driver is the one who crashed it, not me."

"Is that so? Let me give you a lesson in life, buster. You know who has the right of way in LA? Me!" The man bellowed that last word so loudly, it almost knocked Evan back a few steps. He'd experienced very few people with this kind of high-voltage anger and knew they were to be avoided. "You don't know who I am, but I'm gonna make sure you find out…and never forget!"

The man took a few menacing steps toward Evan, who refused to back down. That made the guy stop—a typical reaction of most bullies who feed on fear.

"I am Arthur J. Strickler, you foul-mannered moron, and let me lay somethin' on ya. I'm a very powerful producer around here. You ask anyone about Arthur J. Strickler, and they either praise me to the heavens, or their knees shake.

By the time I'm finished with you, you'll be doing one or the other."

Evan's fury boiled over as he stared down Arthur, just another angry man who got their way by venting fury and stomping their feet. Connor Alcott had used this tactic, and so did this Strickler guy. It was a nasty perfume to Evan.

"I'm new in town. Didn't catch your name. What is it again?" Evan asked, breezy and cheerful.

"Why you…" Strickler took off his coat to roll up his sleeves. Strickler's driver, a heavy-set man built like a fireplug and snugly wrapped in a black suit, intervened.

"Boss, he ain't worth it. We gotta be on set in a few. Car's dented but drivable. I'll take care of it." The driver's voice was thick and masculine but soothing. Clearly, this wasn't the first time the man had tried to calm his furious boss down.

Strickler got in Evan's face, eyes burning into his intensely, and shook his head. He looked away in seeming disgust, then grabbed his Brooks Brothers jacket, slipped it back on, and climbed back into the Bentley.

"Let's go, Jack," Strickler said to his driver before pointing an accusing finger at Evan. "Better not let me see you again, reprobate. I never forget a face, especially a smug one like yours. And should I see you? Your knees better be shaking, or you should be praising my name! One or the other!" he repeated.

Evan shook his head. The guy reminded him of a cartoon villain.

The driver got the engine started, backed the car up, and they were on their way.

"How about if I do neither!" Evan shouted at the back of the car as it wheeled away.

Coop now approached Evan from the opposite end of the street, shaking his head faintly the entire way. "You sure know how to make a good first impression. That guy? He's my boss. I was hoping to get you on the movie I'm working on for him. That might be difficult, but there's always a solution to every problem." Coop smiled.

Evan stared at Coop, brow furrowed. "That guy is your producer?" Evan asked, wondering if he heard Coop right. "I mean, his name sounds a little familiar, but…"

"Just on this movie. These people come and go. I can tell you this: Stay as far away from that man as possible if you ever see him again."

Evan seemed worried as he followed Coop down Laurel. Arthur seemed to have a lot more anger in him than most, and if he was half as bad as their encounter made him seem, Evan had no problem giving the guy a really wide berth.

Evan's train of thought was derailed as a familiar-looking man furiously pedaled a bicycle right over to Coop and Evan.

Evan would have sworn the fellow was his old friend Hank from 2021, just slightly younger. Evan noticed the bicycle had a sidecar like the old-fashioned motorcycles did, the kind the Germans had in WWII. On the sidecar's seat, Evan spied a few movie props: prop books and a wad of fake movie money. He could see the cover of the book on top, which read, *Tom Sawyer* by Mark Twain.

"Coop, you headed in?" the man on the bicycle asked.

Coop nodded. "Always headed to the salt mines of audio, Henry."

Henry? That's formal for Hank, thought Evan. *Could this guy be my Hank from 2021?*

"Hank?" Evan blurted out.

Henry's eyes moved his way. He looked surprised. "Last time I checked, I believe I was Henry Richards. Don't go by Hank, not yet at least. And you are?"

Evan had to pinch himself. This was extraordinary. His Hank, clearly a prop master, working for a studio and driving a bicycle with a sidecar instead of a golf cart. Evan stared hard at him, confused. Hank was in his seventies at most in 2021, yet this Henry looked to be in his forties. Evan's mind was reeling—he'd just reconciled the crazy idea that he'd gone back in time, and now he had to grapple with the fact that he was looking at his old friend Hank—who'd apparently barely aged over the course of seventy-five years.

This can't be the same guy. No way....

"Evan West," he stammered out, recalling that Henry had just asked him a question." Evan stared at Coop, who was watching them.

"A word to the wise, Mr. Evan West," Henry said, motioning Evan closer. "You just made a mean enemy, my friend. Mr. Strickler is a man who holds a grudge for life."

Evan nodded. No surprise there. He threw a thumb in Coop's direction. "He told me the same thing."

Henry seemed to size up Evan. "Coop, you mind if I borrow your friend?"

Coop shook his head. "Not at all, Mr. Richards. I gotta get to the sound shack and set up for today."

"Good luck, Coop. See you on the set. You hungry, Mr. West?" Henry grinned. "Follow me. I was just heading to the

Rail Head Diner. They got the best bean soup at this joint."

Despite having just eaten a couple of hours before, Evan was hungry…ravenous, in fact. Evan waved to Coop and asked, "When do I see you again?"

Coop shrugged. "Don't worry, Evan, I'll find you. I always do." Coop grinned at their inside joke and made his way to the studio lot in the distance.

Evan walked beside Henry, who pedaled slowly along. He eyed the older man, whose concentration was on steering. "Why are you taking me to lunch?" Evan finally asked, his twenty-first-century mistrust kicking in.

Henry's bright eyes flashed in his direction. "You look like a guy who needs a break. Have a little trust in the kindness of strangers."

Evan regarded the props in the sidecar again. "Where you taking these?"

"The picture I'm working on. Same one Coop's doing. And off we go!"

Henry pedaled toward the Rail Head Diner, just off Ventura. Evan walked beside him, his stomach grumbling. He was hungry. Again. The smell of a grill and fried food wafting from the diner was enticing.

"Here we are," Henry announced, parking the bike and climbing out with ease. Evan noticed an American town movie set down the way from their location.

Evan looked at his watch but found just a bare wrist. With a frown, he recalled that he had hocked his for a tow from Sal the day before.

"You got the time, Henry?" Evan asked.

Henry pulled a pocket watch from his shirt pocket like

a train conductor. "Just past two. Not exactly lunch or sup-pertime, but this place makes you hungry any time of day."

Evan wondered where this was going. *No sense stressing about it*, he decided. He was here now. Might as well let the adventure roll over him and take him wherever it wanted. After all, he was in the era he had always loved so dearly, and to Evan, there was no better place to be.

CHAPTER 9

COUNTERFEITER

Evan and Henry entered the diner. Evan had to clamp his mouth shut to stop his drool from leaking out. The smell was unbelievable and kicked Evan's hunger into overdrive. Henry found them a table by the window facing out toward the gravel road they had traveled in on.

An attractive young woman dressed in a blue waitress uniform approached them. Her name tag read, "DOROTHY." Her hair was pulled back in a ponytail, and she had on just enough makeup to look like she wasn't wearing any. She wore low-slung, white nurse shoes, which made sense, considering her job. Her dress, a pale blue with a sewed-on white apron, completed her *Alice in Wonderland* ensemble. She walked with a kind of extreme confidence rarely seen in a young person. That alone set her apart.

Evan turned to watch her. The very second Evan laid eyes on her, something happened. He'd never felt such a chain reaction of astonishment, awe, and amazement. It was as if a nuclear reactor was nearing critical mass. His entire body flushed, awash with deep attraction. For the first time in his life, a woman he'd never even spoken with had smitten him.

Evan had trouble keeping his balance. Suddenly, he was on a ship in a wild storm, the bow lifting with the crest of a very big wave.

And it felt good.

"You boys ready?" Dorothy looked to both men and smiled brightly. She had auburn hair pulled back in regulation restaurant-server-style, inquisitive eyes, and a depth to her that appeared infinite.

"Evan, what's your fancy today?" Henry asked. He gave Evan a quick once-over, then glanced at Dorothy and smirked a little. "As for me, bean soup and an iced tea, if you please?"

Evan fumbled with the menu, so nervous he could barely read the items.

"Take your time, mister," Dorothy said, sounding a little impatient.

He didn't want to make a bad first impression on the most beautiful girl in the world. "I'll have what he's having," Evan answered, trying to look cooler and more breezy—Dean Martin-style—than he actually was. Though he was sure right now he was more Woody Allen than cool cat.

"Anything to drink?" she asked. Evan just stared in response, unable to speak. He'd never been more captivated by a human being before, and it made the synapses in his brain overheat and malfunction.

Dorothy raised her eyebrows and cocked her head. "You okay? Cat got your tongue, mister?" She flirted in that way that seemed genuine but surely got her loaded with tips.

Evan snapped out of it. "Coca-Cola. Always Coca-Cola. It tastes better here than..." Evan stopped himself. Henry looked at Evan with a curious expression.

"Yeah, ours is the best Coca-Cola in all Encino, or so I heard." She laughed and winked at Henry. "Nice visiting with you, mister. I got your order."

She moved away, and Evan watched her longingly. She glanced back at him, and he averted his eyes with embarrassment. Her presence was so compelling. Had he known her before?

"This place is somethin', isn't it?" Henry asked, then pinned Evan with a hard look. "So, tell me about what you've edited before."

"Mostly trailers, but I'm eager to get on into the big leagues…edit movies," Evan said. A half-truth.

"You new in town?" Henry asked.

"Yeah, you might say that," Evan answered, averting his eyes. "Just got here."

The food arrived, and Evan dug into the bean soup after taking a long sip of Coca-Cola. An enormous brick of bread accompanied the soup, slathered with a pound of butter. It was magnificent, the taste and substance of it hitting every nerve receptor in his body. The dense, tasty meal, combined with his falling hard for Dorothy, had left Evan high as a kite. He laughed to himself.

"What's on your mind, friend?" Henry asked, watching him.

Evan just shook his head. "If I told you, you'd think I was crazy."

Henry frowned at him, then checked his pocket watch and abruptly lurched out of his seat. "I'm sorry, buddy, I got to run. I'm late to the set with that stuff. Good havin' lunch with you!' Before Evan could protest that he had no money,

Henry was out the door, on his bike, and peddling away faster than Almira Gulch in *The Wizard of Oz*.

Dorothy appeared, a check in hand. Evan gulped, wondering what to tell her.

"Hi," Evan said, trying not to look at the scrap of paper with its sum of charges on it, a sum he had no hope of paying.

"Hi there, you!" Dorothy chirped and snapped the check on the table. "Pay for this up front when you're ready."

"I'm sorry. This sounds impossible…but have we met before?" Evan asked, sheepish and unsure if he should have brought it up.

"I don't know, maybe? We live in a small town, although it seems a little bigger every day." She smiled brightly.

"You do this full time?" Evan asked, dreading the process of paying that bill and doing anything to waste time before the inevitable.

"You mean, work as an indentured servant for peanuts? No, sir. I'm an actress, or at least, would like to be. Still looking for my big break. I'm proud to say I take some business classes at Glendale Community College, so you might say I'm a well-rounded girl." She grinned broadly, winked, and then sashayed away from him and took her position behind the register.

Evan just stared at her, captivated again.

"Come on up front to pay," she said again and batted her eyelashes because she knew how effective a weapon it was when a girl was pursuing higher-than-20-percent tips.

This was the moment of truth. Evan sighed. Maybe his money would pass muster. He stood and reached into his wallet, heart beating so fast his face was turning red. Evan took a few steps toward the gallows and pulled out the $20 from 2021.

Dorothy took the bill and took a close gander at it, her brow furrowing. Evan's heart sank; he bit his lip.

"Say, what are you tryin' to pull, mister? I didn't figure you for a chiseler," she said, frowning. "Hey, Butch, get a load of Andy Jackson's big *cabeza* on this phony funny money!"

A big man dressed in white—Butch, no doubt—came around the counter, his ugly scowl making it apparent he was in no mood for jokes.

"Kid, unless you can spot me some real jack, you're washing dishes. Your call!" he boomed out in a voice as unpleasant as his glare.

Evan shrunk back, his eyes wide, wishing Henry hadn't left him hanging. Evan didn't blame him. Hank had no way of knowing he was traveling light.

From behind Evan, a man's hand passed a 1946 genuine prime fin note into his hand. Evan craned his neck to see who his savior was. No doubt one of the good Samaritans who seemed to be in plentiful supply in this time period.

It was Jimmy Stewart, rail-thin and larger than life. In Evan's mind, Bogart was ethereal, but James Stewart shone like the brightest sun in the universe—second only to Dorothy. Jimmy was a walking fourth of July fireworks show, one of the world's most familiar and winning faces.

Evan could hardly believe it. Lanky, good-natured Jimmy Stewart, the father he never had, standing right in front of him. Jimmy wore casual slacks; an open-necked, light-blue shirt, and a tweed sport coat. A dark-brown fedora was parked on the back on his head.

Evan had always seen Tom Hanks as his generation's Jimmy Stewart, but compared with the real thing, Tom was a distant second.

"I got this, Dorothy," Jimmy said in his familiar drawl. He glanced at Evan. "Looks like you brought the prop money from the set, young feller." He leaned to Evan and winked. "I've been ten cents and a dollar short myself on occasion." Jimmy took the $20 from Dorothy and handed it back to Evan. "Might want to give this back to Henry in props."

Dorothy seemed astonished by Jimmy's kindness toward Evan, whom she had no doubt pegged as a small-time crook. Jimmy jerked a thumb Evan's way. "Friend of yours, Dorothy?" he asked.

"We just met, but he came in with Henry. Seems nice enough to me," she said and cast a glance at Butch, who went back behind the counter, disarmed by Jimmy Stewart's kind-hearted charisma.

Evan stepped toward Jimmy Stewart, who seemed larger than life and twice as glorious. His dark hair was swept back in its signature style, his face as smooth and perfect as it looked on the silver screen.

"Saw you guys come in together," Jimmy remarked with a friendly smile. "Any friend of Henry's is a friend of mine."

"Mr. Stewart... Mr. James Stewart, I'm Evan West. So good to meet you, sir!," he blubbered.

"Last time I checked, I was just plain, old Jimmy," Jimmy said, eyes twinkling at Evan before shifting to Dorothy. "Say, Dorothy, keep the change on that and bring us a couple of coffees. Evan, you're on the picture? Come with me. We can walk off our late lunch."

Evan saw everyone in the diner looking his way; any friend

of Jimmy Stewart's was someone to notice. Dorothy handed both Jimmy and Evan small paper cups of coffee, nothing like the enormous "Grande" cups sold at Starbucks seventy-five years from now. Evan nodded with gratitude.

"Thank you for lunch, Jimmy," Evan said, then he turned too quickly and ran smack-dab into a man standing directly behind him. The coffee exploded from the impact and sloshed all over the man's chest.

Evan's heart fell when he saw who he collided with—Arthur Strickler, now dripping with hot joe.

"Excuse me. I'm so sorry," Evan blurted out.

"You again? What's with you?" Strickler was angry, not as angry as before, but still at near-boil, which Evan assumed at this point was just his natural state.

"I'm sorry, mister, I didn't see you behind me. I just turned, and there you were," Evan explained, fear in his voice.

"I'm very well aware of your propensity for error," Strickler said, snatching the napkins dabbed with water Dorothy tried to hand to him to clean his suit.

"Aw, come on, Arthur," Jimmy offered in his best "aw, shucks" voice, taking a step toward Strickler. "It was an honest accident. The kid didn't mean it." He nodded at Evan, who still looked stricken. "No reason to get sore with him."

It was as if someone had popped Strickler's anger balloon. His whole demeanor relaxed, eyes softening. Evan watched his total transformation from the scowling madman he'd been before into a reasonable facsimile of a human being in surprise.

"I never get sore, James. You know what a good-natured fellow I am," Strickler said, his voice lifting up a few octaves, sweet as can be.

Jimmy sized him up, and Evan could see the brief skepticism in Jimmy's eyes. Obviously, the star knew him better than that.

"Uh-huh. See you around, Arthur." Jimmy cast a glance at Evan and motioned for him to go to the door. "Let's go."

As soon as Jimmy was out the door, Evan heard Strickler boom out from somewhere behind him, "Coffee, young lady. To go and make it snappy." His lighthearted cheer had already evaporated like rainwater in the desert.

"Yes, Mr. Strickler. Right away, sir," Dorothy said nervously.

Evan grimaced, not daring to look behind him. He made his way to the door, but Strickler grabbed his shoulder and half-spun him, forcing the two men to stand face-to-face.

"How does an accident-prone reprobate like you know Jimmy Stewart?" Strickler hissed.

Evan bristled, tired of men like Arthur Strickler who wore their anger on their sleeves and used it to pummel the world into submission.

"Jimmy's a nice guy. I'd like to think I am, too," Evan said in a calm yet loud tone. He caught a glimpse of Dorothy back by the counter trying not to snicker. Good—he'd won her over.

Evan looked at Dorothy, avoiding Strickler's baleful glare. "See you next time, Dorothy."

Dorothy didn't smile. "Make a deal with you: Next time, bring real money if you want to eat."

Fair enough, Evan thought, heading out the door to join the great Jimmy Stewart on a walk that would change his life, or at the very least, the 1946 version of it.

CHAPTER 10

CLIMBING MOUNT OLYMPUS

Evan joined Jimmy, still feeling a bit shaken from his second encounter with Arthur J. Strickler...and still in a daze over the fact that he was actually walking next to his cinematic idol.

"You in the picture, kid?" Jimmy asked.

"I'm not an actor, Mr. Stewart," Evan explained. "I'm an editor."

"You're working with Bill Hornbeck. Good guy." Jimmy nodded in approval.

Evan managed not to grimace. "To be honest, I only cut trailers. I'm not on this movie."

Jimmy went silent, seeming to absorb this…although Evan sensed no change in his demeanor. Jimmy didn't seem to be judging him.

And because of that, Evan's admiration of the man only grew.

"Thank you for the lunch, and I am so happy to have met you. I've seen all eighty-eight of your pictures, Mr.—"

"Jimmy, remember?" Jimmy corrected him with lightning speed. He probably had a lot of practice at correcting the formal way people tried to address and treat him. Obviously, the man wanted none of that.

"Oh, sure. Sorry, Jimmy, but yes, I've seen all of them," Evan proudly stated.

Jimmy glanced at him, frowning slightly. "Well, now wait a minute. Aside from this picture I'm on now, I've only done thirty-two flicks. Let's see…" Jimmy pursed his lips thoughtfully. "Yep…thirty-two. Something like that… Not sure exactly."

"What is this one?" Evan asked, and Jimmy lit up.

"It's called *The Greatest Gift*, and I gotta tell ya, I had my reservations at first. Still do, but I think me and Frank might be onto something."

A light turned on in Evan's head. It must have shown on his expression because he noticed Jimmy looking at him curiously.

"You know something I don't, kid?" Jimmy asked, still eyeing him.

"What? No sir," Evan lied. He didn't know what else to say.

"Well, all right then." Jimmy faced forward as they walked together, though his face still held that heavy expression. "I just get that feeling from you, son."

Evan didn't answer. He had too many thoughts racing through his head. The Greatest Gift…*that must be* It's A Wonderful Life, Evan realized, *just with a different title. It can't be anything else!*

"*It's a Wonderful Life* is going to be one of your greatest films!" Evan exploded.

"What's that?" Jimmy asked, eyebrows raised.

"Oh, nothing," Evan said. "I loved *Mister Smith Goes to Washington*, truly one of your greatest."

Jimmy looked pleased. "I thought so, too."

"Say, why don't you get lunch on the set, Jimmy? I'll bet they cater in great stuff for you."

"Aw, sometimes I get tired of that fancy stuff they bring in from Chasen's or the studio commissary. Stroganoff and caviar and cheesecake. I like a plain, old burger now and then. Know what I mean?" Jimmy asked with a smile.

"Sure do," Evan answered.

They passed the guard gate that protected the studio lot, called The Encino Ranch. The letters RKO were stenciled below it.

"Don't worry, he's with me," Jimmy told the guard, pointing to Evan. The guard waved Jimmy on through.

The two men passed a series of buildings; in the distance, larger sets could be seen.

Jimmy pushed his brown fedora back, showing more of his forehead. "Not to say it's not a wonderful life. I'm grateful I can still make a living in this business after the war and all. Bad business, that war. Any war, when you get down to it." He glanced at Evan. "Trailers, huh? Very interesting. We're going to need a good trailer for this picture. Anyway, did you know they actually brought in dogs and cats and pigeons to roam around the set for a few weeks? Kinda gives it a real-life small-town feel."

"I didn't know that, Jimmy," Evan remarked, grinning broadly. Jimmy again gave him an odd look.

"That Frank…," Jimmy continued after a moment, "he thinks of everything. Pigeons. Yes, sir. Hope people like the film. Deals with angels and stuff. Not sure myself. Some things in it I'd like to change, but I'm just an actor," he said ruefully. "Don't get much say in what's going on past a certain point."

"No, Jimmy. You're not just an actor, you're a star," Evan insisted.

Jimmy didn't answer. He looked burdened and a bit weary, though Evan couldn't fathom the reason. Why wouldn't a big star be forever on cloud nine?

Abruptly, Jimmy switched gears. "Say, that little Dorothy gal is a plum, isn't she? I noticed you noticed."

Evan's cheeks grew hot. "Yeah, she is. She's an actress too. Says she really needs a break."

"That a fact?" Jimmy mused thoughtfully.

"Maybe you could get her a part, Jimmy? An extra, or something? You know, something small."

"That's a great idea, Evan. I'll talk to Frank. Nice kid, that Dorothy. Awful pretty."

"And Jimmy…?" Evan started as they reached the front of the set. Jimmy stopped and fully faced Evan.

"Don't worry," Evan enthused. "This picture is gonna be huge!"

Jimmy's eyes twinkled with good-natured mirth. "What, you from the future, or something?" Little crystal ball in your jacket?" He laughed.

"You'll see," Evan said confidently.

Jimmy heaved out a big breath. "Okay, end of the road for me. I'm sure I'll see you around. I think we're shooting back at Paramount tomorrow, but I'll talk to Frank about Dorothy."

"Thanks, Jimmy," Evan said, his attention now completely focused on the set. "Wow. Bedford Falls." Now Evan knew for sure…this was the set of *It's A Wonderful Life*.

Unbelievable. He stared in awe.

Jimmy's hand on his shoulder, giving it a hearty yet friendly pat, brought Evan out of his trance. "See you around."

"See ya', Jimmy." Evan waved, then just stood there and blinked a few times. He had no idea where to go or what to do. He was beginning to wonder if he was in dreamland again. What were the odds he'd end up in 1946, on the set of the movie he was trying to save from Connor Alcott? He'd just shared a stroll and friendly chat with his top movie icon, Jimmy Stewart, who'd even showed up when needed to pay his lunch tab.

Evan shook his head. Either way, he was enjoying this ride. No reason for it to end. He headed toward the main street of the movie town ahead and took a few steps on the street. A huge sign fastened in place to a nearby building read, "BAILEY BROS. BUILDING AND LOAN." Evan stopped and almost had to pinch himself. He exhaled a long time, then had to stop himself from shouting at the top of his lungs, *This is it! This is really it.* He was standing before movie history, as big as it got, and so far, it had not disappointed.

Evan spotted a camera crew setting up a dolly shot at the far end of the street. Extras were already in place, and he could see Gloria Grahame, dressed in a dark, tight-fitting dress, her blond tresses shining in the sunlight."

Evan, still in a state of nervous shock, was becoming overwhelmed from sensory overload.

"Hey, Evan!" a voice called from behind him, making him jump a little. Henry rode his bicycle toward him and waved. Coop was close behind Henry, walking as fast as he could to keep up with the bicycle's decent speed.

Henry pulled up beside him. "How much do I owe you? I skipped out on you earlier. Bad manners on my part."

"Jimmy picked up the tab," Evan said.

"Jimmy, huh? Well, that's something he would do. Generous man," Henry remarked, then gave Evan a serious look. "Listen, you got a place to stay for the night? The only reason I'm askin' is you did say you were new here, and good hotels cost a fortune."

Evan wasn't sure how to answer, so he figured he'd tell the truth. "I haven't thought about it much, Henry. Figured if worst comes to worst, I can shack up somewhere here on the set."

"You could do that, but it's the last day of shooting out here for a week. We're doing a company move back to Paramount, in Hollywood. I can get you bunked there easily on a sound stage. No one would notice," Henry offered.

Coop nodded enthusiastically. "Yes, that's a good idea. My place is too small, cramped, and filled with equipment. Take the deal, Evan."

Evan looked at Henry and nodded. "Why not? Beats sleeping on a park bench!"

Henry reached into his sidecar and then held up a large, black sweater. "Got you this. Help yourself to some warm clothes from wardrobe. You're gonna freeze tonight unless you change."

"Thanks," said Evan, taking the sweater.

"Evan, the bus'll pick us up across the street there in a few hours. Why don't you go change in the dressing room in that house over there?" He pointed to a small home on the corner. "I'll meet you there after the last scene."

"Sure thing," Evan agreed, and Henry pedaled away."

As soon as he was out of earshot, Evan looked at Coop. "What are we gonna do?"

Coop, clearly concerned, shook his head. "I figure we just go with whatever transpires at this point. I saw you walking over with the lead actor in this picture," Coop remarked. "Did he seem like a fair man?"

"Sure, he's fair enough," Evan answered, but Coop looked lost in thought. "We need to stick together," he said, "and find our way back to wherever we came from. I hope you can get a job just by being around these people. They always need someone." Coop rubbed his chin. "I will leave you to Henry's goodwill and then meet you at Paramount tomorrow. I have to get to work, need to prepare for the upcoming scene. Good luck." Coop eyed him. "You gonna be okay?"

"Sure." Evan shrugged. "I'm still not completely sure this isn't a dream or a concussion-induced hallucination that I'll simply wake away from, but to quote Mr. Spock: "Once you have eliminated the impossible, whatever remains, however improbable, must be the truth. So, here I am."

"Who's Mr. Spock?" Coop asked, then just shook his head. "I'm sorry, Evan, but you're really trapped here, just like me."

Coop then turned and hurried toward the crew in the distance. Evan wondered how the heck they were going to get home.

He looked around Bedford Falls, noting that the sun was already on its way down. He found a nearby chair and watched the crew members as they moved portable lights across the streets. The activity on a movie set might be intoxicating for those immersed in the chaos, but at the moment, to Evan, it just seemed tedious. Evan's eyes drooped, the two heavy meals he had consumed earlier putting his body into sleep mode. He drifted off, the sounds of the crew calling to one another and footsteps working their way into his dreams.

When he awoke, the sky was approaching what filmmakers called "Magic Hour"—the time when the sun was orange in the sky, slipped over the horizon, and created a red, blue, and purple tableau above the edge of the world.

Evan headed for the small house Henry had pointed out to him earlier. He entered and looked around. Plenty of open rooms, all with wardrobes appropriate to the people of Bedford Falls. He found a pair of trousers his size and another white, casual shirt. He changed out of his old clothes and into a pair of very itchy, wool trousers and an equally prickly wool sweater. He made another observation about the time period: the air smelled bad, the food tasted better, and the clothes were a lot more uncomfortable. Suddenly, 2021 didn't seem so bad to him. Evan kicked off his shoes and examined his swollen big toe. He winced at the purple mess of a bruise, but at least he could bend his toe. Evan was relieved it wasn't broken, but it still hurt. Maybe a little rest on a movie set would do him good.

He left the house and watched a herd of extras in raincoats and umbrellas moving toward the town square near the Building and Loan. Big, 35mm Mitchell cameras were set up, and the lights blazed hot. Cranes were in place for an upcoming shot. Evan immediately recognized the scene they were preparing to shoot. It was the moment when the townsfolk were about to make a run on Bailey Bros. Building and Loan, and George would save the day by using his honeymoon money to ward off the panic.

Rain machines were ready on standby.

Evan saw a man in a white shirt with dark hair on the crane next to a camera, his hand raised. He stared at the man…who was none other than Frank Capra. Even from a distance, Evan was impressed.

"Okay, rain machines! Let 'em run for a few minutes, get the street wet! Sound on. I want the sound of that rain!" Capra, looking sharp in a white button-up, crisply starched and collared shirt and a dark tie, shouted through a megaphone, his piercing eyes scanning the scene as he smoothed back his full, dark hair. The rain machines commenced the showers.

Evan spotted Coop holding up a microphone on a boom; he then glanced at the nearby audio recordist. He had his thumb up to indicate he was rolling. Capra noted it and held up one hand dramatically. "This is panic, people. All your money is gone. It's the middle of the Great Depression, and the Building and Loan is your only hope. Got that? We all remember those days. I know I do!"

The extras nodded; some laughed politely.

"Okay, quiet everybody!" A burly AD shouted. "Places!"

Capra waited for the set to settle. He looked over at Jimmy. "Jimmy, I see you! Ready to save the day?"

Jimmy stood next to a 1930 Franklin painted in taxi-style gold and black. He gave a slight nod.

"Sound?" Capra barked.

"Rolling. Speed!"

"Camera?"

"Rolling!'

"Mark it!" Capra shouted.

The second AD held up a clapperboard. "Scene Ten Bravo, take one!" He snapped it closed.

"Action!" Capra shouted, and Evan felt a chill go through him. This was the magic that had him hooked from day one. It was the most wonderful feeling in the world to him, watching a movie get made, especially this one—one of the greatest movies ever.

Jimmy stepped away from the taxi and rushed toward the bank entrance; the camera craned up. Some of the extras didn't swarm as Jimmy approached the Building and Loan.

"Cut!" Capra commanded, then pulled the megaphone up to his mouth. "We need a three count here. I need everyone heading toward the building at once behind Jimmy. Understood?"

The extras nodded. Capra waved to them; the crane went down to its starting point. "Let's do this again. Ready? Sound?"

"Rolling!" Coop shouted.

"Camera?"

"Rolling!"

"Mark it! And…action!"

The magic unfolded again. A few more takes were necessary, with Jimmy repeating his action each time. The extras found their sync and rhythm with the scene. Several cameras covered the action.

Frank Capra seemed pleased. He finally waved to the special effects men.

"That's it for the rain. Thank you, gentlemen!" Capra called. He looked at his cameraman. "Print takes three, five, and ten, if you please. That's it for today."

The artificial rainstorm stopped.

"Let's call it, Mike!" Frank said. The crane came down. He climbed off and lit a cigarette.

Evan watched in wonder. *So, this is what it's like watching a genius at work.*

"That's a wrap, people. Tomorrow on the Paramount lot, RKO Stage 7. Those of you who are done for now, collect your pay vouchers from me on the way out! Thank you, everybody!" Bill, the AD, called out.

Evan heard the sound of diesel engines and took a look over his shoulder, watching the production buses come up. Most of the crew were headed back into Hollywood proper and to the studios where they had parked their cars for the day.

The extras lined up to get their vouchers for their day's pay. Evan headed to the bus just as Henry rode up.

"Well, you look like a new man!" Henry declared. He locked his bicycle in place along a nearby bike rack and then joined Evan. "Climb aboard, matey." Henry waved his hand with a flourish toward the bus.

Evan boarded the bus. The crewmen took large cans of beer out of large, steel lunch pails, opening them with steel can openers. Henry sat up front behind the driver, and Evan took a seat next to him.

"Light 'em up if you got 'em, boys," Henry called out in a jovial voice. "Next stop, Paramount Studios!"

Almost every man and woman on that bus flicked Zippos and lit cigarettes from packets Evan never heard of, including Old Gold, Wings, Philip Morris, Green River, and Fleetwood.

The bus roared to life, and they were off.

The driver took a different route back to Hollywood, heading down Burbank and then hanging a left on Vineland before motoring down Ventura Boulevard. The street turned into Cahuenga Boulevard, where things were getting more and more interesting for Evan.

After half an hour had passed, the bus lumbered down Highland Boulevard, heading for Melrose. Evan peered out the window to see the full moon and Venus, close together in the clear, turquoise sky. Cigarette smoke and good-natured laughter filled the bus. The crew was having a time of it, smoking and drinking what they could before they hit the point that a hangover would have crippled them the next day, and that wouldn't be good for any of them.

Evan glanced at the crew, envying those hardworking people. They were working on some of the greatest movies ever made, being paid well, and most would never live to see the eclipse of the grand studio system that took care of them.

Evan realized he and Henry had not said a word since they got on the bus, and he was grateful for Henry's silence. He began to go over his situation again; Coop, who was clearly smart, didn't know what to do at this point. Evan didn't either. He was going to be stuck here forever, never again to see the twenty-first century. Gwen wasn't even born yet. His landlord would wonder why he stopped paying rent. He'd be another missing person in Los Angeles, another Hollywood casualty. There would be a cursory search, but Evan had no family. No brothers, no sisters; his parents were both deceased. He would not be missed, and those dreams he clung to so desperately would never happen. He'd never be that great movie director who made an imprint on entertainment history. No Oscar ceremony for Evan West, no immortality in film history books—or any books for that matter. Evan never had a social media presence, no publicity except that awful movie trailer for *Rage*, and that would only live on in association with one of many tragic school shootings. Evan would never be married or have kids; he'd just be remembered as a felon who stole a movie that had already been stolen, if that. He winced at the thought of his wasted life; he'd gambled everything on towering Hollywood success that only a few had managed to obtain and keep.

"Something tickling you?" Henry asked.

Evan glanced at his friend. "Just thinking, Henry." Evan sighed. "Life is truly like a box of chocolates. Never know what you're gonna get."

"Say, that sounds like a great line for a movie," Henry said enthusiastically. "You want to be a writer? Remember that one."

"Somebody's gonna beat me to it," Evan muttered.

"You should be a little more optimistic," Henry encouraged him. "For I know the plans I have for you, plans to prosper and not to harm you, plans to give you hope and a future." Evan looked at Henry with confusion. "It's from Jeremiah." Henry scrunched up his face. "Forget which verse."

Evan took his advice, focusing on the positive, and Dorothy's face came to mind. Dorothy was his dream come true. Plus, He had become friendly with Jimmy Stewart. Maybe he could make it here. Not as a movie director—too many greats to compete with he could never overtake, but perhaps as an editor, he could make a name for himself in 1946. He felt such strong feelings for Dorothy he realized he'd be happy as a janitor if she returned his affection.

Another happy thought hit Evan: He'd be able to watch Frank Capra's film *It's A Wonderful Life*. What could be better than that? He could watch dreams being woven into reality, with the added bonus of knowing what an incredible impact the film would make on the world.

Then it hit him like a bowling ball flying at 100 mph to the head—he had to save the movie. He could not allow Frank Capra to shoot those scenes!

Evan nodded to himself. He would somehow find a way to stop this travesty from ever transpiring. The resolution hit him plain as day. If Evan had ever been sure of anything, it was about this…100-percent sure.

He felt alive again, not so directionless. It was as if he had been sent back on purpose. He enjoyed the thought of that. Evan West, savior of *It's A Wonderful Life*. He could dig that. He felt suddenly buoyant. He slapped his thighs and grinned ear to ear, realizing this wasn't a curse or horrible fate. It was the best thing that had ever happened to him.

Henry looked up, startled. "You have a happy thought, friend? Share."

"Yeah, just happy to be alive in the year of our Lord 1946, Henry. It's good to be here," Evan said, maybe a little too loudly.

The bus was nearing Paramount; Evan could feel it slowing.

"It's good to be alive, period, but I agree with ya," Henry said, holding onto the seat. "I think this is our stop."

The bus pulled through the Paramount gates.

The grip bus pulled in front of Stage 10. Evan and the others disembarked, most heading to their parked cars in the lot. Henry led Evan inside of the hanger-like area of Stage 10. Evan glanced to the archaic lights and equipment, strewn haphazardly and abandoned for the evening where they stood—to be reinvigorated upon the following day.

Henry led him to another set, which looked deeply familiar.

"I know this place," Evan whispered.

Henry overheard. "Have you read the script?"

"Uh...sure," Evan said. "Of course. This is the last scene of the movie. Christmas Eve at the Bailey House."

"Good going," Henry said, looking genuinely impressed.

They walked from set to set in the Bailey House. Evan reverently entered the living room, where Zuzu's upright piano sat dormant. Evan went to the piano and sat down. He tested the keys and smiled. All perfectly in tune. He remembered the piano lessons his conscientious mother had forced him to take.

Evan played "Auld Lang Syne," complete with left-hand harmony for feeling. He wrapped up with a big "G" chord. Henry smiled and applauded. "Bravo, maestro." He then pointed to one of the bedrooms annexed to the dining room. "There's a bed in there, Evan. You can use it for the night. No one will care. Crew isn't on call until seven. Washroom is right down the hall. Sink actually works. Don't trip over the sound cables," he instructed.

"Thanks, Henry," Evan said.

Henry headed toward the exit. "See you in the morning."

"Not if I wake up from all this, but thanks," Evan said, then added, "Guess you'll be earning your wings soon."

Henry looked at Evan with curiosity, then grinned and exited.

Evan knew it must be late. He wished he had his watch, then remembered the $6 he needed for Sal. He wondered what his car repairs would cost and reconciled himself to the fact that he needed to start earning a paycheck, pronto. He sighed, figuring he'd wake up and deal with whatever the new day brought.

As soon as his head hit the pillow (which smelled freshly washed with strong detergent), he fell asleep, not at all dissatisfied with the day he had just experienced.

Again, he fell into a deep, dreamless sleep. A part of Evan was sure that when he awoke, it would be in his old bed at his apartment, and he'd finally step out of this very long, lucid dream.

But he was wrong.

CHAPTER 11

APPOINTMENT WITH THE KING

Evan awoke to a wet dog's tongue scraping like sandpaper across his face from his ears to his mouth. The dog was panting, half barking and crying simultaneously, sounding very excited. Evan opened his eyes and met the gaze of a shaggy sheepdog; it seemed awfully familiar.

A woman's voice sounded, "Shag, stop that. You're being rude!"

Evan blinked away the last of his drowsiness. His eyes focused, landing right on the face of a stunningly beautiful woman. She looked like anyone's idea of female perfection. Evan stared, taking in her kind eyes and the way she moved, like she was very utterly secure in who she was, without a trace of anxiety or self-doubt. She looked at Evan sympathetically while pulling the collar of the shaggy dog, which seemed happy now that Evan was awake.

"I'm sorry to bother you, sir, but you probably shouldn't be sleeping here," she said. "You need to go."

The remaining cobwebs cleared from Evan's head, and he propped himself on his elbow, eyes swelling. The great Donna Reed, co-star with Jimmy Stewart in *It's A Wonderful Life*, was talking to him.

"No...it's all right. I'm sorry," he managed to croak.

127

"I just don't want you to get into any trouble." Donna's voice was soft and sultry, yet her tone held an urgency that broadcast *You need to go now.*

"You're Donna Reed!" Evan half-shouted.

Donna smiled shyly, and Evan glanced around, realizing that the movie set was coming to life. Gaffers and grips rigged cables and lights on stands, and production assistants mobilized and carried various props in and out of rooms.

"We're setting up to shoot." Donna looked at him sternly.

A thundering voice bellowed out at Evan from somewhere behind Donna. "And just who the hell are you, and what the Sam Hill are you doing lounging in Zuzu's bed?"

Donna and Evan both turned toward the large, red-faced man marching their way.

"I...I just needed a place to crash for a few hours," Evan said to the big man. He looked to the sheepdog Donna still held. "And you're Shag, Jimmy's dog in the movie!"

Shag barked as if acknowledging Evan's declaration.

Donna looked to the angry man. "Bill, I don't think he meant any harm..."

"Don't you worry, Ms. Reed. I know this guy's type. Another drifter who snuck on the lot, looking for a place to flop. All right, fella, I'm gonna deal with you now!"

Evan's eyes nervously flew around the set as if looking for an escape route. His jaw dropped. Miraculously, Jimmy Stewart happened to be ambling past at that very moment, nose in his script. He looked up, and his eyes met Evan's. "Evan? That you? You need some money?"

"Oh, hi, Mr. Stewart—I mean, Jimmy. No, don't need any money," Evan stammered.

"I have a policy: only one bailout at a time." Jimmy smiled.

"No, sir, Jimmy. I'm just, uh…" Evan was at a loss.

Bill, whom Evan had correctly assumed to be assistant director—since only a man in that position would yell so rudely on a set—turned to Jimmy. "You know this guy, Mr. Stewart?"

"Why, sure, Bill. Old friend of mine. Evan West," Jimmy said easily. "He's an editor. Trailer editor if I recall. I asked him here. So, Evan…" Jimmy called loudly, facing him again. "You came in a little early and fell asleep again?"

Bill looked to Evan. "Well, why didn't you say so, mister?" Bill gave him a friendly nod, suddenly his new bff, thanks to Jimmy's timely intervention.

"Sorry," Evan said, scratching Shag's receptive ear.

Donna extended her hand. "Nice to meet you, Evan West."

"The pleasure is mine, Ms. Reed," Evan said. He hoisted himself off the bed, brushed his clothes off, and clasped Donna's small hand.

Jimmy looked at Bill. "Could you get some coffees for us, Bill? Donna first."

"No, I'm fine, Jimmy. Thanks. I'll leave you two to chat. Gotta get into my Susie Homemaker dress now." Donna smiled infectiously before hurrying off. Bill gave a final nod to Jimmy, then ambled off in the opposite direction, probably in search of some hapless crew member to bark orders at.

Evan heaved out a breath. "Thanks, Jimmy. Thought I was toast there for a minute with that guy."

"Toast?" Jimmy drawled out, brow furrowing. "What's that mean, toast?"

"Never mind," Evan chuckled. "Just an old saying."

"Hmm, new to me. Toast. Actually, that's kinda funny. So, whatcha doing here at Paramount? You working with Frank on those trailers you mentioned?"

Evan withered a bit. "No, wish I were. I cut trailers on smaller films. I'm, well… I'm…"

"Completely unemployed at the moment?" Jimmy asked sagely. "I see."

Evan had been pegged. He shrugged and grinned. "I'm so poor right now, I can't even pay attention."

Jimmy froze, then doubled over laughing. "Oh, my, that's rich." He rubbed an eye. "Hot dog! Well done! I like it…so poor, I can't pay attention. Gonna steal that one from you, kid!"

"It's all yours, Jimmy," Evan offered, beaming over how much entertainment he was providing to his cinematic idol.

Jimmy settled down in a nearby chair and motioned Evan over. "Okay, here's what you're gonna do. Stop by old Capra's office right now." He gestured. "Just across the lot there on the west side, the RKO area. Tell him you're a friend of mine and to hire you. Finesse it, of course, but you get where I'm coming from."

"What?! You're kidding me! Ask Frank Capra for a job?" Evan couldn't believe it.

"Yep. He's bound to be there by now as we're all setting up and getting into makeup and wardrobe. Good a time as any," Jimmy told him emphatically.

Evan absorbed Jimmy's suggestion, wonderstruck. After a few seconds, he realized that Jimmy was eyeing him keenly.

"Say, you stayin' with Henry? Got a place of your own? Seems to me you're kinda drifting if you don't mind me saying," Jimmy observed.

"I'm in-between places at the moment, so to speak," Evan lamented.

"Tell you what. You get that job out of Capra and then come back here, and after the shoot today, you and me'll head back to my place. Got a little guesthouse out back, empty at the moment. It's yours for the taking."

"Are you serious, Jimmy?" Evan could barely form the words.

"Well, you need a place, don't you?"

"Yes, sir. More than ever. But...why are you helping me? You don't even know me, Jimmy. I could be an ax murderer." Evan chuckled, then realized he was probably being a bit too flippant.

"I'll take my chances and guess you're somewhat less than homicidal," Jimmy said, grinning. "And as for the why? Well, you have the look of someone who simply needs a bit of help at the moment. We don't want you ending up like...like toast, right?"

Evan burst out laughing. "Right! Good deal."

"Now go talk to Frank, and don't make me embarrassed I vouched for you—twice now if I recall," Jimmy instructed. He gave Evan a little salute with his script, then rose and wandered off, nose buried in the pages again.

Evan half-ran out of the sound stage and smacked into Coop, who had a big microphone in hand.

"So, you made it! I knew you'd figure this stuff out," Coop said.

They shook hands.

"I've been thinking about your trip from 2021 to 1946. You said you were driving, and the car lost control. How fast were you traveling?" Coop asked.

"I remember exactly, because I looked at the speedometer…I hit 80."

Coop lit up. "Eighty miles per hour, and then you slid into the pole?"

"Exactly, and at that point, I must have been going faster, maybe 85, but…," Evan trailed off.

Coop's face was a mask of concentration. "I think I might have a way of getting us out of this time," he suddenly blurted out, enthused.

"Great. Take your time," Evan said.

Coop looked to Evan with surprise. "I thought you wanted to go back to your own time as much as I wish to go to mine."

"I do," Evan answered, then confessed, "but I've found an incentive to stick around a while."

Coop grinned. "You meet a girl?"

"As a matter of fact, yes. I did. But that's not why I'm in no hurry to leave."

"Then what is it?"

Evan took a breath. "Coop, you're working on this film, right?"

"Right."

"What if I told you this particular film is gonna be one of the most spectacular films in history?"

Coop looked stunned.

Evan pressed on. "So…Jimmy Stewart, the film's star, just invited me to stay at his guesthouse."

"Okay, so now you're best friends with a movie star," Coop teased.

"Funny. No, it's just that…this whole scenario, it's unbelievable," Evan breathed, somewhat aghast. "I'm gonna be a part of film history. You worked for Nikola Tesla, one of the most well-known and notable scientific geniuses in history. What could be better than that? What could be better in life than knowing you were so close to greatness? I want to be part of this."

Coop nodded, thoughtful. "Makes sense. This must be an exceptional time for you."

"It is. And I'd like to make it last a while longer before I head home," Evan concluded.

"Rest assured, we won't be leaving here anytime soon. If I'm right about this, we need another lightning storm, and those don't come around all that often. The weather reports show clear skies for the foreseeable future, and I'm just not sure how to get us back, me to my time, you to yours. This will take a great deal of work on my part."

"Thanks," Evan said, and Coop grinned.

"We will solve this problem, Evan West." He gave Evan a quick salute, and Evan headed over to Frank Capra's office.

On the way, Evan spotted Boris Karloff dressed in an eighteenth-century gentlemen's costume, looking like a cross between Frankenstein's monster and Thomas Jefferson.

Evan approached the horror icon and cleared his throat. "Sir, may I ask where Liberty Films is located?" he asked in his nicest voice.

"Why yes, old boy, just right over there," Boris said in the nicest English accent. Evan loved hearing him speak; no one on Earth came close to Boris Karloff in terms of eerily creepy voices. Maybe Vincent Price's was creepier, but Karloff got the prize from Evan.

Evan thought for a second. *What movie was Karloff making*

at RKO in 1946? A more careful look at Karloff's costume answered the question. *Bedlam*, one of the great horror films Val Lewton produced.

"Thank you, Mr. Karloff," Evan said, and Boris seemed pleased.

"Why, it's my pleasure, young man. Even more so to be recognized. Good morning to you." Karloff flashed that familiar smile that almost looked like a leer. He headed away, script in hand just like Jimmy, memorizing lines.

Evan headed west, and then he saw it—Liberty Films. He spotted the placard for Frank Capra, and in the indicated lot space was a 1940 Lincoln Zephyr.

Evan admired the vehicle. Classy car, not too ostentatious. A few spaces down, he saw another familiar name and car: Arthur Strickler, and there was that Bentley Torpedo.

"Oh, brother," Evan muttered to himself. "My lucky day."

He headed into the Liberty office. There was no secretary out front, but he could hear shouting from an inner office around twenty feet or so from the main entrance.

"No, no, no!" a man yelled loudly. "I shot that damned footage you wanted me to, but I'm not going to use it in my film! I'm sorry, Arthur!"

Evan sidestepped to the half-open door and peered in at two men in the middle of a heated exchange. Evan recognized Strickler at once and was filled with dread. He wondered if he should leave. The other man in the exchange was the one and only Frank Capra.

"Frank, listen to me," Strickler sounded remarkably calm, obviously using the same "nice guy" act he had put on for Jimmy the day before.

"I'm done listening to you, Strickler," Capra snarled. "I have the last say and final cut approval in what I shoot. It's in my contract!"

"Of course," Strickler oozed like a hissing stream of lava. "You're the boss. But maybe just one scene, you know, just in case."

"Absolutely not! You have me waste my time on extraneous garbage just to please—"

"Just to please a paying audience and a few select people who are *paying* for the production of your film, Frank! Keep them in mind as well. I answer to them."

Frank waved him away. "Shouldn't you be producing a movie?" he asked, glaring.

Strickler was silent for a second, then rumbled, "Now listen to me. When you and Stewart were off in Europe fighting the war, I was here making movies. A lot has changed, Frank. It's a new business. We're one year out of the biggest war in history. The days of 'Capra corn' are over. It's not what people are looking for anymore. The post-war world isn't the one you left in 1942. People want realism. They don't want to be pandered to with sentimental schlock!"

"So, they want more violence, that's what you're telling me? Just like the war? Really?" Frank growled.

"Maybe." Strickler shrugged. "Who knows? All right, I won't argue with you anymore. Just shoot this last scene..."

"Shoot a terrible scene with George Bailey slapping his wife? Is that what you're asking me to do? Jimmy Stewart, all American hero, hits Donna Reed, America's sweetheart, right in the puss? Are you really asking for that?"

Strickler put two hands flat on Capra's table and leaned in until the two men were face-to-face. "I'm not asking, Frank.

Do it, for your own sake. For all of our sakes." Strickler, a lean, elongated man, towered over Capra. Capra, at five feet, seven inches, looked miniscule next to the hungry vulture standing before him.

Capra pointed a finger at Strickler. "You go to hell, mister, you and the horse you rode in on!"

Capra headed toward the door, right beyond which Evan was standing. He retreated, saw a water cooler, and pretended he was drinking something. Capra exited the office, stood there for a moment, fuming, then stomped his foot.

Evan pulled free a small cup, filled it with water, and approached the livid Capra. "Mr. Capra, a little water?" he asked.

Capra turned to Evan, his face a mask of fury, then suddenly softened. "Thanks, kid." He took the water, knocked it back, then studied Evan. "Who are you?"

"Evan West," he said quickly. "Jimmy sent me to see you."

"Jimmy? You mean Stewart?"

"Yes, sir."

"Why are you supposed to see me?" Capra snapped.

"He said..." Evan shifted his weight. "He said…"

"Spit it out, West!"

"He said...you should give me a job."

"Fine," he growled. "You're hired. More water, please," he commanded and stuck out his empty cup. Evan took it dutifully and refilled it.

"I'm up against the wall with this film, West," Capra muttered.

Strickler was at the other side of the room and had just snapped on his black fedora. He was heading for the door when he turned back and looked at Evan. He paused mid-step, and for a minute, there was a downright ugly silence.

"You again?" Strickler hissed in a withering voice.

"Yes, Mr. Strickler, me again. I'm sorry you have developed such a disliking to me," he said, and then could hardly believe that had come out of his mouth.

"Well put, West," Capra chortled, slapping Evan on the shoulder. "You gutsy little son of a gun. I wish I would have said that to you, Strickler!" Capra's eyes narrowed as he turned toward Strickler. "Why have you developed such a disliking to *me*? If we get to the bottom of that, maybe we can have a real partnership. So, tell me, what is it you do here exactly?"

The two men faced off from across the room. Strickler seemed to project aggression and a desperate need for power across the space between them. "To answer your question, I'm a partner at this studio! Whatever you want, whatever you're expecting, it will all have to go through me! Is that understood?"

Capra stood rock-still for an instant, eyes filled with fire. Abruptly, he stormed over to his desk and came back with a big ledger of checks. "I'd like to buy you out, Strickler. Name your price," Capra announced, dumping the ledger on the nearest table surface and unscrewing a fountain pen.

Evan interjected, bridging the space between the men to get into Strickler's face. "Mister, I'd really love to know what your problem is with me."

Strickler blinked, seeming to consider the question in earnest. "I don't know, precisely, but I've banked my career on feelings, and my gut hunch about you is that you're trouble, the kind of trouble I don't need."

Frank Capra watched this exchange with fascination, almost like he was viewing a movie. Finally, the director waved flippantly at Strickler. "Oh, Arthur, just disappear, will ya? Scram. You've had your morning cup of hate and turbulence. Be on your way now, will ya? I've got a long day ahead of me."

Strickler visibly bristled, seeming to weigh his options as several emotions passed over his face, none of them good. Finally, he pulled the brim of his hat lower and yanked open the door, storming out.

As soon as he left, it was like a black cloud had vanished.

Capra turned to Evan, wide-eyed, then burst out laughing. "I think you're my new hero, kid!" he exclaimed.

"I don't know what came over me. But the guy is such a clown!" Evan blurted out.

"Yeah, I agree. A clown, hah! And don't get too worked up about Strickler. He doesn't own much of the studio, maybe 2 percent. He sure manages to bully his power around, being the head of production at RKO. He's a jackass."

"So, he's your boss?" Evan inquired.

"Technically." Capra shrugged. "But to hear me rail at him, you wouldn't know it, would you?" Frank grinned and slapped Evan on the back. "C'mon, my new friend. Let's go talk to Jimmy and figure out what the hell I just hired you for, aside from telling Arthur J. Strickler what's what!"

As they left the office, Capra broke out in song: "*Should old acquaintance be forgot and never brought to mind, we'll take a cup of kindness yet and drink to auld lang syne!*"

Capra stepped out into the California sunshine with Evan and stretched a bit, seeming content to soak in the pleasant heat and light. *"Bello essere vivi!"* he shouted, and Evan knew enough Italian to understand: Good to be alive!

A young intern, looking quite eager and intense, stepped out of the Liberty office and hailed Frank, requesting his signature on a few documents.

Evan walked a few feet away, then caught a glimpse of Strickler at his car with Jack, his driver. Strickler was so intent on his conversation, he missed Evan hovering only ten feet behind him.

"His name is Evan West," Jack, was saying as he stood near the Bentley. "He's an editor, but I never heard of him. Jimmy Stewart has taken a shine to him."

Evan squinted. Strickler had his driver look into his background? Why?

"Indeed?" Strickler responded. "Do you know the story of Icarus, Jack?"

Jack looked confused. "Can't say I have heard dat story, boss."

"It's the story of a young man who built himself some wings with wax and feathers. He thought he was invulnerable to everything, protected by the Greek gods." Strickler nodded to himself, lips pursed. "Thought he could fly close to the brilliance of the sun with impunity. Know what happened to him?"

"I don't know." Jack shrugged.

"He flew so close that his wax melted, and he tumbled to his death in the sea," Strickler intoned with a mirthless chuckle.

"Mr. Strickler, don't get me wrong, but with all due respect, that guy is just some smart-aleck kid. Why are you so interested?" Jack asked.

"I smell a poison rat, Jack. I don't know what it is, but this guy bothers me," Strickler explained.

Evan sidestepped back to Frank Capra, who was still humming "Auld Lang Syne" while signing documents with an oversized flourish. He realized that, for as long as he was in 1946, he was going to have to watch his back where Arthur Strickler was concerned. The man just didn't have it out for him; he wanted Evan gone. Strickler was the same variant as Connor Alcott, just a 1940s version, who was a great deal stronger with supercharged hate venting from the furnace of his heart. Evan had never met a guy like Strickler before, only lesser versions with the same twisted character traits. Evan vowed he'd stay as far away from Arthur J. Strickler as humanly possible.

Frank Capra signed two more documents, all expense-related. He could see the movie might be headed toward the danger zone of going over budget even though they'd just started shooting. The overrun was mostly because of the new process Russell Shearman had come up with to create fake snow that didn't crunch under the actor's feet, but whatever it cost, it was worth it. The sounds of actors crunching over white corn flakes, the usual process of Hollywood snow, was terrible for the audio edit.

Frank caught sight of Strickler glowering in his direction with his big lug of a driver, and anger filled him. He'd busted his hump making movies for the war effort with his fellow directors, only to go home and take orders from a misanthrope like Arthur J. Strickler. He'd seen his kind in the Army, insecure, angry martinets who wielded power through anger and intimidation. Those were not men to be trusted. Frank remembered the Abraham Lincoln quote: "Nearly all men can stand adversity, but if you want to test a man's character, give him power." Strickler failed Lincoln's test.

Heck, Frank thought, *that man would fail almost any true test of character applied to him.*

Thoughts tumbled in Frank's mind as he walked to the set with Evan: Strickler wanted a rewrite of the script, which included some wildly unpleasant scenes: George Bailey going to war and machine-gunning Germans who were attempting to surrender. What the heck was that all about? And that scene Strickler kept insisting on filming with George Bailey slapping Mary... Frank felt nausea every time he contemplated it.

This kid, Evan West... Frank liked him for some reason. What could he do for the kid? He had to get him a job, for one thing. Jimmy was expecting it, and quite honestly, Frank didn't think he'd mind having him around. Anyone who could stand up to Strickler like that was a friend of his. Also, the kid looked and sounded smart. PA work wouldn't be good for him. It'd be a waste of talent.

Like any good movie director, Frank was happy to surround himself with talented people—and if he could, claim credit for their ideas.

Frank Capra passed onto the sound stage and smiled; the feeling of entering a movie set was always a thrill for him. It never got old.

Frank saw Jimmy get to his feet from the living room couch, a newspaper folded in his hand. It was almost as if Jimmy was standing at attention as his commanding officer entered the room. *Old habits die hard*, Frank mused.

"Hey, Jimmy," Frank called out. "Morning to you, sir."

"Morning, Frank," Jimmy hailed, then glanced behind Frank. "You met my young friend, Evan, I see."

Frank turned to look behind him. There Evan was, seeming not so much meek or hiding but simply standing quietly, content to be out of the way for a moment and just absorb the Hollywood setting. "Sure did," Frank said, chuckling and nodding at Evan. "Kid has intestinal fortitude. I hired him on the show!"

"Wonderful, Frank," Jimmy said through a guffaw. "Hired him for *what?*"

Frank paused and again looked to Evan. "What can you do on a film set, kid?"

"Pretty much everything, Mr. Capra," Evan replied.

"That a fact?"

"Yes, sir," Evan responded.

Frank thought for a second, then shrugged. "I'll figure someone out for you, bub. I gotta get to work now. Stay by my side." Frank looked around, then caught sight of his AD, Bill, in the distance gesturing at an extra, probably giving last-minute instructions. "Bill, prep this, please. Thanks," Frank commanded loudly.

"You got it, Mr. Capra," Bill responded. He scanned the ceiling, the lights, and the actors who were in costume but not quite ready for the scene to start. "Five minutes, folks."

Frank stood there, glumly dwelling on those deplorable scenes Strickler insisted he shoot. The very thought of it was about as appetizing as a plate of garbage for dinner.

"What's wrong, Frank?"

Frank looked up, too absorbed in his unpleasant thoughts

to notice the star's approach. "You look about as happy as a cobra square-dancing with a mongoose," Jimmy observed.

Frank was boiling hot. He knew he shouldn't appear angry in front of Jimmy, but he couldn't help but make his feelings known. "That darned Strickler," he said. "Those scenes he wants us to shoot—you know the ones I'm talking about—he wants me to actually use them in my final cut."

Jimmy looked like he'd just sucked on a lemon. "Aw, for cryin' out loud, Frank, you can't do that. Those scenes are dreadful. You know it, and I know it. You and me have everything riding on this picture."

"And he wants me to shoot the scene where you slap Donna!" Capra's voice broke with emotion.

"Well, I won't do it," Jimmy snapped. "I'll tell Strickler to go jump in a very deep lake."

Frank regained control of his emotions and clapped a hand on Jimmy's shoulder. "Don't worry. I'll shoot the darned thing. Get the powers that be off our backs. But I guarantee you—those scenes will never see the light of day. An unfortunate accident is gonna happen in the lab, I'll see to it."

Jimmy grinned. "That's why you're Frank Capra," he said with a chuckle.

Frank glanced to Bill, then yelled out, "Bill, let's shoot Scene 26. Where the hell is Thomas? He ready?"

Thomas Mitchell wandered onto the set at the call of his name, looking haggard and drunk. He was, in reality, as straight as an arrow but completely in character as the drunken Uncle Billy. Frank watched him with admiration, taking in the slightly glassy look in his eyes, the subtle stumble in his gait. He loved seeing great actors doing what they do best.

Frank approached Thomas and Jimmy. "You boys ready? You know the action?"

"We got it, Frank," Jimmy said easily.

Frank looked to his camera crew. "Number one, people. Camera?"

"We're ready, Mr. Capra," Tony on the "A" camera replied.

Evan sidestepped away from the action, hovering in the background. Frank took one look at him, then faced the camera crew. "Set?"

"Set!"

"Bill, you call it."

Bill beamed. Clearly, the man loved it when Frank turned the controls over to him—a sign of intimate trust between the director and AD.

"Sound!" Bill yelled out with some pride.

Coop was standing by with his boom mic stand. The audio mixer called out, "Speed!"

"Cameras!"

"Rolling!"

"Scene 26 Alpha. Marking!"

The clapboard came down.

Frank raised his eyebrows, and Bill said the magic word, "Action!"

Evan watched in awe. He witnessed the great Thomas Mitchell stagger onto the set, looking every bit the drunkard he was playing, while the extras, some carrying camera equipment, headed back into the house. Thomas shuffled over to Jimmy, and the famous scene unfolded.

"Old Building and Loan, pal. Huh...," Uncle Billy slurred.

"Now you just turn this way and go right straight down

there," George pointed, patting Uncle Billy on the shoulder, aiming him camera left.

"That way?" Uncle Billy pointed, weaving, unsteady on his feet.

Evan was awestruck by Mitchell's performance; it was so intense and gripping. He came across as the perfect drunk. Uncle Billy walked away from George Bailey, and Evan stepped back, so engrossed in the scene he didn't see the cables snaking around his feet. He stumbled over one and hastily tried to recover, only to trip on a two-by-four in the process. He flailed, arms pinwheeling as he attempted to regain his balance. He wound up colliding with a stack of twenty paint cans, knocking them over with a massive clatter and metallic crash.

The sound was deafening.

Evan's face went deep red as more cans tumbled down around him, all crashing onto the concrete floor. Evan glanced over, seeing Jimmy Stewart's surprised reaction. He could feel Thomas Mitchell's anger directed toward him, but the actor quickly recovered. Not losing a beat, he called out, "I'm all right, I'm all right! Oh, the sweetest flower that grows…"

Capra yelled out: "Cut!"

Bill stomped toward Evan, furious. "Idiot! You killed that whole scene!"

Capra held up his hand. He looked at Bill and then Jimmy. "That was actually very funny," Frank said. "You know, that works. Looks like old Uncle Billy plowed into some garbage bins. And Jimmy—your reaction was terrific!"

Jimmy looked genuinely surprised. "It was?"

Everyone on the set looked at Evan as Capra strode over and patted him on the shoulder. "That was pretty funny, kid," Capra said, smiling. "You hurt yourself?"

"No," Evan stammered. "I'm sorry, Mr. Capra. Dumb clumsiness."

"Not at all. I call that a happy accident. Works for our movie." Capra glanced at his camera team. "Print that take. Let's move on!" He then looked back to Evan. "You weren't kidding when I asked you what you could do on a set. Obviously, you can improve a scene!"

"What?" Jimmy asked. "Evan, didn't you tell Frank here you were an editor?"

"Never came up, Jimmy," Evan replied defensively. "We had only just met—and that crazy creep Strickler was giving Mr. Capra here a doozy of a time."

Jimmy looked at Capra with raised eyebrows. Capra scowled. "Strickler. No-good hack!"

"Forget about Strickler, Frank," Jimmy cajoled. "It's not good for your blood pressure. So, what job are you gonna find for our boy here?"

Capra seemed to give the matter considerable thought. He snapped his fingers and pointed to Evan. "Assistant editor! I could use one. You think you can cut it, kid?"

"No pun intended?" Evan shot back.

"Fast. I like that." Capra nodded with approval.

Evan's mind whirled; Capra's question had literal merit. In 1946, there was no digital world. Film was still manually cut off an editing track, spliced, and glued together. Evan had studied and even tried the technique after years spent in fascination with the nostalgia of Hollywood-past, both creatively and technically. He did not hesitate to answer.

"I'm made for the job, Mr. Capra," he said, now filled with self-confidence.

"Congratulations, Evan West, assistant editor of *The Greatest Gift*. Not bad for a very good morning!" Jimmy said.

"Thanks, Jimmy." Evan grinned.

Jimmy shook his head. "Nah. Got a feeling about you, kid. Ya got talent. Anyone who can fall over a bunch of cans and have Frank love it, well, he's gotta be working miracles."

Evan laughed.

"Now we knock off in a few hours. You come with me after. I'll show you the guesthouse, okay?"

"Sure thing, Jimmy," Evan replied, then he looked toward the opened door to the stage, and there she was.

Dorothy was now dressed in a dark-blue dress with a sailor collar, and the overhead movie lights made her hair, now flowing loose and free about her shoulders, seem to shimmer. Her features appeared more defined and polished now, more colorful, and Evan realized she was wearing a bit more makeup than when he had last seen her. A golden necklace gracing her neck gleamed as bright as her smile.

Evan's face flushed as she headed their way with a big smile brightening her face.

"Hi, Evan, passed any phony money around here?" Dorothy looked at Evan first, then at Jimmy. "Mr. Stewart, thank you so much for inviting me down to watch the shoot."

"That's not the only reason, Dorothy. I'm glad you got my message. But you're here to work."

"What?" Dorothy asked, clearly confused.

"Go talk to Bob Miller in casting, just down the lane," Jimmy explained slowly.

"I don't understand." Dorothy looked to Evan for help. All he could do was shrug.

"Honey, you're now an extra in our last scene. It's all taken care of. Go see Bob in casting, sign in, and give him your details so you can get paid," Jimmy said. "Don't know the exact date of shooting, but you're in!"

Dorothy's look of pure happiness sent Evan's heart into the stratosphere. She hugged Jimmy, her eyes closed. "Thank you, Mr. Stewart."

Jimmy smiled, patted her gently, and said softly, "Don't thank me, Dorothy. Thank Evan here. It was his idea."

Dorothy pulled back from her embrace with Jimmy and took both of Evan's hands. "Thank you, Evan." She leaned in and gave him the sweetest kiss on the cheek that he'd ever experienced in his short life.

It was a magical moment, interrupted only by the dulcet voice of Donna Reed as she stepped into their private space.

"I'm sorry to interrupt, but...Jimmy, can we talk about this next scene? It's a tough one as you know." Donna looked anxious. She tried to muster a laugh but couldn't.

Jimmy lifted his eyebrows at Evan and leaned in. "It's a big smooching scene. We're all a bit on edge," he explained.

Evan knew the scene he was referring to—one of the best in film history.

"Excuse me," Jimmy said and headed toward Donna. "Okay, Mary, old girl, let's get down to some serious lip-latching!" he said with almost cartoonish flourish, no doubt trying to lighten the mood.

"Jimmy, you're horrible," Donna giggled.

Evan smiled. *Mission accomplished, Jimmy.*

Dorothy looked back at Evan; they were alone at last.

"Evan, thank you for getting me a job on the film. That's

the nicest thing anyone's ever done for me," she said, her face only inches from his. She smelled wonderful; he inhaled the combined scent of her clean hair and just enough perfume to entice. Evan's stomach was fluttering along with his heart; a fireworks show was going off in his head.

"Have you ever heard of déjà vu?" she asked him out of the blue.

"Sure," Evan responded. "That feeling where something has already happened and is happening again. Or...will happen again." He paused, staring intensely at her. "Or..."

"Or...?" she prompted.

"Or...the feeling you've known someone from long before," he said in a whisper.

"It's so strange, Evan. I can swear we've already met," Dorothy murmured, a wistful smile on her face.

"But we have met before. Yesterday. At the diner!" Evan joked.

She sweetly smiled. "I think you know what I mean."

"I do. And in all seriousness...I feel the same way. It's odd... and kinda magical. For me anyway," Evan confessed.

"For me, too, Evan," she said. She looked at the set; the characters George and Mary stood near an old-fashioned telephone on an end table. Jimmy and Donna faced each other, both engrossed in the pages in their hands, no doubt studying their lines, then Jimmy walked away from Donna, seemingly lost in thought.

Evan glanced at Dorothy. "Excuse me for a moment, Dorothy."

"No problem, Evan. Remember, I gotta run to casting for my big moment!"

"Go, go," he prodded. "See you later."

"Promise?" She lifted her eyebrows.

"Count on it." Evan winked, then headed over to see what was eating Jimmy.

Jimmy glanced over at Evan as he approached.

"You look like you have a problem, Jimmy. Something with the script? You want to run lines?" Evan offered.

"Well, shucks, Evan. This scene just makes me nervous. I haven't done a kissing scene in six years. Not since before the war. I think I forgot how to go about it!"

Evan had to all but bite his tongue to keep from laughing. "Nah, you didn't. C'mon, you never forgot how to fly a B-24 on all those missions over Germany, did you?"

"That was war and flying with the Eighth. Much easier than a love scene. In the Army Air Force, you're so trained to do it by the numbers, it only gets rough when nothing goes to plan, which was almost every mission. But doggone it, kissing a girl on camera is much tougher," he mumbled. "You try it if you think it's so easy!"

"No, thanks. I have enough trouble leading up to a kiss with a girl in real life, forget about on camera." Evan laughed.

"Well, that makes two of us. Anyway...I don't mean to blubber and be a crybaby." He smiled wanly. "Just nerves, I guess."

"Jimmy, you gotta believe me. This scene coming up with you and Donna… It's gonna be a tearjerker for years to come," Evan assured.

"Now how could you know a thing like that, Evan? That's crazy." Jimmy cocked his head, seeming to study Evan closely.

"Would you believe I'm a time-traveler from the year 2021 and know every scene from this movie? *It's a Wonderful Life* is gonna be huge for the next hundred years!" Evan grinned.

Jimmy squinted at him, then shook his head. "That's a tall tale, kid, and yeah, you got me. I almost believed you," he said. "And there you go again with calling *The Greatest Gift* by another name. *It's a Wonderful Life…?*"

"You never know. Maybe?" Evan suggested, acting way too bold.

"I like it, actually," Jimmy said thoughtfully. "Has a kinda ring to it."

Evan spotted Coop heading toward him. Capra stepped between them and addressed Coop, "You fix that issue we had on the boom the other day?"

"Yes, sir, Mr. Capra," Coop responded confidently. "We repaired the problem and can assure you we will no longer have that 60-hertz hum."

"Good deal, son," Capra said, then looked at the cast and crew. "Folks, listen up. This is a very emotional scene we're about to shoot. I want absolute silence—and I mean absolute. Not a peep." He glanced to Jimmy and Donna. "George and Mary, you ready?"

"Yep," Jimmy rasped.

"Yes, sir," Donna said softly.

Capra looked at an actor Evan didn't recognize who stood off-camera. "Johnny, you ready on the Sam Wainwright lines?"

"Ready to go, Mr. Capra." Johnny gave a thumbs-up.

"Sound! Rolling!"

"Speed!"

"Scene 62 Alpha, take one, mark!"

"Action!"

Jimmy and Donna leaned in together, cheek to cheek, in one of Evan's favorite scenes of *Wonderful*. She spoke softly into the telephone, "We're listening, Sam."

Johnny, off-camera, called out Sam's lines: "I have a big deal coming up that's gonna make us all rich. George, you remember that night in Martini's bar when you told me you read someplace about making plastics out of soybeans?"

Jimmy nodded slowly, per character, and answered, "Huh? Yeah, yeah...soybeans. Yeah."

The scene continued. Johnny continued with his off-screen lines: "Mary, would you tell that guy I'm giving him a chance of a lifetime? You hear? A chance of a lifetime!"

Mary looked at George. "He says it's a chance of a lifetime."

Evan could see Jimmy gearing up for the explosive climax. He dropped the phone, grabbed Donna by the shoulders, and shook her. Donna pulled tears from deep inside. It was masterful to behold.

"Now you listen to me," Jimmy said fervently. "I don't want any plastics! I don't want any ground floors, and I don't want to get married—ever, to anyone! You understand that? I want to do what I want to do. And you're...and you're..."

Jimmy pulled Donna close to him in a fierce embrace. "Oh, Mary. Mary!"

"George. George… Oh, George!" Donna cried out.

Evan glanced at Dorothy who was watching the scene from nearby. She was in tears. Her eyes found Evan's. They shared a moment.

George kissed Mary with passion. It was perfect!

A moment passed. Evan heard sniffles from people around him and realized a tear was in his eye as well.

Capra called out, "Cut!"

He looked toward the camera team, his eyes glittering with tears. "Print that *now*!"

The script supervisor ran over to Capra, dabbing her eyes. "Mr. Capra, they missed a whole page of dialogue. Jimmy skipped right to the hug and the kiss!"

Capra laughed. "With technique and feeling like that, who needs dialogue?"

The script supervisor smiled and nodded. "I agree. It was beautiful."

"Just mark it as shot. Draw a line through that page if you please." Frank asked.

Dorothy headed over to Evan and took his hand. "That was the most beautiful love scene of all time," she said. Then, clearly swept up in the feeling of it all, she nearly bowled him over with a surprise kiss—and a nice, long kiss at that.

Coop saw this, looked at Evan, and started shaking. Evan, still in Dorothy's embrace, caught Coop's eye and realized the man was trying to keep from laughing.

"Sorry," Dorothy said after breaking off the kiss and taking a step back. "I don't know what came over me."

Evan was staring at her, a bit dumbfounded. And then it hit him, finally.

How could I have been so blind? This is Dorothy, the Dorothy I met in 2021 at the party. This is her young self, per history, now an extra in It's A Wonderful Life*! Wow! This is all so incredible. So...*

The thoughts combined in his mind, surprise and shock and wonder and...something more. "Dorothy," he muttered. "Don't apologize. I hope... I hope that happens more often with us." He smiled softly. "Any more romantic movies shooting on the lot? We can go watch another kissing scene."

Dorothy smiled broadly. "Can we see each other later?" she asked quietly after a beat.

"Sure. If not tonight, maybe tomorrow."

"Okay," she murmured. "See you around. My shift at the diner begins at 11 a.m. I'm off at three." She glanced at Frank, Jimmy, Donna, and Coop, then headed out. Evan wondered if she was embarrassed after being so forward. Maybe not.

Evan, now full of life, made a beeline for Jimmy. "Jimmy, great scene!" he said, then looked at Donna. "Ms. Reed, you were sublime!"

"You think so, Evan?" Donna sounded sweetly sincere.

"I'm still tearing up," Evan said from the most honest place in his heart.

"Oh, thank you, Evan," Donna said, then smiled at Jimmy. "I like your friend's opinions."

"Yeah, well, no accounting for taste," Jimmy quipped. He pulled Evan aside out of earshot and whispered, "Did the kissing thing look real to you, kid?"

"The kiss was perfect, Jimmy," Evan assured.

"Not too fake?"

"Not fake at all."

He nodded. That seemed to settle him. "Okay, see you around." He began to amble off, then looked over his shoulder. "We're leaving at a decent hour today, so be ready for wheels up at six."

CHAPTER 12
HOUSES OF THE HOLY

The day went by quickly. Evan was just happy to watch the extraordinary process of his favorite movie being filmed. He knew every scene by heart, but to see them played out by fine actors who sometimes had trouble with the lines, or other times knew them perfectly, was a joy.

Evan and Coop conferred, and Coop slipped him his address so they could talk privately.

"What time do I come by?" Evan asked him.

Coop looked at Evan like he didn't understand the question. "Come on by anytime. I said I'd be there. I have some exemplary devices to show you, Evan. You will be most impressed," Coop said.

Then Evan remembered that this was a simpler time; you didn't have to fit yourself into someone's "busy" day. If they said to come by, they would be there. People in 2021 seemed to need to constantly distract themselves from the daily minutia of life. Here, they seemed to be just happy to have a life at all, or maybe he was overthinking it.

Evan hung around the set, watching crew members come and go, everyone moving busily about. At six, Jimmy emerged from his dressing room in a pair of slacks, a white shirt, and a casual jacket, his fedora perched on the back of his head.

"Ready? Let's call it a day," he said, and Evan turned and followed, pinching himself that he was actually going to be driving from Hollywood to Beverly Hills with the great Jimmy Stewart.

Evan was impressed when Jimmy headed toward a dusty-blue, 1946 Series 62 Cadillac Coupe. They climbed in (no locked doors—not in this age), and he noted how much bigger this car was than his own Ford. Jimmy cranked the engine, and they headed west on Melrose.

Stewart glanced at Evan. "I'm still not sure about that scene, and I'm not looking for platitudes, but level with me. That look okay to you?"

Evan searched for the right words. "It felt real, Jimmy, I mean…" Evan stopped himself from leaning on his constant refrain of *You're great, Jimmy*. Evan needed to get used to the fact that he was here, now, with Jimmy Stewart and needed to act like it. "George has so much pent-up anger toward how his life has worked out this far, and here he is, listening to Sam Wainwright, his friend who actually turned his own dreams into gold, and he has the woman of his dreams near him. The tears you shed and the emotion you displayed seemed very real. It's like you really did have a lot of pent-up anger and resentment in you." He faced Jimmy, watching him thoughtfully. "Did you draw on that?"

"Anger and resentment? No. That was fear," Jimmy said and left it at that. They drove in silence for a while. Evan knew what he was referring to: the fear he felt before flying a mission over wartime Europe. Fear that came from the deepest, darkest part of Jimmy's soul. He must have struggled with that every hour of every day he was stationed in the UK with the Eighth Air Force.

Jimmy turned the sleek Cadillac onto Roxbury from Wilshire Boulevard. Evan noticed Beverly Hills in 1946 seemed far more rustic and quainter than in his own time, with low-lying buildings, dusty streets, and lots of trees. Evan wondered when the genius city council decided to cut all those down to make way for astronomically expensive restaurants and jewelry shops no one went to.

"Almost there," Jimmy announced.

They pulled into Jimmy's driveway soon enough. Evan noticed the house was in no way ostentatious, overly large, or opulent. It was simple, actually, looking like any average nice house you might see in 2020s' Beverly Hills with a price tag of over five million dollars. Jimmy pulled into the driveway, put on the parking brake, and looked at Evan. "They say any landing you can walk away from is a good one. I'm thirsty. Want some lemonade?"

Evan followed Jimmy into the house. He marveled at the interior. It was casually decorated with modest furniture. A plant adorned the foyer that led into the main living room. One staircase led to the second floor.

"Welcome to my humble abode," Jimmy said, spreading his arms slightly. "Let me get that lemonade."

"Sure," Evan said, realizing how thirsty he was after the sweltering heat from the ride over from Hollywood. It was hot for April; he wondered if "global warming" was already transpiring in 1946, or if, more than likely, it was just a heatwave without the sinister connotation.

A knock came at the front door. Jimmy doubled back from the kitchen and opened it.

"Well, hello, Henry!" Jimmy exclaimed and returned to Evan with a man only an inch shorter than Jimmy. Evan looked to see yet another familiar face, as familiar as Jimmy's… and he was gobsmacked.

"Want you to meet an old friend of mine," Jimmy said, motioning everyone toward the kitchen.

The man leaned in with an outstretched hand. "Hello," he said in a lazy drawl. "Henry Fonda."

Evan did his best not to blubber. "Mr.…Mr. Fonda. Yes…a pleasure, sir" was all he could manage. He looked Henry Fonda up and down…not as tall as he seemed in the movies, nor nearly as taciturn or mercurial. His roles had simply cast him as such and made him famous.

In person, Evan felt Henry Fonda was just a regular guy.

"I'm Evan West. Great to meet you," which was all he was able to say.

"Just Henry, please." He yawned. "I believe we have some airplanes to build tonight if I'm not mistaken?" Henry then looked toward a gleaming statue on a high shelf. "How's that Oscar of mine, James?"

"It's doin' just fine, Henry," Jimmy said and looked at Evan. "He's just sore at me for winning that ole thing back in '40. We were both nominated."

Evan spotted that gleaming gold statuette and stared reverently. Jimmy hoisted it and handed it to him. The title on the plate was *THE PHILADELPHIA STORY*.

"Wow," Evan sighed. "Great movie, Jimmy."

"Yeah, it was okay, but frankly, I think I got robbed!" Henry laughed.

"You were brilliant in *Grapes*," Evan offered and meant

it. He'd seen *The Grapes of Wrath* more times than he could count.

"Oh, Henry. Stop bellyaching. You were terrific in that picture. Heck, I woulda' voted for you!" Jimmy quipped. The men went to the kitchen, and Jimmy poured two lemonades from a bottle he kept in his Frigidaire.

Jimmy and Fonda turned their attention to the 1/48-scale model airplanes Evan noticed were scattered across the dining room table. Evan had seen those around as a kid; they had appealed to the generations before his own.

Jimmy glanced up and noticed Evan's curious look. "Little hobby of mine and Henry's. Model airplanes," Jimmy explained, picking up a small container of Testors glue and carefully gluing the seam of a wing, which he pressed against the flank of a model plane.

Jimmy set it down carefully. "Lost my port wing on this B-24 last week when I dropped the darned thing," he said, then carefully set the repaired model upright between two empty glasses while the glue dried.

Evan glanced at Fonda, who was deeply immersed in the construction of a B-25 Mitchell bomber, and tried to recall what film Fonda had done this year or the year before. It came to him a moment later while at the same time marveling over the fact that he was in Jimmy Stewart's dining room, watching two of the biggest movie stars in film history building model airplanes.

"Henry, I really liked your last film, *My Darling Clementine*," Evan said, trying to sound less like a fawning fan and more like he was part of the exclusive movie club he had now entered.

"Yeah?" Fonda said, looking up. "I thought it was good, but I did a little research on Wyatt Earp. Wasn't exactly fact that they put up on that film screen. The man was a stone-cold killer who happened to be the winner."

"True, and they didn't even cover Earp's love affair with Josephine," Evan agreed. "Or that Morgan Earp was just a kid. Ward Bond wasn't exactly the casting I would have gone with. And Doc Holliday? He was a smallish man, dying of tuberculosis. Victor Mature looked too healthy."

"You know your history, kid," Fonda nodded, sizing Evan up. "Also, the OK Corral was small. Could barely fit a horse or two in there, cramped. They made it seem like a rodeo stadium. And the gunfight itself only lasted about thirty seconds."

"Hollywood hyperbole, making it bigger than it really was!"

"That's a fact," Fonda agreed. "Now, I didn't mind playing Wyatt, but did you know, according to history, he wasn't particular to fighting the Clantons? He didn't mind most fights, but this was one he didn't want."

"Right!" Evan agreed, pointing to Fonda enthusiastically. "It was his brother, Virgil, the marshal, and his kid brother, Morgan, who were worked up to bringing down those guys."

"Exactly," Fonda said, then he resumed work on his B-25. "Ah, well. Good picture, though."

Jimmy looked at his B-24 Liberator model, lifting it carefully; the wing had finally stuck in place. "The wings were always situated too high on this plane. Just like real life, they tended to fall off with too much stress." Fonda stayed focused on his B-25, tapping on the greenhouse nose for the bombardier.

"Look at that, James. Not one glue smear," Henry boasted.

"Evan, let's take a look at your new home," Jimmy said, setting down the model and then standing up and heading out the back kitchen door with Evan.

"Pleased to meet you, Mr. Fonda." Henry nodded in response.

They passed through his modest garden and into a small casita annexed to the main house. Jimmy opened the door. Evan glanced inside and saw that it was comfortably furnished, housing a small sofa, two chairs, a bed, and a little kitchenette in the corner.

"Will this do you, son?" Jimmy asked.

"It'll do just fine," Evan said.

"Then I'll leave you to it. Day off tomorrow. Any plans?"

"Think I'm gonna ask Dorothy out," Evan said slowly.

"Good call, young man," Jimmy said. He nodded to him, then opened the door. "I'm making some sandwiches later if you want to come in and join me. Nothing special, just ham and cheese. There's something I like about simple meals. I've had a hard time with rich food since I got back from the war. Doesn't sit well with me. So long, friend." He closed the door.

Evan was once again alone. This time, he knew when he woke, he would be living at Jimmy Stewart's place. He was okay with the thought he might never go back to the twenty-first-century home he once had. He was on a grand adventure, and he was buckled in and planned on enjoying every minute of it. He went to a big cabinet, 1940s-era Philco radio and turned it on. The Lux Radio Theater was playing before a live audience, and Evan sat back and enjoyed the show. He loved podcasts, and radio shows were no different except they had that "live" thing going for them that was so refreshing.

Evan stepped into the small bathroom and looked around, surprised to see it fully stocked. Apparently, Jimmy kept his guest home ready to be occupied at a moment's notice. Evan opened the medicine cabinet, finding a shaving mug with soap, a heavy "safety" razor (which looked more like a weapon than anything that could be claimed as "safe"), extra Gillette blades, several new toothbrushes still in their box, and a tube of Pepsodent toothpaste. Seeing the unopened tube made Evan slump in relief more than any of the other hygienic products now in arm's reach. He surely had the worst breath imaginable at that point. Uncapping the tube and squeezing out a big dollop of Pepsodent onto a new brush, he went to work, scrubbing away whatever foul bacteria had made a home in his mouth. That task blessedly completed, he slathered shaving soap onto the brush Jimmy had provided and shaved—a bit gingerly—with the military-grade razor, nicking himself twice in the process, but it was worth it. Evan noticed Jimmy had even provided his favorite aftershave in the entire history of the product: Aqua Velva. Evan splashed it on, reveling in the sting. For the first time in what seemed like forever, he felt like a clean, refreshed man. He went back to the Lux Radio Theater and dozed off while listening to an advertisement for the Hudson Motor Car Company.

CHAPTER 13
MEETING MISS RIGHT

A few miles away in Los Angeles, Dorothy Paige woke to a new day. She was living with her parents, had been since she lost her husband in the war. She looked forward to her day off from the movie *The Greatest Gift*, but she still had a later shift at the diner and afterwards, had to head to Glendale College. Her first class, business and management, started at 9 a.m. She was already in her second year, and the subject material came easily to her. She loved the experience of learning; it was more gratifying than almost anything she had ever done in her life. Her father had dabbled in the stock market with penny stocks. His advice had been well-meaning but uniformly incorrect. For example: Coca-Cola had to be a fad and would be soon out of existence. And Dorothy had no doubt that anyone who was cultivating cow manure as a future source of skin cleansing had to be off their rocker. Dorothy had only taken his advice once and wound up losing the entire $50 she'd invested in a penny stock for a company that claimed it would replace oil with coal for use in automobiles. It only took one bath in the NYSE to realize money was best invested wisely, and she learned to listen to her own voice rather than anyone else's. She made a vow to nod and smile when her father gave advice over the dinner table, but not take him up on it.

Dorothy went to the bathroom, washed her face, and smiled at herself in the mirror. She could not get Evan out of her mind. There was something about him that was oddly curious and compelling at the same time. He didn't seem like other guys she'd met before; he was worldly, yet somehow innocent, a combination she had never encountered in a man. He was mannered and well-spoken, yet didn't seem to realize how fortunate he was to be where he was in his life. She'd love to know where he came from, what his family was like, if he had served in the war… Most young men his age had, but he didn't have the "stare" most of the soldiers and sailors came back with, a result of all the horrible things they had to see and do in the Pacific or Europe.

She had to admit, she liked him. The more she thought about him, the more that feeling grew…as did her guilt. Robert, her husband, who had been killed in France almost two years ago now, had been her one true love. Even thinking about someone else, especially someone as strange and unique as Evan West, seemed wrong and exciting at the same time. Robert was a good man, dutiful but boyish. Dorothy never could imagine someone as sweet-natured as her husband training to kill for the US Army, and yet he had and paid the ultimate price for his service. He always assumed he would make it home in his letters to her; he never seemed at all worried that he'd not be back by Christmas 1944.

Robert didn't live to see that December.

He'd been laid to rest in a cemetery in Normandy along with so many other soldiers who would never make it home.

Dorothy swore to herself someday she'd go to visit him, but not anytime soon.

The wound was still too raw. He had given her the gift of her beautiful son, Richie, who was more than likely still asleep in the next room. Richie never knew his father, and Dorothy couldn't bring herself to talk about him—even that was too painful. She wanted Richie to know about him, but how could a little boy even begin to contemplate a father he never knew…would never see?

Now, Evan West had come along, and for the first time since she'd received that telegram in June 1944, she felt alive. Different…lighter, not weighed down as much by that anchor of grief. She marveled at how Evan had gotten her a part in a movie, just like that, and expected nothing in return. She had kissed him—pretty impulsively, she admitted, and had felt a thrill, but did he feel the same way she did? She didn't know. Would Robert mind?

How could he? He's gone.

Dorothy looked away from her reflection and sighed. She knew he'd wish her well, wherever he was. She looked around her room, seeing the same four walls that had surrounded her as a toddler, a child, and then a teen and beyond. It was much the same as it had ever been. Lots of little-girl items were still in evidence; a large doll with rosy cheeks regarded her from the floor. Framed prints of flowers and lambs dominated the walls, along with a cross on a necklace over her vanity. Everything in Dorothy's room screamed, *HOME. SAFE. COMFORT.*

She crept down the narrow hall and headed into Richie's room, a cozy, brightly lit space with shelves lined with fire trucks, cowboy toys, and blue drapes to match his bedding.

Richie was fast asleep in his bed, which was shaped like a Spanish galleon, his head nestled on a pillowcase dotted with airplane renderings. She had to wake him, feed him breakfast, and get to class. Dorothy put a hand on her son's open door as if to steady herself, feeling a wave of emotion. Every time she saw Richie's serenely sleeping face, she felt certain she was in the presence of the Almighty. There was something so precious about a sleeping five-year-old. It was almost too much to take in. Dorothy was so grateful for Richie. All of the challenges…all that extra hardship that came with raising a child was nothing compared to the unique, unconditional love she felt toward that little being sweetly asleep under the blanket…that being that was a part of her forever.

In Beverly Hills, Evan woke up feeling like a new man. Today was an off-day for the shoot, so he decided to take it easy. His first order of business was to pay Coop a visit and go over their plan, but then he wondered: What was their plan, exactly? Did Coop have a way home? The more Evan thought about it, the less he liked the idea. And did Coop really want to go back to 1899? Seemed like a bad time to Evan, especially for Black people. But considering his mentor and friend was Nikola Tesla, perhaps returning to his time would be worth it for Coop.

Evan dressed and reached in his pocket to feel his precious three dimes and the remains of the rose petals Gwen from 2021 gave him. Though they'd broken up only a few days before, there was now seventy-five years between them, and he was glad for it. What he had been missing in his relationship with Gwen he had found in spades with Dorothy. Sweet, gracious, charming Dorothy. He would keep the petals to remind him that the love he'd longed for was here, in 1946.

Evan was unsure if he should just walk into Jimmy's house or knock. Walking into a Hollywood star's residence still felt a bit presumptuous to him, even though Jimmy had done much to make him feel at home. He got to the kitchen door and knocked for a second but heard nothing. He walked inside, and the kitchen was quiet except for the hum of the Frigidaire. Jimmy must still be asleep, or maybe he was out playing golf at the Wilshire Country Club with Henry Fonda. Evan noticed an envelope on the kitchen counter addressed to him. He opened it and pulled out the note inside, which read:

Good morning, Evan West! Good having you here. Eggs and orange juice in the Frigidaire, help yourself to anything you need. I'll be away until later tonight. Here's $20 to get you through the day. A man can't survive long in Los Angeles without a little jack.
—Jimmy

Evan almost teared up at Jimmy's generosity. He helped himself to a glass of orange juice, then cleaned the glass thoroughly. He pocketed the $20 and headed out.

He walked to Wilshire, hailed a cab, and told the driver to take him to 4356 Clarissa Avenue in Los Feliz. The driver wordlessly drove him through Beverly Hills to Santa Monica Boulevard, then north on Highland all the way up to Franklin. Evan suddenly remembered that he still had to pay Sal back. He made a mental note, then went back to enjoying the drive to Los Feliz and the colorful show outside the cab window comprised of big metal cars, Spanish-themed buildings, and an endless stream of palm trees. Not once in his life had he just sat back and enjoyed anything; he was always in such a hurry to get to the next stage of life. But here…now…he felt he could stop, if just for a second, to enjoy life and take in everything without the anxiety that came with "making it."

Actually, just being in 1946 made Evan feel like he'd made it. He noticed as they drove along that there were no homeless people wrapped in blankets, no graffiti on the walls, no beggars on the street corners looking for handouts. Whatever went wrong between 1946 and 2021 had been profound, and it wasn't lost on him that the United States, in his time, had become an empire in sharp decline.

He was daydreaming when the taxi stopped at 4356 Clarissa, a classic LA-style bungalow in a quiet neighborhood. Evan spotted a 1938 Dodge parked out front—presumably Coop's wheels. Evan paid the man, then headed up the sidewalk to Coop's house. He knocked on the door, and Coop answered wearing dress slacks, a dress shirt, and a vest. Coop graced Evan with a wide grin.

"What took you so long?" Coop laughed. "Betcha my house is nicer than Jimmy Stewart's… Then again, perhaps not."

Evan regarded Coop's formal wear, recalling that he was from the nineteenth century, an era in which men dressed far more formally than their twentieth-century counterparts, even on their day off.

Old habits are hard to break, no matter what time period you're in, Evan mused.

"Please come inside. It's about time you see my laboratory." Coop lifted his eyebrows and ushered Evan in.

Evan's jaw dropped. "Laboratory" was an understatement. Coop's home was a replica of Dr. Frankenstein's workspace, complete with enormous machines strung together with heavy wiring from wall to wall. Not so much a laboratory as it was a nuclear power plant.

Coop had taken out the ceiling, and wires fell from what used to be an attic; it was pure "steampunk"—late-nine-teenth-century knowledge using 1946 electronic trappings. Evan was astonished by the house, which was a lot more 1931 *Frankenstein* than 1946 living space. And that movie's action had taken place in a tower on a hill somewhere; Coop had apparently managed to replicate the same effect in a bungalow—a marvel in itself.

"What does the landlord think?" Evan finally asked.

"He doesn't mind since the landlord is me," Coop answered. "The electricity bill is somewhat expensive, but I can manage. There's not much point in saving money if you're not in your own time and don't plan on living out the rest of your life forty-seven years in the future."

Evan was still taking everything in, all those machines strung together, with ladders and catwalks, antennae and oscillators.

"Where'd you find all this stuff?" Evan murmured.

"It's astonishing how much technology you can find from radio shops and the newer military surplus shops springing up all over town. You can buy aircraft radio, radar sets, naval sonar and its British equivalent, ASDIC, field generators, frequency boosters… You name it, it's available."

Evan walked toward the equipment, knowing better than to touch it. He'd hate to get electrocuted, and this stuff looked like it could fry a man alive.

"So…what are your plans with all this stuff?" Evan asked.

Coop seemed surprised by the question. "The plan is to return to the time we belong," he answered as if stating the obvious. "I'm zeroing in on how we can get back. I have been laboring on this the last two years. It's my only purpose." He walked slowly among his machines, clearly proud of what he'd constructed.

"You weren't kidding when you said your place was cramped," Evan observed.

Coop nodded, then pulled down a massive knife switch. The room began to hum, slowly at first and then with fury. Evan could feel the entire room fill with electricity, buzzing like a thousand angry hornets.

"You might feel a little weird now, but you'll get used to it." Coop threw another switch; this one threw off sparks when it came to life. A bright, yellow "spinner" on top of the machines began to rotate and whirl at an impossibly high speed. Evan couldn't help but be amused at the Jacob's Ladder machine near Coop throwing up sparks, one after the other.

"What does that one do?"

Coop seemed annoyed. "If I had to explain what all of these did, we'd be here all day, solving nothing. Let's just say they generate power on an immense scale."

"Enough to revive a corpse stitched together?" Evan asked, not able to resist.

Coop looked puzzled, clearly not getting the reference. He twisted a knob on one machine, and a "sphere" of golden electricity, not at all unlike the one Evan had seen on Lakeridge and Cahuenga, formed above Coop, who reached into the electronic protoplasm, fashioned an electric ball, and then threw it Evan's way.

Evan panicked and ducked, but the ball of electric proto-plasm wisped into nothing before it reached him. Evan slowly straightened up, then began laughing hard. He motioned for Coop to make another one. Coop obliged with a grin, making the next one bigger. It splashed over Evan, who didn't duck this time. It washed over him, and his hair stood on end.

Evan blinked, feeling hot all over, his body tingling almost pleasantly. Almost.

Coop laughed. "Nikola taught me that trick!" he exulted. "Scared you. You have to be forthcoming!"

Evan nodded. "Ever thought about using that as a self-defense weapon?"

Coop's brow furrowed. "Why would I do that? It wouldn't be portable, but perhaps that's something I could work on. The crime in this area is lacking, but it is something to con-sider. Now, however, our task is to get us back to our time. Again, how fast was your automobile going?"

Evan took a seat (in a very small chair) and told Coop the entire story from beginning to end. The chase, blowing stoplights, the heavy rain, the car reaching speeds it never had before, hitting 80, hydroplaning, the skid into the electric light pole. Coop took notes throughout Evan's explanation, face furrowed with concentration.

"Did lightning strike nearby when you hit the pole?" Coop asked. Evan nodded. "Acknowledged," Coop murmured. "More current than I could ever generate with these. The governing dynamics of a current that intense could, in fact, open a hole in the Earth's magnetic field but only in certain places. The field itself is not uniform. There are areas where it is more… What's the best way to describe it? More porous.

I believe the area at Lakeridge and Cahuenga is one such area, but I don't have the proper instrumentation to affirm my theory."

Evan thought about it. Everything Coop said made sense. "Let me ask you this: The porous magnetic field… Is this something that is a constant, or does it come in waves?"

Coop nodded to himself, thinking. "The magnetic field is alive, sometimes stronger, at other times weaker in any given point on the globe. If it does undulate with waves, they are difficult to predict. Nikola thought the magnetic field's rippling correlated with sunspots and solar flares, much like the aurora borealis. Again, this is just a theory, but I feel Nikola was onto something. Should a large thunderstorm erupt, we can't very well hurl your car with us in it into that very same light post at 80 miles per hour trying to prove a point unless we have a grasp on how the magnetic field operates. Insufficient facts always invite danger."

Evan smiled—another Spock quote. Coop was a human version of Spock and didn't even know it, which was fine with him. Spock in those classic *Star Trek* episodes always thought his way out of danger; the guy was loyal and unflinching. That was exactly the kind of partner Evan needed on this strange adventure, and he silently thanked God for it.

Coop went to his table and picked up a device Evan thought looked like an old-time Bakelite alarm clock, round and steel-constructed. "I want you to carry this at all times," Coop instructed.

Evan took it, examining the device closely. "This a radio?"

Coop shook his head. "No. Well, in theory, it is. It generates a radio signal. It's something I recently came up with. I never needed it until now. I need to know where you are at all times."

In a normal situation, Evan would have been offended by such a request. But now, yes, he could use all the monitoring he could get.

"Thank you, Coop," he said, then cocked an eyebrow. "Look, we barely know each other. Why do you trust me at all? I could make off with this or rob you. Who knows what I'm capable of?"

Coop mulled that over. "Yes, I do have some reservations about you. To me, you are a man from a very distant future whom I know very little about. However, we are two strangers in a time in which we do not belong. It's akin to being on a ship or train where everyone speaks a different language. I will find that man or woman who speaks my language. It's simple human bonding, nothing more. We also have a similar goal, do we not?"

Evan could buy that; he doubted Coop was anything more than he appeared to be or said he was. And everything he said rang true: They were indeed the only ones from another time in a world of strangers.

They discussed more theories, and then Evan asked Coop to drive him by the Sinclair on Franklin and Highland since he still owed Sal money. Coop offered to pay, but Evan declined. He still had $18 from Jimmy's $20 and knew how easily money could spoil a friendship. Evan and Coop climbed in Coop's '38 Dodge and drove to the Sinclair. Sal spotted Evan and looked pleased. He told Evan that if he needed anything else, he'd be there for him. Sal also told him to go check on the repair of his car in case Big Mike wanted some money upfront.

They headed to Big Mike's. Evan looked over the lot filled with cars in various stages of repair. He spotted his Ford, which Mike clearly had not gotten to yet. He marveled at how the car seemed more "alive" now than ever. He wondered if machines could somehow "revive" themselves if transported back into the time in which they belonged. *An interesting theory*, Evan decided. He was new to time travel, so he had to take such concepts one step at a time.

He spoke briefly to Big Mike, who promised to get to Evan's car done soon before rumbling off with a wrench toward another broken-down vehicle.

Coop and Evan chatted on the lot, forming a plan for the day. Coop agreed to drive Evan to Encino, after which he would return home and get back to work.

"How did you meet Nikola Tesla?" Evan asked after they were on their way.

Coop smiled as he drove. "Long story for another time, but don't worry. I'll let you know, the best thing to happen to me in my short life was being hired by the world's most brilliant man. I'm a Horatio Alger story, Evan. My parents were former slaves, never educated, and I entered the halls of glory with a certifiable genius on a level most people could never understand."

They pulled up to the Rail Head Diner and Evan could see Strickler's Bentley, now repaired, parked awkwardly filling two spots. Evan's heart sank. *Oh, no, not this guy again.* He supposed he could lay low, but that wasn't Evan's style. He was going to go in there, order a burger, make eyes with Dorothy, and then maybe he'd try to make peace with Strickler. Not an alliance, surely, but a non-aggression pact might be possible. Maybe.

Coop clapped him on the back. "I'll see you later, Evan. Tomorrow on the set, or tonight? Could we have dinner? Maybe I could tell you my life story." Coop laughed.

"Let's shoot for that tomorrow. Tonight, I'm hoping to hear Dorothy's life story, if she'll share it with me." Evan got out of the Dodge and shut the door.

Coop nodded, looking suddenly more serious. "Don't get too close to anyone in this time, Evan. I'm speaking from a place of caring. Saying goodbye is always much harder to those who've captured your heart." Coop gave Evan a small salute, put his Dodge in gear, and headed off.

Evan entered the diner and was relieved to see Strickler in a far booth, completely engrossed in a conversation with a man he had not seen before. He glanced at Dorothy, who looked at Evan with pure delight. He waved, she waved, and then Evan moved a bit closer to Strickler—though not enough that his presence was conspicuous—and overheard a bit of the conversation between Strickler and the stranger. Evan inched still closer so he could hear better and quickly wished he hadn't.

"I need your assurances, Arthur, that the scenes we asked for will end up in the final cut, contract or no contract." The other man leaned into Strickler, a huge stogie cigar in his chubby, soft hand. The man had male-pattern baldness, wore wire-framed glasses, was overweight, and seemed to be having troubling breathing. He looked like the quintessential studio stooge for the Big Boys upstairs.

"Capra's a genius, Bob." Strickler spoke as smoothly as he had to Jimmy Stewart. *He knows where his bread is buttered,* Evan thought with mild disgust. "But he's annoying as a result thereof," Strickler continued. I assure you, though, he will use those scenes…"

"You can do that?" Bob sounded surprised.

"I had copies of the rushes made from day one." Evan could see Strickler in profile, and caught sight of that smile of his, reminding Evan of the proverbial snake in the garden.

"It's a done deal."

Evan was incensed. *This weasel Bob is behind the corrupted version of* It's A Wonderful Life *that eventually made it into Connor's greedy, greasy hands.* He knew he had to step in. Evan hoped to appeal to Strickler's sense of decency, if he had one. He headed toward the booth, then felt a tap on his shoulder.

"Going someplace, sir?" Dorothy flirted charmingly.

"Just gotta have a word with these fellas," he said quickly, indicating Strickler and Bob.

"Now why would you want to go and do something like that? You and that Mr. Strickler had some pretty strong words the other day." Dorothy looked genuinely concerned. "I'm ready to go."

"So am I." Evan smiled and squeezed her hand. "Give me a moment."

She gave him a cautioning look, but Evan had to do what he had to do. He approached Strickler, convinced he had to say something important.

It was a mistake.

"Mr. Strickler…," Evan began.

Strickler glanced at him, his pleasant, honey-filled expression deteriorating. He shot a venomous eye at Evan. "What are *you* doing here?"

"Uh, well I'm here to… Never mind." Evan collected himself. "Mr. Capra hired me on as one of his editors. Mr. Strickler, it would be a mistake to use any of those scenes you made Mr. Capra shoot."

Strickler stood quickly like an Old West gunslinger, and Evan was suddenly aware that he was John Wayne-tall—easily six foot four. He leaned into Evan and poked a finger into his chest like a dagger.

"Are you following me?" Strickler hissed.

"No," Evan stammered. "I just know what you're planning. Your voice carries in this place."

Strickler looked around and spotted Dorothy, who stared at him nervously. Then he glanced at the other patrons, who all seemed disinterested in them. Strickler returned his predacious look to Evan.

Evan backed away; there was no point in pushing this issue with an incredibly tall man who seemed very fit for his age. Diplomacy would not work with Strickler. He was too cunning and cruel. Evan held his hands up in the universal conciliatory way of one man telling another *I don't want a fight*. Strickler, smelling blood and weakness, pounced.

The other patrons went dead quiet; they could "feel" the energy rippling off the larger man.

"This is none of your business." Strickler's spit hit Evan partially in the eye. "And if you mention anything you've heard here, I'll do something to you you'll never forget."

Something snapped in Evan. He'd had enough of Connor Alcott and Arthur J. Strickler and all the other bullies of the world who were accustomed to controlling situations with their anger and malice. Evan found a burst of energy and shoved Strickler away. Strickler, like most bullies, was surprised, and for a second, afraid.

Evan could feel someone behind him; he quickly turned and saw Bob's alarmed, fleshy face. "Problem, Arthur?"

Strickler snatched Evan's hand away, turned to Bob quickly, and offered a greasy smile. "Not at all, Bob. Just dealing with a small problem. Back with you in a minute."

Strickler looked at Evan, sizing him up. Then abruptly, as if reaching an unsavory decision, he pushed past Evan and sat back down at his booth without a word.

Dorothy waited near the door for Evan, her eyes wide with fear. Evan felt a swell of new confidence now that he had stood up to Strickler, but he was uneasy about it as well.

"I guess you showed him, huh?" Dorothy said in a low voice. "Ready?"

Evan loved it, smitten by her reaction to his dustup with Strickler. It didn't seem to affect her at all, but maybe she was a good actor.

Evan touched her hand. "So, where are we off to? I'd love to take you to dinner. Anyplace you like."

"Would you mind coming over and meeting my mom and dad at their place?" Dorothy squeezed Evan's hand, eyes bright.

He smiled. "Not at all. I'd love to."

"We'll take my car," she offered.

"Outstanding."

Dorothy walked to her car, a 1940 Chevy Master Deluxe Coupe that had obviously been driven hard. He noted the big visor over the top of the windshield—one of his favorite embellishments, destined to only ever adorn American cars from the 1940s.

He climbed in, then hastily checked the right-side rearview—he could see Strickler leaving the restaurant and heading to his Bentley, where Evan spotted Jack, Strickler's goon, waiting for him. Evan's heart sank when he noticed Strickler pointing his way. Evan slumped down in his seat, hoping they couldn't see him.

"Your car—1940 Chevy. Nice set of wheels," Evan stammered to Dorothy. "What I mean to say is that I like your car."

"Thank you." Dorothy beamed. "I got it used, but I take good care of it, and it returns the favor. Here we go!"

She cranked the engine, smiled at him once more, and pulled out onto Burbank Boulevard, toward the North San Fernando Valley. Evan noticed far fewer houses along this street in 1946 than were present in his native era. What Evan realized would eventually become Roscoe Boulevard was still a dirt road, cobbled together with a combination of brick and primitive asphalt. Dorothy pulled into one of several small, tract home complexes—clean and neat but not pretentious—and stopped in front of a charming home surrounded by a reticular picket fence.

Evan marveled at the smell of orange groves and, of course, the ubiquitous exhaust smoke. He was witnessing the beginnings of the American dream here, a dream that was fading rapidly in 2021.

Dorothy parked and looked at Evan. "Welcome to Chez Dorothy!" She was so sincere and sweet, it made Evan's heart hurt. *Why don't they make people like this in the twenty-first century?* he lamented. *Eh, why bother asking?"*

They walked together through the front gate, and Evan noticed that Dorothy had her hand in his as if she'd already taken him as her boyfriend. He was mystified yet exhilarated. There was something about this girl that got his stomach in knots and his heart beating like a marching bass drum.

"I'm glad you're here." Dorothy turned to Evan and gave him a light kiss on the lips. She smiled. "Ready to meet the folks?"

"Hold on a second," Evan said because he had to tell her the rules. He would not, could not, break this woman's heart. "Look, I'm not sure I'm ready for a real relationship because I don't want to hurt you."

Dorothy took Evan's hand. "How about if we see where this goes? I'm pretty tough. Let's not lay down the rules now. Let's just try to have some fun." Her smile was so infectious, Evan was seduced. "I hope you don't mind me being so forward, but that's just how I am and who I am. Lotsa guys don't like it or take me the wrong way. You're not one of those fellas, are you?"

Evan shook his head and smiled. "Just let me take the lead now and again," he replied. Dorothy smiled and stepped onto the front porch.

They entered the house, and Evan's eyes adjusted to the darker light. A middle-aged woman walked into the foyer from the kitchen and looked at Evan, giving him the once-over from head to toe. Twice.

"Well, hello there, stranger," she said to Dorothy. The older woman had an honest, open face and held a freshly baked peach pie in both hands. It smelled like heaven.

"Hi," Evan said. "Evan West."

"I'm Dorothy's mom, Ellen. But you can call me Mrs. Paige."

"Nice to meet you, Mrs. Paige." His eyes slid down to the aromatic concoction in her hands. "That looks like some fine pie you have there."

"Peach. My favorite," Ellen Paige remarked, smiling.

"Mine, too."

"Evan just came into town a few days ago, Mom. He's working on the film with Mr. Capra," Dorothy explained. "He's a movie editor."

"How lovely," Ellen said, approval in her tone.

"Anyone care to say hello to Dorothy's dad? Or am I just more wallpaper around here?" Mr. Paige appeared behind his wife. The mid-sized man wore reading glasses, farmer overalls, and a Colonel Sanders-style western tie.

"Evan, this is my very sensitive and easily offended dad." Dorothy blushed and waved at him.

"Donald Paige, son," the older gentleman said. "Doggone good to meet you."

"Likewise, sir," Evan said and shook his hand.

"Where do you hail from, son?"

"I… Here and there, and may I say, you both have raised a wonderful daughter here in Dorothy."

"Good family makes for good kids," Mr. Paige quipped and chuckled. At that, a little boy rampaged into the room wearing a Moe Howard bowl haircut of dark hair. He finished tearing through the space and stopped abruptly before Evan, staring at him with big, round eyes.

"Howdy, pardner!" the boy said and waved at him.

Evan waved back. "Hi, yourself."

"Hi, Mommy." Richie ran to Dorothy, leaped into her arms, and hugged her.

Dorothy smiled down at him. "How's my big boy today?"

Evan stared. *Dorothy has a child? How?* She was so young and, well, she seemed single.

"Fine," the boy shouted, then squeezed out from her embrace, dropped to the floor, and called out, "Hey, Rancher! Come on, boy!"

A moment later, a shaggy mutt of a dog padded out, panting. Evan was struck by the humanity of Rancher's appearance; the light eyes poking out from the fur were filled with expression. The way his mouth opened wide—he even looked like he was smiling.

"This is Rancher," Richie announced. "And I'm Richie. Who are you?"

"I'm Evan," he replied and scratched one of Rancher's ears as the mutt approached him to give him a curious sniff.

"Richie is my son, Evan." Dorothy looked at Evan a little tensely.

"Richie, you look a lot like your mom," Evan commented, then knelt down. "And Rancher here… Buddy, I feel like I've known you all my life. Your breath smells about as bad as…"

"He eats anything, Evan. Including cat poop and grass," Richie explained.

"All right, enough canine culinary talk," Mrs. Paige commanded, setting the pie on the kitchen table. "I'm about to cut this pie, and I'd like to keep my appetite, if no one minds too much."

Richie turned to Evan, eyeing him warily. "Maybe I like you. Maybe I don't, mister, but why are you here?" he asked, furrowing his brow.

"Your mom invited me," Evan said, his hands on his hips.

"Well, I don't know why," Richie said. Everyone laughed at his boyish honesty.

The pie was excellent, the sugar and crust beyond anything Evan had eaten in 2021; he would never get used to how good the flavor of food was in 1946 after growing up on a staple diet of sawdust.

Richie raced to the table, where Mr. Paige was collecting plates and glasses.

"Hey, Mom." Richie looked to Dorothy. "Can I show Evan here what Uncle Moe gave me?

Dorothy patted him on the back. "Of course, honey." Richie ran off, and Dorothy turned to Evan. "Richie's dad was killed in the war just after he was born. Afterward, we moved back here with Mom and Dad. It makes things easier for me since I go to school and work, as you know," Dorothy explained.

"What's your favorite subject?" Evan asked, knowing the answer based on the investment-savvy Dorothy he had met in 2021.

"Business administration at the college. I even dabble in the stock market, just like Dad."

Evan smiled. "You don't say?"

"Yep. I'm actually pretty good at following hunches too. Better than my dad," she whispered as Mr. Paige turned around and flashed a false frown.

"I heard that," he said, then snickered. "And my daughter here is just plumb lucky, that's all. She don't know squat about stocks," he grumbled to himself as he headed to the kitchen.

"He put some stock into pigs' knuckles a month ago. I put it into Coca-Cola. He lost all his money when the pigs got gangrene and lost their feet," she giggled.

Evan laughed. "I think the Coca-Cola investment is a sound one, Dorothy."

She looked to Evan, her eyes twinkling. He was struck by her inner beauty, which seemed so infectious.

"Evan, I know this is really none of my business, but..." She hesitated.

"Go on," he urged.

"I was just wondering if, you know, you... Well, if you have a..."

"A girl?"

"Yes. A girl."

Evan sighed. "Yeah, I did. For a while. But I blew it. She was great, but—"

"But what?"

"She and I just weren't a match, didn't like the same things."

Dorothy shrugged and smiled. "Why would you want to be with that person then?"

Evan wondered about that too. Why had he been so "into" someone he had absolutely zero in common with?

Evan's attention was seized by Richie flying into the room, making whirring airplane noises. He shoved a model airplane into Evan's hand.

Evan examined it in detail. "Wow. A P-80 Shooting Star."

"Pretty spiffy, huh?" Richie beamed.

"I'll say."

Dorothy nudged Evan and smiled. "You know your airplanes. My brother works at Lockheed, and this is one of their prototypes. They call it a jet. Imagine, a plane without propellers. What'll they come up with next?"

Evan nodded enthusiastically, forgetting himself for a

moment. "Yes, the P-80 is really the precursor to the F-86 Sabre, and those were Korean War heroes," he said.

Dorothy furrowed her brow. "Never heard of a Korean war…"

Evan flushed. How could he recover from that? He had to keep playing his part; no one would ever believe he was a time traveler, and the last thing he needed was to be considered crazy.

"Neither have I," Evan said. "I meant…you know, Korea, Japan, Germany, all the same. You hang on to that, buddy," he suggested to Richie, handing the plane back to the little boy. "That's gonna be a collector's item one day."

"You're a visionary, that's what I think," Dorothy said without any trace of sarcasm or skepticism.

"Nah, Dorothy. I'm just…traveling through time. Metaphorically speaking, that is." Evan inwardly cringed. Had he said too much?

Dorothy seemed to like Evan's answer since she leaned over and kissed him quickly. Richie didn't miss this at all.

"You guys gonna get married now? 'Cause you better ask me first."

Dorothy blushed, then looked to Evan. "Well. We'll just have to see about that, won't we?" The answer seemed to satisfy Richie, and he fired away, varooming the airplane around the room.

Dorothy and Evan ended up talking for a few hours about anything and everything; she told Evan about her husband, the day she got the telegram from the War Department, her worries about raising Richie, about her enthusiasm for business, numbers, and the American economy. She related how she lived through the Great Depression and how the experience changed her and everything else she knew.

Evan was enthralled. Dorothy didn't talk like the women he knew from his own time; she didn't talk about herself so much as make observations about the world she saw around her. She was intensely curious about everything; history, economics, human emotions and behavior. Evan added what he could when he could with his twenty-first-century wisdom, but he realized Dorothy was far more insightful than most people. He had to be cautious.

Mrs. Paige asked Evan if he would stay for dinner: a pot roast with some baby carrots and squash. He couldn't say no. The food was amazing. Afterward, they loaded up on ice cream, each having three servings and coffee. Evan was stuffed—he couldn't remember eating so much in his life. After they finished, Dorothy offered to drive him back to Jimmy's house.

They rode in silence on the way home; Evan was exhausted from the day's events and the huge meal. Dorothy pulled up to Jimmy's house after Evan gave her directions. She never asked how he knew Los Angeles so well because maybe, in some way, she felt he belonged here as much as she did.

"Evan, thank you for spending the day with me," she said, putting the car in park. Her eyes slid to his. "I know it's not like going out and kicking up your heels. You being a single, eligible bachelor, and all. I'm sure it was pretty boring compared to the nightlife you're used to."

Evan smiled and put his hand on the wheel. "It was a perfect night, Dorothy. You must believe me, I'm not exactly Mr. Nightlife." He leaned in and kissed her delicately yet firmly on the lips. He drew back, eyes locked on hers. "I'll see you tomorrow on set?"

"I'll be there. My big scene is tomorrow, I think." She laughed.

Evan got out. She waved, started her car, made a quick U-turn, and headed back to her parents' house. He looked up to the stars and sighed with contentment.

Two shadows abruptly appeared before him. Evan recognized Strickler's lackey, Jack. The man was on Evan before he could react. Evan noticed Jack's arm raised high. Something that looked like a blackjack was clutched in his hand. The weapon came rushing down toward Evan's head.

Evan slipped into darkness. It didn't even hurt when he hit the sidewalk.

CHAPTER 14

SHANGHAIED

Evan awoke an hour later and swiftly realized he was in the trunk of a car. He smelled the exhaust and the stench of grease, felt the cold dread of fear crawl up his spine, then passed out again.

The next time Evan woke up, he stayed that way. He realized after a moment that he was on his back, lying on a hard floor. He turned his head from side to side slowly. As his vision un-fuzzed, he looked around, thinking he must be in a warehouse somewhere. Huge crates surrounded him, and he could make out chains dangling from the ceiling. Outside could be heard the oddly calming lapping of water. The floor gently bobbed.

Not a warehouse. A ship…I'm probably in the cargo hold. In the distance, Evan heard a ship's horn blow. He couldn't feel the vibration of the ship's engines running, so he knew they must still be in port. He could hear men's voices above him, some speaking in another language he thought might be Chinese.

Evan sat up slowly and glanced at his watch. It was 2 a.m.—he'd been out for at least four hours. He tried to shake the cobwebs out of his brain, adjusting his eyes to the dim light. His hands were bound with heavy rope. Evan struggled to his feet and immediately began walking—which was harder than anticipated. His brain was a bit short-circuited, the blow to his head making even simple actions nearly impossible. He stumbled around, searching for something sharp and jagged… anything to get his hands free. He knew Arthur Strickler was behind his abduction, which made his situation even more chilling.

He lurched over to what appeared to be a jagged beam, broken off out of the side of the bulkhead. Evan positioned himself with some difficulty and began the tedious process of sawing through the ropes. He heard more voices above; men were tromping across the deck directly above him.

New sounds, far too nearby, made Evan wince. A heavy click…and then the sound of the hatch to the cargo hold opening.

Company was coming. Evan deduced the same goons who had dumped him here were about to pay a visit. He glanced down at the ropes in the half-light; the beam had cut midway through the hemp. He knew if he were caught like this, they'd just tie him up again, and maybe even bind his ankles and legs this time. He thought it best to pretend to be unconscious, so he went back to the crates where he had awakened and slumped down.

Evan prayed this would work.

Footsteps clambered down the ladder from above. Evan nearly closed his eyes, keeping them open a tiny bit, hoping to get a good look at his captors. From his slumped position, he spotted two big sets of legs coming toward him, belonging no doubt to two very large men. He did not recognize their muttering voices, but considering Arthur Strickler's power and reach, the man more than likely had an army of mercenaries in his employ to do his bidding.

They loomed over him; one kicked Evan in the leg with a hard sailor's shoe. Evan did his best not to react or cry out, but the pain was sharp, biting.

"If this kid only knew where he's gonna end up," one of the men laughed.

"You said, it, Joe. You couldn't catch me dead in a place like Madagascar," the other guy mumbled. "Musta done something pretty big to piss off the big man."

"Eh, Big Man has always got it out for someone. Amazing how many of his enemies he has on any given day. Then they just disappear."

"We could kill the kid now, dump him overboard, and not be bothered taking care of him for the next month," the bigger of the two men suggested.

"Nah, too risky. We'll do what we got paid to do. Dump this boy in the jungle and let the natives eat him, or whatever they do over there. We throw him over now, and they'll fish out the body. The law will put two and two together, link him to Strickler, and then he'll roll on us. I know how it works."

"Aye, aye. Let's tell the chief to light the boilers and inform the captain we're ready to shove off."

The two men headed back up the ladder, and the hatch soon shut with a *clang* that made Evan's bones shudder. He blinked slowly and rose to a sitting position, back against the wall, mind going to all the bad places, the dark passages that most people avoid at any cost. He felt hopeless; the idea of spending weeks on board this awful steamer, heading to such a faraway place, was torturous. He doubted the inhabitants of Madagascar would eat him, but he would not be welcomed. Just another stowaway with no money. He had to get out of there and fight. That was what he'd always done in life. Evan was a loner, a survivor, and this was going to be one of his biggest wins against all odds, if he could pull it off.

Evan looked back at the jagged beam nearby. Slowly, he got to his feet and approached it, still woozy, his head pounding from the brutal blow he'd been dealt hours ago. He got back into the necessary position and resumed sawing at the ropes. Time passed with agonizing slowness, but the ropes were becoming more frayed, wearing away, and that gave him hope. He doubled his efforts, sawing more furiously, sweat dripping down his throbbing head. He could feel the rope was thinning, weakening.

Rip!

It was done. He rubbed his tender wrists slowly, then spun his arms, getting his circulation going again. He felt a great sense of victory.

Okay, one problem down. About another fifty to go. Evan glanced at the ladder and took a deep breath, hoping those two sailor goons hadn't locked the hatch behind them.

Hopefully, they were so secure in Evan's unconscious state, they hadn't bothered. The bruise on his thigh barked at him; that damned guy didn't need to do that, but then again, it might as well have been Arthur Strickler who jabbed his pointy-toed Florsheim into Evan's leg.

He got to the ladder and started climbing as quietly as he could, trying not to grunt with each step. Slight nausea overcame him—he likely had a mild concussion. Deciding that vomiting would have been too loud, he squeezed his eyes shut, took a few deep breaths, and kept climbing. After an eternity, he reached the hatch and was pleasantly surprised when it opened easily.

Evan emerged from the hold and climbed out on the blessedly empty deck. The air was chilly; the LA harbor tended to cool down at night considerably. The area was relatively bare, displaying only the typical working-boat trappings one would expect on a deck. Evan headed to the starboard side railing and looked out over the side. The ship was about 100 meters from the dock. He swung back around to take in his environment. From the looks of it, he was standing aboard a surplus Liberty ship; the Kaiser shipyards had made over two thousand of those nautical wonders to help win the war. Evan considered jumping to the black water waiting about 30 feet down. It would have been ice cold. Plus, they'd hear the splash more than likely and be waiting for him at the dock if he survived the jump.

A big "if," his beleaguered brain reminded him. He wasn't a bad swimmer, but he was no Olympic athlete either. There were no boats tied to the ship he could climb down to, nor did any gangplanks lead from the ship to the dock.

It's jump and swim or stay on board, Evan. He stood there, weighing his options anxiously. A deep groan went through the ship; he could feel the deck vibrate. The boilers were coming online.

"Hey! You!" a voice shouted behind him. Evan looked over his shoulder and spotted "Joe," recognizing the voice. "Get your butt back here, boy!"

The burly man broke into a run toward Evan, who ran

toward the stern. He saw a gangway that led below, and he hurried down it, mini-leaping three stairs at a time. He then found another ladder heading down to a lower deck.

A gunshot rang out. He heard the bullet ricochet off a few surfaces, just like in the movies.

"That was a warning. If I wanted to kill ya, you'd be dead!"

Evan didn't care or believe him. He just kept running, then leaped down another ladder that led to the engine room. It was well lit there, but too many stokers were at their respective boilers and snapped their heads Evan's way. Most were Chinese—and looked surprised to see him.

Evan doubled back to the gangway, which led him to the mess. There, he found what had to be the other goon who had captured him, judging by his muscle mass, seated at a table drinking coffee when he spotted Evan hurrying by. He dropped his cup and followed Evan at a full run, soon only a few feet behind him.

Evan ran faster than he ever had, hit the next ladder he found, and clambered up it, a flood of high-powered adrenaline flooding his body and conquering his sluggish brain. Evan climbed faster than he thought possible. These men meant to kill him, and he had no intention of allowing that to happen.

He emerged from the deck and almost collided with Coop, who was dressed in a black suit and fedora. His look was dead serious. He raised his hand a bit, which held some kind of steel contraption, and motioned for Evan to get down.

The biggest goon emerged from the hatch first, face red with exertion. He spotted Coop, so surprised he stopped in his tracks. "Who the hell are you, some kind of undertaker?" he bleated through heaving breaths.

Coop didn't answer. He just raised his right hand in a "windup," like a baseball pitcher, and threw a massive blue ball of electricity at the goon. The man gaped for an instant, then turned to go back down the ladder in a panicked attempt at escape, but it was too late. The electro-protoplasm swept over the man, paralyzing him just as he reached the hatch. He toppled over and landed on the steel deck below with a sickening crunch.

"That worked very well, I'm happy to say," Coop said, taking a breath.

Evan felt a wave of relief—which disintegrated as he looked beyond his friend Coop, seeing a tall, heavy, familiar man step out of the shadows.

"Put that thing down, or I'll fill ya full of lead!" It was Joe, the other creep. Coop quickly turned, and Evan lunged after him. Joe, confused over which one to shoot at, aimed at Evan and then lost his footing when the ship lurched forward. He fired and missed.

"Clear out of the way, Evan!" Coop commanded and then threw another ball of electricity from his metal contraption at Joe, who flinched back but was still hit full-on. Body laced with electricity, he fought like a man trying to ward off a swarm of bees. Finally, he staggered to the rail and toppled over the side, splashing into the harbor. He didn't come back up for air.

"Let's go!" Coop yelled to Evan and hurried to the accommodation ladder down the ship's port side. Evan, paralyzed with awe, didn't move at first. "A bit more alacrity on your part, Evan. That would be helpful!'

He snapped out of it and followed Coop to the ladder.

Evan noticed at the bottom was a rowboat tied to the bottom step. Coop got in, and Evan sat before him in the bobbing boat. Coop manned the oars and pulled them toward the docks.

"How many others?" Coop asked.

Evan shook his head. "I dunno. Those were the only two I saw."

Coop rowed faster. "More than likely, there are more. I came as quickly as I could."

Evan felt the device Coop gave him earlier in his pocket, realizing that was how Coop knew he was there.

Coop noticed rope bracelets on Evan's wrists. "I take it they bound you?"

Evan nodded, realizing that he had escaped whatever ghastly fate Arthur Strickler had designed for him. He knew then that if he was going to stick around for a while and find a way home—or work on a way to live out his days in this time period—he was going to have to have eyes in the back of his head. Speaking of his head, his was throbbing.

"I tracked you from Beverly Hills to San Pedro using the monitor I gave you. I knew there was no way on Earth you'd come to this godforsaken place on your own," Coop said. They reached the shore, and Coop tied up the rowboat to a dock hidden among several tugboats. "I doubt this fine vessel's owner minded me borrowing it for an hour," He remarked and pulled Evan from the boat to the dock. "As soon as I saw you were headed this way, I got in the car and hurried down here. I saw Strickler's car leave the area and deduced which ship they'd taken you to by simple process of elimination."

"How?" Evan asked, intrigued.

"Simple. Strickler is a cheap hustler. He's surrounded himself with the dregs of society. People of that ilk do not travel on tankers, which are expensive, or even modern cargo vessels. They travel on rust buckets like that one. I found the oldest, dirtiest ship in the harbor and made plans to board her. Despite the wonderful novel by Agatha Christie, most killers don't travel on the Orient Express. They travel in war surplus Liberty ships with names like the SS *Cyclops*."

Evan cast a glance at the Liberty ship that was now up to steam and slowly heading out of the harbor. The name emblazoned on the forecastle: SS *Cyclops*.

"What about the goons?" Evan asked without a lot of sympathy.

"What of them? If you for one second feel any sympathy for them, remember what they were more than likely going to do to you without remorse."

"I didn't know you had it in ya, Coop" was all Evan could come up with.

"You're my friend. I will not allow anyone to harm you, and yes, I have it in me. We all do," Coop answered simply.

They made their way to Coop's Dodge, which he had wisely parked in a darkened area behind a seaman's paymaster store and a bar called The Sea Hag.

Evan climbed in the car, countless questions still swirling in his brain. He watched Coop carefully place the metal gizmo that produced the electronic fireballs into a carrying case that looked like an old-fashioned suitcase.

"How'd you come up with that?" Evan asked.

"I have you to thank for this. Don't know what to call it yet, though for now, 'Evan's lifesaver' has a good ring to it. You had suggested I weaponize the electric ball 'trick' I showed you. The idea stuck with me, and I put this together in a few hours. Good thing there weren't any more of those miscreants. This machine is only good for two discharges, then it must be recharged for hours. Lucky for us, there were only two goons, and my aim was true."

Evan was astonished. His friend had basically engineered a sci-fi ray gun and saved his life with it. And this was not sci-fi, this was real. The thing actually worked and was extremely effective from what he could see.

"I'm overwhelmed, Coop. You have made something so complex, intricate…," Evan muttered.

"It's not overwhelming at all when you consider all the things I learned from Nikola," Coop replied matter-of-factly. "Since arriving here, I've learned more utilizing technology from this era. You'll see in time."

He cranked the engine, and they headed north to Los Angeles along the Arroyo Seco Parkway and SR 11—as evidently there was no I-110 in 1946, just expansive boulevards that were largely empty at this time of night. Even the Red Car trolleys were not operating at 4 a.m., and what few vehicles were on the road seemed to be mostly LAPD black-and-whites.

Coop promised he'd pick Evan up at 7:30 to get him to the studio by 8:30.

CHAPTER 15
TOMORROW'S YESTERDAYS

Evan quietly made his way to Jimmy's guesthouse as the sun peeked over the hills. Once inside, he realized there was no way he was going to sleep. After that experience, who could? Winston Churchill had once said, "Nothing in life is more exhilarating than to be shot at with no result."

You couldn't have been more right, Mr. Churchill. Evan took a breath. First, he'd been shot at, and today would be his first full day working for Frank Capra.

Frank Capra! Evan suddenly realized that his goal of directing a great film before he turned twenty-seven was being partially realized. He'd be working with one of the greatest directors in motion picture history. Evan was flying as close to the sun as he ever could. The only trick was to make sure the wax on his feathers didn't melt.

Of course, Evan still had Strickler to deal with. The man had tried and would try again as soon as he discovered he'd failed. Until then, Evan had to make his way through this experience as carefully as possible. He might be here for the rest of his life, which struck Evan as both a good and bad thing. In some ways, it felt like a Vietnam War-like decision—bad if you stay, bad if you go. Lose, lose. Aside from the threat of Strickler, being with these people and Dorothy was worth never going back…and to what? Connor Alcott? He'd have no job as an editor, Connor would see to that. Connor was disrespected, but like Harvey Weinstein - in Hollywood, you can be disrespected *and* feared. Plus, when a guy like that had money, people tended to tip-toe and acquiesce.

Evan considered. Stay here, maybe get killed. Go back to 2021, and die slowly, his dreams never coming true. Probably meet someone like Gwen and pretend to be someone he wasn't just to "get by." Either way, his life would be difficult.

Evan paced a while, then finally changed clothes, trying to make himself as presentable as he could. He needed a fresh wardrobe, that was for sure. Two outfits—one from 2021 that was really starting to smell, and one "on loan" from the RKO costume department—was all he had. Evan glanced at his watch: 6:45. He could *not* be late his first day for Frank Capra. Evan silently prayed Coop would be on time.

Thinking of Coop, Evan made sure to carry that device he had given him everywhere from now on. Evan wondered if the batteries would ever run down on the thing, but then again, considering it was made with Tesla technology, the chances of that seemed slim.

Evan heard Jimmy in the kitchen, which was nice. He loved the guy. Evan peeked out the window and spotted the star sitting at the kitchen table in his robe and slippers reading the paper. Evan would skip coming in to make small talk; Jimmy loved to chat, and he had no time for that. He slipped out past the kitchen unseen and slinked to the front yard to wait for Coop.

Evan waited a long time. Seven o'clock passed…then 7:25, then 7:30. No Coop, and no cell phone to call him to see what was up. 7:45. Now he was going to be late. *Damn it.* Evan could only make a good first impression once, and he was blowing it.

Coop arrived at 7:50 apologetic; the traffic was absurd. Construction everywhere. It seemed to be a Los Angeles constant.

They made their way to Paramount/RKO, encountering more construction, traffic jams, and horns blowing constantly. Evan looked to his watch, panicking. It was already 8:40, and they were only at Sunset Boulevard and LaBrea.

"Evan, I deeply apologize for being late. I did not know there was so much road construction scheduled today. I don't recall the road being in need of repair, but I suppose someone felt it was necessary."

He didn't need to apologize. Evan knew it wasn't his fault. His nerves were already on edge from his night-time excursion, and now the adrenaline rush of almost being shanghaied to East Africa was wearing off. Evan vowed to drink as much coffee as he could to get through the day.

"Also, I was up the entire evening working on our problem. I need you to know we might very well be stuck here," Coop said darkly. "I might not be able to get us back."

Evan just nodded silently. Stay or go, either way, he had a hard road ahead of him. And right now, that road seemed rockier because he was late.

Coop dropped him off at the Liberty Films offices. He hurried, out of breath, sweaty, hair askew, and made his way into Capra's office as quietly as he could. According to his watch, it was 8:49. Not only was he several minutes late, but he also looked terrible, like a guy who'd been up all night. An attractive young lady behind the front desk clocked Evan immediately. "Excuse me, sir? May I ask your name and what business you have here?" Evan couldn't guess her age based on all the makeup the woman wore. She could have been anywhere between her thirties and middle age. And judging by the piercing look she gave him over her glasses and her commanding voice, she could have easily quit her day job and enlisted as a drill sergeant.

"Yes, I'm Evan West. I'm…," Evan stammered, intimidated by the commanding woman.

"Yes, the editor." Her rock-hard demeanor softened, and he relaxed. "Nice to meet you. Vera Stone, Mr. Capra's assistant. I have some paperwork you need to fill out for us and the union before you begin work today." Vera handed him a clipboard and stack of papers with a fountain pen attached.

Evan took what was handed to him dubiously. "Could I fill this out later? I'm already late."

"I've noticed, and no, this must be done before you do any work. Questions?"

Evan sighed and sat down, examining the paper attached to the clipboard. He saw the line for the applicant's social security number. *Uh-oh*. His was from the twenty-first century; it would never jibe with the SS numbers from 1946. He'd just have to take his chances. He filled out the form, then signed it and handed it back to Master Sergeant Stone. She took the clipboard and motioned toward Frank Capra's office.

"He doesn't like it when people are late," she warned. Evan could hear him shouting on the phone behind his closed door. "He prefers three short raps on the door, then open it a crack. He doesn't like shouting 'Come in' through a closed door. Good luck."

Evan swallowed, then followed her instructions carefully, knocking three times on Capra's door before opening it just a crack. He heard Capra slam down the phone, then he threw a script down on his desk with a loud *crack*! Evan poked his head in.

"Good morning, Mr. Capra," he said mouse-like.

Capra looked to him, frowning. "You're late, West. We're off to a bad start, but come in!" Capra looked at an assistant standing next to his desk, a woman in her late twenties wearing black glasses with her hair bound up in a twirly-doo that vaguely resembled an upside-down ice cream cone.

"Well?" Frank asked.

"Well…?" the poor girl repeated, looking in Evan's direction.

"Oh, sorry, Mr. Capra," Evan said, picking up the slack. "There was a lot of construction on Sunset today…."

"I don't care, West. We've got bigger problems right now," he muttered. Capra picked up the script, glanced through it once more, then slammed it down on the desk again.

The girl beside him jumped at the angry sound.

"I have no choice," he said dismally. "A terrific scene, and I'll have to shoot the damned thing on a sound stage, cheat it all to hell. It'll look phony as heck, but there it is!"

Evan cleared this throat and spoke up: "Mr. Capra, may I ask which scene?"

"The prom night dance sequence scene. I need a floor that opens with a swimming pool below it. Now where the hell can I find one of those? Answer: Nowhere!" He slammed his fist into the script just for good measure before glaring up at Evan. "You might want to read the script if you're going to help edit this madness."

"I know it by heart," Evan blurted out, catching himself.

"Do you?" Capra said, somewhat amused.

The assistant raised her hand. Capra snapped, "What, Sally? Spit it out. You're not in high school. You don't have to raise your hand."

"Might we shoot the prom scene at night up by Lake Hollywood?"

Dudley, another assistant Evan did not notice at first, a prematurely bald, thirty-five-year-old man on a chair behind Capra's right side, chirped in. "Right. And when things get exciting, everyone jumps in the lake with Jimmy and Donna. Same effect, just no pool."

"And Mr. Strickler will certainly like the budgetary aspects of not building a pool on a sound stage," Sally piped in, smiling.

Capra's face turned two different shades of purple as he roared, "I don't give a damn what that pencil-pushing dilettante would like! Don't ever mention that bastard's name in a creative meeting again!"

Sally looked like she was about to cry.

"No, we need a platform that opens over a damned pool," growled Capra. "Not a lake. Not a river. Not the bloody Pacific Ocean. A pool!"

Evan stepped forward, raising his hand even though Sally had just been chided for that action. "I...uh...I know where you can get one of those," he interjected quietly.

"You jerking my chain, West?" Capra said in a deadly voice.

"No, sir. It's…the Beverly Hills High School. They have one. Right in the gymnasium. I remember reading about that um, someplace. The pool, I mean," he corrected himself on the fly.

"You sure about this, West?" Capra said, his tone lightening.

"Damn sure, sir," he said. "Sorry. I meant scout's honor, um, yes."

Capra glanced at Dudley and Sally. "Well, don't just stand there, go out and make some calls. I want that damned gymnasium with the pool!"

The two assistants fled the room as if the devil were chasing them. Capra looked at Evan, grinning. "I took you on as a favor to Jimmy. But that's the second time you've been useful, kid. I like that! Next time, *be on time*, or there will be no next time!"

"It'll look great. The pool is exactly what you're looking for, Mr. Capra," Evan insisted, relieved that the tense moment had passed.

"Let's go take a look at some of those rushes you'll be helping on," he said, rising and clapping a hand on Evan's shoulder. Evan and Capra walked to the front door as it opened—and there stood Arthur J. Strickler in all his glory. His head was buried in papers.

"Capra, we have to talk.…" Strickler looked up and saw Evan. His face blanched.

"Good morning, Mr. Strickler," Evan said cheerfully.

Strickler merely stared, frozen.

"What the hell is it, Strickler?" Capra wasted no time. "We have too many porta-potties on set for your budget?"

"Uh, no," Strickler muttered, recovering from the shock of seeing Evan, who he must have figured was either dead or in the middle of the Pacific by now.

"My new assistant editor, Evan West." Capra indicated Evan.

"A distinct pleasure," Strickler hissed, eyes narrowed.

"Likewise, sir," Evan said.

"New boy on the block?" Strickler added, lifting his eyebrows and staring pointedly at West.

"Yep. Like a new ship ready for sea," Evan said, enjoying himself. "Sorry for the maritime comparison but…I have a yen for all things nautical." Evan stared hard at Stricker, smirking a little.

"Quite so," Strickler parried, then looked to Capra. "Do you have a minute, Frank?"

"Later, Arthur," Capra said, waving him off. "I've got a picture to cut."

Strickler was left there, standing alone, a combination of rage and confusion on his face. He added two and two, but it came up five. Nothing made sense to him right now. Finally, Strickler returned to his office upstairs in the RKO building. He sat at his desk, reflecting a minute after looking around his environment; the big one-sheets of new releases and the gleam in these offices didn't come naturally to Strickler. He had fallen into this profession after his construction company went broke during the depths of the Great Depression.

He stared at the gleaming wood of his desk, the surface so shining and smooth it reflected his weary scowl back at him. He had lost it all, despite putting everything he had into Strickler/Flannery Construction. His entire soul had been poured into a company that in 1926 alone built over one hundred low-cost homes in Baldwin Hills, twelve doctors' offices and the Ocean Park Hotel in Santa Monica. He'd been living high, paid good wages to his workers, and never doubted his business partner, Pete Flannery.

But he should have…and then should have murdered the man earlier than he had.

Strickler stood up, went to his cabinet, and poured a gin straight up—no ice, no mixer. He thought back to Pete Flannery. The man was a swindler, a man whose moral compass was broken if he ever even had one. Strickler met Pete in the service, both having served in France during the Great War. Both were Marines and had seen their share of combat.

Those experiences never left Strickler. He never forgot or forgave. Before the war, Strickler was a man who never paid religion any mind, but after he got back stateside, it became all he could think about. God had both exalted and betrayed him; God had allowed Strickler to survive. Yes, he had done that, and for God's mercy, Strickler was grateful. But surveying the horror of battle, the anguished howl of violent death, made Strickler angry with God for allowing it all to happen. His mind went back to the faces of the dead; mouths hanging open and filled with flies, eyes sometimes staring into nothing, sometimes closed forever. Strickler cursed the god who gifted him life and cursed the optimism so brutally crushed from the dead. He hated the world and the god that made it. There was no love to be found in Arthur J. Strickler from that day forward.

Strickler picked up a copy of Frank Capra's script for *The Greatest Gift*. He stared at the cover, finishing off his straight gin in one melancholy gulp. There was nothing about life that was great, nor was it a gift. More like a curse, and Arthur Strickler would do anything in his power to remind the world of that. The only people who seemed to enjoy it were the stupid and gullible.

For the next few hours, Evan felt like he had died and gone to heaven. He huddled in a hot room about the size of his apartment living room with Frank and his editor, a very competent, good-natured man named Bill Hornbeck. Bill and Frank apparently went back a ways. Bill had edited Frank's *WWII: Why We Fight* series of films. Evan marveled at the way Bill and Frank worked in sync, finding a few frames to cut here and there, storing trims, and asking Evan to label everything. Evan had done all this before but on Avid, a virtual software. But at Liberty Films in 1946, it was all done by hand; 35mm work print cuts and trims were stored in a trim bin and hung like laundry on a clothesline. Each shot, scene, and accompanying sound were kept neatly together.

They reviewed the Potter/George Bailey scene where George begged Potter for help, then studied the near-George-suicide scene on the bridge; after that, the scene with George getting news from Mary about a new baby on the way. It was a journey through history as Evan watched Bill manipulate the ancient upright Moviola, slicing film by hand and pasting it together while Evan stood by with extra cement (Evan was pretty sure it was just glue, but they called it cement).

They broke for lunch. Capra said he had no choice but to speak with Strickler, which gave Evan time to catch a quick catnap in Capra's outer office within an enclave out of sight to anyone entering the place. Master Sergeant Stone had just left for lunch, so he was afforded some welcome quiet and privacy.

Evan awoke to Capra roaring from within his office. "Get out, you ignominious hack! You damned jarhead piece of cod swallow! Get out!"

The door opened, and a paperweight sailed out the door and smashed into the outside window just above Vera Stone's neater-than-neat desk. Arthur Strickler emerged and hastily closed the door behind him as yet another crash exploded. "Come back again with an idea like that, and I'll shoot you with the .45 here in my desk! You hear me? I'll shoot you deader than the lapdog from hell that you are!"

Strickler frowned. He glanced down in thought, then turned to go. Then he paused, eyes locking onto Evan's from across the room.

"Hard day at the office, Mr. Strickler?" Evan asked, yawning.

Strickler just stared for an instant, then he walked over slowly, body tense. He stopped less than a foot from Evan, pulled out a handkerchief, and mopped his brow. "Have a hard time getting to work today?"

Evan frowned. "What do you mean?"

"Don't get smart with me, boy-o. We both know what's going on." Strickler got in his face. Evan could smell pickles on his breath.

"Not sure what you're referring to," Evan said with a shrug. "But let's suppose you did want to do something, like kidnap and send me somewhere far away. No…you wouldn't do that, would you, Mr. Strickler? That's illegal. Besides, once you've crossed a line like that, there's no turning back."

Evan was rather amazed at his own courage at the moment—and his sudden ability to conjure up a movie-like hero line like that on the fly. "I'm full of surprises."

Strickler's face transformed into an ugly mask of hatred. This was the *real* Arthur J. Strickler, a man with an evil soul and heart of stone.

Strickler seemed to catch himself, morphing quickly back into the grim-faced reaper he appeared to be. A smile cracked his thin lips. Evan knew Strickler; he was simply a better-controlled Connor Alcott, a man without the crippling malady of alcohol clouding his thinking. Unlike Connor, Strickler was calculating and knew when to use his anger, but for just that one moment, he had lost control and dropped the mask he used to get through in society, allowing his "soul to come up." It was a phrase Evan had heard his grandfather use once when referring to a banker he knew who lost his temper and called in a loan from a poor man who was doing his best to pay the bank back and had missed a few payments. The banker had eviscerated the poor guy just to vent his anger—and no doubt the banker would do it again to the next soul who had the misfortune of getting in his path—just as Strickler would.

Evan braced himself for whatever was about to come.

Strickler studied him. "I may have underestimated you, West." His voice was chillingly quiet. "How about this? We put a stop to our hostilities and turn an eye to something more productive."

"What did you have in mind?" Evan asked.

"Collaboration," he said easily. "Something along creative lines. You are, as you say, resourceful. I could use a man like that in my corner."

Evan just glanced pointedly at his watch in response.

If that fazed Strickler, he didn't show it. "Think about it." He offered Evan a crisp smile, turned on his heel military-style, and marched out just as Master Sergeant Stone was returning from lunch.

She glanced Strickler's way before glancing at Evan. "Talking with the big man?"

"Not so much talking as exchanging blows," Evan said, smiling offhandedly as if it meant nothing to him.

"I think he's a jerk," Vera Stone volunteered. "I don't like the way he looks at me either. Like I'm prey."

"The man is a hunter of souls, a destroyer of worlds," Evan intoned darkly.

Vera chuckled. "Yeah, you got his number. Thing with guys like him, they always assume they're fooling everyone, but the reality is quite the opposite."

The door to Capra's office flew open with the director's typical fiery gusto. Capra stepped out and glanced at Evan. "Let's go, West. Back into the trenches we go to fight on. Stone, get me those contracts when you can, if you please."

"Coming, boss." Vera saluted. Evan watched her go. Master Sergeant Stone indeed.

Capra and Evan headed back to the editing building and examined the existing footage with Bill. Evan marveled as he always did at the scene where Jimmy and Donna were enjoying their time together, post-swimming-pool prom party, lounging in robes and sweat clothes and singing, "*Buffalo gals, won't you come out tonight.*" The scene ended when George was pulled away by Uncle Billy, who informed George that his dad had died.

Evan glanced at Capra, who stood next to him, eyes intent on the footage. Capra leaned into Bill, who was huddled between Evan and Capra. "So, this too grim?" Capra asked the editor.

"It's dark, Frank, but the scene before has to be a happy one. It'll take the edge off."

Evan nodded. Bill knew his stuff.

"The swimming pool sequence will be funny. No, hilarious!" Bill continued. "How do we do that? I'll tell you how. Jimmy and Donna will fall into the pool after the doors slide open, thanks to our two pranksters. Then the rest of the kids just go ape and do the same—they jump in and splash to hell and back. Then we're out of it. Slow dissolve to Buffalo Gals. Now that is what I call cinema!"

Evan stepped forward, fighting the urge to speak up.

Capra picked up on it and eyed him. "What?" he pressed.

"I mean, that's fine, Mr. Capra. But…" Evan hesitated.

"But what?" Capra snapped.

"I just thought—"

"Thought what? Damn it, speak up, boy!"

"Well, call me crazy, but wouldn't it be funnier if Jimmy and Donna kept dancing in the pool as if nothing had happened?" Evan mimicked their dance, the Charleston, a mindless two-step. Capra didn't say a word for a minute. Then suddenly, he burst into a big guffaw. "My goodness, West, that's hilarious! It's absolute, 100-percent genius! You should be directing pictures, not editing them," Capra shouted.

Evan decided in that moment that if he died on the spot with that compliment firmly locked into his soul, his life would be complete.

"Thank you, sir," Evan said quietly.

Capra picked up his script and scribbled some notes. "Okay, West. Now let's see you do some splicing for Bill. Lotta work to do. Bill, make him earn his paycheck."

"I plan to," Bill said and threw Evan a smile.

Evan returned the gesture. The more Evan sized up Bill, the more he liked him. He wasn't the intense introvert most editors were; he looked more like a nice bank president—the kind who didn't call in overdue loans from poor people.

"Bill, let's go out for a smoke," said Frank.

Bill stood and handed the moviola over to Evan. "You have the plane, kid."

Evan got to work. Bill had marked all of the cuts coming up in the next reel with a white grease pencil. Now this was the test of tests. Evan had to splice all those scenes together as Bill had marked them exactly to the frame.

Evan took a deep breath and dived in. He found the scenes and the marks and spliced the film together, one cut after the next. At first, the work was slow-going, but he built up speed over time. All the old movie technology he had studied was coming back to him: four sprocket holes to the frame (two on each side), thirty-two frames per each foot of film, twenty-four frames a second, 45 feet per minute of film. He had the entire sequence cut together in twenty-five minutes, not bad for a guy who had only done this once as a home experiment with some old 35mm he got from a theater going out of business.

Bill and Frank returned, both with cups of coffee in hand. "Let's run it," Frank commanded, and so Bill hit the power. The scene with Gloria Grahame, in all her sexiness, walking across the street as a car came to a screeching halt while Jimmy Stewart watched on flashed by. Evan turned to Capra, waiting for a slew of criticisms. Instead, he merely sighed.

Bill patted Evan on the shoulder, showing his support.

"It's a damn shame they're forcing us into an early release on this," Frank exhaled. "I hate editing while I'm still shooting. Feels rushed."

"Don't worry, Mr. Capra. We'll make it all work for you," Bill said. Frank nodded absently.

Evan could not tell him that seventy-five years into the future, filmmakers shot and edited simultaneously while fighting timetables, studios, and diminishing budgets. It was hard for Evan to be too depressed for Capra. At least the director would have had the blessing of knowing the brilliant future of *It's A Wonderful Life*.

CHAPTER 16

LEGEND OF A MIND

Coop was in a bad mood. A man not usually given to the normal ups and downs most people felt was having a rotten day. His duties on the movie were minimal today; he simply had to transfer from optical tracks recorded from the set to mag-full coat for the editor who, with Coop, worked simultaneously as the crew shot since they were behind, which was causing Coop's workload to expand tremendously. That didn't bother him; he was no stranger to work. It was, in fact, all he knew.

The term "workaholic" may not have been in vogue in 1946, but it was the best word to describe Coop. If "work-aholic genius-engineer-inventor" was an actual job title, it would have fit the man to a "T." But all of that was a heavy burden, and as a result, sleep did not come naturally to Coop. If anything, it was a distraction. Coop, grappling with another sleepless night, was plagued by the headaches that had been consuming him for the past year. They were debilitating, unbelievably wretched, and when they came on like a hurricane, he'd go into a death spiral for hours on end, a cold rag on his head, unable to think or move. They were what Winston Churchill referred to as his "black dog"—an affliction that followed you everywhere.

Now that Coop's power-headache was coming on fast, he wasn't making any progress toward getting him and his new friend, Evan West, back to their respective eras. Nothing was going to help or work. He was stuck in 1946, which he could manage, but he was very aware that Evan was also stuck here, and that could lead to potentially fatal consequences. Arthur Strickler had Evan kidnapped, and now that Evan had thwarted him, Strickler's goal was likely to have him killed. Evan could not stay in this time; he had to return to his own - or move on to another. Coop would not, could not let anything happen to his friend. Coop knew too well what men like Strickler were capable of. He had seen it on his face when he first met the man.

Coop drove home, thinking back on his upbringing. Poor in New York City. He was born in Tennessee; his parents moved to New York when he was two. Coop had no memories of Tennessee or living as a sharecropper's son. He remembered only 125th Street in Harlem, the cold-water flat he grew up in, and the smell of those cramped rooms and the sounds of traffic, horns, and trash cans rattling.

In New York, he grew into a very precocious and alien-like child who read by the time he was three, spoke French and Italian at four, and could quote Shakespeare at five.

Coop's mother worked at the Brooklyn Women's Hospital; his father did plumbing jobs around Harlem, sometimes all the way up to Upper Manhattan and Washington Heights. His brothers and sisters went to public school, and Coop went to the New York Public Library, a place that did more for Coop than a full PhD program at Harvard or Yale would have done for anyone else. His brain was like an enormous, thirsty sponge that sucked up every bit of knowledge, and unlike most, he retained it.

Coop did go to Columbia University, but only to attend lectures given during the fall semester of 1890 by leading physics theorists and scientists. Coop could spot the frauds from a mile away and noticed the distinct frown on the face of one man in particular—a heavyset man with a balding head and thick spectacles. Coop immediately knew this man was the smartest in the room, and Coop had boldly introduced himself to Thomas Cummerford Martin, an adjunct professor of electrical engineering at Columbia and former president of the American Institute of Electrical Engineers. Martin took an immediate liking to Coop, admiring his manners, polish, and mastery of language. He offered Coop a job as his assistant, and not knowing better, Coop happily accepted.

During that magical winter semester of 1891, Coop helped Martin prepare his lecture materials and always double-checked his mathematics to make sure Martin's calculations were correct.

Martin chaired the Engineering Council for Professional Development that defined engineering as "that profession which utilizes the resources of the planet for the benefit of mankind." Martin and Coop came up with that phrase together. Both men soon found something to be especially excited about: the work of a Serbian immigrant, a former Edison employee, and an utterly brilliant man named Nikola Tesla.

On May 10, 1891, Martin brought together an enormous gathering at a Columbia lecture hall. Not only were there members of the academic world, with representatives from Columbia, Cornell, MIT, Yale, and Johns Hopkins, but also the giants of industry from Westinghouse, Edison General Electric, along with delegates from various trade journals who spread the news of this great discovery and "revelation to science and art unto all time." Coop sat in the front row as Nikola Tesla, who barely spoke before he began his lecture, walked out on stage, and the entire room was filled with electricity.

Tesla presented his discoveries in the realm of high-frequency engineering and demonstrated the principle of coupled tuning. He Introduced and demonstrated a technology that would raise the average power developed by RF sources five orders of magnitude.

Coop was in awe; this was a man who was taking existing technology and approaching science like an artist. He didn't take the rules seriously (most scientists, Coop noticed, were more interested in following the rules than breaking them) and was doing more for innovation than anyone else, even Edison. During the lecture, Tesla held up long poles of glass, and they lit up with a soft light with *no wires attached*. He called this "cold light," wireless electricity that would activate when near an active source of power. Coop found this astonishing as did everyone else in the room.

In his own unknowing, clumsy way, that night, Nikola Tesla declared war on his former employer, Thomas Edison. Edison, a practical man who could see exactly where to make money with any invention, was also attuned to seeing threats, and Tesla's "cold light" certainly fit the definition. Anything without a wire could not be regulated, and power was the last thing Edison wanted to give away for free. Edison was planning a war with Tesla. Winning was all he knew.

Coop reflected on the fact that Edison's war with Tesla was what drove them to Colorado Springs, which in turn, led to Coop's strange time travel adventure to 1946. Coop shook his head as if to clear away the memories, then turned left from Franklin to Hillhurst and made a right on Clarissa. He was still brooding, headache going from mild throbbing to a full-on sledgehammer against his forehead.

He held his eyes closed once he parked the Dodge, afraid he might lose consciousness. Coop was tired from being up all night, the adventure that led to him killing two men—which he had no remorse over—and the long drive to and from San Pedro. He had saved his friend's life. Though he barely knew Evan, for all intents and purposes, the young man had become his traveling companion through 1946.

Coop, for whatever reason, felt a deep kinship with Evan. He'd never really had any friends. Tesla came the closest to having that distinction, but the man had been so solipsistic and closed off, Coop doubted he ever even confided in his own mother. Tesla had been a vast wasteland when it came to human relationships and only sought out working partners who were subservient to him, Coop being perfect in that role.

So why do I want to go back to 1899 and to Nikola Tesla so badly?

Coop, who had always longed for a girlfriend but never could see the practicality of having one, had nonetheless felt the emptiness of his life nagging at him. He had his science, his inventions, his deft maneuvering around obstacles, but all that was growing old. He wanted a friend, someone he could learn from and who simply liked Coop for who he was. Evan was exciting, a man from the future, the real future, where all the scientific excitement was bound to be. Since Evan's arrival, they never had time for "the talk." Coop wanted to know everything, but as a man with manners and scientific imagination, he understood all came in due time. He would ask Evan all those burning questions eventually, but right now, his focus was to save him.

The dark thought crossed his mind to develop another electric plasma gun that would disintegrate Arthur J. Strickler and his goon Jack to nothing. It would be easy to develop a more focused version of the device that stunned two killers and led to their deaths (or at least severe injuries), but he didn't want to go there. Malicious thoughts were easy to conjure but hard to dismiss. He had a lot of anger inside of him that was unresolved, though he normally shrugged it off with bursts of creative energy that kept him up all night developing something for work, such as a microphone that was extremely directional or an advancement of the cardioid microphone that picked up sound from a "heart-shaped" recording zone.

Right now, he had to fight off his headache and get back to work. If he couldn't go back to 1899, well, to hell with it. Coop could live with firing forward to the twenty-first century if that was a possibility.

With any luck, and considering what Evan had said, maybe a man with his level of melanin would not be so damned afraid to go out at night. Although, he had found in 1946, there were just as many Black predators roaming the streets at night as White.

Coop entered his house, still careful to lock the door and stuff the keys back in his pocket.

In the kitchen, he took a cold washcloth, soaked it in the sink, filled it with ice cubes (an amazing invention from 1946 he would never take for granted), and stretched it across his forehead. He reclined on a sofa, letting the coldness sink into his forehead, hoping it would permeate his brain and cool it off, bringing him back to reality—or at least a semblance thereof. Coop's migraines came on so strong that for days afterward, his vision and sense of taste and smell would be affected. His sense of smell became acute and blue lights danced in the corner of his vision that under any other circumstances he would have found beautiful. When he had succumbed to these headaches as a child, his mother would say he had too much going on in his head and his pipes overheated. She was smarter than she knew—because that was exactly what was going on. He had such an enormous problem to solve, it had temporarily blown out the circuits of his brain.

Coop felt himself sinking into the quagmire of his sofa, such a soft bit of furniture he bought new from Wertz Brothers. He loved its luxury. Coop squished a pillow under his head and pondered how they could go back to their respective times, or at the very least, how he could get his friend Evan forward to his own time. Coop, who was current on all things scientific, also knew the Einstein theory that compared time to a winding river, with humanity in a boat, drifting along between two high banks. One can't see the future beyond the next curve or the past behind them, but it's all still there, as real as the moment around them. Coop knew this to be true, and he also knew something else: Whatever

Nikola and Evan had chanced upon was breaking every rule of science and physics.

Yes, the winding river was the correct analogy, but those banks were high for a reason. Although his "sort of friend" Nikola Tesla had not been a believer in the Almighty, Coop believed very strongly indeed in His existence.

Perhaps it was his Baptist upbringing, or maybe even his righteous feeling of right and wrong. But Coop knew there was something out there, something so massive and beyond human understanding that to accept this thing—God, for lack of a better term—was better than to dismiss his existence.

Without God, there would be no existence at all.

The high banks that forbid men and women from seeing into time past or time forward, in Coop's mind, were guardrails constructed by God for a very good reason. And because of two random but almost connected encounters with electrical power so immense it had diminished those banks, both Coop and Evan had crossed into the same time.

But why here? Coop mused. *Why Los Angeles in the 1940s, and why a man from 1899 and a man from 2021 both ending up in the same decade, same place? What was the calculus behind that? Was it by design?* Evan went back seventy-five years in time; Coop had gone forward forty-five. Coop had done the math, looked for any variables in the equation. Their backward and forward travel were both divisible by five and were thirty years apart in total. But those figures provided no answer.

Coop suddenly recalled the quote Evan had mentioned earlier from someone named "Spock:" "*Once you have eliminated the impossible, whatever remains, however improbable, must be the truth.*" Coop could see the impeccable logic of the statement, but it was hard for him to reconcile the idea that he and Evan were here for a reason.

If there was a reason behind all of this, he simply couldn't fathom what it might be.

Coop's headache was crushing him now, a heavy dinosaur stomping on his head, smashing him into eternity on that nice, soft, velvet pillow. Before he drifted into a dreamless sleep, Coop considered the pillow he had his head resting on, and how in the 1700s, a pillow like this would have only belonged to a king or queen.

Time is like a winding river, with humanity in a boat drifting along between two high banks...

Coop's last thought was that he'd have to be the one to discover how to scale those high banks, get to the top, climb over, and get into the next bend of the river, all while holding tight to the boat.

Indeed, Coop needed a boat of some kind. Without one to hold him on that journey, he'd drown and pull Evan down with him.

Coop would not allow that. Ever.

CHAPTER 17

THE DUKE OF MATCHMAKING

Evan had a big day. He took a quick break after he got word on the set that his car was ready at Big Mike's. He hailed a cab for the few blocks to LaBrea and Sunset and paid for the Ford, which now looked as good as new.

Getting into the seat and driving it back to RKO/Paramount was a joy; he felt like a million dollars driving a car that wasn't so completely out of place. Never before had he so believed that he was exactly where—and when—he was supposed to be. The car seemed to drive smoother now, or maybe that was his imagination. The gears whispered as they changed; the tires felt steadier on the road. Maybe the Ford had been as out of place in 2021 as Evan was in 1946. Maybe, just maybe, time had a way of rejecting such objects and people it didn't know what to do with.

Evan worked with Bill on the set until 5:30 p.m., then Bill asked if he could go through all the edits and double-check the splices to make sure they held. Evan was hoping to run by the Rail Head Diner before then and pop in on Dorothy. Life was so exhilarating for him at the moment, he could barely keep his thoughts straight.

After he finished all the tasks Bill set before him, he drove his Ford to the diner. As Evan looked through the diner's front entrance window, Dorothy turned his way, looking out at that exact same moment. Their eyes met, and she smiled and waved. Evan walked in.

Now face-to-face, they regarded each other for a brief instant as if both were too awash with anticipation...and other burgeoning emotions...to move or speak.

"Wow," Dorothy finally breathed, red-painted lips parting in a smile. "Nice surprise!"

Evan couldn't help but return her sweet smile—it was that infectious. "I figured if we got lucky, we could go to the movies tonight," he offered, raising his eyebrows.

"And I know just the one," she said, leaning against the counter playfully. "Very romantic—and with an actor you know."

"Really?" Evan said with mock surprise.

"Yes, sir, Mr. West!" She grinned and took Evan by the arm. He walked her to his Ford, which looked absolutely at home, then opened the door for her like a gentleman should.

"You sure I'm not stealing you away from Richie or school tonight?" Evan asked, circling around the car to hop in on the driver's side. As soon as he sat down, Dorothy reached for his hand.

"You are, but a little hooky now and then never hurt anyone," she said with a smile. And so, they were off, rolling through the Valley and finally pulling into the El Patio theater, which offered a "revival" of *The Philadelphia Story* with Cary Grant, Katharine Hepburn, and Evan's favorite, Jimmy Stewart.

"Don't you love oldies?" Dorothy asked as they parked.

Oldies? From six years ago? Evan mused. Then he remembered—in the days before TV and reruns, movies got a run of a few weeks at most, then were stored away for safekeeping. Rarely were movies shown again after their first release. TV, with its insatiable appetite for content, changed all that in the '50s and '60s.

It was a Wednesday night; the house was mostly empty, not many movie-goers present. Evan had seen the film before, but his attention was fixed on Dorothy and her blazing presence beside him. Even in her modest waitress uniform and apron, her hair done up in a basic bun, she radiated a kind of sweet, one-in-a-million uniqueness and timeless elegance. She just seemed…perfect.

"You want to hold hands?" she asked, her lips upturned in a coy grin. Without waiting for Evan's answer, she pulled his hand into her lap. Evan grew nervous. This was turning out to be one of the most satisfying moments he'd had in his life. She smelled great, she felt great, and being near her was intoxicating. The way she smiled, how she truly "glowed" with inner happiness, was overwhelming to Evan. Everything she wore was perfect, not because of the clothes but because of the confidant woman beneath them. Evan had never in his life met someone more comfortable in their own skin.

The film played, and all throughout the experience, Evan fought the urge to steal a kiss from her, but he held out. It wasn't due to fear. It was something else…

He respected her too much.

The movie concluded, leaving them both teary-eyed. They walked slowly back to Evan's Ford, neither seeming to want the moment to end. Dorothy stopped and pointed to a very bright object in the sky.

"I see that one first every night. Brightest star and always near the moon," she said.

"It's not a star," Evan corrected.

Dorothy screwed up her face and cocked her head. "Of course, it's a star," she sighed. "What would you call it?"

"It's a planet," Evan explained. "Venus. Poets called it the morning and the evening star. Brightest object in the sky aside from the moon." She turned to face him, and Evan dived in for a kiss.

"I love smart men," she cooed when Evan broke away, to which he smiled and then dove back in. They kissed for a long time. Evan was in heaven. They sat in the car, and Evan put on the radio. "Just A Little Fond Affection," played by Gene Krupa and His Orchestra, set the tone as they drove to Dorothy's house. They didn't speak—the moment seemed too magical for that. Evan pulled up in front of her house, put the car in neutral and tugged the parking brake on. He looked into her eyes and then to the wedding ring she still wore.

Dorothy noticed, and for a second, she looked afraid.

"Where did your husband die?" Evan asked gently.

Dorothy took her time answering. "In France, on the beach at Normandy. June sixth."

A long silence transpired between them. She wiped a tear from her eye. "He's buried in France and will be twenty-four years old forever. He was my first love, and I swore I'd never take the ring off until the day I died." She took both of Evan's hands, looking deeply into his eyes. "You ever been in love before? Not just 'in lust' or 'Maybe I like her,' but really, really in love with all of your heart?"

Evan wasn't sure how to answer because he didn't know.

"Yeah, maybe. I think so. Never told her, but maybe."

"Then you weren't. When you're in love, you know it. You know it through and through. You know it in your heart, your soul, your intellect. And when you do know it, you have to tell her. If you don't, the opportunity will pass, and you'll lose her. When they're gone, they're gone. Just ask me. I know all about it."

"Okay." Evan nodded fervently. He looked into her eyes, those hauntingly beautiful eyes. He kissed her what felt like a long time, and during what couldn't have been more than a minute, he had an out-of-body experience. He floated away on a blissful, silver cloud. Then she pulled away.

"Good night, Evan West. See you on the set tomorrow." She gave him one last look, then left the car without a good-bye glance over her shoulder. *It's best that way*, Evan thought. Lingering glances are pointless if you know how you feel about somebody.

Maybe Evan was in love with Dorothy. Maybe... He couldn't imagine he was anything else with her but in love. And if that were indeed the case, how could he go back to 2021 with all its ugliness? Life wasn't life in 2021; it was slow death.

Evan returned to Jimmy's house around 8:30, where he found Jimmy in a tuxedo waiting for him.

Jimmy watched him walk in, eyes twinkling. "Nice night out?" he asked.

"Yep." Evan couldn't help but grin. "Saw a good film. Maybe you've heard of it?"

"Could be," Jimmy said, straightening his jacket.

"*Philadelphia Story*. Grant and Hepburn were exceptional." Evan smirked.

"Yeah, it's okay. But that Stewart fellow needed some work," Jimmy quipped. "Come on, get dressed. We got a party to go to."

"On a school night?" Evan asked.

Jimmy picked up on the reference right away and chortled. "Yep, a school night. I like that. Come on."

Evan frowned. "I don't have anything nice to wear," he pointed out, hoping to get out of the obligation.

"Yes, I'm way ahead of you on that." Jimmy moved to a hall closet and took out a dark blue suit, pants, a jacket, a red tie, and a white shirt. "I passed by my favorite thrift shop—used to shop there all the time in my lean years—and picked this out for you. Figured it might come in handy." Jimmy had a jolly glimmer in his eyes. "You'll like this party, kid."

"Really?" Evan asked, unconvinced. "Not really the party type."

"Old friend of mine's invited us. Ever heard of John Wayne? My buddy Gary Cooper says he's got a girl he wants me to meet, and I'd be lying if I told you I wasn't interested. So, see what you can make of yourself and be ready in ten. I need a wingman, someone who can get me back to base."

Evan admired the suit. "Jimmy," he said slowly. "That was very thoughtful of you."

He waved it off. "Off you go. Get dressed. Your shoes are fine, by the way. You buy those at Wexler's?"

Evan wasn't sure how to answer. Wexler's? Must have been some men's shop or shoe shop that probably died in the Kennedy era. Jimmy headed to his bar and poured himself a Johnnie Walker Red.

Evan made his way to the guesthouse to work on getting party-worthy. He cleaned up fast and, in his opinion, looked pretty darned good.

"You about ready out there?" Jimmy yelled to Evan from the kitchen.

Evan smiled at his reflection in the bathroom mirror. "Think so."

The Duke's shack—as Jimmy referred to John Wayne's house—was also in Beverly Hills, just off of Sunset Boulevard near Beverly Drive. It was a magnificent mansion with two pools and a waterfall. The Packard limousine carrying Evan and Jimmy swung into the huge driveway, already populated by a dozen cars and a few motorcycles.

Evan noticed that Jimmy was not himself as he nervously fidgeted with his sleeve and tie throughout the trip. Evan thought it was just the prospect of meeting that girl who Gary Cooper wanted him to meet, though he had the feeling it was more than that. Once at the party, Jimmy's worry was even more pronounced.

Jimmy got out of the car and smoothed his jacket, eyes flickering around. "Let's go out back, Evan. It'll be stuffy in there, and I don't like cigarette smoke."

Evan followed him out back to the garden pool area, where Jimmy paced back and forth, hands stuffed in his pocket. "I'm really tired of Strickler harassing Frank about this movie," he finally said. "Bad enough we had to shoot those dreadful scenes, which Frank did out of studio pressure, but now he's forcing Capra to actually use 'em. It screws everything up, Evan. Those scenes will sink both me and Frank. We'll be done. Finished. Know what I'm saying?"

Jimmy reached over to a passing waiter who had a tray full of whiskies and snatched a glass. He downed it in one gulp. "I've been out of the game now for too long to come back and foul up everything."

"I agree completely, Jimmy. I personally think the guy's a philistine. A nickel and dimer who thinks he knows movies, and worse, thinks he knows better than people like Frank who's been doing this a long time. And he looks like a guy who used to be a criminal," Evan said emphatically. *Used to be?* he thought. *Ha! Still is, considering what he did last night.*

"Well, it won't wash in the long run." Jimmy nodded to himself. "If I have to throw my weight around on the issue, then so be it. I'm not going to let that suit with a mean face throw my career off track. I've worked too hard, and frankly, he's not proven himself to me at all."

The pool was occupied by a colorful mix of young people in bathing suits. Near the swimming partygoers stood a more mature crowd dressed in evening gowns, suits, and tuxedos. As Evan approached the group mingling poolside, he saw the man towering above them all.

John Wayne, in a black jacket, gray tie, and gray slacks, was absolutely massive. He grinned big, waved at Jimmy, and lit a Camel. As he approached them, cigarette in hand, Evan noticed a very pretty young woman behind him.

"Jimmy, glad you could make it," the Duke said in his famous growl, standing opposite Jimmy. Evan gazed at the man's lined face, slightly squinting eyes, and graying hair, smoothly combed to the side. The man projected calm and casual despite the lavish crowd, his high-class clothes, and expensive surroundings.

"John, glad to be here. This here is one of our new editors on *The Greatest Gift*, Evan West. And a friend now as well." Jimmy clapped Evan on the back. The Duke extended his hand—which was unbelievably huge—to Evan.

"Good meeting you, West." He flashed his signature smile. "Well, so far, it looks like it's gonna be a good party. Grab yourselves some drinks. I only stock the best liquor and finest grub. I need to make the rounds as host, but I'll catch up with you later." He took a pull of his cigarette as he moved away.

Evan was pleased but not surprised that the John Wayne on the silver screen was basically the same man in real life. And just as unforgettable.

Another familiar face stepped their way—Gary Cooper. His wife, Rocky Cooper, was slim, elegant. Her face was honest but beautiful. Evan's eyes moved from Rocky to the straight and delicate mouth and perfectly coiffed hair of the woman next to her—a striking young lady who stood out even next to Rocky. Jimmy seemed genuinely happy to see them.

"Great seeing you!" Jimmy exulted.

Rocky's austere yet elegant features were striking. At the moment, her petite, darkly painted lips were turned down in exasperation. She tugged at Gary's sleeve before turning her brown eyes on Jimmy. "James, help me out here. Gary's had three martinis and wants another." Gary looked like the cat who swallowed the canary.

Jimmy laughed. "If the man wants a drink, then let him have one. Or two. But no more, Gary. You're gonna ruin tomorrow's takes." Jimmy laughed.

"I need the blur of booze to get me through the days working with Fritz Lang," Gary slurred.

"Aw, come on. He can't be that bad," Jimmy said.

"Want to trade? Frank and me get along great," Gary offered.

"Thanks for nothin', James," Rocky said, arching her pencil-thin eyebrows, half-joking, half-serious.

"I'm just doin' my best, Rock," Jimmy said, then noticed the young woman with them.

Rocky's black hair, curled up at the ends, bobbed as she turned toward the young lady as well. "This is Gloria McLean, James. I mentioned to you earlier I wanted you to meet her. She's quite the fan. Ever since *Mr. Smith*," Rocky explained.

Evan knew she was referring to *Mr. Smith Goes to Washington*, which introduced Jimmy to the movie-going world in earnest.

Gloria looked at Jimmy demurely. Evan could tell she wasn't just putting it on. She was genuinely starstruck. Gloria didn't seem to belong in this crowd of perfectly made-up faces and plastic-surgery recipients; she radiated a genuine quality, just as Dorothy did. They both had that edge that made them stand out in the palm-tree-studded, fantasy land that was Los Angeles. Gloria's blonde hair was swept to the side, and she had an innocence about her that matched Jimmy's perfectly.

"Of course. I only saw the film for the first time last year, Mr. Stewart," Gloria said in a charming voice. "But I was hooked!" She smiled, and her lovely face, with its perfectly sized lips and long nose bobbed cutely at the tip, lit up like the sun. Her hair, sweeping down to her shoulders in a wave, was a light, straw-colored blonde that shined fetchingly.

"Now you go ahead and stop that Mr. Stewart stuff, young lady," Jimmy said in a drawl, his eyes glued on hers. "Jimmy'll do just fine. Mr. Stewart's my dad. I'm just plain, old Jimmy."

Evan immediately felt sparks fly between them. Evan knew Jimmy Stewart would marry her someday. It was exciting to be a fly on the wall for their first encounter. Clearly, the two of them just "fit" together perfectly from the start.

The night wore on. Evan, who remembered the old maxim "look like you belong," did so, mingling with starlets, would-be writers and directors, and the established elite of Hollywood. He shook hands with Clark Gable, Joan Blondell, Friz Freleng, Otto Preminger, Billy Wilder, Paulette Goddard, Laurence Olivier, and Fay Wray. Now immersed in the inner circle of a John Wayne party, Evan realized there were no hurdles to prove himself. He was among the Olympian deities, and everyone could take off the mask and not worry. They were, overall, nice and unpretentious, just ordinary people enjoying a party with other movie stars they shared a common bond with. They were all "in," and everyone else was "out." Evan knew very well what it meant to be the latter, being a perpetual outsider himself.

It was already past midnight, but considering the energy level of the crowd, Evan felt this party could go on well into the dawn. Evan saw Robert Walker, who later would go on to star in the phenomenal *Strangers on a Train* five years in the future. Walker was another GI who had returned from the war and was at present mostly known for his part in *Thirty Seconds Over Tokyo*. Walker had lost his wife, Jennifer Jones, to David O. Selznik, and Walker wasn't over it. Not by a long shot. Inebriated to the point of incoherence, Walker buttonholed Evan in a long conversation about life on Mars, the possibility of life on Venus, and whether or not the Earth had been visited by travelers from another world.

Evan finally escaped the strange conversation when Walker excused himself to the bathroom, where more than likely he was going to hurl. Evan shook his head. He had never been fond of alcohol. The idea of getting completely whacked out of one's mind and then spending the next two days recovering wasn't something he had any interest in exploring. To Evan, all liquor tasted like lighter fluid anyway.

Evan searched for Jimmy and saw him pulling the "Walker" treatment on Gloria McLean. He stood and listened as Jimmy sang "Danny Boy" and other numbers, then switched to a few vaudeville-style jokes, then offered her an overblown imitation of Ed Wynn, all while she smiled at him indulgently. As Jimmy started in on the Frank Sinatra hit "South of the Border," Gloria flashed a look of desperation Evan's way.

"Jimmy, let's get outta here," Evan said, gently taking him by the arm.

"Nah, party's just getting started, young man," he sang, then broke into an awkward jitterbug.

Evan winced. "Believe me," he muttered, "you want to leave now. You asked me to be your wingman, and the wingman gets his partner back to the airfield."

Evan tilted his head slightly to Gloria, now standing off by herself, bored and ignored. "If we make a graceful exit now, Jimmy, you can make amends later."

Jimmy stared, eyes slightly glassy as his liquor-muddled brain slowly processed Evan's suggestion. "Ya think so?"

"Sure of it," Evan said. "I'll say good night for us. Why don't you head back out front and call for the limousine?"

"Sure, good idea." Jimmy nodded as he wobbled through the garden gate.

Evan approached Ms. McClean, who turned to him and smiled. "Leaving so soon, my new friend?"

"Early day tomorrow."

"How is Jimmy?" she asked hopefully.

"Oh, he'll be fine. Just one too many," Evan said waving it off. "He's only like that when he gets nervous."

"Why was he so nervous?" she asked.

"Because of you, Gloria. You're beautiful. And he really likes you. I can tell."

Gloria smiled sweetly. "I like him too."

Evan raised his eyebrows. "So, you'll give him another chance? Like another date?"

"What girl could say no to a date with Jimmy Stewart?" she asked with complete sincerity.

"I'll let him know. Good night, and nice meeting you," Evan nodded to her and headed out to the limo.

Evan heard her say goodbye and hoped that in his own small way, he had set history on its right path and Jimmy Stewart on the way to the altar.

Evan was pleased to see Jimmy make it to their limo without wandering off-course. He got in next to Jimmy, settling into the dark, cushioned seat. The limo started, and they were back at Jimmy's home within eight minutes. Evan tipped the well-built but soft-spoken limousine driver, a Hispanic driver who was wearing a uniform clearly tailored for a much bigger man. The driver helped Evan get Jimmy into his house and into bed. Jimmy was asleep before he hit the pillow. Evan sighed. At least Jimmy had a late call tomorrow, unlike himself, which meant the star could sleep off what was sure to be one helluva bad hangover. Evan's heart went out to him.

Whatever fun he might have had back at Duke's house wasn't worth the headache, exhaustion, and bleariness that always came with overindulgence.

Evan abruptly realized he was exhausted. He had not slept in two days and was starting to hallucinate, seeing weird shadows where none should be. Evan headed to the guesthouse slowly to ensure he was going the right way as his senses were starting to betray him a little. He undressed and hit the sheets.

Feverish hallucinations immediately overwhelmed him; dreams came on like fireballs thrown from Zeus. Evan dreamed he was back in 2021, and Theodore Martin Huckabee, the mass shooter who was influenced by Evan's terrible trailer for *Rage* was seated across from Evan. Half of Huckabee's head was missing, and blood dripped from an open wound. He leaned toward Evan, a horrific grin on his face.

"I knew I'd find you somewhere," Huckabee mumbled, his eyes shining. "You can't hide, I'll follow you anywhere. I'm your biggest fan!"

Evan awoke with a start; tendrils seemed to hold him to the bed. He was paralyzed. He finally fought his way clear of the invisible ropes tying him down and sat up. He blinked in the darkness, which still seemed very alive with Theodore Martin Huckabee's presence. Evan realized he was still burdened by the killer's horrific actions.

Evan wiped the sweat off his face and leaned forward, catching his breath. Yes, it was guilt that had led him to do something as crazy as steal those film cans from the monstrous Connor Alcott, which in turn had led him here, to 1946. How, he still didn't know.

But Huckabee had set the wheel in motion. Gwen broke up with him, Connor desecrated *It's A Wonderful Life*, and then came the final trigger: Huckabee shooting nine people to death and wounding countless others, both mentally and physically. Some of those wounds would never heal.

Evan, exhausted beyond comprehension, fell back to sleep and saw Theodore Martin Huckabee again, and it wouldn't be for the last time.

"I'll follow you anywhere. I'm your biggest fan!" was all Huckabee ever said, but he just kept saying it. Evan dreamed he was with Jimmy at the Duke's party, and across the pool stood Huckabee, blood dripping, waving to Evan like a child. The dream switched to Huckabee in the editing room, peering over Evan's shoulder, flesh falling onto the long spools of film, smearing the masterpiece he was working on. Evan woke up panting after each dream. He was hoping for at least four hours of sleep that night but managed only about forty minutes before waking up at seven to get ready for work.

Hopefully, Huckabee wouldn't follow Evan to the editing room. That was the last thing he needed.

Evan swallowed hard as he got in his car and drove off.

CHAPTER 18

WEARING OUT THE WELCOME

Evan got to work a little after 8 a.m., and all he could think about was the image of Theodore Martin Huckabee at the end of his bed leering at him. He half-expected to look in the rearview and see him in the back or driving alongside him in the DeSoto that pulled up next to him at one of the stoplights along the way to the set. When Evan arrived, he walked in on Bill and Capra seated in the editing room having a quiet discussion while Bill spooled up the rushes from the most recent shooting days. Evan grabbed a cup of coffee (he still couldn't get over how good the coffee in 1946 was) and offered them a polite "Good morning." They watched the scene he had spliced together the day before; he waited for the inevitable torrent of criticism from Frank, but all he said was "Very nice."

Bill turned and pointed to Evan. "You got a knack, kid," he said. "And it was this kid who threaded it for us."

Frank looked at his editor. "Why don't you take ten, Bill? We'll pick up where we left off."

"Good enough," Bill said. He reached in his pockets for his Lucky Strikes and Zippo and headed out.

Capra walked up to Evan, studying him closely. Evan

waited, wishing he didn't wear his emotions on his sleeve.

Capra cocked his head. "Something on your mind, West?"

Evan closed his eyes and dove in. "Do you ever wonder, Mr. Capra, if your films affect people? You know, I mean, affect them negatively? Like, if they're watching folks on screen shooting other people?"

Capra frowned. "I don't think I follow."

"Well," Evan struggled, nearly spilling his coffee as he stood there. "I mean, look… I know movies are entertainment, but…" He paused, digging deep for the right words. "What I mean, is…suppose a kid somewhere saw this cop up there shooting at George Bailey and then got it into his head that shooting a gun was cool."

"Cool?" Capra shook his head, confused.

"I mean, slick. Nifty. Um, swell."

"Got it."

"And then he gets hold of a gun and hurts someone. How would you feel about that?"

Evan thought Capra would just wave him off. He was sounding a bit goofy. But instead, Capra scratched his head and nodded, sighing.

"I've wrestled with this problem before, West. It's not an easy one. The question I've asked in the past is how damaging is it for kids to emulate their movie war heroes by shooting off machine guns, playing dead, throwing grenades… They don't know the foulness of war, the finality of…the ungodly evil inherent to it. Because they're kids. It seems like high adventure."

Capra shoved his hands in his pockets and leaned against the edit table. "Are we responsible as filmmakers to regulate what we create? Arguably, all we do is imitate or recreate what has already transpired in the real world—except our version is all make-believe. No one dies, no one bleeds, and yet, are we to be held accountable for what we produce? Are we to be held up to judgment for how our stories may impact the young?"

Evan had no immediate answer. Not that he thought Capra expected one. He bit his lip and shook his head. "It is a question. Yes, indeed…"

Frank approached Evan with his devil eye for detail. "That you would ask such a question, a question from one so young and not yet fully indoctrinated in the scope of horror in the world, I must admit that leaves me curious."

Evan sensed where Frank was going. He decided not to evade the unspoken question. "Before I came here, a while back, I cut a trailer for a small movie. Back in a small town you've never heard of, for a small film company you've never heard of either."

"That's a questionable assumption," Capra smiled.

"But the bottom line," Evan pushed on, "is the trailer I made had some gratuitous violence in it that was pretty bad."

Capra remained silent, attentively listening. "Anyway," Evan continued, "we showed the trailer in the local theater in front of the larger picture about to play." Evan put down his coffee, thought back on what had happened, and shuddered. It was hard for him to hide his emotions. "Couple of days later, a kid sees my trailer—with lots of gunplay—and then goes off and shoots up a school classroom. When asked why he did it, the kid said…the trailer made him do it. Inspired him to take a gun and pull the trigger." Evan shuddered again. "Inspired. What a word to use for such a thing…"

Capra nodded. "And you're blaming yourself for that?"

"Who else is there to blame? He was inspired by my creation!" Evan knew he was borderline screeching, though Capra did not bat an eye. "A few days ago, I found ways of talking myself out of believing I was responsible in any way. But so much has changed now, and I believe *I've* changed."

Capra didn't move a muscle, but when he spoke, he could have brought down the walls of Jericho. "The problem with that kid was intrinsically who he was and had nothing to do with a movie clip. Did the boy have good parents? Was the father a drunk, a louse, on drugs? Do you know the answers to these questions?"

"No, but—"

"No buts. A kid who has no belief system of what is good and bad is a kid in trouble. Improving the individual, building up his moral fiber, his hopes, his aspirations, and offering him a more hopeful outlook on life is the only way to make that kid into a viable human being. That goes for a nation as well, and ultimately, a world."

Powerful words, and Evan knew they were true. He began to pace. Capra just stood there, waiting until Evan calmed himself and looked at the director.

"Can you ever foresee a time, Mr. Capra, where images of violence and wrongdoing are bombarding kids on a daily basis? Television, film, streaming twenty-four hours a day, desensitizing them to the consequences of their actions and subliminally teaching them how and with what equipment to kill to wreak havoc?"

Capra frowned. "Television. Yep, it's the newfangled thing. I predict it will be big ten years from now, but I don't know what streaming is. More of your technology you've read about?"

Evan nodded. "Something like that."

Capra took a moment, then looked at Evan with sincerity. "You're an odd kid, West. But to answer your question, such an assault on a kid's senses, day in and day out, could have profoundly dismal ramifications. Anger, despair…kind of like what George Bailey goes through in our script."

"George Bailey is a gentle man confronted with personal ruin and disaster. He's not a deranged sociopath," Evan countered.

"No, but despair is a dreadful thing and can manifest itself in many forms, violence being one. Suicide, another." Capra looked at the big screen at the end of the room. "That's why I'm making *The Greatest Gift*. Perhaps kind of along the lines of what we've been gabbing about. The war wore me out, wore the whole world out. Strickler, that bastard, and the studio lackeys think the world can't buy into old-fashioned schmaltz again, but…" He paused, turned to Evan. "But I'm not buyin' it. Life has a way of rebounding, turning itself around. By the way, I've thought of a new title. How does this sound?"

Evan spoke automatically: "*It's a Wonderful Life*."

Capra froze, staring at Evan as if he were an alien from Mars. "How did you know that? I've told no one!"

"Uh, well, you mentioned life just now and how turn-aroundish it is. The word 'wonderful' came to mind, and I made a lucky guess."

He chuckled. "Remarkable. Sometimes you scare me, West. You're strange but fun to have around."

"I love the new title," Evan said quickly. "Much better."

"I know." He nodded, then glared at Evan fiercely. "You feel guilty about that kid. Let me give you some advice."

"I'm listening."

"Do something about it!"

"How?" Evan stammered.

"Give the world something in return for that pain, which you think you've caused. Write something inspiring. I have the feeling you have that in you, Evan. Or…"

"Or?"

"Do something hopeless and reckless for a hopeless and reckless cause. The more hopeless and reckless, the better. But I gotta tell ya, Evan, you need to know you are not to blame for that crazy kid's actions. You got it? Forget about it. Dwelling on something like that can drive a man crazy."

Evan swallowed hard, his heart in his throat. Capra smiled, and Evan did the same.

Then the director's expression grew suddenly dark. "Now. I have one of my favorite meetings with Strickler, who, unlike us, has no conscience about what he owes to the world as long as it makes a buck, and he can deposit it in his already very full bank account." Capra turned on his heel and headed out.

"Mr. Capra," Evan called out to him. Capra stopped and looked back at Evan. "Don't let that creep ruin your film, sir."

Capra grinned. "I won't. But Strickler's a snake of the first order. If there's a way he can muck with it, he'll find it." Capra stopped and reached into his jacket. "Hell. Almost forgot." He held out some papers to Evan. "West, can you take these papers to business affairs? They're the copyright for *It's A Wonderful Life*, and they need to go through due process. Very important."

Evan took the papers, knowing just how important they were. "Yes, sir."

Capra looked at Evan. "I like you, kid. And don't feel like such a failure. Remember, no man is a failure..."

"Who has friends." Evan smiled.

Frank smiled bigger.

Evan headed directly over to Capra's office as opposed to business affairs. Evan knew if he followed Frank's instructions, Strickler would somehow get his hands on it and run wild, maybe even title the film something like *The George Baily Rampage.*

He was met again by the very severe Vera Stone, clacking away at her typewriter with gusto.

"And what may I do for you, Mr. West?" She gazed at him through her thick spectacles. "Aren't you supposed to be editing?"

"Yes, we are doing that, but if I may, could you do something for Mr. Capra? A favor?" he entreated.

Vera Stone folded her arms over her chest, wearing an expression that made it clear she wasn't fond of doing favors for anyone, not even her own boss.

Evan pushed on anyway. "Can you maybe run to the commissary and pick up some pastries for Mr. Capra and myself please?"

Vera Stone's face turned to stone. "Is this coming from Mr. Capra, or you?" she demanded.

Evan froze. "From me," he admitted after a beat. "Frank needs some refreshments. The guy is not happy right now. I figured anything we could do to make him happy..."

"Then why don't you get the pastries? It's not like I don't

have anything to do," Vera said very quickly, her face turning red with anger.

"That may be, but we're on a schedule, and…"

She snatched up her purse and swung it over her shoulder. "You could have gotten them yourself in the time it took you to walk over here and order me to do it. I know what you're up to, Mr. West, and I don't like it one bit."

She fired out of the office so fast, Evan was sure that he saw papers fly off her desk as she stormed past. As soon as she was gone, Evan knew he had to work quickly. He entered Capra's office and then looked down at the papers in his hand. He remembered Dorothy's words—the old Dorothy, that is, seventy-five years in the future at Hank's party.

"Did you know that because the paperwork was lost when the film was made, this movie fell into public domain in 1974?"

Evan knew it was up to him to keep this part of history intact. He walked over to Capra's desk, and then it hit him. This was Connor's desk! He saw the GEORGE LASSOS THE MOON mark near one side. Connor must have gotten it somehow after Capra vacated the RKO offices and it went into storage. Perfect. He noticed a small niche above one of the drawers large enough only to shove a wafer-thin paper or two. He jammed the papers inside the niche and shoved them forcefully until they were out of sight. Then he manipulated the paneling above and below to completely cover the crack. It was all so tightly fused, it would take a screwdriver to get in there and get the papers out.

And then he heard the voice from Hades.

"So. We meet again," Arthur J. Strickler said from the front door.

Evan snapped his head up and gazed at his enemy.

"Hello, Mr. Strickler. What may I do for you?" Evan asked, as bright and chipper as a man could be who had recently been kidnapped and almost shanghaied to Madagascar by order of the man standing in front of him.

"I was supposed to have a meeting with your boss, not that it's any of your business," Strickler said with oily disdain.

"He went looking for you," Evan responded dryly.

"Indeed? How's the editing going?" Strickler shifted gears in an apparent attempt at casualness.

"Very well. The movie will be perfect."

"Oh, I know that. Believe me, I do," he said, smiling that smile of his that made Evan vaguely nauseous. "Well, I'll be on my way. Perhaps Frank and I missed each other in transit."

Evan chose not to say anything; he just kept a steely eye on Strickler, very aware of how to conduct himself around a dangerous man. Strickler picked up on it and took two malevolent steps toward Evan. "This won't end well for you."

"It won't? Why on Earth not?" Evan lit up with a big smile that infuriated Strickler.

Strickler advanced until only the desk separated the two men. His eyes, as black as a tiger shark's, drilled into Evan's. He pointed a long finger. "I do have the right to final cut contractually," he mentioned, raising an eyebrow. "Just so you know."

After a brief stare-down between the two men, during which neither of them moved a muscle, Strickler spun on his heel and left the room, not bothering to close the door behind him. Evan looked down at the desk and patted it.

"Safe for posterity," Evan said to himself. As for Strickler…

he would remain a problem, one that would no doubt only get bigger with time.

Evan headed back out to the editing room. On the way, Coop ran up to him.

"We're in trouble," he said, panting.

"Why?"

Coop pulled him aside and motioned him closer. Evan leaned toward Coop as if they were making a drug deal.

"I think I know how to get us back," Coop began. "But it could kill us."

Evan was taken aback. He wasn't ready to go back and certainly wasn't ready to die trying.

"Are you sure?" Evan asked.

"Pretty sure. We'll only be able to go back to your time, but I'd rather go into the future than back to where I came from."

"Why not stay here?" Evan asked.

Coop nodded toward Arthur Strickler, who was loping his way toward the editing room. "That's reason one. Reason two? We're not supposed to be here. We're tampering with elemental forces of nature. Us being here is… It's wrong. Science does not tolerate aberrations, and right now, we're an aberration. If we stay, we're opening a door to the unknown, an unknown that's very dangerous."

Evan thought about what Coop was saying.

"Am I getting through to you?" Coop asked fervently.

Evan nodded. He thought of Dorothy, being in the regal presence of Frank Capra, and his burgeoning friendship with Jimmy Stewart and could not bear the thought of returning to 2021 and everything that went along with it: pandemics, canceling people for their political views, wokeness, the roiling anger and 24/7 pity party the United States indulged in, the politicization of art, sports, movies, music, Twitter and any social media, smartphones, streaming services, and the non-stop celebration of ignorance and stupidity. Rampaging mobs storming the US Capitol… no, he didn't want to go back. The very thought of it was like eating a huge bowl of broken glass.

"I don't want to go back," Evan declared.

Coop's frustration was immediate. Do you understand we cannot stay here?" he asked, raising his voice.

Evan wasn't budging. "I can't go back to 2021."

"And you can't stay here, Evan," Coop said with finality. "It's not allowed. I know you hate your own time. If I really thought long and hard about my own, I'm sure I'd conclude that I don't like it either. But we have to go back to where we belong. The two of us being here is about to upset something far bigger than we can contemplate. What that is, I can't say. For me to try and understand how big the universe is would be like an ant trying to decipher a skyscraper. However, I do understand there are certain rules that we're violating, and slowly but surely, you're about to see some changes to your own physicality. It, whatever 'it' is, wants us out."

This troubled Evan. "Explain."

"Okay, we're here, in an era we shouldn't be. At first, that's fine, but over time, things start to go wrong. Changes will happen because you're being attacked by, for lack of a better term, the universe's equivalent of white blood cells—antibodies that attack and destroy an infection. At present, we're an infection in this era. We should not be here. Time might tolerate us for a little while, but it will eventually spit us out."

"You've been here over two years," Evan pointed out.

"True, I have been, but as of last night, I'm colorblind. My right hand has no nerve sensations. I'm losing sensation in my feet, my hair is going gray, and my eyesight is dimming. In other words, I am aging rapidly."

Evan grimaced, looking over his friend and checking for gray hairs around his temple beneath his fedora. He spotted a few but shook his head stubbornly. "That could be from anything."

"Since when does something like this happen to someone?" Coop asked, eyes fierce. To Evan's surprise, He removed his shoe and sock and stood awkwardly, balancing on one leg just enough to raise his other foot to reveal the problem. To Evan's surprise, a sixth toe was growing next to Coop's small toe.

Evan's jaw dropped.

Coop, despite his balancing act, managed to hold Evan's gaze. "One could postulate what else is about to go awry, Evan. But the final conclusion is: We can't stay here."

Evan was shocked and backed away. He saw a nearby bench against a wall and collapsed on it. After a second, he held his breath and yanked his own shoe off. So far, so good—no sixth toe. Evan exhaled in relief.

But God only knew what else might be happening to his body. If Coop's theory was correct, the longer he stayed here, the more deterioration would occur.

"Have you noticed anything different about your physicality, and I would also include your mental state, since you've been here?" Coop asked.

Evan thought long and hard and knew he had to tell the truth. "Okay, I'll come clean.... I've been seeing things."

Coop cocked an eyebrow. "Continue."

"I keep seeing someone from 2021, a killer…. I can see and feel his presence. Heck, I can even smell the guy."

Coop seemed fascinated. "I envy you, Evan West. I'd far prefer mental hallucinations to colorblindness and a sixth toe. But either way, the great guardian we call time will not allow us to stay here without consequences."

"How do we get back?" Evan asked. When Coop told him, he wished he hadn't asked. They headed to the sound stage together. Going into the editing room was not an option with Strickler in there. Evan could only inhale poisonous fumes for so long, and he's already taken enough drags from Strickler's foul carbon monoxide for one day.

Coop explained what would be needed to take them to 2021.

It would be dangerous and physically grueling, and it had a high chance of not working.

But they had to try.

All they were waiting for was the right weather.

CHAPTER 19

UNTHINKABLE BUT NECESSARY

Coop and Evan made it to the sound stage just before Capra called, "Action." Evan waved to Dorothy, who stood out in the rear of a crowd scene near where Jimmy and Donna Reed stood by the Christmas tree. She looked so pretty and excited to be part of the film. Evan again took special delight over the fact that he was responsible for her getting the part—with Jimmy's help, of course.

Evan waved at Jimmy, and he gave him a thumbs-up, wiping his brow and shaking his head as if to say, *What a night.*

The scene was shot in a few takes, with close-ups of Jimmy, of course, followed by two shots of both Jimmy and Donna, and then a wide-angle master including the whole town in Jimmy's living room. At the end, everyone broke out in the familiar "Auld Lang Syne" song. Finally, an insert shot of the little angel on the Christmas tree, and Jimmy's final line ended the movie.

A moment later, Capra called out: "Cut! And print!"

Dorothy ran off set and hugged Evan, just as Bill the AD called out, "That's a wrap for the day, folks. Tomorrow, 7:30 a.m. call time, Stage 5. Thank you!"

Evan squeezed Dorothy's arm and leaned toward her. "Want to have dinner with me tonight?"

"More than anything else in the world," She said and froze a little in surprise as Evan kissed her. She melted, returning the kiss, then held his eyes as he pulled away. She blushed a little as Jimmy ambled up to them.

"How are you feeling, Jimmy?" Evan teased.

"You want it harsh or sugar-coated?" He smiled and winked at Dorothy.

"C'mon," Evan prodded.

"I feel like I have a bull kicking me in both the stomach and the head, and I'm about to explode," he said.

"Is it too late to get it sugar-coated?" Dorothy asked.

"That *was* sugar-coated," Jimmy said, then looked at Evan. "How did it look from out here?"

"Jimmy, it was outstanding," Evan praised with full sincerity. "It will be one of the great scenes of the movie, a real tear-jerker. I look forward to cutting some of it. If Mr. Capra lets me."

Dorothy grabbed Evan's hand. "Back in a jiff. It was beautiful, Mr. Stewart, I mean, Jimmy." She turned to Jimmy quickly for one last look and then ran off.

Evan and Jimmy both watched her go, a vision of loveliness. Jimmy nudged Evan.

"So, you gonna make an honest woman outta that girl, or what?"

Evan reddened. "What? You mean marriage?"

"Well, you don't have to make it so gol-darn grim, doggone it." He chuckled. "She's awful pretty, and something tells me no one better's gonna come along."

Evan sighed. "It's not really like that, Jimmy…"

"Kid," he said. "I may not be the best judge of character, but that girl is smitten with you." He winked and slapped Evan on the shoulder, then moved up as Capra approached.

Capra's eyes moved to Evan. "Papers taken care of, West?"

"Absolutely," Evan assured. "Safe and sound."

"Excellent. Now. I've made an executive decision."

"What's that, sir?"

"I'm gonna give you credit in the movie. Editing associate, or something like that. I'm sure the union won't mind."

Evan thought back to what Coop said: "*We're an infection on this era. We should not be here.*" And then he realized he was inserting himself in history that for all intents and purposes was already written. He was altering the chain of events and the film by having his name in the credits. God only knew what kind of chain reaction that would set off in the sequence of things. Or worse, maybe he'd grow a third eye or even a second nose.

"Mr. Capra, I think that's a grand gesture, and I appreciate it, but I'd like to remain anonymous on this movie."

"But you were of great help to the picture. Still are. Not only on the editing side but creative too," he said. "Post-production rules—everyone who's anyone knows that, and your name on this picture… Why, it's only fair!"

"I have my reasons, sir," Evan said softly.

Capra looked at him for a moment and shook his head. "You're a strange fellow, Evan. But I've done a few strange things myself in my day. Suppose every man has. All right, I'll respect your wishes, and if you're hiding from the law, Jimmy here will be the first to turn you in." Frank went to the assistant director to go over some paperwork.

Jimmy approached Evan, a bashful grin on his face. "Evan, about last night," he began. "That girl. Gloria. She say anything to you about me after I left?"

"I know she wants to see you again," Evan told him.

"She said that?" Jimmy beamed.

"Told me she could hardly wait."

"Wow. Even after I made a horse's—"

"Yep, even after that." Evan laughed.

"Well, okay then." Jimmy turned to go, then looked to Evan. "Thanks for being my wingman, pal, and getting me back to base."

Evan smiled. "Anytime."

Dorothy approached. Evan laughed as he could hear Jimmy whistling *Buffalo gals, won't you come out tonight.*

"What's so funny?" she asked, smiling.

Evan looked at her and laughed again. "Everything. Now, you and me, let's go out for dinner, what do you say?"

"Where?"

"How about a place I know called Dorothy's Eats? A nice, home-cooked meal… Did your mom make another pie?"

"That's presumptuous of you, Evan, inviting yourself over like that," Dorothy teased.

"Best food in town. How could I turn that down?"

"I'll go get the car," she said and smartly stepped out of the room, all class. Evan watched her go, thinking, *Some people have more than they bargained for, and Dorothy has it in generous quantities.*

"I'll follow you!" Evan shouted, and she gave him a thumbs-up.

Evan headed toward the rear of the sound stage, then froze as a horrible thought hit him out of the blue. He remembered that Connor, seventy-five years in the future, had the atrocious reels of the movie. Evan now knew Strickler must have succeeded in duplicating and re-editing the film. Evan's heart sank. Nothing Evan did in this present time would change the inevitable—Strickler would win at the end of the day because time and events are absolute.

Evan peered into a darkened corner of the stage and saw the shape of a man sitting on an apple box. Evan looked closer. It was Huckabee. He was just sitting there, staring, not saying a word.

"I'm going insane," he said aloud. Evan was an aberration whose time was running out.

While Evan followed Dorothy toward her house that lovely early evening, Evan kept thinking about his conversation with Coop—and more importantly, what he was going to do to try to stop Strickler's plan to destroy *It's A Wonderful Life* and turn Frank Capra and Jimmy Stewart into national laughingstocks.

There were several options open to Evan; he could kill Strickler, but that wasn't really an option as he wasn't a killer. And as bad as Strickler was, he didn't deserve to be murdered. Secondly, Evan could go to Capra and warn him of Strickler's evil plan, but then Capra would think he was certifiable. He already felt Evan had a few screws loose. Third, Evan could steal the final master of the movie and make sure Strickler never got his grubby hands on it.

Evan stepped out of his car and strolled over to Dorothy's window.

"Penny for your thoughts?" Dorothy looked to Evan briefly, her dainty hands on the wheel.

"Nothing," Evan said. "I was just thinking how beautiful you looked today on set."

"How romantic." She smiled. "And sweet."

"And true."

Richie exploded through the front door and ran to his mother.

"Mommy!" he yelled happily. He then ran to Evan and hugged him. "Evan, I think I might like you now," Richie said very matter-of-factly.

Evan was too overwhelmed to do anything except embrace the boy back. "Good to see you again, tiger."

Dorothy reached for one of Evan's hands while Richie got the other. They walked toward the open door, where Mrs. Paige was waiting for them, smiling.

"Evening, ma'am," Evan said.

"Evan, lovely to see you again," she replied, standing aside to let the trio in.

Dinner was served half an hour later, a sumptuous meal of pork chops and mashed potatoes, which just so happened to be one of Evan's favorites.

Grace was particularly memorable as Richie was the one who said it for the family.

"Dear God, thank you for the food. And thank you for Evan."

Evan turned glum when he heard his name in prayer. He knew he could not stay there and might end up losing his life in his effort to leave. Under the table, Dorothy squeezed his hand.

Later that night, they played Monopoly, which was regularly interrupted by Rancher, who would often zoom into the room barking and then topple the board and pieces. Evan pondered, *Was this what it felt like to have a real family?* He kept stealing looks at Dorothy, flirting at close quarters. Everything felt thrilling and nostalgic. That night, Evan wanted more than ever to stay in 1946 forever, make a go of it there.

But that was impossible.

For now, he contented himself with pretending and was lucky enough to get a Monopoly on Boardwalk and Park Place. He sold them to Dorothy for Baltic and Mediterranean Avenue, then pretended he was cash poor. He'd rather lose to Dorothy than lose her. The harsh reality was, he was going to have to.

It was unthinkable but necessary.

CHAPTER 20

99-PERCENT PERSPIRATION

Coop sat in one of his tiny chairs, pondering his equipment and current dilemma…and was positive the area at Cahuenga and Lakeridge was a "special area," a place where the Earth's magnetic field was porous, or thin. He was also fairly certain that if they hit a certain rate of speed during an electric storm and hit the same pole, or at the very least, passed into that area at that speed, even without hitting the pole, they would propel themselves into another time. But which time would that be? He was working with very primitive tools, trying to replicate an experiment that was an accident—not just any accident but a freak accident. With science, the only way to solve problems, he knew, was to conduct experiments over and over and then replicate the results over and over.

Coop frowned. *But how does one replicate a freak accident?*

A dark thought entered Coop's mind: What if he was dead wrong, more wrong than he'd ever been about anything? What if they hit 80 mph in the rain, swerved, smashed into a pole, and both ended up the subjects of a police crime photo?

Coop rubbed his eyes, then abruptly stood up, dashed to his Dodge, started the engine, and tooled over to Cahuenga and Lakeridge. He parked and walked in a slow radius around the area, glancing occasionally up at the newly repaired power lines. He sensed there was something here. He could feel it—a certain energy, a vibration in the air.

This was it. Coop had been here a thousand times, and every time he stood in this spot, he could feel it—and taste it. A strange, coppery taste that coated his tongue every time he stood right there.

This was it, had to be!

The problem lay in how to re-open the door. Coop thought he had the solution. Speed, plus energy…an energy at an exceptionally high level. That would get them through to some other time.

They had to go. They didn't belong there.

Coop would have to use Evan's car. Coop's Dodge couldn't reach the speeds necessary. They needed an electrical storm—a rarity in LA. Then they could ram the car right through the time portal to…who knows where.

The more Coop rolled the problem over in his mind, the more convinced he became that they could do it.

Coop crossed his arms, staring daringly up at that infamous pole. *To heck with the consequences!* He'd construct something transportable that could generate enough power to open the portal.

Coop rubbed his chin, hitting another mental snag. *How could a device built with only commercially available 1946 technology hold that much power?*

Coop sighed. He'd just have to work on it night and day; sleep was not a luxury either of them could afford. Their time was running out.

Having grown up in a church-going family, Coop had always tried to find faith and the voice of God wherever he could.

He looked up at the sky, closed his eyes, and thought:

So…is this the place, God? Am I correct?

Thunder boomed in the distance. Coop's ears perked up; he felt rain falling. This was it. He had to go now! He hurried to his car and drove toward Evan in Beverly Hills.

Coop roused Evan from his sleep at 2 a.m. Light rain was falling, and the forecast called for more precipitation.

"This is our chance," Coop said for the second or third time, sitting tensely in the passenger side of Evan's Ford as Evan drove them through the wet streets. "We have to try now."

Evan stared glumly at the road ahead. He glanced in his rearview and saw a pile of Coop's steampunk electrical equipment jumbled in the back, held together by thick, rubber-coated cabling. Coop reached back, turned to the biggest machine in the pile, and switched it on. It began to glow.

They made their way east on Sunset and passed over Fairfax, which Evan noticed in 1946 was just as sleepy as it was in 2021. The glow from Coop's machines lit the car up in warm colors.

Evan glanced nervously at the luminescent metal humming directly behind them. "What do those do?"

"Interesting question. They tap into the Los Angeles power grid and, using electromagnetic forces, build up enough energy to take us through the portal," Coop explained. "I'm not sure it will work, but we must try."

A fork of lightning lit up the sky, but this storm wasn't

near as charged as the storm from 2021 that propelled Evan into 1946.

"Shouldn't we wait for a bigger storm? I mean, this is far from the storm I passed through in," Evan mentioned a little desperately because, in his heart of hearts, he hoped this wouldn't work. He could maybe deal with Huckabee, maybe learn to like him….

Or worse, he could start seeing more apparitions and slowly be driven insane. He'd seen enough horror movies to know how things worked once you pass through forbidden doors. Evan's heart pounded hard. He could feel the electricity in the air.

"Okay, Evan. Let's hope we don't burst into flames when I hit this switch," Coop muttered. Before Evan could object, he flipped said switch. The entire car began to glow red. Evan could feel heat and prepared to bail out. He glanced out the window—just in time to see all of the stoplights go out in unison.

"Well…this should be interesting," Evan said through slightly gritted teeth, and not too far behind him came the first car accident—a boom of glass and steel. He passed through the LaBrea and Sunset intersection, barely missing an oncoming 1931 LaSalle. He dodged several more cars as he made his way east, his Ford looking like quite a spectacle as it glowed orange through the streets of Hollywood, barely dodging the few cars out at this hour. They hit Cahuenga, and Evan swung north. The weight of the machines dragged the car down, slowing their progress.

"Evan, here we go," Coop said, voice intense. "I need you to get the car to 80 to 85 mph *now!*"

Evan floored it and had to chuckle a little. This was just like *Back to the Future* except without the DeLorean. The car was sluggish, hard to handle. Coop turned around and hit another switch. The machines grew hotter.

Not one house or streetlight shone—Coop had sucked every kilowatt of power from the Hollywood area, maybe beyond. Evan loved the insanity of it and sped the car up. The V-8 was singing as his foot prodded the pedal down…70, 75…80.

"Here we go!" Coop shouted.

Evan got it up to 88; he could see the light pole up ahead, but it was dark. No giant portal of electricity, no spectacular lightshow. He could feel the car hydroplaning. He corrected the skid, but nothing otherworldly was happening this time.

"Watch out!" Coop shouted, and Evan did exactly that. He steered the car away from the pole, slowed, and finally braked. They waited. Nothing happened.

No bright flash of light, no electrical excitement. The machines in the back were humming but otherwise seemed dormant.

Evan steered the car toward Lakeridge and parked. "Wanna try again?" he asked. Above, there was no lightning, just a thin sheen of oily mist that covered the streets and landscape.

"Well, that was a disappointment," Coop grumbled. "Let's chalk this one up to my over-enthusiasm and not really understanding the problem. Shall we return home?"

"Let me help you unload all this, and whatever I can do to help you with these incredible machines, I will do."

Coop took him up on it. They returned to Coop's house on Clarissa and Evan helped Coop unload the machinery.

Once inside, Evan assisted Coop in hooking back up all the machines to prepare for the next round of experimentation.

"Evan, pass me the Phillips. Let me show you how all this works together," Coop offered, and for the next three hours, Evan got a crash course in quantum physics, energy, and Tesla's velocity squared times mass/length. Most of it went over Evan's head, but Coop's impressive explanation made him realize that Coop had missed his calling; he would have made a magnificent university professor.

They ended their day with a Coca-Cola toast to their next attempt.

"When do you think we could try this again?" Evan asked.

Coop shrugged and smiled. "Weeks, maybe months. Who knows?"

For weeks, Frank, Bill, and Evan lived, breathed, and ate *It's A Wonderful Life* eighteen hours a day. The studio had instituted a fierce deadline on completion of the picture, and while exhaustion had set in for many on the team, Evan was thrilled to be a part of history in the making.

The day finally came when Capra put his seal of approval on the final product, and this was, of course, when Evan became the most concerned. Strickler had remained conspicuously invisible throughout the editing process, and though he had threatened to decide the final cut, he never made an appearance in the editing room, never sent notes or called with suggestions…nothing.

In Evan's mind, this could only mean he was working in stealth and was planning his sneaky next move.

Evan drove home from the studio that day filled with a huge sense of relief and wondered if all filmmakers felt like this when their picture was locked. A big moment for everyone except the composer and sound editors who then had to weave their own special magic over the final picture. He pulled up to Jimmy's house, cranked the emergency brake up, ambled to the front door and knocked. Jimmy opened the door, flashed a rather anemic grin, and motioned for Evan to enter.

Evan frowned. "Something bothering you, Jimmy? You look a little down."

"Gloria," Jimmy stammered. "I—she—she accepted a date proposal from me, and…"

"That's great! I told you!"

"Yes, you did, Evan. You did at that," he stuttered.

"But?"

"But…I don't know where I should take her. You know, to impress her. First date and all."

Evan nodded. "Ah. Yes. Good point."

Jimmy looked to Evan expectantly, waiting for suggestions. So, Evan ticked off the usual suspects. "Uh, Musso and Franks is nice."

"Naw, too Hollywood. Too obvious." Jimmy waved this off quickly.

"Chasens?"

"Too Beverly Hills. I want to impress her, make her think I know something everyone else doesn't, you know, the 'Jimmy knows about cool, out-of-the-way places' thing."

"Jimmy…"

"Yeah?"

"El Cholo, over on Western," Evan said. "It's like being in a Carmen Miranda movie. Not many of the usual Hollywood types hang there. It's subtle, romantic, and has authentically Mexican food."

"Romantic. Right." Jimmy nodded. "Good thinking. Not too spicy, is it? I got a weak stomach, you know. A souvenir from the war."

"There are alternatives on the menu, carne asada, a basic steak with some rice and beans that shouldn't tear up your gut too much."

"Yeah, by golly, I'm a meat and potatoes man myself. That just might do it." Jimmy smiled, suddenly his old self again. He set the drink down and walked over to his phone, dialing a number. "Gloria? It's me. Jimmy. Jimmy Stewart. Listen, I came up with a perfect spot for us for dinner tonight."

Again, Evan congratulated himself on being not only a part of 1946 movie-making history but a 1946 matchmaking legend as well.

Jimmy hurried upstairs to get dressed.

Evan glanced at himself in the mirror that hung beside the stairs and noticed something alarming; his dark brown hair was going gray at the temples. He had wrinkles under his eyes, and he looked tired.

Old.

Evan straightened up, shook his head, and looked again. Same wrinkles, gray hair, and look of exhaustion. Coop was right. They had to get out of this time, and the sooner the better.

Coop paced before his enormous Dr. Frankenstein-like machines, his mind in knots. When he took long, late-night walks, he could conjure things in his head, solve complex problems. Coop poured himself a glass of water, broke a tray of ice, and savored the liquid. One thing he loved most about 1946 was refrigeration and the freezing mechanism above the main cooler. Ice. The glory of ice. Yes, ice was available in the 1800s but was always in short supply. The ice man would come, Coop could enjoy his cold drinks, and within a few days, the ice would melt in the older "icebox" he had owned. It was expensive and unreliable, the worst of combinations.

Coop stepped outside onto Clarissa Avenue and breathed in the fragrant Los Angeles air. In April, the hyacinth bloomed, and its scent graced the warm city. Coop made his way east, stopped at North Hoover, and then made a right. It was already quiet at 8 p.m. Los Angeles was an early to bed, early to rise town with a few late-night spots, but for the most part, it was a well-constructed mining town. People came here to get rich and either re-invent themselves or move back to where they came from, healthier and wealthier but not wiser.

Coop knew how to get away from the current time period, which would be the equivalent of leaping out of the boat they were in (using the river analogy), scaling the high bank, and scrambling over onto the other side. The last experiment was a failure, but the more he thought about it, the more he felt it had been due to lack of energy. He couldn't build up enough pure voltage to break the membrane of the portal, even while drawing from Los Angeles' combined power. He needed fire from the heavens, the electrical fireworks of the Almighty. The earlier storm was puny, not enough ions in the air. They could not do this jump without God, and Coop would have to allow his faith to guide him.

The inherent problem was: When and where would they be deposited? In 1348 Europe, with the Black Plague raging and the living hell that was the Middle Ages? Or what if they wound up in 1940 Poland with a brutal Nazi occupation underway? Considering Coop's skin tone, a concentration camp would likely be his final destination.

Coop hung his head, hating that he didn't know what to do.

CHAPTER 21

THE GLORY IS FLEETING

Arthur J. Strickler lounged in his Hancock Park Mansion on Ridgewood Place and stared out the front window. Evening was coming on, and as always, his mind was unsettled.

He lived alone with the exception of a maid who came to clean up his dinner plates and wash his windows. A Japanese gardener came by once a week to trim his enormous hedges and mow his impeccable lawn. He had no dog to keep him company nor cat to lounge on a nearby pillow. He preferred the silence at home save for a large, grandfather clock that ticked away every minute he was convinced had escaped him, leading to his inevitable death—the one thing he could not control.

Strickler thought about Capra and that meddlesome kid Evan West, and then he thought back to his old business partner again. He didn't know why he kept thinking about crooked Pete Flannery, but for some reason, the man clung to his brain like a leech. Strickler stood and took a walk across his living room as the evening shadows came on from the picture window. He stared at the framed presentation of his medals, and the memory of the day he met Pete Flannery came back again.

Strickler had been wounded, bleeding, but had managed to walk five miles back from the battlefield. Pete spotted Strickler first and rushed over to him. The medics got him water and a cup of coffee, and Flannery helped carry Strickler to the aid station where Strickler ended his great war service.

Flannery stayed with Strickler and made sure he was sent back to a military hospital in Paris, and they promised to stay in touch.

Flannery had big plans to start a construction company in Los Angeles and was looking for men to go into business with—veterans and survivors like Strickler. A partner like that could go a long way.

Strickler came back to the United States as a decorated Marine. Purple Heart, the Navy Cross, and the Croix de Guerre from the French government.

He thought back to how he later found Pete Flannery in Los Angeles. Together, they incorporated Strickler/Flannery Construction and went to work. Over the course of the 1920s, Strickler was married, had a son, and got divorced after the company folded in 1929.

Strickler was destined never to see his son again. The boy died in 1932 from pneumonia, and in 1933, his wife drank herself to death in Chicago with a mountain of debts and a trail of broken hearts behind her.

In 1928, when Strickler was still riding high with his construction company, the bank manager discovered discrepancies in the company's accounting ledgers. Strickler was asked to take a look at the books with an accountant, and that's when he experienced his second and perhaps more deadly trauma: His trusted partner Pete Flannery had embezzled from the company over the years. For the first time since 1919, when they began the company, they couldn't meet payroll. Strickler put in his own money to cover payroll and new construction, and when he confronted Pete Flannery, the situation deteriorated farther than he could have imagined. Not only did Flannery deny the accusation, he also blamed Strickler and threatened to sue him for malfeasance. Strickler left the meeting, drove home, got his M1911 service pistol, drove back to Flannery's house, and shot the man in cold blood. After he killed Flannery, Strickler dumped his body into a tub of wet cement and poured the sloshing gray liquid stone into the foundation of what would someday be the Mayfair Supermarket on Hyperion Avenue.

No one ever asked about Pete Flannery, and Strickler's assurances to anyone who asked was that Pete had stolen a lot of cash from the company and skipped town—and that was the end of that. No police investigation, no inquiries from relatives. Pete had no friends that he could tell; no one cared about him one way or the other. He was better off dead, and Strickler was a lot worse off broke.

Strickler/Flannery Construction folded in 1929, Arthur's wife had left him with their son, and he faced a mountain of debt and unpaid bills. He paid off every employee he owed wages to from his own accounts, obliterating ten years of built-up savings. He moved from his home in the Hollywood Hills and started over as a construction foreman at Republic Studios. He built one Old West town after the other using the same crews he once utilized in his own company, starting over as any survivor would.

In 1931, because the movie business was literally the wild

west, Strickler was asked to help produce a series of "singing cowboy" movies starring the then-unknown John Wayne. From there, he was given an office at Republic and more assignments, moving from Gene Autry films to cops and robbers movies—mostly two-reelers—but by 1936, he was hired at Universal to produce *Dracula's Daughter*, his first full-length feature. The film did so well that the Universal front office then hired him to produce *The Phantom Rider* and *Ride 'Em Cowboy*. Strickler built up a reputation as a penny-pinching, hard-charging executive who gave directors a lot of leeway and was able to deliver a good product on time, on budget, and without complications. He wasn't known for his wit or conversation, he wasn't liked or invited for golf at the Toluca Lake Country Club with Bing Crosby, but he was reliable. Strickler made money, accrued power, and kept to himself, putting distance between himself and the Hollywood drama that occurred every day. He never complained and kept his nose to the grindstone.

Strickler looked to men like Jack Warner and Harry Cohn as his idols. Like him, they were ruthless and hungry, willing to do whatever it took to impose their will on others. Arthur had already killed; the act meant nothing to him. He never gave life a second thought. Like Stalin said, *"Death solves all problems. No man, no problem.* Arthur J. Strickler was a man who would look up to Stalin.

Strickler still cursed the god that gave him a second chance because, with every business associate he encountered, he saw the German who brained him with his Mauser or Pete Flannery. They were all out to get him. Unless he got them first.

When Pearl Harbor was attacked in December 1941, Strickler saw an opportunity with so many young executives, directors, and actors joining the war effort. He had no interest in serving the United States; he'd already fought his war for Uncle Sam. From now on, his wars were his own, on battlefields he chose. No more charging up Hill 142 with a bunch of green, eager Marines. From now on, he would lead the charge up Hill 142 with a brigade of tanks, poison gas, and artillery all of his own making. He would lose no battles and win every war. There was such a vacuum of executives, Arthur was able to take his pick of empty desks to fill. In March 1942, he first chose to work for "David O. Selznick ("a drug-addicted, pathetic skirt-chaser" was how Strickler summed him up), and then he went on to RKO, where he found he pretty much could run the place as he chose.

He would make movies that he chose, too, and he chose to make movies that depicted life as he saw it. If anyone needed an education on the bitterness of life, Arthur J. Strickler was the man to teach that lesson. He never forgot Ernie Rodriguez, Merle Olson, Sam Miller, Alfred Spencer, Steve Brill, Reed Hastings, Peter Beinhardt, Richard Sears, and John Hastings all faceup, rotting under a French sky fighting a war that only made the world a worse place to live. They lived for everything and died for nothing.

Arthur J. Strickler, a bitter, powerful, and lonely man, had chosen his one task on Earth: to make sure everyone saw how deplorable life could be. He knew the reach of motion pictures, their power. He knew he could easily control the vast audiences that lined up every day to see Hollywood's latest product wash over them. He now had the opportunity of a lifetime; Hollywood's greatest "feel-good" director was now working for him. In his own little way, Arthur J. Strickler was about to steer the world his way. He would wave his wand and magically evaporate optimism and dreams, leaving behind a planet inhabited by men and women like himself. In some ways, he was very much like Mr. Potter (his favorite character in the story), and in time, he'd remake the world into a Pottersville of his own.

He paced the floor and schemed. For whatever reason, the Evan West that suddenly appeared on the set of *It's A Wonderful Life* was a new opponent, the likes of which he'd never faced before. Something about that kid bothered him to his core, but he couldn't put his finger on it. He couldn't stop him, couldn't cajole or bribe him. That he already knew.

He'd have to banish him to the same concrete foundation Pete Flannery now slept, the sooner the better. The very thought of that made Strickler happy. Not overly so because Strickler didn't know true joy, but the idea did hold a hint of satisfaction for him, and that was all he needed to keep going.

While Strickler was scheming, Evan was alone in Jimmy's house. He went to the refrigerator and made himself a ham sandwich, poured a glass of water from the tap (and this, sadly, tasted strange—even 1946 LA had bad tap water), and contemplated while he ate. The movie was finished. He'd been blessed to have been a small part of it, he'd fallen deeply in love with Dorothy, and although he'd been here for several weeks, he knew he had to go back to…where? Where would he go?

Evan could only trust that Coop would somehow figure out how to make it happen. Evan was no scientist; he was a film geek and a darned good editor, but science eluded him.

Evan made his way back to his guesthouse but then stopped, spying a shadowy figure ahead of him standing in the door to the guesthouse, a big grin on his face. Evan didn't have to venture farther to see who this was: Theodore Martin Huckabee, beckoning him. Evan shook his head to clear the vision, hoping it was just a dream or mirage.

But no. There he was, Theodore Martin Huckabee, or at least a pretty good facsimile of him. Evan tried to rationalize why he'd seen this ghoul two nights in a row and realized it must be because this was what Coop was talking about. "*We don't belong here*," Coop had told him, and rather than growing a sixth toe, Evan could see visions of lost souls who were trapped in the timeless void, and they weren't benign; these souls were out to drive him mad.

"Damned good work you did on that trailer, West," Huckabee said, grinning ghoulishly, face splattered in blood. "It got me going!"

Evan was not about to go anywhere near the guesthouse. No way. He stood there, weighing his options.

"You want to come talk with me? I want to know how you know me so well. I mean, your work touched me, man. Got my motor going."

Evan backed away from Theodore Martin Huckabee, hoping he would vanish, hoping against hope he would somehow fade back into the rippling currents of time.

"What's the matter, you too good for me, West?" His hideous grin started to slide down, turning into an angry scowl. "Before you turn your back on me and go back into Stewart's house to hide, I think you need to know something."

Evan held his tongue; the last thing he needed to do was engage evil. He knew that much from the countless horror movies he'd watched over the years. Once evil called your name, if you engaged, it never let you go.

"You think you're above me, West, but let me tell you something, and I want you to remember this forever: You and me, we're alike. If you had half a chance, you'd shoot Arthur Strickler and Connor Alcott, but it wouldn't be from some obscure ambush point. You'd do it up close and personal so you could see the fear in their eyes."

Evan had heard enough. He backed up against Jimmy's door and opened it hastily, closing it behind him with a bang. Evan glanced over his shoulder and through the window. Huckabee was still there, staring at him. Then he made an obscene face, his tongue rolled out, eyes open wide. It chilled Evan to his marrow; he'd never forget that face for the rest of his life.

He made his way into the kitchen again and turned on the small Philco Jimmy had on the counter. *The Jack Carson Show* was on; Jack's distinctive voice was wisecracking about the strange relatives that came by to visit his house on 22 North Hollywood Lane. Evan peered out the back window. Huckabee seemed to be gone, if he had indeed ever been there. Either Evan's mind was playing tricks on him, or he was losing it. Probably both. He felt himself getting sleepier, the overwhelming "newness" of being where he was fatigued him. Still, he had no intention of going back to the guesthouse.

Evan walked into the living room, more asleep than awake now. He stumbled to a large, comfortable leather chair, sank into it, and drifted into an uneasy slumber.

He was awakened by the sound of the front door opening, then closing, then uneven footsteps. Evan stood up, brushed himself off, and tried to look presentable. Jimmy noticed Evan and gave him an offhand wave.

"Hello, Evan, old boy, old pal," Jimmy said, speech slurred. "Sit down, have a drink."

Evan quickly ascertained that Jimmy was far more inebriated tonight than at the party at John Wayne's. It wasn't like him, Evan knew that much. Jimmy wasn't exactly the drinking type; Bogart, Huston, Cooper, Wayne, yes. Jimmy, no. It looked wrong on him, like wearing a bright green suit with a yellow tie.

Jimmy weaved his way over to the bar and poured three fingers of Pinch Scotch. He handed it to Evan, then poured himself four. He gulped it back and plopped down in a chair across from him.

"I never asked you this before but I might as well: What did you do over there in the war, kid?" Jimmy asked.

"Nothing like you, Jimmy. It's a long story but nothing like what you went through."

"I respect that," Jimmy said, nodding absently. "Better than being over there. It was the worst thing…worst thing you could imagine." Jimmy knocked back his drink, finishing half the glass in three gulps. "You see, I was Eighth Air Force," he explained. Evan nodded—he knew. "I commanded the 703rd Bomb Squadron. We flew B-24s, a beast of a plane. You know the B-24? Flying that bus gives you a big left arm, holding the yoke with one hand, controlling the throttles with the other." Jimmy demonstrated, holding out his left hand and making his right a claw, pretending to hold onto four engine throttles. "I was appointed operations officer of the 453rd Bomb Group, and later, the chief of staff for the Second Combat Wing, Second Air Division of the Eighth. Any of that ring a bell?"

Evan nodded again. "I knew you were a pilot in the war, wasn't sure of which unit. But you flew over Germany?"

A haunted look passed over Jimmy's face. He finished his drink, got up to reload. "Sure, sure. I flew over Germany. Eighth was based outta England. We had some missions over occupied France, Holland, Belgium, and yeah, Germany."

"How many combat missions did you fly?" Evan asked.

Jimmy sipped more of the Pinch. "Twenty in all. Yeah, twenty. When you're in the air, in combat, you count every minute because you know one of them might be your last. Cold as hell up there. You know, the planes are built to be as light as they can be." Jimmy's speech had become even more garbled. "When I was up there, I forgot I was an actor. You know, all I wanted to do was bomb the target with a good, tight pattern and get my men back home."

Evan leaned forward. He took a swig of the Scotch and it burned. "Did you?"

"Not always, no. We always lost a few on every mission. Every. Single. One. We never came back without a bloody nose," Jimmy reminisced with a grimace. "The Germans were good. They had radar. They knew when we were coming and where. The flak was bad enough, but when they sent up fighters, that's when you…you got nervous. The fighter was, he was the boogeyman… The fighter had eyes, and in a great many instances, the fighter had a pretty competent fella at the controls, and when he latched onto ya, you were in trouble.

And I was in trouble plenty of times. Evan, you can't imagine how terrifying that is up there, a long way from home, and you just gotta get through it. Not like you can close your eyes and make it go away. You just had to go through it. And it got to me, I'm not ashamed to say. It got to everybody."

"What got you through?" Evan asked.

Jimmy looked wistful, then half-grinned. "91st Psalm, my dad sent it to me in a letter before I went to England. *'For He shall give his angels charge over thee and keep thee in thy ways.'* Dad knew what he was doing."

Rather than respond, Evan allowed the silence to remain.

"When we finally got back to base and saw all those planes limping in, unloading their wounded and dead, I was never relieved. I never felt like we'd accomplished anything other than surviving."

Jimmy stood and headed over to his library. He pulled out a book entitled *Second Air Division 8th Air Force USAAF*. He hobbled over to Evan and flipped open the book, pointing at the photos of grim-faced American airmen posed in front of their parked bombers. "Half of these guys never made it home. We took 50-percent casualties, Evan. Newspapers don't report that, but it's true. Half. Civil War-era casualties, and the Germans kept fighting even up to the end, when they had jets. Can't blame 'em for not giving up until they did."

"Why?" Evan asked. "They knew they were beaten. Why keep fighting?"

A grim look crossed Jimmy's face. "Would we quit even if we knew we were beaten? We'd never quit, just like those fellas in the Philippines in 1942 didn't. They fought until the bitter end, so…even though they were Nazis and terrible, such a terrible regime…I understand why they wouldn't quit."

He plopped back down on the chair and stared off into the distance. "Not a day goes by when I don't think about those young men under my command who didn't make it back. Not one."

A long silence lapsed between them. There was nothing left to say. Jimmy stood again and headed to the bar. "When I remember this stuff, sometimes it's better that I forget it." He poured another drink, this one not as full as the last. Evan downed the last of his drink. The warmth of Scotland filled his bones. The "water of life," as the Scots called it. He watched Jimmy down his, hoping to stretch out his time with the star. He didn't want to go back to that guesthouse, though he was not about to tell Jimmy why.

"How did your date go?" Evan asked, and Jimmy cheered up—or at least appeared to.

"She's a sweet girl, really. We had a good time yuckin' it up. I think I like her, Evan."

"How was the food?" Evan asked.

"Better than I thought. You were right, I dug into the steak and kept away from the peppers. Drank a few too many beers, but I guess that's where I'm at right now, been thinking too much about the war. Gloria took my mind off it, but it's always right here." Jimmy tapped his forehead. "Gives me the blues." Jimmy yawned, stretched. "Okay, Ev, stay down here all you like. I'm going up."

Jimmy went into the kitchen, poured himself a glass of water, and gulped it down. He returned to Evan and clapped him on the shoulder.

"Glad you're here, Ev," Jimmy said. "Stay down here as

long as you like. Like having you around." Jimmy trudged upstairs slowly, taking every step carefully like men who've had too much to drink do. Evan studied Jimmy and saw his face etched with anguish. He couldn't begin to imagine what Jimmy had gone through, and although the alcohol was designed to kill the bad memories, it was failing at its task, simply dredging up the darkness and punctuating it with the cold dread that drink brings on.

Evan got up and peered out to the guesthouse, which now looked more like some haunted house from a horror movie than the friendly, Jimmy Stewart-owned guesthouse he'd been so fortunate to stay in while there. He couldn't see Huckabee, but he could feel his presence, like staring into the alligator pit at the zoo or handling a sack full of snakes. It was a madness he could feel creeping in, just like the conversation he just had with Jimmy. He was right when he stated Evan couldn't begin to imagine the terror at 25,000 feet above the Third Reich, the sky filled with clouds of red and black death, Luftwaffe fighters screaming in at impossible speeds at the lumbering bomber formations, spewing machine gun and cannon fire at those fragile planes. He couldn't begin to imagine the terror of keeping those planes on target, dropping bombs, and then having to fly all the way back to England with fighters following, repeating the 91st Psalm over and over and hoping it was true.

For Jimmy, that Bible verse got him home. Evan had read too many times about the guys who felt they were doomed and actually were; their minds convinced them they were going to die, and in time, they did.

Evan went back to his chair, deciding he'd have another

drink. That Scotch was incredibly good. If he had enough, he might actually develop a taste for it. Evan sunk into the chair, picked up the book Jimmy had shown him, and leafed through it. He gazed at those young men in their leather jackets standing or kneeling before their bombers, with names like Bouncin' Bettie and Big Time Operator, with pretty Varga girls emblazoned near the nose. Evan wondered who those young men were…whether they made it home or not. He wanted to ask Jimmy sometime, but maybe he shouldn't. He did remember an incident when he was a kid that happened sometime in the 2000s. A neighbor came by who had served as a Marine in the Iraq war. When they went in the pool, Evan noticed ugly scars along his torso, and he asked his mom what they were. His mother told him those were war wounds, and Evan wanted to ask the Marine what happened.

Evan's mother said something he never forgot. "Real heroes don't tell stories."

He remembered that and then heard Jimmy coming back downstairs, now dressed in his pajamas. Jimmy reached for the bottle of Pinch. "I'd like to spend a little time with my friend, Ev, if you don't mind. Sorry I'm stinko. No way for one man to see another, it's just that, doggonit, I get gloomy thoughts sometimes."

Evan handed him the album, and Jimmy stumbled back, caught himself, then headed back up the stairs, missing a few as he stomped his way up. Evan was left alone downstairs, his fear of Huckabee and that guesthouse too great for him to leave the room. He might as well make a night of it. It helped that Jimmy's living room was one of the best places he'd ever stayed in.

Evan dwelled on Jimmy Stewart. Whatever he saw and experienced in the bloody skies over Europe would never leave him.

A 50-percent casualty rate…he hadn't known that. Evan had always thought the Americans came through the great wars somewhat unscathed and didn't get hit hard until Vietnam. He was such a Hollywood rat, he got most of his history from the movies, and in the movies, WWII was a grand adventure. Even *Saving Private Ryan* with its horrible opening ended with a handful of GIs taking out an entire German SS Panzer Brigade. But the idea that one out of every two bomber crewmen didn't return home was, well, to Evan, a punch in the face. That meant the Americans had *Das Boot*-like casualties. It modified Evan's gauzy viewpoint of what had occurred between 1939 and 1945. His generation had never faced anything that dire. Hell, the people in his generation seemed to think that being eyed suspiciously by a shopkeeper or asked to change their haircut by an employer was the equivalent of Stalingrad or the Rwanda massacre.

Evan heard Jimmy's bedroom door open, and the man emerged, empty bottle in hand. He came downstairs, weaved to the bar, but noticed there was no more Scotch. He set the bottle down gently, looked to Evan, and shrugged. Jimmy plopped down on the couch across from Evan, reclined, and drifted to sleep. Evan went to the linen closet and pulled out a blanket and pillow. He went to Jimmy and shook him awake.

"Jimmy, wake up. Here's a pillow."

Jimmy stirred and squinted up at him. "What's up, West? Oh, a pillow, thanks. Man can't sleep without a pillow," he muttered and then conked out as soon as his head hit it.

Evan covered Jimmy with a blanket and watched him a while. Jimmy wasn't a sound sleeper, squirming, shivering, and shaking his head. He muttered in his sleep, gasped, and at one point, shouted. Evan watched him reliving the horror in the skies again; it was hard to see a man in so much mental anguish. Jimmy hid it well during the day, but he couldn't subdue it during his sleeping hours. No one deserved that... No one.

Evan's eyes were weary again; the alcohol, fear of Huckabee, and fatigue were getting to him. He sunk down low in the chair and fell asleep. He dreamed of USAAF B-24s, Luftwaffe fighters, men screaming over the intercom, and flak bursts, all while Huckabee looked on and laughed at the horror, reveling in it.

Dorothy reclined in bed next to Richie, watching him sleep. She thought about her life, where she was. Between the waitressing, business courses, and Richie, how could she have time for Evan West? And yet she would make time for him. There was something about him she could not put her finger on, something indefinable. She felt wonderful when he was around; maybe it was because he was different. He was nothing like any other man she knew. He was smart, polite, incredibly open-minded, and seemed to genuinely love her. She found him most enchanting when he smiled and laughed.

Dorothy shook her head. Some people were just too good to be true.

She went to the kitchen and poured herself a glass of lemonade. She thought about everything facing her, a young widow, a single mother still living at home with her son. She couldn't sleep. She felt uneasy about something, nothing she could put her finger on. She'd bitten her nails down to nothing worrying about unseen phantoms in the night.

Dorothy sipped her lemonade and stared off into the distance, trying to remember the old Chinese saying: "*That the birds of worry and care fly over your head, this you cannot change, but that they build nests in your hair, this you can prevent.*"

CHAPTER 22

THE NITRATE JUNGLE

Coop was up all night. Dawn came, and he could hear the chirp of morning birds outside, alerting the world that a new day had arrived. He finished his drawing, went over the equipment he had on hand, deciding he had everything he needed. Then he paused as a dark thought crossed his mind: *What if they failed?* He believed they could jump to another time, that he could create the combination of speed and power needed in that very same spot in which they had arrived. Then again, maybe he couldn't. Maybe nothing would happen. They might just stay here in 1946, age rapidly, growing more toes and maybe a third eye and a second mouth. In the final analysis, Coop knew that he had to try, because true scientists aren't afraid to try and fail.

The weather forecast was on the radio; Coop hurried over and turned it up.

"…in Los Angeles, a high-pressure zone is coming in from the west over the Pacific with a 60-percent chance of heavy thunderstorms and rain that will come in around between 7 and 9 p.m. and continue through Friday."

Coop felt an electric thrill go through him. This was good. Thunderstorms meant the extra power they would need. He scurried around the lab, picking up everything he could to take with him. Wherever they ended up, the supplies might come in handy. Coop wouldn't miss his house and lab; he could always buy and build another.

He just hoped they would go into the future, not back to a time that was pre-electricity or even worse, pre-refrigerators.

Coop hurried to his Dodge. He wanted to head Evan off before he started his day; they needed to prep and say goodbye to everyone as inconspicuously as they could. He checked his watch: 6:21 a.m. Not too early to pay a quick house call on Evan.

Coop frowned, a little grimly. *Nothing will be the same after today.*

He started the Dodge and made his way through the surprisingly light early morning LA traffic.

Evan woke bleary from the Scotch he drank the night before. Jimmy was no longer on the couch across from him; the pillow and blanket had been neatly returned to the linen closet. Evan sat up, stretched, and stood. His clothes from the night before stuck to him, he didn't smell very good, and his mouth tasted like bread gone bad. He noticed movement in the front window that looked out to the front lawn. He first thought it was Huckabee and looked quickly away. He took a breath and looked again, surprised that it was Coop.

Evan checked his watch, then hurried to the front door, opening it quietly. Coop was dressed in his usual dark suit, white shirt, tie, and black fedora.

"Evan, come outside. We need to have a discussion," Coop said quietly, pointing him toward the middle of the front lawn where they wouldn't be heard. Evan followed him, wary of what was about to be discussed.

"Tonight," Coop stated. "We go tonight."

Evan was taken aback. *Tonight? So soon?*

Coop noticed his melancholy. "I know you've fallen hard for Dorothy. Who wouldn't? But we have to go soon, Evan. A massive thunderstorm is on its way, and who knows when another of this size might come? Southern California isn't known for its tropical climate. We're an arid desert that's been thoroughly irrigated. A thunderstorm like this is rare and exactly what we need."

"I need to talk with Frank," Evan decided. "And say goodbye to Dorothy."

Coop nodded in understanding. "I'm going to get everything together, and then we'll be ready for tonight."

Evan thought for a second. *The wrap party.* He had to attend. He couldn't just leave.

They said their goodbyes, and Evan hurried around back to the guesthouse, not giving Theodore Martin Huckabee a second thought. He grabbed what clothes he had, tossed them in a small bag Jimmy had left in the room, shaved, and went out to meet the last day he would be living in 1946… unless, perhaps, the experiment didn't work. He realized he was hoping that maybe it wouldn't.

He ambled toward his car, then glanced through the home's back window and noticed Jimmy in the kitchen drinking coffee and watching the hummingbirds outside. He had to say something to his friend before he left, so he knocked on the back door. Jimmy motioned for him to enter.

In the kitchen, Jimmy looked right as rain. You'd never think he drank almost an entire bottle of Pinch the night before.

"You want some eggs and toast, Evan?" Jimmy asked.

"Jimmy, I wish I could, but I gotta go in. There's some stuff I forgot to do yesterday," Evan stammered.

"Aw, sit down. Eat something," Jimmy demanded with a wave. "You drank almost as much as I did. All that Scotch in your belly needs to get soaked up. Tell Frank I kept you late." Jimmy then went to work beating the eggs. Evan could smell toast already in the toaster. Burning. Jimmy went to the toaster and plunked out two slices of steaming bread.

Nausea overcame Evan; the last thing he needed now was burned toast in his already queasy stomach. The Scotch last night was still in him, a ghastly blend of alcohol and stomach acid.

Jimmy noticed Evan's discomfort. "Want to sit down, Ev?" he asked. "You don't look so good." Evan took his advice. "Here, have some toast." Jimmy gingerly buttered a piece for him and presented it. Evan grimaced at the charred bread slice; he couldn't imagine putting that in his mouth.

Jimmy buttered the frying pan and poured in the eggs. That created a new smell that didn't help Evan's stomach either, but he was hungry. Alcohol was gross; it tore a hole in his stomach and reminded him again of why he didn't drink. Whatever levity Evan experienced the night before was replaced with a dark specter of self-loathing, doubt, and confusion.

Jimmy put a plate of eggs in front of Evan, who tore into them with a relish that surprised him, considering that the very smell of cooking made him nauseated a few seconds before. He was *that* hungry.

"Evan, I wasn't too crazy last night, was I? I can't remember much," Jimmy admitted as he ate. "These okay? You like 'em?" Evan nodded. Jimmy looked thoughtful, eyes distant for a minute, then continued. "You know Alfred Hitchcock?" He smiled. "Strange bird. Hope to work with him someday. I heard he gets physically ill at the sight or smell of eggs. Imagine that, a big guy like that who refuses food. They say he's a genius."

Evan smiled, knowing someday Jimmy would work with Alfred Hitchcock on what some would consider to be his finest film. "I hope you do get to work with him."

"Well, I'm not Cary Grant, but anything can happen in this business."

Evan finished, wolfing down his eggs but avoiding the toast. He stood, thanked Jimmy, and hurried out. As he got to the front door he heard Jimmy yell out, "You forgot your toast!"

Evan pretended he didn't hear that and piled into his Ford, cranked it up, and headed for RKO. Traffic was light that early in the morning, and Evan left the windows down, loving the cool Los Angeles air as it whistled through the car's interior. His Ford's engine threw off just enough heat to keep his feet and lap warm. He turned onto Melrose and made his way east toward the big studio he'd always wanted to be a part of in 2021, a time that now seemed long ago.

Evan turned into the lot, waved at the gate guard, and headed to Liberty Films, relieved to see Frank Capra's Lincoln already there. He went in and was equally relieved that the master sergeant at arms wasn't in yet. He could only handle the bare minimum of obstacles in his hungover state.

Evan knocked on Frank's office door, and Frank grunted out, "Who the hell is here this early?"

Evan entered. Frank looked startled; he held a newspaper open, and a Lucky Strike burned in the ashtray on his desk. "West, you're a man always filled with surprises. What brings you by?"

Evan looked Frank directly in the eyes. "Please tell me those sequences Strickler forced you to film are gone."

Capra's face went hard. "I wouldn't allow those awful scenes anywhere near my movie."

Evan took a seat across from him and leaned forward tensely. "It's been my experience anything on film can be found. Don't ask me how, but I know it can. Is there any way you can burn the negatives?"

Frank looked troubled. "I can't do that, Evan. My name is on the movie, but it belongs to Liberty Films and RKO. That's contractually forbidden. I just can't, as much as I'd like to."

Evan thought fast. "Okay, despite your contract, what if there was an accident? You know, an unfortunate event?"

Frank sat up and shook his head. "You're talking like a gangster, West. I cannot in any way condone or allow you permission for anything like that to happen." He leaned forward, motioning for Evan to come closer. "And now that we got that outta the way…do it," he whispered. Capra fumbled in his pocket for keys, snatching a small one off the ring. "Negative vault is down the hall past editorial. Reels 7, 9, and 12."

Evan nodded.

"Now get outta my office before I call the police," Frank said, then smiled.

Evan stood and left the office. He made his way past editorial, then to the negative vault down the hall, gripping that exquisite key in his hand. He unlocked the door and entered a dreary, poorly lit room.

The negative vault was as ugly and dingy as any janitorial closet at a middle school. Evan found it hard to reconcile the fact that such an area could be where Hollywood dreams were kept. The smell of nitrate film kept in a fireproof vault hit Evan's nostrils—a thick, acrid smell. Evan found it thrilling in a dangerous kind of way, knowing all that film could create an enormous explosion if a match were set to it. The vault was like a nuclear reactor—as long as the rods stayed in place, it was benign.

Evan headed over to the *It's a Wonderful Life* row of film cans and found reels 7, 9, and 12. He took each down, then unlocked the clasp that sealed reel 7 and opened it.

The can was empty. Fear crept into Evan's throat. *No!* He opened reel 9. Empty. Reel 12: the same.

Strickler had gotten there before him. Evan had to admire the man's dexterity and cunning. Strickler was no film illiterate; he knew the process inside and out. The negative was the foundation of every movie. More than likely, Strickler had hired an outside editor to strike prints from the negative and cut them onto the master, creating the monstrosity Connor Alcott would sell to the highest bidder over a rainy weekend in 2021.

Panic set in. Evan couldn't do anything now to stop Strickler and the movie from being desecrated. He didn't have time to sleuth around the studio and turn over rocks. He had to say goodbye to Dorothy at the party and then somehow hook up with Coop and try to leave 1946 for destinations unknown.

Evan thought about telling Frank, unsure if there would be anything the director could do. Still, Evan had to try. He headed to Frank's office and saw him at his desk, lighting another Lucky and going over budget reports.

"Mr. Capra?" Frank looked up, and Evan reluctantly told him, "The negative is missing."

"That son of a…!" Frank shouted, his face going shades of red Evan had never seen on a human being before. Frank got up, shut his door, and pulled Evan close to discuss their next step.

And while it was fun to plan a "film heist" with Frank Capra, Evan knew the clock was ticking on his time there.

It was going to be a long day with a very uncertain outcome.

Evan put in a quick call to Dorothy to tell her he was coming by for a visit. He left Liberty films and turned right onto Cahuenga, heading over into the Valley and toward Dorothy's house. The overwhelming sadness of what he was about to do choked him up. He felt as if a vise had seized his heart and was squeezing it flat. What would he tell her? *Uh, Dorothy, I'm from 2021, and now I'm seeing a dead man from that time who killed a bunch of people, and uh, well, I'm going crazy, and my friend has a sixth toe. He seems to be aging rapidly, and I gotta go back because I'm disrupting the time/space continuum.*

He seriously doubted that would go over well and decided the best thing would be not to say anything at all. He'd spend the best few hours with her he could. Besides, he figured, Coop could still be wrong. Perhaps they'd just speed toward that light pole—and hopefully not hit it this time—and still be in 1946.

Evan pulled up in front of Dorothy's house and saw her waiting outside. She wore a smile as big as the sun as she hurried over to his car, her arms open wide.

"Ready for the big party tonight?" she asked. Evan pulled her close and kissed her. She tasted like heaven and smelled even better. "Ready as I can be. Say, I need to buy a suit. You want to come with me to buy one?"

"A suit?" She scowled. "No way. You're going in a tuxedo, sir."

"Aw, I don't need anything that fancy," Evan said and realized that he was sounding more and more like Jimmy Stewart every day.

"If you're taking me to the ball, Prince Evan, then you're going in a tuxedo, and there will be no further discussion of it," she said. "I know just the place."

While Evan and Dorothy walked into the I. Magnin store at 6340 Hollywood Boulevard, Coop was busy with a mission of his own.

He raced about his house, gathering everything he'd need for tonight's time jaunt. He hoped for another forward trip in time. Coop hated the idea of going back. Besides having to deal with rampant racism, there was no refrigeration, ice cubes, dry cleaners, quality Pepsodent tooth paste, or mouthwash. Just itchy wool clothes, painful shoes, outdoor toilets, and no radio.

No thank you to that, Coop thought fervently. As much as he cared for Nikola Tesla, the affection was never returned. He knew that even if he went back to Nikola and tried to convince him to "go along" with the powers that be, he'd never do it. Nikola, as brilliant as he was, was on a collision course with his own obstinacy and ego. He was destined to become a laughingstock and there was nothing Coop could do about it.

He gathered up his tools, along with the newly configured "Evan's Lifesaver" electric plasma gun he'd hastily fabricated. He also packed up a generator, heavy wiring, and an energy "container" that he had filled with pure, thermomagnetic electricity that he'd captured and kept activated. Coop loved the heat the device threw off. Perhaps with a little helpful lightning, it would be able to throw them into either the future or the past, come what may.

The last thing he did was empty his cash vault. Coop didn't believe in banks. Having grown up in the 1890s, banks were about as reliable as a paper hat. He stuffed about five thousand in his wallet and another one thousand in both socks.

They would not be traveling through time light.

Back on Hollywood Boulevard, Evan had picked out his Sy Devore black tuxedo with a wing-tipped collar, along with a silk bow tie and cummerbund. He also picked out a nice pair of black formal Florsheim shoes he would probably never wear again after that night. At the register, he was shocked when Dorothy insisted on paying.

Evan noticed the shop clerks exchange a look. He knew they saw him as a sad excuse for a man, but what did he care? He'd never see those two goons again—although, given the fact that he was now a time traveler, he wasn't so sure about that.

"Dorothy, you are wonderful to offer, but I insist I pay. Still, I have to say…you are magnificent." Evan opened his wallet.

The tuxedo was packed in a nice, white and blue I. Magnin box, and they bounded out to Evan's car. He was more brokenhearted by the minute, knowing he wouldn't see Dorothy again until she was almost one hundred years old. Evan drove her back home, and she kissed him a long time through the open car window and asked if he could pick her up at six by the latest. He assured her he'd be there. Maybe earlier.

"I want to see you in that tuxedo, Ev. Tonight is gonna be very special."

Evan drove back to RKO with a lump in his throat. It felt awful. He already knew in his heart he'd never love anyone like Dorothy again. He was about to leave her, and what made it worse was the knowledge that he was going to break her heart as badly as the fallen soldier she was once married to.

His heart ached. Should he tell Dorothy who he really was, where he was from? How would that lessen the blow of him leaving her life forever?

He pulled into the studio and rushed toward Liberty Films, noticing both Strickler's Bentley and Frank's Lincoln in the lot.

Good. The gang's all here. Time to get to work.

Evan loped into the building, noticing Vera Stone at her post. She gave Evan a quick nod and pointed to Frank's office, where he heard raised voices. They shared a look, and Vera made a gagging gesture when Strickler raised his rumbling voice: Evan smiled, went to the door, knocked.

"Come!" Frank shouted, and Evan entered. Strickler looked at Evan with a blank expression while Frank stood up and gestured for Evan to have a seat.

"West, Bill's gone on to his next job, and I need you to oversee the print strike for the 16mm we're sealing in the time capsule. You up to do that?" Frank asked, his face a mask of innocence.

"Yes, sir. I just need the inter-positive and the final negative cut," Evan answered.

Frank looked to Strickler. "Studio have the IP/IN?" Frank asked, and Strickler quickly nodded.

"I just had the final cut printed. It's ready to go," Strickler assured.

"You mind if I have a look-see before we go to the ceremony tonight?" Frank asked.

Strickler was as cool as could be. "I already have the projector laced up in four."

Frank and Evan shared a quick look, silently agreeing that the man had to have another print stored somewhere.

"Then let's go into four. Evan, do me a favor and lock all our negatives in the vault." Frank pushed Evan the same key across the desk. Strickler watched with hungry eyes as Evan picked it up.

"You put the negative back in the vault, right?" Frank asked Strickler, who squinted. Then, he straightened up slowly.

Evan realized in that moment that Strickler knew they were onto him.

"It's still in the lab. I'll make sure they put it away," Strickler said carefully.

"You comin' to the party tonight?" Frank asked, and Strickler nodded, stood, and swept his hat off the desk.

"Wouldn't miss it for the world," Strickler answered, did his best to give Evan one of his withering blue-eyed stares, and had reached the door when Frank said, "Strickler, let's you and me take a look at that print."

Strickler glanced back. "Thanks, Frank, but I've seen the movie."

"Then let's see it again," Frank insisted. "You and me, let's share our triumph of a film."

Strickler glanced from Frank to Evan.

The director addressed Evan. "West, head on down to the lab and put all the negatives away. Lab's over in the Hughes Building, second floor. Just follow your nose. You won't miss it." Frank laughed. "See you tonight at Stage 4, then we're going to caravan over to Grauman's for the time capsule ceremony. It's gonna be a doozy of a party."

Evan headed out of the office, with Strickler watching him all the while. Evan looked at Vera Stone, who motioned to him with her head.

"I already authorized the transfer. They know your name," she informed Evan in passing as he headed out the door and into the blazing sunshine of LA on his way to the Hughes Building 400 yards away.

Bicycle riders passed as he navigated the studio sound stages. Then he saw it. Hughes Building.

He walked in, and Frank was right; he could smell the heavy chemical odor of a film processing laboratory from yards away. He bolted up the stairs to the second floor, walked into the lab, and was greeted by a sleepy-eyed negative cutter named Potsy.

"I'm Evan West. Came to pick up the negative for *It's A Wonderful Life*," Evan informed the man, but Potsy didn't look like he was going to accommodate him.

"I gotta have second authorization from Mr. Strickler," Potsy said, seeming pleased at the opportunity to exercise some authority over another human being.

"Frank Capra is asking for this, and if I were you, I'd accommodate him. Strickler is with him now. He was in the room when Frank asked me to pick this up," Evan explained.

Potsy shook his tiny head. "No, sir. I need to hear from Mr. Strickler or no dice, friend."

Evan found his deepest, craziest indignation gene and brought it to the surface. "Are you going to get in Frank Capra's way?"

"I'm not gonna go around Mr. Strickler. If I did, it'd be my job."

"And it'll be my job if I don't bring this back," Evan countered.

Potsy was unmoved. "Sorry, bub, but I can't let you in here without permission."

"I was hoping I wouldn't have to do this, but if I go back to Mr. Capra, who is in a screening with Mr. Strickler, and bring them both back here, it will not go well for you."

Potsy's face registered fear.

"You don't want to see an angry Sicilian," Evan added, piling it on even thicker. "Believe me, I have seen it and never want to again."

Potsy seemed to think about it but just shook his head a moment later. "No can do, buddy."

Evan held out his hands in supplication. "Well, I hate to do this to you, but I'm going to get Frank Capra."

Potsy's jaw clenched; his eyelids fluttered.

Evan ambled away down the hall, whistling without a care in the world.

He didn't make it very far before he heard Potsy's stammering voice behind him. "Okay, okay, okay. What the heck?

It's on you, bub. Cans are stacked over there, 16mm prints. One runs longer than the other."

Evan's eyes widened. *Runs longer? That's it!* The longer print had to be the rotten, sour apple Strickler wanted to unleash on the world. Potsy watched Evan pick up the cans, then shook his head.

"Need you to sign this first," Potsy officiously said and handed Evan a sign-out form. "When Strickler hears about this, it's your hide, not mine."

Evan quickly signed, getting ink on his fingers from the leaky fountain pen, then hauled up the prints and headed out.

On his way to the vault, Evan suddenly felt a lightning strike of dread. What if Strickler had already had a print struck from the negative? There was no way to know if he had. Evan couldn't worry about that now. He hurried back to the Liberty Films building, strolled in past Vera, and headed down the hall to the vault. With one hand, he unlocked the door and went in. He found reels 7, 9, and 12—all had film in the can now. Whatever trick Strickler had just pulled, Evan hoped that somehow he and Frank had just stopped him.

He glanced to two 16mm prints of *It's A Wonderful Life*, contained in the dark gray cans with their negative counterparts. Two were Strickler's versions; the others belonged to Frank. Evan looked closely at the label. One read: "A. STRICKLER-RKO." The other just said **FRANK CAPRA'S IT'S A WONDERFUL LIFE.** He grabbed them all, stacked them up to his chin, and locked the door behind him.

Evan passed Screening Room 4, then paused. He could hear Jimmy's voice behind the closed door:

"Just a minute…just a minute. Now, hold on, Mr. Potter.

You're right when you say my father was no businessman. I know that. Why he ever started this cheap, penny-ante building and loan, I'll never know. But neither you nor anyone else can say anything against his character because his whole life was... Why, in the twenty-five years since he and his brother, Uncle Billy, started this thing, he never once thought of himself."

Evan looked at his watch. It was already 2:14 p.m. The day was flying by. Hoping Vera would turn a blind eye to his thievery. He passed her desk with the cans. She didn't bother to look up. He slipped into Frank's office, set down the two cans labeled **FRANK CAPRA'S IT'S A WONDERFUL LIFE** on Frank's desk, then hurried to his car, tossed the two 16mm reels into his back seat, and headed to Jimmy's house.

CHAPTER 23

THEY HAVE BEEN, THEY ARE, THEY WILL BE

Evan got to Jimmy's house, made a bee line to the guest-house, and tossed his I. Magnin box on the couch. He stopped dead in his tracks when he saw who was sitting on the bed. Huckabee appeared to be decaying; the skin on his face was mottled. His hair was falling out in large clumps.

"I'd love to know why we can't be friends, Evan," Huckabee said in a slow, rumbling voice.

Evan's heart almost stopped from fear. He knew Huckabee wasn't real, that he was just a projection from Evan's imagination because Evan being here was wrong. Evan heard thunder—the really loud kind. That startled him even more. He hurried out of the house and looked up just to make sure he wasn't going completely insane.

The once clear-blue skies were now filling with dark clouds. That was real, not a figment of his imagination. Evan was confused since it had been sunny out just a few moments ago. He peered at the sky, watching strange, dark clouds beginning to swirl and converge on one another like ghosts fighting for celestial supremacy. He heard a distant boom again and thought back to what Coop had said about the future being immutable. He knew that he must not have stayed here. After all, Dorothy had remained alone, made a fortune, and now lived in tomorrow.

Evan went back inside, relieved to see Huckabee gone. Specters tended to do that, after all. Evan carefully dressed, fighting with certain aspects of the starched shirt and particularly the tie. When he looked at himself in the mirror, he was pleased at how well he cleaned up, despite the smattering of gray in his hair. He wasn't exactly Humphrey Bogart but felt he was at least on the level of Robert Cummings when it came to tuxedo presentation.

Evan reached into a pocket of the pair of black, wool trousers he'd worn from 2021. He found the dried rose pedals Gwen had given him and which he'd kept near his bed since he arrived. He'd stored them in a small napkin, mainly out of superstition. Should he carry them with him? He figured he might as well. It couldn't hurt.

He headed over to the main house and found Jimmy sitting in the living room also dressed in a tuxedo, though he wore it much more elegantly than Evan.

"Ready for a little party tonight, Evan?" Jimmy asked, standing up and tugging at his jacket.

"I am," he replied. "You picking up Gloria?"

"I sure am." Jimmy smiled. "Waiting for the limo now. You're headed to pick up that wonderful Dorothy? Sweet girl, Evan. She's as good as they come. Don't let her go, or you'll regret it the rest of your life," he said, a warning that hit Evan right in the gut.

"I'll see you there," Evan croaked, not able to talk about

Dorothy without becoming emotional. He couldn't believe it. This was it. He was about to say goodbye to the woman he loved, more than likely for eternity.

"Be careful out there," Jimmy said with a wink, then headed out.

Evan made his way to his Ford parked out front, sure he'd never be back here at Jimmy's house again. Coop could be incorrect, but he didn't think so. Evan looked up at the sky, still roiling with that bizarre mix of gray, purple, blue, and orange.

He made his way to the Valley and checked his watch with a grim frown. It was almost six. Traffic was heavy. There was no way he was going to make it on time. Evan finally pulled up to Dorothy's house at 6:15. He jerked the parking brake on and remembered the film cans in his back seat. He'd forgotten to toss them into a trash can as Frank had asked. Evan stuffed them under a floor mat. Anyone peering in the back window would still see them.

He hurried to the front porch.

Dorothy's parents were happy to see Evan and demanded he have a piece of pie while he waited for Dorothy to get ready.

"You can't go to a party on an empty stomach," Ellen reminded Evan - he didn't have the bad manners to remind her there would be food served at the event. Don Paige was also pleased to see him, though Evan could barely look at either parent. For a second, he allowed himself to believe that he could stay, marry Dorothy, and make a life for himself here.

But that isn't in the cards, is it? he mused sadly.

Dorothy entered with Richie; both were beaming. Her dress was beautiful beyond words, a pale silk beige that shimmered, and her shoes were shiny black with low heels.

"How do you like it," she asked, completing a perfect swirl.

"I think it's beautiful."

"What's wrong, Evan? Go over there and stand next to her. I want to get a picture of this," Ellen commanded.

Evan stood uneasily and joined Dorothy, who positioned Evan's arm around her waist. She stood so close to him he could feel ripples of electricity from her—it was intoxicating.

Richie hurried over to join them in the picture, and he hugged Evan as close as he could. "I changed my mind about you, mister. I'm willing to give you a sort of chance with my mom. I'm so glad you're with us now," Richie said, and it was all Evan could do to keep from bursting into tears.

"I'm glad I'm here too, sport," Evan managed.

Don Paige used one of those old Spartus Spartaflex cameras with the viewfinder on top. He kept trying to focus on everyone, which seemed to take forever.

"Okay, hold on…," he muttered.

Evan, Dorothy, and Richie stood there for what seemed like an eternity while Don Paige lined up his focus points, and then a huge flash went off, the flashbulb crackling.

"Yay!" Richie shouted and pointed to the small wisp of smoke that curled from the flashbulb.

"You ready, Prince Evan?" Dorothy asked coyly, then turned and casually alerted her parents. "This is my first of many important Hollywood parties. Get used to it, folks!"

Evan walked her to the door and took one last look over his shoulder at the Paige family. Richie was waving broadly. Ellen had her hands clasped in front of her, and Don wiped tears from his eyes.

Evan grimaced. He slowly stepped over to them and dropped to his knees, giving Richie a long hug. Then he stood and shook Don's hand. Finally, he embraced Ellen. "Goodbye," he told them.

"Goodbye? Got news for you, son. War's over. You're not going anywhere." Don smiled.

Evan nodded, holding back tears, and walked out.

When they reached the car, he opened the door for Dorothy. She stepped in and gracefully took a seat. He jumped in on his side, cranked the V-8, and they were off.

On the drive over, they talked about everything; Evan encouraged Dorothy to maintain her stock investments in IBM and Coca-Cola, and if she had more money, to increase them—exponentially if possible. She told him she'd soon be saying goodbye to the Rail Head to attend school full-time. If Butch needed extra help now and again, she'd go in, but for the most part, she was intent on making her future a bright one.

They arrived thirty minutes later at Paramount Stage 4, pulling up to an area marked with rope and an awning. Evan rolled up in his Ford, which looked out of place with the Cords, Cadillacs, Lincolns, Rolls-Royces, and Bentleys.

Two uniformed valets opened their doors, and they headed toward the huge entrance. Evan noticed Dorothy was elbow to elbow with Vivien Leigh and Clark Gable, while he was flanked by John Wayne and Errol Flynn.

Waiters in white coats holding trays of champagne and caviar attended to the well-dressed guests. The rich and beautiful of Hollywood mingled easily with one another. The royalty of a bygone era, now animated and alive under Evan's nose.

Evan scanned the enormous stage, looking over the heady scene of wealthy, beautiful people mingling. Products of one of the greatest machines ever created, the Hollywood studios in 1946 exerted more power than General Motors and US Steel. Evan's appreciation of the time and place he was in was interrupted when he spotted Strickler across the room. He was reminded that the night was far from over.

A nearby dance orchestra began to play "Cheek to Cheek."

Evan took Dorothy's hand and bowed. "May I have this dance?" She nodded happily, and together, they glided toward the roomy dance floor.

As Evan watched her move, his heart fell apart all over again. He could not stand the idea of losing her. Dorothy was so elegant and danced with such grace; her closeness was exhilarating. She smelled of fresh jasmine and strawberries.

"Did I tell you how beautiful you look tonight?" he asked softly.

"Only once, but I'll give you an hour to cut it out," she answered and kissed him sweetly on the cheek.

Though he was enjoying the moment immensely, he found his gaze constantly shifting to Strickler. Evan was astonished he was here tonight. Somehow, Evan had pictured him skulking around the negative vault throughout the evening, trying to find his version of the film. It bothered Evan that Strickler's lapdog from hell, Jack, wasn't present. That meant he could be anywhere.

Jimmy and Gloria walked through the massive doors, and every eye in the room was fixed on them. Applause broke out, and the music stopped. Jimmy gave a slight bow and clapped in return.

Errol Flynn and Clark Gable passed next to Evan. Errol took a look at Dorothy and stopped as any red-blooded seahawk would.

"Hello, old boy. Could I pick you up something from the bar? I'm quite familiar with it." He eyed Dorothy. "And you, young lady, look a bit parched. A Gibson or gin rickey would do you right up."

Dorothy smiled. "How about a champagne?" she asked, and Flynn looked gobsmacked.

"Champagne seems like such a terrible waste at a party, but champagne it shall be," Errol said and gracefully made his way to the bar. Dorothy looked back at Evan with an exasperated expression.

"When I tell Mom Robin Hood got me a glass of champagne, she'll pass out," Dorothy giggled. Evan laughed with her.

Coop pulled into the Paramount parking lot, his Dodge's running boards almost scraping the ground from the weight of the heavy machines he had packed. He trolled the lot and spotted Evan's blue Ford parked nearby and began the ugly, sweaty work of transferring his machinery into Evan's car. The Ford's trunk was just big enough to carry the battery and generator, the backseat barely providing enough room to hold everything else. Coop poked a hole behind Evan's backseat (he was sure Evan wouldn't mind) and snaked wires through to connect the main power generators to the batteries, which were full but losing power with every minute that passed. This era's technology was superior to that of 1899, and Coop thanked God for that. He checked his connections, then turned everything on. The machines glowed to life. He breathed a sigh of relief. His contraptions were not meant to be portable, but he had nothing else that would serve his purpose.

Coop wiped sweat from his brow with a handkerchief. He smoothed down his tuxedo, closed Evan's car doors, and made his way to the party. He could hear music lilting into the darkened parking lot and mused to himself, *Hollywood, where dreams are made.*

Evan noticed that he was standing near Gregory Peck, who was chatting amiably with Cary Grant. He leaned in to eavesdrop.

"Fred sent me this script the other day about this whale," Gregory was saying. "The filming of this is a few years off, but he insisted I should take the role."

"A whale? Who wants to see a movie about a whale?" Cary Grant scoffed. "Never act against kids or animals, remember that old rule. If I ever had to act alongside a monkey, I'd have to rethink my career."

"Right. I think I'm going to pass," Peck said.

Evan turned to Peck. "Excuse me, Mr. Peck. I know that script," he said nervously.

"You do?" Peck lifted his eyebrows.

"Based on the book *Moby Dick* by Herman Melville. It's a classic."

"I've heard of it, of course. Read it at Berkley," Peck admitted.

"Trust me, sir, you'll want to do this picture," Evan insisted. "A seminal role for you is Captain Ahab, a lunatic, yes, but compelling!"

"Yes, that's the role. Ahab. I doubt they'd cast me as Moby," Peck said with his customary deadpan humor.

"I hope you will seriously consider that part," Evan persisted.

"All right, then." Peck grinned at Evan. "I'll take it under advisement, young man. Thank you."

Evan nodded, then ambled over to Dorothy, Jimmy, Gloria, and Capra, who were all by a banquet table sipping champagne. Strickler, Henry Fonda, and Donna Reed were also in their circle.

"Your movie is sensational, Frank," Strickler bellowed. "You were right, and I was wrong. I see that now. We never needed those dreadful scenes we shot. What was I thinking?"

Capra eyed him warily. "Well, I admire a man who can own up to a mistake, Strickler."

Ha! Evan shook his head.

Strickler kept laying it on thick. "I looked at the movie with those scenes, and it just didn't work. It will be your film that the world will see and remember! A triumph!"

Capra nodded approvingly. "Well, then, if you're that taken with the film, you'll no doubt remember the young man who helped with the editing and other creative aspects: Evan West."

Strickler fixed his gaze on Evan and nodded. "Of course. Congratulations, young man. Quite a victory for you, I'm sure."

Dorothy tugged at Evan, but Frank Capra suddenly had his arms around them both. "Rumor has it I'll be hearing wedding bells soon. Why am I always the last to know about these things?"

Dorothy blushed. "Oh, Mr. Capra, right now we're just having a wonderful time."

"Right. Let's not start throwing rice quite yet," Evan said as he held Dorothy tight.

"All evidence is to the contrary," Capra said, eyes merry. Evan swiveled his head and noticed Strickler talking to someone out of earshot. He then saw who Strickler was chatting with.

It was Jack, sweaty and looking like he'd eaten a pound of peppers. Jack was leaning into Strickler, who was trying to talk above the band's rendition of "Ole Buttermilk Sky."

Evan stepped away from Frank, who was busy flirting with Dorothy. He got just close enough to hear Strickler.

"Capra doesn't even know that the copy of the print he's putting into the capsule tonight is really my version of the movie. I cut it behind his back knowing I couldn't win in the short run, so might as well have my version ready for some lucky soul to find in the future. My version, not Capra's! I like to think long-term, Jack."

"Good thinkin', boss," Jack grunted.

Thoughts tumbled in Evan's mind at warp speed. Connor would ultimately get Strickler's copy in the capsule, which meant Strickler *had* struck a 16mm print from the negative, and that meant Evan had stolen the wrong print. He knew tonight he had to get the right print to Frank before he buried Strickler's and burned the negative from those awful scenes. It was nitrate film, so it would go up in seconds.

Evan checked his watch. The ceremony at the Chinese Theatre was an hour away. He saw Jimmy, who gave Evan a salute. Evan headed Jimmy's way and leaned toward him.

"Thank you, Jimmy, for everything. I really do appreciate it," Evan said.

"Aw, Evan, you're talking like I won't see you again, and that's just nonsense," Jimmy replied, his eyes warm.

"I just wanted you to know how much I appreciate

everything," Evan said. He knew he was repeating himself, but he couldn't help it.

"Well, uh, pleasure to have you around, Evan. You're a heck of a guy!" Jimmy was distracted by John Ford, who waved him over. "See ya round, buddy," Jimmy said, as he walked away.

Evan then looked over the crowd and spied Coop, easy to spot due to his height and skin tone. Coop saw him in nearly the same instant and headed his way.

"I transferred my equipment into the trunk of and backseat of your car. I hope you don't mind," Coop announced loudly over the music and gaiety of the crowd.

"You gotta help me," Evan shouted. "We have to get over to the Chinese theater!"

Coop was stone-faced. "We have a rendezvous with destiny," he objected.

"No choice," Evan said. "I have to do this, and I need your help."

Coop looked like he was about to put up a fight but then nodded. "As long as we do this mysterious task with alacrity."

"Don't worry. It'll be quick. I gotta think of something to tell Dorothy." Evan bit his lip.

"Tell her you got to do something for the ceremony. You know, for Mr. Capra," Coop suggested. "And that you'll meet her at Grauman's afterward."

Evan nodded with admiration. "Not bad, Coop. It should work. She's a cool girl. She'll understand."

Evan heard Capra's voice behind him. "I'm going to head on over now to Grauman's with the print."

Evan glanced backward. Capra was talking to Jimmy.

Just then, Evan saw Dorothy heading in his direction, a

wary expression on her face. She stared at Evan and then at Coop. "What's going on with you two?" she asked, looking as if she knew she wouldn't like the answer.

"We have to do a favor for Frank. You remember Coop, right?" Evan asked.

Dorothy nodded and squinted at Coop, who tipped his hat to her politely before moving toward the door. Soon, Evan heard the distant roar of thunder outside. No rain yet, but he knew a storm was coming.

"It's for the ceremony," Evan explained to a wary-looking Dorothy.

"Why can't I come and help?" she asked.

Evan paused. *Why not bring her? She might as well know the truth.*

"Sure, come along," Evan invited. "But I gotta warn you, what we're doing is right but maybe not legal."

Dorothy furrowed her brow, then smiled. "Then let's go!"

A massive boom of thunder clapped, and then the room went dark for a moment. A titter of concern passed through the space. An instant later, the lights returned, and Evan and Dorothy were gone.

They hurried out of Stage 4 and toward the valet. Evan didn't have time to wait—he had to get there before Frank. Evan hurriedly asked the valet for his keys and gave the guy his ticket.

"I can get that for you," the sleepy valet replied, starting to walk off in the direction of the lot.

"I'd like to get my own car," Evan objected hastily.

"No, sir. Them's the rules. I'll go," and before Evan could stop the guy, he trotted off into the lot. Evan looked at his watch, nervous. Then he heard the familiar sound of a nearby engine and turned—only to watch Frank's Lincoln heading out of the lot in a hurry.

Evan's heart sank. There was nothing he could do. The right version of the film had been deliberately mislabeled and was under the mat by the back seat. The wind was already picking up; it was about to be a humdinger of a storm.

Coop walked over to Evan. He looked nervous, and Evan realized why when he looked over his shoulder and spotted Strickler's muscle-bound lackey, Jack, strutting out the building door. He was headed right for them. Evan grimaced. He didn't want to get into it with this guy or have Dorothy get hurt in the process. Strickler was close behind Jack. The pair must have seen Evan leave the party.

"Uh, Evan, I sense we're about to be in a great deal of danger," Coop said, his voice quavering.

"I see 'em, I see 'em," Evan muttered.

The bicycle bell startled all three of them—it was Henry on his old bike with the sidecar.

"Evening, Mr. West," he said. "Hi, Coop."

"Why aren't you at the party, Henry?" Coop asked.

Henry gave an odd smile. "I made a quick appearance, then ducked out. Got too much work to do. That's kinda my mission, you might stay. Work, work, work."

"Listen, Henry," Evan said quickly. "I don't have time to explain, but I need you to buy me a few minutes."

"Buy you minutes?"

Evan nodded to Strickler and Jack, who were both picking up their pace. "Keep Strickler busy for us, okay?"

Henry looked to Strickler and Jack. "Why…I'd love to be of help, Evan."

Dorothy wrapped her arms around him and gave him a quick peck on the cheek.

"You're an angel, buddy!" she said.

"You could say that," Henry laughed. "Next time you're in town, fellers, look me up." He peddled over to Strickler and turned his bike sideways, creating a small roadblock.

Evan could hear Henry talking loudly. "Evening, Mr. Strickler. Why, I thought you'd be at the party tonight!"

"Yes, well, business, Mr.—?"

"Henry, just Henry."

The sound of Evan's V-8 winding through first gear came nearer. The sleepy valet eased over with agonizing deliberation and pulled up to the curb.

Evan, Coop, and Dorothy climbed in as soon as the valet got out. Coop could barely squeeze in the back seat on account of all the heavy machinery he had stacked there so neatly.

Evan made sure not to give the guy a tip even though he held out his hand, and just buzzed off and waved to Henry with a laugh. Strickler and Jack noticed Evan's departure, circumvented Henry, and rushed over to the valet.

"They're not using the valet," Coop warned from the back seat, staring out the window. "They just decked the poor guy and dropped him. Stricker took his key from the box and is heading into the lot."

Dorothy looked over her shoulder, then to Evan. She slapped his thigh. "This is turning out to be one heck of a fun night!" she laughed.

Evan floored it, passing through the studio gates and peeling out onto Melrose. The first drops of rain started to fall, and they were not normal drops. They were enormous. Evan drove through the deluge, feeling as if he were in a car wash. He jammed down the gas pedal and fishtailed north onto Highland, then headed for Hollywood Boulevard. Dorothy cheered him on; she didn't have a shred of fear in her.

"Evan, are you sure you should be driving this fast?" Coop asked nervously.

"Yes, I need to be driving this fast!" Evan shouted back.

"If you slow down, I'll kill you!" Dorothy giggled. She was having way too much fun.

Traffic was heavy, brake lights were up ahead, and Evan felt like he was about to lose his mind from the anticipation of what he knew was about to happen.

"Come on, go! Go!" Evan shouted at his Ford. The rain pelted down on the car roof; it felt exactly as it did that Sunday that now seemed so long ago. He put the pedal down, got to Hollywood, and fishtailed a hard left, just missing an ice delivery truck.

Dorothy shouted with glee, "Man, that was great! *Great!*"

They made it to Grauman's just as the awnings were put in place, and already, a small crowd had gathered, all holding umbrellas and brimming with curiosity. Evan parked behind Frank's Lincoln, already sitting at the curb.

"Coop! I need those film cans!" Evan shouted.

"Where?"

"Under there!" Evan pointed. They were directly underneath one of Coop's heaviest devices.

"I need help!" Coop yelled, and both Evan and Dorothy ran around the back and did their best to muscle the heavy generator out of the way. Coop reached under and grabbed the film cans, then handed them to Dorothy.

Frank was at a podium near the spot where the time capsule was located, practicing his speech.

"Ladies and gentlemen, we're all here tonight to take a look at how good men can be, how strong they're required to be, and how resilient they are." Frank looked over to see Evan hurrying toward him with Dorothy and Coop, completely drenched.

"Sorry, Mr. Capra," Evan panted, holding up the film cans. "He tricked you. Those reels are the wrong cut. Put these reels in those cans."

Frank stared at him, shocked. "Are you positive?"

"Absolutely, 100 percent," Evan assured him. "Please trust me on this. Give me those reels, and take these for your time capsule. Mr. Capra, thank you for everything. Everything!"

Capra took a moment, then nodded. "All right, West. You haven't let me down yet, kid. Give me that!" He snatched the reels from Evan and gave Evan the ones he had held originally. Evan looked back at Coop, who was pointing to his watch. In the distance, they could hear police sirens. Strickler was on their tail and bringing the law with him.

Evan was running out of time. He looked at Dorothy, who smiled. Then she registered the look on his face, and her smile fell away.

"I gotta go," Evan murmured.

"I'm coming with you," she decided.

Evan took her in his arms and held her close. "You can't come where I'm going," he said quietly. "I'm sorry, Dorothy. This is a horrible thing to tell you, but you can't come with me."

Dorothy broke away and stared at him with wide eyes.

"What do you mean, I can't come! That's crazy! Of course, I can. I want to be with you, Evan West, I love you. No one else. I'll never love anyone but you!"

Oh, no, Evan thought. *This is so painful, worse than I ever thought it would be.* He grabbed her shoulders and looked into her eyes.

"It's too much to explain, but I'm not from here. You can't go where I'm going, I'm—"

Dorothy slapped him. "Wake up, Evan. It's me. We're together. You're not going anywhere without me because I won't go anywhere without you!"

Evan tried to pull back, but Dorothy refused to let him go. "No! You can't go away! No!"

"I have to go someplace… You would not believe it if I told you," Evan said, his voice thick with sadness.

"Tell me. I knew there was something about you that couldn't be explained." Tears streaked her beautiful eyes. "Tell me because I won't let you go! I will not allow it!"

She pulled him close and wept into his shoulder as the sirens grew louder.

"Okay, here goes," Evan said. "I'm… How do I say this? I…aw, to heck with it. I'm from 2021. I'm from another time, and I have to get back. I'm so sorry, but I have to get back, or bad things will happen to you and me."

Dorothy drew back, face screwed up in horror. "Are you crazy?"

"I know, I know. It sounds that way, but I'm not. If I were crazy, I'd never love someone as wonderful as you. Just please listen to me, please believe me, I want to stay with you here, forever, but I have to go," Evan pleaded.

Dorothy just stared, tears trickling down her cheeks, clearly struggling to process all that Evan had told her.

"I'm going to see you again, I promise. I'll be back. I don't know where or when, but I'll find you," Evan swore, then kissed her deeply. He broke away silently and hurried to his car, holding onto Dorothy's hand until the very last minute.

They locked eyes one last time. Evan knew it was now or never.

He broke away from Dorothy and ran to the car. Coop was already in the back seat fiddling with his machines. Strickler's Bentley seemed to come out of nowhere. Strickler, uncharacteristically, was at the wheel; the car was just yards away from Evan away from Evan and moving fast. Jack leaned out the open car door on the passenger side, ready to take a running leap at Evan.

"Frank! I need your lighter!" Evan shouted back toward the podium, and Frank knew exactly what Evan was about to do. He tossed Evan his well-worn Zippo. Evan caught it, opened the negative can of Strickler's version of *It's A Wonderful Life*, and tossed the reel into the open door of the Bentley. The reel spilled out like an inky, rolling tongue. Evan held the end of the film as it uncoiled.

Jack leaped from the Bentley's running board, his arms outstretched to grab Evan. The reel whirled in and clonked Jack on the side of the head. He stumbled and slammed head-first into a lamppost, sliding unconscious onto the sidewalk. Evan lit the nitrate negative, and like an angry fuse, it boiled a snake of smoky sparks and flame all the way to Strickler's Bentley. Strickler stopped but didn't get out.

Evan got in his car, looking one more time at Dorothy,

who stared back at him in awe. They locked eyes again for an instant. Finally, he had to release himself from her gaze. He cranked the engine and fired away with a screech.

He heard an engine roar behind him and looked back. Strickler was gunning it, chasing Evan, who made a sharp right on LaBrea and Strickler followed.

All the police vehicles Strickler had summoned had converged and were now also close behind Evan.

Evan gunned it to Franklin and turned the corner, and the heavy equipment in the back of the car made the Ford rear up on two wheels for a second.

The car slammed back down, jostling Evan and Coop. Evan was flooring it as soon as he stopped bouncing.

"Okay, Evan. Now the fun begins," Coop announced and hit a switch on one of the machines in the back seat. A loud buzzing sound erupted. The entire back seat lit up as if filled with a police helicopter's spotlight. The bluish-white light pouring out from the Ford was blinding.

Evan blew red lights, approached the corner of Highland, and glanced in his rearview.

Strickler was leaned over his steering wheel, a skull-like grimace on his face. The backseat of his car was in flames, but he didn't seem to care. Evan knew at that moment that Strickler was completely insane.

Evan skidded a long left onto Highland heading north, Strickler right behind him.

"And now, we go to phase two. Say goodbye to the power grid, Los Angeles!" And with that, Coop hit another switch in the back seat. Sparks flew, and smoke began to pour out of the side windows.

Every light along Highland winked out. The stoplights sparked out as well, and all of Hollywood suddenly went dark.

The entire city of Los Angeles, from Santa Monica to Pasadena was curtained in darkness. Every kilowatt of power, gone.

Lightning streaked through the skies above; rain was beating down harder than Evan thought possible. The water was so thick it streamed down the windshield, blinding Evan to what was in front of him. He was now flying on instruments only. The trunk of Evan's Ford shone red from the intense power being generated.

"Are we close?" Coop shouted over the enormous buzz and sparks.

"We're close!" Evan hollered back, blowing the Cahuenga light, skidding to the left, and heading up to Lakeridge and Cahuenga, where the thin membrane of the Earth's magnetic field invisibly hovered. As soon as Evan hit Cahuenga, he slammed the accelerator all the way to the floor.

Strickler's car was faster and still raging with flames. The LAPD Fords that followed were now holding back, their drivers having no desire to approach a car that was about to explode. Strickler's Bentley revved faster with its huge 12-cylinder engine, and he slammed into the back of Evan's Ford.

Evan kept the car under control.

Coop grunted with anger. "Final stretch, Evan. This is where we find out if—"

Strickler smashed into them a second time. Evan struggled to keep the wheel steady.

"This is it, Evan. Go as fast as you can!" Coop shouted.

Evan obliged. His speedometer read 76 or so. He would have to go faster. Coop hit another switch. Evan could smell something burning, and it wasn't Strickler's car, which was preparing for another thrust.

Coop reached for something, his eyes wide with anger. Evan saw what it was in the rearview—that same "plasma gun" that had saved him before. Coop leaned out the open window and fired it at Strickler's car.

Strickler never knew what hit him. A green and red plasma bubble splashed over his car with the force of King Kong's fist. His Bentley lost control, went into a spin, flipped twice, and then exploded.

Strickler was thrown from the car, but from what Evan could see, he got exactly what was coming to him and more.

Evan looked ahead. He saw it. The gateway. A vortex of rippling light, fueled by enough power to rip a hole through the thin membrane and break the laws of time and space.

Coop pointed at the shimmering vortex ahead. "Go Evan, go! Right at it! Right at it!"

Evan had the car going so fast he was surprised the engine hadn't blown. The roaring noise of Coop's machines was deafening. Lightning struck the electric pole in front of him; sparks erupted. Evan could see electro plasmic tendrils forming on the sides of his car.

Something was happening....

"It's working! It's working!" Coop screamed at the top of his lungs. Evan could see the pole approaching fast. Sparks were coming down, his car was about to burst into flames, and he could feel extreme heat. The car was barreling crazy-fast right toward the enormous "doorway" opening, a yawning chasm so majestic and horrible at the same time it scared him to the core of his soul. This was otherworldly, a bridge to another universe, and he was driving right toward it.

Evan prayed aloud, "God, don't let me down!"

Before he was consumed with a bright, white light, the last thing he thought was, *At least I saved it this time.*

And then he went unconscious.

At Grauman's, the lights came back up. Dorothy didn't notice.

Her heart was shattered. Teary-eyed, she looked around and saw Frank. He headed over to her, face soft with sympathy.

"What happened?" he asked.

"Evan left," she stammered.

"What do you mean, left? He's with us!" Frank said.

"No, he said he was from somewhere else, and he had to go." She broke down sobbing.

"Now?" Frank shouted. "We're just getting started! What the heck!"

Two LAPD officers in a nearby black-and-white pulled up fast. One officer hurried out and went to Jack, who was still unconscious on the sidewalk. Jack still had a gun curled in one of his hands. The officer, a young man with a military haircut who looked like he had just returned from Okinawa, reached down and picked up the weapon.

Sirens could be heard all over Hollywood, throwing an "end of the world" vibe over the already rain-soaked evening. Dorothy could hear the radio from the nearby LAPD black-and-white crackling.

"10-50F on Cahuenga and Lakeridge. LAFD and LAPD respond immediately. Possible fatalities." The two LAPD officers exchanged quick glances and rushed back to their vehicle, leaving Jack out cold on the sidewalk.

Dorothy's eyes were wide with fear. Capra charged over to the two cops.

"What kind of car was involved. Do you know that?" he asked. The cops looked unsure. "I think we know who's involved in the accident," Frank explained impatiently.

The officers motioned for Frank and Dorothy to climb in the back seat.

Dorothy's heart fell. Something terrible must have happened to Evan and Coop. Her mind flashed through everything Evan had told her. She couldn't help but wonder if he had gone insane somehow. And the car chase… What had she just witnessed?

The two officers cranked up the siren and made a U-turn, heading toward Cahuenga pass.

Dorothy burst into tears all over again. She could not go through this again. She couldn't lose her only two loves. What had she done to deserve this? Where was God?

Frank sat next to her, hand around her shoulder.

"Miss, I'm sorry. I just hope to heaven this wasn't someone you knew," one of the officers said from the front seat, sympathy in his voice.

They made their way through the pelting rain; ahead, Dorothy could see the roiling orange of high flames despite the heavy downpour. The LAFD was already on the scene, and there were lookie-loos everywhere. The police had blocked off the road with smudge pot railroad flares that burned, bathing everything in an ominous pink/red color.

Dorothy saw the fiery wreckage, and what was left of her

heart fell through the floor. The black-and-white stopped. Both Frank and Dorothy piled out, adrenaline on high. A heavyset woman in a flower print dress, dripping wet, stopped them, eyes wide, red cheeks aflame.

"It was terrible! Terrible!" she shouted. "Two cars going like a bat outta hell. One flipped over, and the other… "I dunno what happened. I can't even think about it! I can't explain what I saw!"

Dorothy knew she had to find that inner control valve within herself and turn it. She was going to get through this, stay strong. This was going to tear up her family, especially Richie, but she had to be a rock. She could not falter.

They walked toward the fiery wreckage and saw a sheet splayed over a fatality. Frank neared, arm protectively around Dorothy.

"Oh, no," Frank murmured. "Terrible."

Strickler's fancy Bentley had been smashed to ruin. It looked like a Sherman tank had run over it.

"Officer," Frank yelled, "that's Arthur Strickler's car!"

"It looks like it's been through a war!" one of the officers exclaimed. "Strickler, you say?"

Frank nodded, saddened. "Arthur J. Strickler. He worked with me at RKO. What a tragedy!'

Dorothy was almost overjoyed, not that she was happy he was dead, but at least it hadn't been Evan and Coop. The heat from the burning car was intense. They stopped approaching when a firefighter blocked their way.

"Don't go any closer, folks. That car might blow at any minute," the firefighter warned.

"Is there another car?" Dorothy asked.

"No, ma'am, this is it. People shouldn't drive so fast at night in the rain," the firefighter grunted.

The heavy-set woman in the rain-soaked dress followed them. She was one of those people who saw an accident and then suddenly, it was the most important event they'd ever witnessed. Dorothy saw her and drew her close.

"What happened to the other car?" Dorothy asked.

"It was terrible. I saw it from just over there. I had a flat and heard a terrible humming noise, and two cars were driving like crazy up the pass! The car in front was glowing…"

Frank came in close so he could hear. The added attention made her puff out her chest and say with added flourish, "It was glowing, mister, and it went faster and faster, and then it just vanished! Poof! Like it was never there!"

Dorothy was immediately relieved. So Evan wasn't dead. He was just…gone?

"It just vanished!" the woman said again as if answering Dorothy's internal question.

"That makes no sense," Frank said. "Cars don't vanish!"

"This one did! Poof!" she repeated.

Dorothy and Frank exchanged looks. Frank shook his head.

"West is one strange bird, I'll give him that. Dorothy, don't worry. He'll be back," Frank assured her.

"How do you know?" she asked.

"I dunno, I got a knack for these things. Whatever happened to him, search me. But I got a feeling, if he ain't dead, which he ain't, he'll turn up again."

That's when Dorothy knew—Evan was telling the truth. She smiled. He was from another time. She just had to wrap her mind around that concept.

Dorothy knew she'd remember this night for the rest of her life, when she went from the highest high she'd ever experienced to the lowest of lows, and finally, to a dull feeling of relief.

Not as good a feeling as she would have had if Evan had returned, but relief.

And one day, she knew that he would return. And she would be waiting.

Dorothy looked at Frank. "I'll wait for him," she declared. Frank looked at her, frowning, then nodded. He understood.

"I would too. Come on, we still have a ceremony," Frank said and headed back to the car. He looked to Strickler's sheet-covered body and shook his head. "Terrible about him, God bless his soul…but people shouldn't drive so fast in the rain."

CHAPTER 24

THE NOWHERE MEN

2021

Connor Alcott was furious; his heart beat like crazy. He knew he shouldn't smoke, drink, and take drugs like he did. It affected his health especially in moments like this. He peered ahead at the downed power lines, sparks dancing off them in the rain. He got out of his Range Rover, keeping back from the lines, but he could not see a sign of Evan's antique junker.

Sirens were approaching; the smell of high voltage and rain seemed dangerous. No point in getting any closer to that electrical swarm.

Connor climbed back into his car. His iPhone was blowing with texts and incoming calls. He read the first text:

GET YOUR BUTT BACK HERE NOW! THEY ARE WAITING!

Connor immediately called the number. Jake Johannsen—Connor's faithful employee whom he often liked to refer to as "J-Jo"—picked up.—

"Hey, man," Connor said. "What's going on?"

"They're here!"

Connor's thoughts were still a blur. "Who?"

"The guys from Amazon. They're waiting. I got the projector ready to go, but they said they want you in the room," Jake explained. "Get back here, dude."

Connor felt like he was going insane. What did he mean? There was no film in the projector? Connor then breathed a sigh of relief. This entire episode must have been a drug-induced hallucination. Connor felt funny and then recalled the last time he had felt so strange—it had happened after a three-day bender on cocaine, Valium, and vodka, followed by four Ambien. He had no memory of the following week, but he did hear embarrassing stories about what he had done during that time. This must be a similar episode.

He decided right there and then, he had to go to rehab someday soon. This stuff was catching up to him. Connor drove back to the studio and headed inside. Jake, whose nose looked like it weighed more than he did, appeared anxious. He was skinny, pale, and nervous by nature, sorely in need of a vacation he'd probably never get.

"Come on, man. They're ready," Jake hissed, then hurried to the makeshift projection booth.

Connor went into the larger editorial room converted to a private screening theater. He got a small round of applause from the Amazon movie executives who had taken the time to come and see this one-in-a-million screening. They all looked pleased to be there, beaming broadly even though their Harvard MBAs had trained them not to.

"Okay, folks," Connor began, raising his hands dramatically. "This is it, Frank Capra's true version of *It's a Wonderful Life* before the studio got its hands on it! Check it out, party people!"

The movie began. Connor was already counting the big bucks in his head. Ten million? Probably more like fifty million when this was over. Connor practically salivated. *Bidding war. Think bidding war!*

Two hours later, Connor was the object of derision. The movie was exactly the same, not one frame shot differently. Connor was slack-jawed with shock.

How could this happen? Why?

His reputation was in tatters. Never again would he command respect from the Amazon people, let alone anyone else. People talk. Amazon would talk to Disney, who would talk to Time Warner, who would talk to Viacom, who would talk to Netflix and Hulu.

He made a vow then and there to never use drugs again. The vow was broken that night when he replayed the horrible scene over and over in his head—the looks on those people's faces, so furious their time had been wasted.

"Did you even bother to look at this before you got us down here on a Sunday in the rain?" an Amazon executive, who looked way too fit, had demanded.

"Bro, I dunno what happened!" Connor pleaded.

"I'm not your bro," the Amazon guy said before he stomped out.

Evan West and Coop were both fast asleep in the Ford parked in the grass just off Cahuenga when a large truck rumbled by, waking them. It was sunny yet hazy from the thick, LA fog that hovered over each day like a heavy wool sheet.

"Coop? You okay?" Evan asked.

"I am, Evan. Yourself?" Coop responded.

"Where are we? WHEN are we??"

Evan heard the Red Car clanking along the tracks and felt a terrible sense of despair. He looked at Coop, who exited the car. Evan climbed out as well and inspected the Ford. No dents or other indications of a crash—just some blackened sections on the trunk from the heat generated.

"Oh, no…we're still here," Evan moaned.

"It would appear so, or we might have inched ahead a few days, but this looks relatively similar to the time we left," Coop responded, then froze. "Wait a second…" He took off his shoe and broke into a grin. "I have five toes! Five!" Coop scrambled over to the rearview and looked at himself. The gray hair was gone along with the wrinkles.

Coop looked at Evan, who rushed over to take a gander at himself in the rearview. His gray hair had also vanished.

Coop almost collapsed with relief.

Evan scanned the streets ahead and across the tracks that would one day be lined with Interstate 101. The cars appeared boxier than before, and he squinted to get a better look as a few roared past. No gas ration stickers in the windshields. He tried to get a closer look at the license plates, but the vehicles were too far away.

A clattering 1930 Chevy sedan passed by closely; it looked like a Model A Ford but built more cheaply. Evan got a glimpse of the gold-on-black license plate.

"Did you see that?" Evan asked Coop, who looked to Evan in astonishment.

"Evan, can you read that?" Coop asked.

"California tag 25 B 821!"

Then they both said it in unison: "1941!"

Evan was angry. *1941?* They had gone back in time. Coop was dejected, and then fury—at least, as much as a guy like Coop would muster, overtook him.

"We went back! I'm most disappointed!" he barked. "Now we're back five years before, and…" He glanced back at his machines. "I'm not sure what went wrong. I feel like someone who's finally invented an engine that only goes in reverse."

Evan thought it through. He'd left Dorothy, broken her heart and maybe her soul…for this? He couldn't meet her now in 1941. She was probably already married to the doomed soldier, and he could not interfere with that—no…never. He couldn't take away Richie just because Evan was selfish and in love.

"What do we do?" Coop asked.

Evan, alarmed and disappointed, shook his head. "When all this is over, and we get back, how do I tell everyone I know in the twenty-first century I went to the 1940s? More importantly, how do we get out of here?"

They exchanged worried looks.

So many unanswered questions… Evan and Coop had work to do.

If you enjoyed reading this book, please take a moment to
write a brief review on Amazon and/or Goodreads.
We would appreciate your sharing your comments
about *It's a Wonderful Time*.

Learn more about this book series at
www.HollywoodTimeTravel.com

Acknowledgments

I would like to thank the following people who were involved and believed in this project when I first came up with the idea back in 1993 and for their encouragement over the years. Lynne Kadish and Barry Bleach; George Saunders, my cowriter on the original script and first draft of the book; Doug Claybourne; Jay Hoffman; Holt Satterfield; Michael Cummings and Lynn Brown; and all my beta readers for the book.

Many thanks to Reinhard Denke, who has been a great co-writer to work with on this book series. Thank you all for your help and encouragement in making this book a reality which is now available for everyone to enjoy.

I would also like to thank our publishing team: copyeditor Andrea Vanryken, our proofreaders, Margaret McConnell and Ted Hollis, Robbie Destocki of Creative Image Design Group for his graphic work on the original book cover concept, Bryan Lopez of The Direct Marketing Agency for his work on web design and social media, Christy Day of Constellation Book Services for her work on the book cover and interior design and Martha Bullen of Bullen Publishing Services, our book coach and marketing consultant. We could not have gotten the book out without her amazing and outstanding guidance, knowledge and advice.

—Doug

I would like to thank Doug Stebleton for bringing me in on this magnificent book and believing in me enough to let me be a part of it. I would also like to thank Michael Cummings for making the introduction.
—Reinhard

About Doug Stebleton

Doug Stebleton has been working in the entertainment business since 1987. Born and raised in Glasgow, Montana, he came to Hollywood at age 19 and has lived and worked in southern California since then. His expertise is music publishing for film and television. His company owns a catalog of songs that are licensed to film and television studios and to independent productions. Some of the company's credits include *Blood Diamond, Borat, Little Miss Sunshine, Zoolander, Big Bang Theory, Blue Bloods, Brooklyn Nine-Nine, The Sopranos, Ugly Betty, CSI, Scrubs*, and *ER*.

Doug is also a film producer. His first film was a documentary titled *Mother of Normandy: The Story of Simone Renaud*. His next film, *I Want Your Money*, was released in over 500 theaters across the nation in 2010. In 2014, Doug produced and directed *Reagan at Normandy*, a short film for the Airborne Museum in Normandy, France, and in 2017, he produced *Heroes of WWII: The European Campaign*. Other projects he is producing include a cable TV show on film and TV cars called *Kars & Stars* and a feature film, *Big Life*.

Doug has a love for history and hopes to keep making films and documentaries that are inspiring, informative and educational. His passion for Hollywood films and time travel inspired him to create *The Hollywood Time Travel Series*. *It's a Wonderful Time* is his debut novel, which he coauthored with Reinhard Denke.

About Reinhard Denke

Reinhard Denke, a native of Texas and graduate of USC Film School, got his start in 2009 with his spec script *Sex, Greed, Money, Murder and Chicken Fried Steak* about the Cullen Davis murders in Fort Worth, Texas. The script was optioned by Johnny Depp's infinitum-nihil company and chosen for the prestigious 2009 Hollywood Blacklist. In 2013, he wrote *Far Below* for David Oyelowo, and was hired to rewrite 2015's *Captive*, starring Oyelowo, Kate Mara, and Michael K. Williams. He also wrote a TV pilot and series entitled *Golden Gate* about 1960's era San Francisco that has been optioned by Demarest Films, and he wrote the limited TV series *Vanished* for Straight Up Films and Truly Original.

Reinhard adapted *The Lives of Beryl Markham* for Rock Island Productions; it is now entitled *Undaunted.* He wrote the screenplay *Ackia* for the Chickasaw Nation and award-winning director Nathan Frankowski. Also for the Chickasaw Nation, Reinhard wrote *The Chickasaw Rancher*, which is to be released in 2021. He adapted *The Madman of Music,* a bio of composer George Anthiel and movie actress Hedy Lamarr. He wrote *Moonchild*, the story of Linda Kasabian and her ordeal with the Manson Family, for director Marcus Nispel and producer Adam Krentzmann. Reinhard also co-wrote *Mizmoon,* about the Patty Hearst kidnapping, for director David Brown and Clear Horizon.

Reinhard Denke lives in Woodland Hills, California, with his wife, Marilee and their two children, Jackson and Winston. He coauthored *It's a Wonderful Time,* the first book in *The Hollywood Time Travel Series*, with Doug Stebleton.

Learn more about both authors and this book at
www.HollywoodTimeTravel.com.